MW00932032

Dancing at Angel Abbey

LAUREN M. BLOOM

For Bishop Jim,
From one believer
to another!
Be blessed,
Lauren

BALBOA.
PRESS
A DIVISION OF HAY HOUSE

Balboa Press books may be ordered through booksellers or by contacting:

Balboa Press
A Division of Hay House
1663 Liberty Drive
Bloomington, IN 47403
www.balboapress.com
1 (877) 407-4847

Print information available on the last page.

ISBN: 978-1-5043-5331-1 (sc)
ISBN: 978-1-5043-5333-5 (hc)
ISBN: 978-1-5043-5332-8 (e)

Library of Congress Control Number: 2016903903

Balboa Press rev. date: 4/19/2016

For Tatyana, with love always.

The angels are nearer than you think.
Rev. Billy Graham

CHAPTER ONE

"*Your father is dying,*" the note said. "*Come home at once.*"

For the life of me, I couldn't have told you how that note ended up on my desk. I had been in meetings all afternoon, arguing with the managing partner, Roy Blackwell, about why our law firm shouldn't close another real estate transaction for Dr. Frank Grandy. The good doctor was a charming elderly man with a lot of old New York money and no common sense whatsoever. Manhattan is among the priciest real estate markets in America, and there is plenty of money to be made there by savvy investors. There are a lot of bad investments, too, though, and Dr. Grandy had an unfailing knack for finding them. Allowing him to spend another several million on a property that was bound to lose value the instant he bought it seemed downright criminal.

I lost the battle, of course. The firm's share of the money involved in the deal would be enormous, and our managing partner's lust for that money easily trumped any argument I could make. Defeated, I stomped back into my office, trying not to acknowledge the triumphant smile on the face of Mark Davenport, a soft, sweaty fellow in a Brooks Brothers suit and Harvard club tie. Davenport made partner about the same time I did, and he was Roy Blackwell's favorite stooge. Davenport's entire legal practice seemed to consist of separating wealthy, trusting people from their money in one way or another.

Blackwell himself was the Hollywood image of a senior partner in a Wall Street law firm. He was fit, tanned, and handsome, in a Spencer Tracy-ish sort of way. Blackwell was always immaculately dressed in hand-tailored suits and Italian shoes, with nary a strand of his silver mane out of place. He wouldn't have tolerated the damp, sycophantic Davenport for an instant if the younger man hadn't been so willing to suck money out of clients on the firm's behalf.

The note was sitting in the center of my desk, its graceful strokes of black ink starkly noticeable on the rectangle of rich, ivory parchment. Even half-buried in the jumble of files, memos, legal magazines, and an unfinished mug of cold coffee, the note was impossible to overlook, seeming to glow as if lit from within by a thousand candles. "*Come home at once*," it insisted, in an elegant, old-fashioned script.

I crumpled it up and tossed it in the trash.

Then I loaded up my briefcase with the Grandy transaction files and left for the day. The note had annoyed me for some reason, and I was annoyed enough already. There are lots of ways to spend a pleasant evening in New York, and reviewing real estate documents isn't one of them. Still, there might be something in the files to bolster my opposition to the deal, which was going to close soon. If I wanted to protect poor Dr. Grandy from losing another big chunk of his inheritance, I didn't have time to waste.

My law firm was located across the street from the Wall Street stop on the Broadway–Seventh Avenue subway line, my habitual transportation home at the end of the day. The trip might have intimidated an out-of-towner, but I found it no worse than usual. Lawyers, stockbrokers, working people of all stripes, students, tourists, and beggars all crammed together in a chaotic mass of jostling humanity. The car was hot, slightly smelly, and intensely uncomfortable—exactly what I had come to expect at the end of a typical workday in New York.

As the subway rumbled north from Wall Street, a big, lanky man of indeterminate age and heritage—Jamaican, perhaps—shoved his way into the car, raspberry-tinted dreadlocks flowing behind him. He was dressed in baggy jeans, a Bob Marley T-shirt, and ratty sneakers, and the combination made him look like some kind of urban fairy. Sure enough, the man was a busker, one of the many street musicians who haunt the New York subways in search of a meager living. I saw more than one tired New Yorker look up and smile as he sang an island working song, conjuring images of blue skies, green fields, and the sweet smell of sugarcane.

Finished, the singer worked his way through the subway car, shaking an empty coffee can. I reached into my wallet and gave him twenty dollars. It was a huge tip for a busker, but his song had touched me, though for what reason I couldn't say. He smiled, revealing one slightly crooked gold tooth, and his chocolate-brown eyes crinkled. "Come home at once," he said to me. He winked and then vanished into the crowd of commuters, looking for his next audience.

Had I misheard him? Was it just a coincidence that his words seemed to echo the anonymous, discarded note? Whatever was going on, the singer's words startled me. That increased my irritation, so I chose to ignore the coincidence.

The train lurched, slowed, and then stopped at the 79th Street station. I tightened my grip on my briefcase, pushed past the other passengers, and left the train. It was late, I was tired, and it was time to go home.

My apartment was on the Upper West Side of New York City, three blocks from the subway and not far from Lincoln Center and Carnegie Hall. I had moved there for convenient subway access but stayed for the neighborhood's bohemian charm and for the kaleidoscope of ethnic restaurants, artsy shops, and chic boutiques—which my work schedule, admittedly, left me precious little time to enjoy. Still, just walking through the neighborhood every day was a treat, so long as I wasn't so preoccupied with some client's legal troubles that I forgot to look around.

My place wasn't huge—no rationally priced Manhattan apartment is—but it was just enough for my elderly Siamese cat, Honoré, and me. The ceilings were high, the woodwork was more than one hundred years old, and the lovely, tall Palladian windows looked north, out onto a magnificent city that came into being centuries before I was born and will continue to thrive long after I am gone.

So I'm a closet romantic, OK? Nobody's perfect.

Given my starry-eyed secret tendencies, I probably shouldn't have been surprised by what happened next. I opened the door to my apartment, and there sat Honoré on the original hardwood floor, preposterously dignified as only a mature Siamese cat can be. A piece of crumpled parchment rested between his paws, and I didn't even have to smooth it out to know what it said. "*Your father is dying. Come home at once.*"

Oh, come on.

If this all seems a little far-fetched to you, join the club. Long ago, when I still had my baby teeth, and a world of incredible possibilities lay ahead of me, I believed in absolutely *everything*: Santa Claus, the Easter Bunny, the Great Pumpkin, you name it. My mother encouraged me, my beautiful, enchanting, and utterly impractical mother, who vanished without a trace one October night when I was thirteen years old. She went out for something—a PTA meeting, a church social, girls' night out—your guess is as good as mine. All I know is that she never came home.

My father called the police, filed the right reports, made the right inquiries, consulted the right people, and soldiered on exactly as everyone said he should. He was a model of perfect rectitude. And if he wasn't able to console his confused, heartbroken daughter, well, who could blame him, when he was obviously trying so hard?

I don't think my father ever realized that after my mother disappeared I left my bedroom window open every single night. I still don't know why. Even if she returned, my mother would hardly have come crawling over my windowsill at two o'clock in the morning. I guess it was sort of like lighting a candle in the window, a symbol of my hope that God or the angels or even Peter Pan would bring her back. It wasn't until early February, after the temperatures dipped so low that I shivered sleepless under two blankets for a week straight, that I finally closed the window. That was the night when I finally admitted to myself that she wasn't coming back.

Shortly thereafter, my father clumsily presented me with a Siamese kitten. He was barely three months old, a fuzzy scrap of fawn-colored fur with bright blue eyes and a brown smudge on his nose that would grow into an elegant bandit's mask. He was so tiny that he could settle down into my two cupped hands, but he had the heart of a lion even then. I named him Honoré for the debonair *bon vivant* that Maurice Chevalier portrayed in *Gigi*, my mother's favorite movie. For once, my father didn't disparage or try to improve on my choice. Little Honoré cuddled up against my jawbone night after night, the warmest thing in my drafty room, purring his tiny heart out and giving me something solid to cling to while I slept.

It's embarrassing to admit it, but Honoré became my oldest and closest friend. We grew up together, lounging for hours at a time on my bed as social studies reports and debate club projects gave way to college term papers and then law school exam preparations. He sprawled majestically across my class notes for hours, forcing me to memorize rules of law and pertinent case details because I didn't have the heart to disturb him. It annoyed me sometimes, but it also sharpened my memory and helped me ace the exams that put me at the top of my class. That, in turn, rendered me eligible for a job at one of New York's most prestigious law firms. Other law students had study groups—I had Honoré. The competitive advantage was definitely mine.

Elderly now, Honoré still slept on my shoulder, his head pressed firmly beneath my jaw. Any casual date who objected to his presence got shown the door fast. Men come and go in New York and all too rarely linger. But Honoré was always there, and I was always grateful for his loving and dignified presence.

Knowing what it said, I nevertheless took the crumpled note from between Honoré's paws and smoothed it out. "*Your father is dying. Come home at once.*" Honoré huffed a little and walked away, tail upright, his messenger duties fulfilled. I thought about throwing the note back into the trash, but couldn't bring myself to crumple it up again. I wasn't ready to drop everything and rush out of town, but it was time to pick up the phone.

The receiver beeped when I lifted it. My father's nurse, Paula, had already left me a message. "Your father's in bad shape, Miss Kate," she said in a thick upstate New York accent. "You better come home right away, OK?"

I hung up the phone with a sigh and set the note down. The coincidence of the note arriving just in time to warn me of Paula's call should have been disquieting. Oddly enough, it didn't trouble me at all.

I went into my tiny bedroom, dragged my overnight bag out of the closet and started throwing things in. Honoré jumped up on the bed and settled in to watch as I packed. This time, though, he didn't crawl into the bag as he usually did, an old joke between us that only another cat lover could appreciate. He just sat there, solemnly watching.

At first, I decided to leave Honoré at home. I would be gone for only a day or two, and we had a reliable pet sitter. Darla was a graduate student who looked in on Honoré daily when business took me out of town. He liked Darla, and she adored him, always bringing treats of lox or smoked oysters from the tiny grocery store on the corner for her "fine French gentleman." Darla's visits would have spared Honoré the stress of traveling upstate, so leaving him behind would have been the sensible thing to do. Still…

I was halfway out the apartment door when, on an impulse, I turned back, grabbed Honoré, and dumped him into his pet carrier. He settled down with his usual equanimity, and I shifted my overnight bag to one shoulder so I could manage my briefcase and purse in one hand while carrying him in the other. Heavily laden, I took the elevator down to the lobby and walked out into the heat, haze, and clamor of the late summer evening.

It can be almost impossible to catch a cab in New York City, but for once we got lucky. I had barely stepped to the curb when a cab pulled up. The driver, an oversize, unshaven man with shaggy dark hair wearing a red plaid shirt, rolled the window down. He smiled broadly, revealing big, uneven teeth. "Need a ride, miss?" he asked, in a thick Russian accent. "You look like you have a lot to carry. Where are you headed?"

It was such a simple question, but the unexpected kindness in his voice caught me off guard. My eyes began to water—I must have been more worried about my father than I had thought. "Penn Station," I replied.

The cabbie got out and opened the trunk. "I'll take your luggage, miss. You just hang onto your little friend there." He quickly stashed my overnight bag and briefcase as I climbed in, settling Honoré's carrier firmly on my lap. In less than a minute, Honoré and I were headed for Penn Station and the train that would take us upstate to my father's house.

For the first time in years, we were going home.

Archangel Gabriel speaks:

For a moment there, I was afraid Kate was going to ignore my message. It isn't easy to communicate with people now, when a cacophony of conflicting voices, real and electronic, distracts their minds and troubles their hearts. Add to that all the myriad complexities around free will, and the work of a messenger angel is a lot more challenging today than it was a few millennia ago. Back then, all we had to do was materialize, emit a comforting glow, and say, "Be not afraid." People fell all over themselves to listen. Those were the days, I'll tell you.

Kate's case was particularly troublesome. Young as she was, unresolved grief, the loneliness that accompanies life in a big city, and the pressures of practicing law in a Wall Street firm had hardened her almost beyond recovery. She was all but deaf to her inner voice, the instrument that my angels and I normally use to communicate. We had tried more subtle means: significant song lyrics on her radio, phrases on billboards and signs that she passed every day, a few meaningful words spoken by someone in a meeting or in a conversation overheard on the street. She had ignored them all, though, and time was running short. That's why I asked for special permission to leave her a note.

We try not to communicate with physical objects like the note I placed on Kate's desk very often. Their sudden appearance is tangible proof that miracles do, in fact, happen, and miracles frighten people in the modern world. They rush to either dismiss miracles as practical jokes or explain them away by science. Even if people do believe, others laugh at them or argue. The message gets missed in the ensuring squabble about whether the miracle was "real" or not. My job is to inspire faith, not conflict.

That note was as real, which is to say, as solid and tangible, as the half-full mug of cold coffee sitting next to it on Kate's desk. As for how it got there, well, let's just say that it took me a fair bit of negotiating and a small mountain of administrative work to get permission to do it. Consequently, when Kate crumpled the note and threw it in the trash I wasn't especially pleased.

Thankfully, though, there are always second chances in Heaven. Had she quietly gone along with the bad real estate deal, it would have been difficult for me to convince anyone that Kate hadn't simply sold her soul for money as so many people do. Even that would have been remediable before she died–everything is, after all–but not in time for the events that we had all choreographed so carefully to unfold as planned.

Fortunately, Kate fought like a tiger to protect the vulnerable old doctor. My angels and I cheered her on even as her managing partner refused to budge. That not only gave us hope for her, it encouraged us about him as well. Does that surprise you? It shouldn't. Remorse can be a marvelous teacher, and Roy Blackwell would have plenty of opportunities to learn from it before leaving the physical world. His angels continue their labors, and remain optimistic that they'll be able to bring him around to repentance once he finally starts to recognize just how badly he behaved.

At that moment, though, my primary focus was on Kate. Citing her magnificent performance as proof that she still could be reached, I was granted permission to keep trying. One of my angels suited up as a subway busker to pass my message along, but she chose to ignore him, as well.

It was frustrating, but not entirely Kate's fault. New Yorkers learn quickly to tune out strangers to avoid being cheated or robbed. My angel admitted later that his costume had probably been too convincing. (He appreciated the tip, though.) Kate enjoys Manhattan's street musicians, but she lost the ability really to listen to them years ago. Pity–they are some of the best messengers I have.

Unfortunately, we were running out of time. Whether she knew it or not, Kate needed the chance to say good-bye before her father passed on, so it was necessary to err on the side of the miraculous. Having the crumpled note that she had discarded in her office reappear on the floor of her apartment was a trifle excessive, but I was flat out of other options. Luckily, Kate finally took the hint, checked her messages, and headed off on her adventure. After a bumpy start, things were finally looking up.

It was one of those days that make me love my job.

CHAPTER TWO

When I took the train out of Manhattan, it always surprised me to see how quickly the city's bustling streets and soaring skyscrapers gave way to the rolling farmland, coursing rivers, and silver birch woods of New York State. People who live elsewhere always think of the city as "New York," but Manhattan couldn't be more different from the lands that lie above it.

Manhattanites, of course, believe that the city *is* the state. The *New Yorker* magazine's most famous cover remains its 1976 "The World as Seen from 9th Avenue" map, which depicted Manhattan as larger than New Jersey and everything to its west, and the Hudson River as only slightly narrower than the Pacific Ocean. Its residents believe that New York City rules the world, and the rest of New York State is usually wise enough to dodge the argument. Still, the quiet beauty of New York beyond Manhattan has a magic of its own. Living in the city, I forgot that sometimes.

Honoré and I were headed to Angel Falls, the little town where I grew up and my father still lived. Perched on the Hudson River between Manhattan and Albany, Angel Falls is a discreetly well-to-do community, established in the 1700s and named for the crystalline waterfall that flows over high stone cliffs in the woods on the northern side of town.

Local legend is more romantic, claiming that the village was actually named for a gleaming white angel who emerged from that same waterfall one dark night. According to the story, the angel startled awake the town founder, Jacob Wittesteen, an ill-tempered drunkard who had stumbled out into the woods to sleep off a binge. Every child in Angel Falls knows the tale, and a mural depicting the moment of Wittesteen's awakening is the first thing visitors see when they enter our town hall.

No one knows what the angel said to the astonished Wittesteen that night, but the story goes that the conversation instantly turned the man's life around. He became a strict teetotaler, married a girl from a good family in a nearby town, and built a successful dry-goods store that served as the anchor for a thriving community. Wittesteen supposedly grew into something of a father figure to his neighbors, praised for his good works and benevolent disposition. When he died at the ripe old age of ninety-four, Wittesteen left all of his land and the store to the community, subject to the sole proviso that the village be named Angel Falls in honor of the miraculous encounter that had transformed him from sinner to saint.

Wittesteen's dry-goods store is still on the town square, preserved as a museum, with a brass plaque on the wall that tells his tale much more kindly than I have. No one really knows whether the story is true, but it adds the kind of local color that tourists adore. They buy angel-shaped lollipops, cookie cutters, and refrigerator magnets, and postcards depicting Wittesteen's mystical encounter, delighting in the quaintness of the shop and its surroundings.

The northern side of Angel Falls is made up of restored antique homes with neatly mowed lawns and manicured gardens. A white gazebo nestles in the center of the town square, its eaves carved to resemble outstretched angel wings. A community band plays there every Thursday evening in the summer. There is a library with wide stone steps and gabled windows, a graveyard filled with the mossy, crumbling headstones of generations of the town's oldest families, and a handful of charming specialty shops and boutique restaurants with angel-related themes. There are also some of the best public schools in the country. Imagine a world of Scott Joplin ragtime piano, white lawn dresses, and ice-cream socials, all watched over from a polite distance by benevolent seraphs, and you will know how the more prosperous citizens of Angel Falls think of their home.

There is a darker side to Angel Falls, though, that the tourists don't see and the locals don't like to acknowledge. On the southern side of town, the homes are less immaculate, the yards scruffy and unkempt. The luckier occupants of those houses, with their weedy sidewalks and grimy windows, work as nannies, housekeepers, cooks, and gardeners for their rich northern neighbors, too busy tending other people's homes to devote much time or energy to their own. Their kids bus tables in the restaurants on the square or take tickets and shovel popcorn at the local movie theater.

The less fortunate don't work at all, but sit outside their rundown houses on rusting metal chairs, drinking cheap beer and staring off into space at nothing in particular. Children play ball in the streets, dogs roam without collars, and it's not uncommon for recreational drugs and money to change hands in the parking lots. I wasn't allowed on that side of town growing up, and my father never spoke of it. Everyone who lives on the north side of Angel Falls knows about the south side, though, and looks away from the troubles of their less privileged neighbors.

The darker aspects of Angel Falls weren't on my mind as we boarded the train. All I could think about was just how sick and antagonistic my father was likely to be when we arrived. I couldn't remember how long it had been since my last visit, which meant it had been too long. Despite the cancer that was slowly overtaking him, I knew from our phone conversations that my father retained his quick wit and uncanny ability to skewer me with a few well-chosen words. This time, I expected his comments to be particularly sharp.

I was lucky enough to find two empty seats together, so Honoré didn't have to make the trip on my lap. Instead, he rested comfortably in his carrier on the seat next to mine. Most cats hate to travel, but Honoré never objected to it or, for that matter, to much of anything else. His equanimity was always a marvel. Reaching into the carrier, I offered him a taste of the smoked salmon cream cheese that I had bought with a bagel and coffee at Penn Station as a light supper. He licked it thoughtfully from my fingertip, closed his eyes, and purred.

Once we finished the bagel, we still had about an hour to go before our stop. That gave me plenty of time to review the real estate documents and find out just how badly Dr. Grandy was about to be swindled. I reached up to the luggage rack to grab my briefcase, and was shocked to discover that it wasn't there.

It's hard to describe the intensity of my panic when I realized my briefcase was gone. It wasn't the loss of the briefcase itself that upset me. It had been a gift from my father when I graduated from law school, and it was *ugly*: big, hard, heavy, and so black that it seemed to devour any glimmer of light that was foolhardy enough to approach it. It had sharp, square edges, and was tall, deep, and wide enough to hold more files than I could ever hope to carry. It was just like the one my father had received as a graduation gift from *his* parents when he began his own legal practice decades before, its weight compounded by the burden of that legacy. It wasn't just a briefcase, it was an unspoken command to follow in his footsteps, equal his successes and then go on to surpass him. Truth be told, I hated the damned thing. It would have been a blessing to lose it—if the Grandy real estate files hadn't been inside.

The thing is, those files were absolutely confidential. Clients need to feel safe telling their lawyers the unvarnished truth, so we can offer them our best advice. They won't do that if they can't trust us not to air their dirty laundry. Consequently, the legal profession insists that attorneys' private communications with their clients be kept as sacrosanct as religious confessions of sin.

Unfortunately, some of my less ethical colleagues have been too willing to hide their clients' misdeeds behind a convenient cloak of attorney-client privilege. That is one reason so many people hate lawyers. In an age where everyone else is focused on transparency and openness, the attorney's duty of confidentiality can seem downright deceitful. Still, it is one of the most important ethical rules of my profession. Client confidentiality must be maintained at all costs, period. A lawyer who breaches client confidentiality can expect to be kicked out of the legal profession in a flash.

And there I sat, having lost about a ream of my client's extremely confidential paperwork, so frantic I could barely breathe.

I had no idea where my briefcase might be, or, worse, who might have it. One thing I did know—it wasn't locked. Anyone, absolutely *anyone*, could look inside and read everything there was to know about Dr. Grandy's upcoming real estate deal, including his private financial information and the confidential memorandum about our negotiating strategy that Roy Blackwell had delivered to him just that morning. Even if Dr. Grandy forgave me, Blackwell never would. Partner or not, unless I found those papers I would be out of a job for sure.

Wildly, I looked around to see whether someone had taken my briefcase or moved it to make room for their own luggage. But the car was almost empty. Its only other occupant was a sixtyish woman seated several rows away who seemed deeply immersed in a *Harry Potter* novel. It occurred to me that I hadn't read a novel for pleasure in over a year. I pushed the irrelevant thought away and tried to concentrate, mentally retracing my steps.

The image of the Russian cabbie putting my briefcase in the trunk of his taxi flashed into my mind. He had taken it from me, but I couldn't remember getting it back. Once we got to Penn Station, I remembered buying my train ticket, picking up the bagel and coffee, and boarding the train. I had put my overnight bag in the luggage rack, but I couldn't recall juggling my briefcase with my other luggage. I had been so focused on taking care of Honoré, I hadn't even noticed that my briefcase was missing.

No question about it—the briefcase was still in the cab.

That realization should have upset me still more. Oddly, perhaps, it did just the opposite. People are forever leaving umbrellas, cell phones, laptops, and, yes, briefcases in New York City cabs. They get them back more often than you might think. If I had the cab company's number, it would be easy to ask them to hold it for a couple of days. My gap-toothed Russian cabbie had been memorable even by New York standards. They would know who he was. The briefcase would still be in his trunk. Heck, he had probably already turned it in to the lost and found.

Rummaging in my wallet, I found the receipt, and sure enough, the cab company's phone number was printed on it. I pulled out my cell phone (not an iPhone, mind you—the senior partners in our firm wanted constant access to us all but didn't believe in "wasting money" on stylish Apple products). I was just about to dial when I heard a delicate "ahem" about two feet above my head.

Looking up, I saw the *Harry Potter* fan standing in the aisle next to me. Seemingly impervious to the summer heat, she wore a pink turtleneck top, a fluffy green cardigan sweater, and a gathered skirt made of some soft, fussy floral print. Her graying hair was tightly curled, and her outfit was completed with sensible brown oxfords and half-moon reading glasses suspended from a chain around her neck. I thought instantly of Maggie Smith and smiled in spite of my worries.

The woman placed one long, arthritic hand on my shoulder and smiled back. The hand was wrinkled and spotted, but her nails were polished a delicate pink, and she wore a beautiful antique garnet ring. "Have you lost something, dear?" she asked, her voice softened by the hint of a British accent. "You seem terribly worried."

"Not really," I replied, trying to hide my concern. "I left something important behind, but I know where it is, and I'm sure I'll be able to get it back."

Her smile broadened. "It can't have been all that important if you left it behind, dear. You strike me as a young woman who knows how to hang onto the things she really cares about." She glanced at Honoré, comfortably asleep in his carrier. "You just hold tight to your friend there. He dearly loves you, and love is a thing you should never let go." She gently patted my shoulder again, and went back to her seat.

My shoulder felt cold where her hand had rested. I glanced at Honoré. He still seemed to be asleep, but for a moment the barest hint of a smile played around his whiskers. "You're not the Cheshire cat, you know," I muttered, and then turned to call the cab company.

I was dialing the last digit when the train went into a tunnel, cutting off my phone. We traveled for a few moments in darkness, the only light coming from the lamps overhead. When we emerged from the tunnel I tried again, but there was no cell phone service to be had. It didn't matter, I decided. It was probably too late to call anyway. I would try first thing in the morning, and would just have to trust that the briefcase would be safe until then.

For a while I watched the Hudson River go by, its rippled surface silvered by the light of the waxing moon. It had gotten dark as we traveled north, but I had been so busy worrying about the briefcase that I hadn't even noticed.

My failure to observe such a gradual shift in the world around me was nothing new. There had been several times since law school graduation when whole seasons had passed without my noticing. Life in the city can distract you from changes in the natural world, and I had been too focused on working toward partnership to pay attention to the subtle but beautiful show that nature was performing outside my door. When the seasonal changes finally became pronounced enough that even I couldn't overlook them, I was always faintly regretful, as though I had missed something important. That never kept me from making the same mistake again, though. Time after time, I would look around and realize that another season of my life had passed away, unnoticed, while I worked.

Moments later, the conductor announced our impending arrival at Angel Falls. I gathered up my overnight bag, my purse, and Honoré, and then turned to say good-bye to the English woman. She was gone. Must have headed to the café car for a cup of tea, I thought. The train stopped, and the doors slid open.

Taking a deep breath, I stepped off the train and onto the station platform. The air was cooler than it had been in the city. A light breeze carried the scents of clean water and fresh, growing green things. Had I been less stressed and distracted, it would have been a wonderful welcome. As it was, the beauty was there—I just wasn't able to appreciate it.

Clutching Honoré's travel carrier, my purse, and my overnight bag, I lumbered down the metal stairs from the train platform to the station entrance, my heels ringing hollowly on each step, to look for a cab. It turned out that I didn't need one. Andrew Eriksen, the dear man who, with his wife Bella, had maintained my father's house for years, was waiting for me in my father's old black Lincoln. The engine purred softly under its perfectly waxed hood. "After Paula left that message, we were sure you would come, Miss Kate," he said in greeting. "It wasn't hard to guess which train. Let's go—your father is waiting."

Archangel Raphael speaks:

Every archangel has personal interests. Mine is good health. My angels and I keep Creation healthy, and we especially love to soothe away the hurts that plague the human soul. We don't usually worry too much about business–that's more Uriel's territory. But when business starts interfering with people's well-being, we step in and help. Kate was under so much stress that it was starting to affect her health. That brought her right into my sphere.

It never ceases to amaze me, how readily human beings hurt themselves and each other in the pursuit of money! Kate's briefcase might as well have been chained to her wrist by a medieval torturer. It kept her totally focused on her job, blind to my Master's beautiful world and unable to enjoy the priceless gift of the life she had been given. OK, the thing was more useful than a rack or an iron maiden. But for Kate, just looking at that briefcase was a torment.

Her father's parents had given him a case just like it years before, wrapped up in exaggerated expectations and their certainty that he would never be good enough to meet them. What they did to him would be hard to forgive if they hadn't been bullied and buffeted by their own parents in turn. Still, they're not the most likable people in Heaven. They have been with us for decades now, and they're just as judgmental as they were when they passed away. We'll keep trying to heal them, of course, but only the Master knows whether they'll ever unbend.

Kate's father passed their harsh ways onto her with the "gift" of that horrible briefcase. His ability to love was so distorted by his cold, critical parents! He thought he loved his daughter, and in some ways he did. Still, he was a lot less interested in loving her than in making her run the same gauntlet that he had. He told himself that he had succeeded despite his parents' disapproval and was bitterly determined to make sure Kate did, too. Hazing takes a lot of forms, and it's hellishly tough to stop once it gets started.

Personally, I was glad Kate left her briefcase in the taxi. It gave her a break from the burdensome expectations she associated with it. With time, she might even realize how free she really was to toss it aside for good if she wanted.

It's too bad that agonizing over those files was spoiling her break. So much worry over a few pieces of paper! I'll never understand why people keep secrets from each other when they do business together. If somebody wants to sell something and somebody else wants to buy it, why not just tell each other everything and work out a deal where everybody comes away happy? It would be healthier, that's for sure.

When she realized that her briefcase was gone, Kate panicked, sending her already stressed body into high alert. We didn't want her getting sick. So, one of my most effective angels went in to work with her, a darling who has been delivering peace to people since before they hung the gardens of Babylon. That little dose of loving energy she gave Kate through a touch on the shoulder would soon start working its magic.

We really need to update that angel's costume, though. It has gotten old enough to seem almost cartoonish. We can't have people realizing how often the charming strangers they encounter "by chance" are really angels in disguise. It would ruin the surprise, and where's the fun in that?

CHAPTER THREE

"Are you warm enough, Miss Kate?"

Just as with the Russian cabbie, Andrew's kindness caught me by surprise. It shouldn't have—he and Bella had always been considerate toward their employer's motherless little girl—but it reminded me again of how few people had spoken kindly to me of late. (Dr. Grandy had always been kind to me, but I wasn't in the mood to dwell on that just then.)

"Fine, Andrew, just a little tired. Thank you for coming to get us."

Andrew chuckled. He was a tall, broad-shouldered man, still lean despite many years of enjoying his wife's excellent cooking. He had a ready smile, a shock of silvering hair, and gray eyes that crinkled more when he smiled than I remembered. How long had it been since I had seen him?

"Glad to see the old fellow's still going strong," he remarked, inclining his head toward Honoré, resting in his carrier on my lap. "They live a long time, Siamese cats do."

Siamese cats typically do live a long time, often into their late teens and sometimes past twenty. I have heard stories of the odd specimen who lived to twenty-five or older. Still, I experienced an uncomfortable moment as I tried to remember just how old Honoré was. I got him when I was thirteen—or was it fourteen? And now I was thirty-two... The thought fell away as a sudden gust of wind blew a swirl of fallen leaves against the windshield. It's colder in the Hudson Valley than in Manhattan, and autumn comes sooner there.

"Bella will have your room ready, Miss Kate, and you'll want to see your father before he retires for the night." Andrew's voice didn't flinch, but I sensed a touch of uneasiness in his tone.

"How bad is he?" I asked.

"Bad enough," Andrew replied. "He's strong and determined, and he has hung on longer than the doctors said he would. No one lives forever, though, not even him."

Andrew was right about that. No one lives forever, though my father, the great Christopher Jamison Cunningham, would certainly strive to be the first. He was born in Tonawanda, a blue-collar suburb of Buffalo, New York, the only child of a Scottish immigrant steelworker and his wife. He grew up poor—as he never failed to remind me—but claimed that his childhood poverty spurred him on to achieve greater success. I have always suspected that my father was secretly grateful for his impoverished childhood, since it gave him added justification to take pride in his accomplishments. Pride was always his greatest pleasure.

Christopher Cunningham was a big, rawboned man in his late sixties, with wintry gray eyes, broad shoulders, and a raptor's beak of a nose. His shock of black hair had not gone gray until the cancer took hold. The sharpness of his expression was rivaled only by the strength of his intellect and ambition. From boyhood on, he devoted his life to achieving more than his parents or anyone else in their working-class community thought possible. He went to college and law school on full scholarships and was valedictorian at every graduation he attended. He built a legal practice representing union laborers like his father and then went on to represent his community in the New York State Assembly.

I was just a little girl when we moved to the great house in Angel Falls that my father bought so he could be closer to Albany. He maintained his parents' home in Buffalo as his local residence for many years, though. He won reelection time and again, brutally crushing the ambitions of any political rival foolish enough to contest his seat.

I have since learned that my father was once widely considered to be a shoo-in for the governorship, and that there had been talk among his supporters about a run for the White House someday. But then my mother vanished, shattering my father's political aspirations as she went. No one seriously believed that my father had hurt her, and the police never found even the slightest evidence of foul play. Still, happy wives do not abandon their families. My mother's unexplained disappearance left a faint but permanent stain on my father's reputation. A promised nomination for lieutenant governor went to a rival, he was passed over for president of the state senate, and then a committee of his closest advisors and contributors quietly approached him to suggest that he not run for office again. My father, no fool, took the hint. He sold his parents' house in Buffalo, retired from public life, and moved permanently into his Angel Falls residence to brood over the unfairness of it all.

My father's house was a mansard-roofed, neo-Baroque monstrosity, built in the 1860s by a robber baron whose name has long since passed from memory. Constructed of damp, gray stone, it featured heavy columns, gables in unlikely places, crawling ivy, and a biliously green copper roof. Inside, the house was dim and musty, with dark-stained mahogany woodwork that no amount of polish and elbow grease could brighten, faded wallpaper, worn oriental rugs, and perpetual drafts from chinks in the walls that no handyman had ever been able to find and plug.

The house was never neglected or unkempt—Andrew and Bella would not have permitted that. But by both design and temperament it was far more a haunted mansion than a comfortable family home. It reeked of bitter old money, faded elegance, and ruined hopes vanished into anonymous dust. The house was worth a fortune, but I had hated it as a child and didn't like it any better as an adult.

While the house was foreboding, the grounds were somewhat less so. The wide circular driveway, formal gardens, and spacious, rolling lawns were handsome enough, so long as my father kept a team of gardeners to maintain them. As the years passed, though, he had dismissed all of his staff except for Andrew and Bella. Unable to manage the grounds alone, Andrew let the surrounding woods reclaim the margins of the property. Inside the house, as my father's social schedule declined and his acquaintances drifted away, Bella closed off the rooms one after another, until my father lived in only two or three of them. The house and my father declined together, growing colder, grimmer, and grayer with each passing year.

The evening sky darkened as Andrew pulled into the drive. I could picture my father, sitting alone in his wheelchair next to the black marble hearth, staring into the dying fire like some mad prophet seeking a sign that the end of the world was finally at hand.

And he wondered why I never came home.

We didn't talk about it, of course. I would call, usually on Sundays, and tell him as much about my legal work as prudence and ethics would allow. When I first started practicing he was tremendously helpful, offering thoughts I hadn't considered and strategies that quickly brought me to the partners' favorable notice. In his later years, though, my father started to suggest actions I had already taken, theories I had considered and abandoned, or methods that would ruin my credibility if I used them. If I questioned him or, Heaven forbid, dared to argue, he would become enraged, hang up the phone, and refuse to take my calls for weeks at a time. Our conversations eventually settled into rote civilities, and at a certain point, it seemed best to end each one as soon as I decently could. Then I would sit, Honoré on my lap, and stare blankly into space for hours before returning to whatever work I had on hand at home.

Thankfully, the life of a young lawyer at a big Manhattan firm is always horrifically busy. I had plenty of excuses not to visit, and I used them all. As Andrew and I climbed out of the Lincoln, though, I realized with a sharp pang of guilt that I had not been back to Angel Falls in almost three years.

Fallen leaves crunched underfoot as I walked up to the front door, a slab of polished walnut with an enormous lion-headed door knocker. The wind was chilly against my face, and I could smell wood smoke from somewhere close by. For a moment, I remembered jumping into piles of fallen leaves as a child, back in a time before everything gathered from the grounds was labeled "waste," bagged in plastic, and shipped off to landfills. The door opened the instant I knocked and Bella stood there, silhouetted in firelight and smiling warmly.

It would be lovely to be able to say that Bella was like a mother to me. The truth is that my mother's absence created a profound emptiness in our household that no one else could ever completely fill. Still, dear, maternal Bella had baked my birthday cakes, pressed my dresses, kept track of my bewildering round of extracurricular activities, and generally looked after me throughout my adolescence. She hadn't replaced my mother—no one could—but she had certainly done her best.

Bella was a lovely little woman, as petite and graceful as Andrew was big and rangy. She had velvety brown, expressive eyes with enviably long lashes, a full but graceful figure, and dark, luxurious hair, streaked with silver, which she wore in a practical braid down her back. On anyone else, the hairstyle would have looked austere—on Bella, it created the impression of a Gypsy queen.

Seeing her again, her face more deeply lined than I remembered, I was immediately awash in shame. I hadn't mistreated just my father, I had also neglected Bella and Andrew. They weren't family, exactly, but they had been very, very good to me for a very long time. I had forgotten how much they had once meant to me.

Bella opened her arms, and I rushed into them for a hug as eagerly as if I were thirteen years old again.

"Come inside, Katie," she said. "He's waiting for you." She smiled down at Honoré, hanging from my hand in his carrier. "Good to see you again, sir," she said to him. She turned back to me. "Katie, why don't you let Honoré out? We thought he would probably be coming with you. His food and box are all ready, right where he'll expect them to be."

Pulling back from Bella, I set the carrier on the floor and opened the door. Honoré sauntered out, stretched, twined once around Bella's ankles, and then disappeared up the grand staircase.

Bella chuckled. "Still the lord of all he surveys, I see." Her smile faded. "Come with me, Katie. It's getting late and your father doesn't do well when he gets tired. You had better visit with him now so he can get to bed."

I followed Bella into the cavernous parlor. The lamps were all turned off, but just as I had imagined, there was a fire on the hearth. Though dying down to coals, it still cast enough light for me to see my father, once the lion of the New York State Senate, sitting in his pajamas and robe in a wheelchair and waiting for me.

His face was yellowed, liver-spotted, and fallen, exaggerating the sharpness of his profile. He had lost weight, and his once-broad shoulders had collapsed into his chest, making him look like some ancient bird of prey. His hair had never fully grown back since the last round of chemo, and it clung to his scalp in uneven patches. An oxygen tube ran from a canister attached to his chair across his chest and up to his nostrils. When he looked up at me, though, his iron-gray gaze was as piercing as ever.

"Thought you would never get here," he said, coldly.

I swallowed hard, a disobedient little girl being rightfully scolded. How was it that, years after I had grown up into a successful adult, he could still reduce me to a puddle of shame with a few sharp words?

"Sorry," I replied, trying not to let him see that he had upset me. "I didn't get Paula's call until after I left the office."

My father shook his head as if I had just confirmed his worst expectations. "Brought that cat with you?" he asked. I nodded. "Figures," he grunted, and turned back to the fire.

After that, I tried a few times to start a conversation, to ask how he was feeling, even to say good-bye. My father ignored me, staring into the flames with all his might. I was so grateful not to be berated that I welcomed his sullen silence, promising myself that I'd make another attempt to talk with him in the morning. Bella brought me a glass of wine, and my father eventually fell asleep in his chair, firelight flickering over his ruined face. Andrew wheeled him away and put him to bed. Alone, I sat and watched the fire for a while, then finished my wine and went up to bed myself.

There are parents who keep their children's rooms untouched out of love. My father left my room unchanged after I left for college, but there was no sentiment involved. He just saw no need to invest time or money in redecorating it. And, in fairness, I never asked him to redo my room, because I was never home long enough to make it worthwhile.

So I went to bed that night in a drafty room decorated for a teenage girl, with faded curtains and yellowing wallpaper. My high school debate medals still hung from the cork bulletin board over my old desk, and well-worn paperback novels sat next to my high school and college yearbooks on the bookshelves. But the sheets were clean and fragrant, the blankets were freshly aired, and Honoré sat waiting at the foot of the bed, as he has every night since he was a kitten. I climbed into bed, he cuddled up under my chin as always, and at last we slept.

Archangel Azrael speaks:

You are more likely to recognize my famous brethren than me. Most people have heard of Gabriel, Archangel of the Annunciation, and who does not know Archangel Michael? Even without all the statues and paintings, not to mention that delightful John Travolta movie, Michael would be the most celebrated among us. After all, Michael is the leader of God's army, a brilliant strategist who is personally responsible for casting the Adversary out of Heaven. What a battle that was! We still tell stories about it, and the mortal souls among us are always enthralled. You people practically worship your warriors—so of course you love our handsome, charismatic Michael most of all.

Please do not mistake my admiration for jealousy. There is no envy in Heaven. How could there be? We archangels are all perfectly capable of doing whatever the Divine requires of us. Any of us could do what another does should circumstances call for it.

That said, we offer our best service when we are truest to ourselves. Michael is every inch a hero. Gabriel plays a spectacular trumpet and could talk the birds out of the trees. Raphael is a gentle, sensitive companion and extraordinarily gifted healer. You understand… Thanks to our Master, we archangels are a talented bunch.

As for me, well, my talents lie in a different direction. You may not know the name "Archangel Azrael," but I would bet my best harp that you have heard of the Angel of Death. People fear me as much as they love Michael, but they would not if they understood what my angels and I really do.

Death comes to every living thing (with one notable exception, of course). Sometimes, for someone like Kate's beloved Honoré, the rules can be stretched, delaying the natural progression that leads to death for a good long while. Sooner or later, though, every soul that was ever born needs help transitioning into the hereafter. My angels and I accompany those souls, guiding them through the transition and providing comfort and compassion as they look back over the lives they have left behind.

I have long suspected that people fear death—and me—because they are terrified to examine the things they did while they were alive. Everyone makes mistakes, even the holiest of saints. Still, nearly everyone also expects to be the one soul who gets everything right from cradle to grave. Departed souls are so ashamed when they look back and realize how many opportunities they lost, how much beauty they overlooked, and how much pain they inflicted on the people they loved. They do not want to admit how much they have squandered, but they cannot look away from the unvarnished truth when it is illuminated by the light of the Divine. All their fond, false illusions about themselves dissolve like smoke, leaving an unpleasant smell behind. Only a very few can stand it at first.

How they suffer! But we never inflict suffering upon them—they do it all themselves. My angels and I do not expect people to be perfect. The Master made human beings to be glorious, fallible creatures, and who are we to argue? We are honored to comfort and support departed souls as they grieve over the mistakes they made, the loving words left unspoken, and the good deeds left undone.

When my angels and I have comforted the departed long enough for their regrets to come into perspective, they are usually able to forgive themselves. That allows them to pass unburdened into Heaven. They are welcomed with open arms, their mistakes pardoned and forgotten by the Master and everyone else concerned. So, you see, we provide a very important service indeed.

Kate's father was in for an especially challenging transition. Having been one of those (thankfully) rare individuals who are so bitter that they want to inflict pain even from beyond the grave, he was going to need all the help he could get. Such a shame—he once had so much promise! No one's life is wasted, but I knew, after centuries of doing this work, that he would think otherwise for a very long time. Instead of passing him along to one of my angels, I decided to handle him myself.

We will meet one day, you and I. When we do, please do not be afraid. I promise not to hurt you. Once you get over your self-blame and regrets, you are going to love it here.

CHAPTER FOUR

I woke, muzzy-headed, to the sound of my cell phone buzzing on the bedside table. I had been so worn out by the time I had gone to bed that I didn't even remembering leaving it there. The sun was streaming into the tall window beside my bed, making dust motes dance. It was still cold, but the room felt cozier and more welcoming than it had the night before or, for that matter, as far back as I could remember. Then again, it had been years since I had last slept there, so maybe my memory was a little off.

The screen flashed as the phone buzzed again, louder than before. It was 8:45 in the morning, and the firm's managing partner, Roy Blackwell, was calling me.

Oh, God.

Quickly sitting up in bed, I grabbed the phone and answered on the third ring. "Hello, Mr. Blackwell."

"We had a strategy session on the Grandy acquisition scheduled for 8:30 a.m., Cunningham," he barked, not even bothering to wish me good morning. "Where the hell are you? Everyone has been waiting, and as you well know, we can't bill for that time."

In my haste to get upstate, I had forgotten all about the meeting.

"There has been a family emergency, Mr. Blackwell," I quickly replied. "My father is terminally ill, and I've been called home. It was very sudden. I haven't had a chance to call you." That wasn't strictly true, but having been startled awake, the last thing I needed was a lecture on billable hours. The firm got plenty of them from me, Heaven knew.

"Our final meeting with the seller is scheduled for ten a.m. Thursday, Cunningham," Blackwell fired back. He was clearly annoyed, but he had known about my father's illness for months. Even he couldn't decently argue with my absence. "That's only three days from now. When will you be back?"

"I don't really know, Mr. Blackwell," I replied. "My father isn't doing well. It shouldn't be more than a day or two, though." I tried to sound polite. Having endured my father's icy welcome the night before, I wasn't eager to ruin the morning by provoking a fight with my boss.

"That's not going to cut it, Cunningham," Blackwell snapped. "Opposing counsel will use any delay to our disadvantage. We can't postpone the meeting and we can't walk in unprepared. You know it's going to take hours to get everything ready. I'll have to reassign the deal to Davenport. He'll be more committed to the negotiations than you were anyway. But we have a problem. When you didn't show up this morning, I had Davenport search that slovenly haystack you call your office. He wasn't able to find the transaction files in all that mess. Where the devil are they?"

My mouth went dry and a cold chill seized my stomach. I had slept later than intended, missing the opportunity to call the cab company and track down my briefcase before facing Blackwell's wrath. At that moment, I didn't actually know where the files were, though I hoped they were safe in the cab company's office. Blackwell's silence at the other end of the phone grew deadly.

Sometimes I wonder what would have happened if I had told Roy Blackwell the truth: that I had loaded the files into my briefcase and accidentally left them in the trunk of a cab in my rush to get to my dying father. Maybe he would have been reasonable, or even offered to help. Maybe I could have given him the cab company's phone number and he could have called them himself, leaving me free to focus on my family. Maybe my Russian cabbie would have delivered the briefcase directly into his hands, the confidential files untouched. Maybe everything would have been fine, and everyone at the firm would have agreed that Kate Cunningham, junior partner, had been understandably distressed over the imminent death of her father and made a perfectly excusable mistake. Maybe.

Nope. Not a chance in the world. Or, at least, not in my world.

I will never know what Roy Blackwell would have done if I had told him the truth. Trust me, though, it wouldn't have been anything helpful, considerate, or kind. He wanted the deal, I didn't, and he was sure to interpret anything I did as an effort to undermine the transaction and subvert his authority for good measure.

Still, I wish I had been truthful with him that morning. That's not because he might have acted differently, but because I have a much deeper appreciation for the importance of honesty now than I did then. At that moment, however, half-asleep and still shaken by my father's animosity the night before, all I wanted to do was stay out of trouble. So I lied, as quickly and adroitly as I could.

"The files are at my apartment, Mr. Blackwell," I said. "I took them home to keep them safe from prying eyes when I left the office, and left them there when I got the call about my dad. They're still in my briefcase. I'll have a friend drop by and pick them up, then deliver them to the firm later today."

Well, it wasn't a total lie. I fully intended to call the cab company the instant Blackwell let me off the phone. The briefcase could be delivered to the reception desk, my "friend" could immediately vanish, and nobody would need to know how careless I had been with Dr. Grandy's confidential files.

He clearly didn't like my reply, but even Roy Blackwell couldn't continue to bully a distraught daughter.

"That will have to do, I suppose," he ungraciously conceded. "But I want those files delivered to me personally this afternoon, do you understand? And I want you back in the office as soon as possible—tomorrow if you can, and Wednesday at the latest. For some reason, Grandy likes you and wants you on the negotiating team. You really should stop trying to sabotage his purchases. If you would cultivate him, he could become your biggest client."

For the merest fraction of a second, I considered resuming my arguments against the merits of the deal. It was still a lousy purchase, and having Mark Davenport rush to assemble the closing documents wasn't going to do Dr. Grandy any good. I needn't have bothered, though. Blackwell had already hung up.

Between Blackwell's unpleasant tone and the fast-approaching closing, there was clearly no time to waste. He had ordered me to produce those files in just a few hours. I would need to track down my briefcase in a hurry, both to find the files and to keep Blackwell from realizing that I had lied to him. Setting down my phone, I reached into my purse for the cab company receipt.

It wasn't in my wallet.

No big deal, I thought, the receipt must have fallen loose into my purse. No amount of rummaging produced it, though. Panicked, I yanked my overnight bag up off the floor where I had dumped it the night before.

Plopping the bag on the bed in front of me, I unzipped it and started rooting around, desperately hunting for the receipt. It wasn't there, either.

Then I heard a soft meow and looked up. Honoré sat on the other side of the bed watching me, the receipt held down by his two front paws. Had he been human, I would have said his expression was one of pity, and perhaps a little reproach.

"Don't look at me like that," I told him. "Do you want us out on the street and living out of dumpsters? You'd miss your organic cat food and your nice clean litter box, my friend." I would have sworn that he shook his head at me. Some coconspirator he was.

Snatching the receipt away from Honoré with one hand, I grabbed my cell phone with the other. I had just started dialing the cab company's number when I heard a quiet knock on my bedroom door. Another interruption—just what I needed. It was probably Bella, wanting to know if I had slept well and what would taste good for breakfast. "Come in," I called, reluctantly hitting "cancel."

It wasn't Bella at the door. Instead, Nurse Paula came in. Her plump, pretty face was pink, a strand or two had come loose from her blonde ponytail, and her eyes were damp.

"I'm so sorry to have to tell you this, Miss Kate, but your father passed away last night," she said gently. "I found him this morning when I went in to get him bathed and shaved for the day."

The cell phone slipped from my fingers, landing with a soft plop on the bed. Paula sat down next to me and began to cry. We hugged each other, but my own eyes wouldn't tear. Honoré watched the two of us, inscrutable, his tail twitching softly behind him.

Archangel Michael speaks:

Why, oh why, do people insist on lying when it always gets them into so much trouble?

When my armies and I cast the Adversary out of Heaven, I really hoped that would be the end of all the lying on Earth. And it was–for about ten minutes. Then the lying started again, as soon as people let the Adversary talk them into believing that lying, hiding, and sneaking around would keep them out of trouble. Dumb, dumb, dumb! It never works, but they almost never learn that until the end of their lives, and by then they've done a whole lot of damage that could have been avoided if they JUST TOLD THE TRUTH.

Yeah, folks, it's that simple.

I love humanity, but I can definitely skip the lies. Even little "white" ones have an ugly ring to them that makes me want to grab my sword and go vanquish somebody, I swear.

You might not expect the commander of the Creator's armies to take time to focus in on one little lie told by one young woman. And it's true that I'm mostly a big-picture kind of guy. But there are a lot of angels working with me, and it's our job to maintain the integrity of Creation. Integrity is the foundation of everything. We can't let the cracks go unmended. The entire Universe would collapse if we did.

You don't usually see us, but my angels and I are always around, bolstering your courage and shoring up your honesty. We're there when a soldier or a cop goes charging into a gunfight. We're there when a brave employee blows the whistle on a corrupt corporation. And when somebody has to deliver bad news or admit to an embarrassing mistake, my angels are standing by to help.

There was an angel hovering near Kate when she answered her phone that morning. We knew she might need support because, like a lot of you, Kate grew up surrounded by lies. Sad thing was, the truth was really a whole lot simpler than all the lies her family members told themselves and each other. Sure, a lot of their story was sad. But who said that every minute of mortal life has to be a laugh riot? You lose all the nuance that way.

So, yeah, I could say that Kate was brought up lying and didn't fully appreciate that there was anything wrong with it. She wasn't a sociopath or a criminal or anything, and she never meant to hurt anybody. That matters a lot here in Heaven. People who mean to do harm get in a lot more trouble than people who don't.

Like I said, though, Kate wasn't a bad person. She was just a clever young woman who thought it was OK to tell a little fib now and then to save her own skin, especially if she made it right later. No big deal, right?

Wrong.

Kate knew what she was doing when she lied to Roy Blackwell. She meant to tell a lie, even if she didn't mean to hurt anybody, and like I said, intentions matter. She had to learn better, especially because Gabriel had such major plans for her. Kate had an important divine destiny involving a whole lot of other people. They would need her to play the part the Creator intended for her. She couldn't start fulfilling her destiny, though, until she had learned that lying never leads to anything good.

Trouble was, Kate had gotten away with so many little white lies over the years that lying didn't bother her much anymore. A minor consequence wasn't going to get her attention. She had been driving Gabriel crazy, ignoring all his portents and tossing that note away like it wasn't a genuine, solid-gold miracle. If we just gave her a touch of remorse or a little self-doubt, she would have ignored that, too. Gabe and I agreed that we had to give her a pretty hard shove to get her back on track.

We didn't want to do it, but trust me–it was for her own good.

CHAPTER FIVE

Eventually, Paula and I pulled apart from one another. She told me again how sorry she was for my loss, an especially gracious thing to say when she had devoted so much more time and energy to my father's care than I ever had. Then she left me, so I could get dressed. I hoped that Paula's gentle nursing had brought my father some comfort in his final days. Heaven knows, I had done nothing for him myself.

Before I could drown in guilt, Honoré walked daintily across the bed to me, purring softly. He pushed his head up under my hand, our time-honored signal for me to pick him up. Even as a kitten, Honoré had always known when I was unhappy and always wanted to help. This time was no exception.

I scooped my old friend up in my arms and held him close for a few minutes, still unable to shed a single tear. It was tempting to linger there with him, but I couldn't hide in my room forever. Like it or not, I had to see what remained of my father.

By the time I threw on some clothes and got downstairs, Andrew and Bella had already arranged my father's body into a dignified position on his bed, closed his eyes, and pulled up his blankets. He looked more asleep than deceased, though there was no mistaking his pallor or the musty smell emanating from his body. The great Christopher J. Cunningham, political lion and attorney-at-law extraordinaire, had breathed his last.

I had no idea of what to do next. Someone needed to be notified, of course, but I couldn't quite focus my thoughts enough to figure it out. Whom do you call, when someone in your family dies? What do you say? Were there papers to fill out? I didn't know.

Thankfully, Andrew and Bella had already taken charge. "I've called Dr. Kaufman, Miss Kate," Andrew said. "He'll be here in a few minutes to examine your father and fill out the paperwork. You don't need to worry about a thing." A smile creased his sympathetic face.

I tried to smile back and thank him, but my face wouldn't move and I couldn't find my voice.

"You've had a terrible shock, Katie," Bella said, wrapping a motherly arm around my shoulders and steering me out of the bedroom. "Come away from there now. You just sit in the parlor, and I'll bring you some tea."

Within minutes, Bella had me bundled into the most comfortable wing chair my late father owned, tucked up under a dark blue afghan with a steaming cup of Earl Grey tea on the side table at my elbow. Honoré jumped up and settled companionably in my lap, still wanting to help, it seemed. I petted him, my mind a blank.

Dr. Kaufman arrived, conducted his examination, and left. He greeted me, I think. I don't remember saying anything to him. In fact, I can't recall speaking a single word for the next few hours. I just sat, my tea gone cold, absently stroking Honoré now and then.

My father's death wasn't the end of the world, but it certainly shook my world to its core. For as long as I could remember he had been the driving force in my life, pushing me toward achievement, demanding excellence, accepting no excuses. He had been a stern taskmaster, and I had often chafed under his hypercritical attention. But he was still my father, and I hadn't been there for him during the last months of his life when he had needed me most. Again and again, I had put off calling or seeing him for just one more day. Now, that day had passed. There would be no opportunity to mend fences with him, no chance to apologize for staying away so long or even to say good-bye. The damage was done, and it could never be repaired.

Both of my parents were gone, leaving me an orphan. It was a difficult thing to accept, so I didn't try. I just sat there, my cat in my lap, staring at nothing in particular and trying very hard not to think at all.

It must have been a little after noon when Bella brought me my cell phone, her face the very picture of concern.

"There's a Mr. Blackwell calling for you, Katie," she said, in a worried whisper. "I told him that your father just passed away and that you're in no condition to talk with anyone, but he insisted. He says it's an emergency. Something at your work, I think."

I roused myself enough to say, "It's all right, Bella. I'll take it." I leaned forward and reached for my phone, and Honoré jumped off my lap, unsettled. Bella reluctantly handed it over. "Yes, Mr. Blackwell?" I asked.

The managing partner's voice was uncharacteristically soft. Had I been more alert, I would have recognized instantly that I was in a world of trouble. "I am very sorry to interrupt you, *Ms.* Cunningham," he said, "but I thought you ought to know that we have the Grandy files."

The Grandy files? Oh, right. "Good," I replied, forgetting that I hadn't yet called the cab company. "I'm glad they got to you."

"Oh, they got to us, all right," Blackwell hissed. "Some hulking brute of a Third World cabdriver delivered them to the reception desk about ten minutes ago. Said he found your briefcase in his cab and tracked down the firm's address from your business card.

"Oddly enough," Blackwell went on, "your business cards and the Grandy files both just happened to be in your briefcase. Or, should I say, your *unlocked* briefcase? Regardless, those confidential files were readily available to anyone who wanted to reach into your briefcase and read through them, including your cabbie friend. For all we know, he made photocopies of every single page of those confidential documents and sold them to identity thieves in Belarus! *Do you have any idea what you have done?*" All of a sudden, Blackwell's voice wasn't soft anymore.

"I'm sorry, Mr. Blackwell," I stammered, but he immediately cut me off.

"'I'm sorry, Mr. Blackwell,'" he mimicked in a saccharine soprano. "'I'm sorry, Mr. Blackwell. The files are locked up in my apartment, Mr. Blackwell. I took them home to keep them *safe from prying eyes, Mr. Blackwell.*' What a load of rubbish!

"You, Ms. Cunningham, are a liar, a manipulator, and an *utter* incompetent," Blackwell snarled. "You have imperiled Dr. Grandy's financial security, endangered an extremely important financial transaction, and put the good reputation of this law firm at serious risk. I would say that you also ruined your own reputation, but that would be an impossibility because, as far as I'm concerned, you never really had any. You're nothing but the spoiled, irresponsible daughter of a rich politician who got you hired here through his connections, and you are fired, effective immediately!

"I'm going to have Davenport go through your slovenly pigsty of an office, salvage whatever we can find of your practice, and chuck everything else into the nearest dumpster," Blackwell ranted. "HR will send your termination paperwork to your home address. And don't even *think* about challenging this, Cunningham, or I will make it my personal business to ensure that you never again so much as wait tables in a greasy spoon in Hell's Kitchen. You are a *disgrace*. I'm embarrassed to know you, and the firm is well rid of you!" He slammed down the receiver so hard that I pictured the phone on his desk cracking in two.

After Blackwell's tirade, the parlor seemed deathly silent. The only sound was the slow, hollow ticking of my father's black-lacquered antique clock, a souvenir he had picked up on some campaign trip or other. I could imagine my father, healthy and formidable as he had once been, shaking a condemnatory finger at me, back and forth in time to each tick of the clock. *You've-been-fired-shame-on-you, you've-been-fired-shame-on-you, you've-been-fired-shame-on-you...* Just hours after my father's death, I had already managed to disgrace him.

Shaking my head to drive the unwelcome thought away, I slowly pressed the "end call" button on my phone and then looked up to see Bella standing there, staring at me. She had heard every word.

"Oh, Katie," she breathed. "Whatever on earth could you possibly have done to make anyone treat you that way?"

I hadn't yet shed a tear that day, but Bella's gentle question melted the hard, dry lump of emotion inside me. I tried to answer, choked, and started at last to cry. Bella put her arms around me and held me as my tears fell, and fell, and fell some more. Honoré jumped back onto my lap and let me pull him close. His fur was undoubtedly getting drenched, but he was too loyal to move and I was too miserable to stop the flow of tears.

Whether I was crying for my father or for myself, I couldn't say.

No one can cry forever, though, not even after losing her father and her job on the same day. Eventually, I dried my tears, sat up straight, and let Bella coax me into eating a grilled cheese sandwich and tomato soup. It had been my favorite lunch when I was six years old or so. Oddly enough, that simple meal was absolutely perfect. My legal practice has taken me to expensive restaurants where I have enjoyed Manhattan's most fashionable cuisine, but nothing ever tasted better to me than the soup and sandwich Bella fixed for me that day. Honoré agreed, happily licking the last of the soup from the bottom of my mug and the buttered breadcrumbs from my plate.

OK, so I was fired, and under circumstances that would probably make it very difficult for me to find another job. There would be time to deal with that later. At that moment, I didn't care very much. Maybe I was still in shock from the verbal beating Roy Blackwell had just inflicted.

My first priority had to be figuring out what needed to be done now that my father had passed away. I had only the vaguest sense of what happens after a death, and no clue where to start. I called for Bella, who, in turn, called for Andrew, and the two of them sat down with me, perched together on my father's old couch.

"Andrew," I asked, "what did Dr. Kaufman say?"

"Your father died of cancer, Miss Kate," Andrew replied. "We've all known this was coming. It's just a blessing that you got home to say your good-byes before it happened."

We didn't exactly say good-bye, I thought, but it would have been rude to correct him. Speaking of good-byes, though, it suddenly occurred to me that I hadn't seen Paula since she woke me that morning.

"Is Nurse Paula around?" I asked. "I'd like to thank her for everything she did for my father."

"She left a little while ago, Katie," Bella answered. "She lives a good distance from here, and it's a long bus ride for her."

Chagrined, I realized that I had not once thought about how Paula got to and from the house, or what her life might be like when she wasn't looking after my irascible father. I would be willing to bet he hadn't thought much about it either. And yet, Paula had wept for him that morning when I couldn't, and had quietly slipped away from the house rather than distract me while I was sobbing over my own concerns. What an incredibly kind-hearted person she must be.

"OK. I'm sorry we didn't get to talk before she left, but I'll get in touch with her when things are more settled," I told them. "I want to thank her for everything she did. Do you know if my father left any instructions for his funeral service?"

"I've already called Pastor St. James," Andrew said. "He's the rector at your dad's church. He said he can come over tomorrow morning, if you're up to seeing him."

My father had a church? That was unexpected. We had attended services regularly when I was a child, but I had always suspected it was for political rather than religious reasons. Elected officials can't afford not to be seen in a pew on Sunday mornings. When his political career fell apart, I thought my father had given up going to church. Apparently, I was wrong.

"Thanks, Andrew. Tomorrow morning will be just fine," I said. "Did Dr. Kaufman say what we need to do with his... um..." Somehow, I couldn't quite bring myself to say "body."

Andrew, thoughtful as ever, spared me the trouble. "All taken care of, Miss Kate," he replied. "The folks from the funeral parlor have already been here to collect him. After you talk to Pastor St. James, he can tell them how you want things done."

Again, I was struck by how considerate and capable Andrew and Bella always were. They had managed everything without my even coming out of my stupor long enough to notice.

"You two are amazing," I said. "I truly don't know what I would have done without you today."

Bella smiled, revealing dimples I had forgotten she had. "Our pleasure, Katie. We're both so happy to be able to help you. Just be glad Andrew didn't take the call from that horrible Mr. Blackwell. He wouldn't have been tactful at all, I can assure you."

The image of Andrew bellowing at Roy Blackwell struck me as so absurd that I managed to smile wanly back.

Late that afternoon, I showered and went through my overnight bag, looking for something clean to wear. There wasn't much. I had packed quickly and with the intention of staying for only a day or two before returning to Manhattan to keep Dr. Grandy's real estate deal from becoming a total disaster. After my calamitous run-in with Roy Blackwell, though, there was no reason for me to rush back. I thought about running a load of laundry, but Bella was bound to insist on doing it for me, and I was reluctant to let her wait on me. Instead, I decided to see if any of the old clothes in my room still fit.

My father had never emptied my drawers or closet, so most of my college and law school clothes were still there. They might not have been the latest in fashion, but denim and sweaters never really go out of style. I grabbed a soft, light blue turtleneck and a favorite pair of jeans. Trying them on, I was surprised to discover that they were a little loose. Then again, maybe it wasn't so surprising. It was common knowledge in the cutthroat world of Manhattan law firms that an overweight woman rarely makes partner. I had forced myself to lose about fifteen pounds after law school, and had worked hard to keep them off ever since. It hadn't been easy, but it had been essential to the tough, professional facade I had needed to survive.

From across the room, Honoré called softly. He had jumped up onto my old bookcase and was sprawled across the top, now carefully washing one mink-brown paw. I perused the various titles. There were several volumes of poetry, collections of short stories, classic novels, throwaway fantasies, and even a few art books. I couldn't remember when I had last looked at any of them.

My old edition of T. H. White's *The Once and Future King*, its spine creased by countless readings, caught my eye. I pulled it out and settled down on my bed to read. Honoré snuggled up beside me. After a few hours of reading, deep into the young Arthur's adventures with Merlyn, I drifted off to sleep until morning.

Archangel Gabriel speaks:

It was hard to watch Kate weeping. Yes, Michael and I arranged for Kate's briefcase to be delivered to the firm, and we had a pretty good idea of what would happen when Roy Blackwell got his hands on it. She had lied to him. There were bound to be consequences. Kate needed to experience those consequences to grow into the person she was meant to be. But even though it had to be done, neither Michael nor I had to like it.

There were so many other things that could have happened! Roy Blackwell could have shown some compassion for once in his life and allowed Kate to explain. He could have given her another chance, or put her on probation instead of firing her. Even if he had insisted on letting her go, at least he could have refrained from subjecting her to a gratuitous torrent of verbal abuse. She had just lost her father. That alone should have been ample reason for Blackwell to show a little pity.

Unfortunately, though, compassion is considered a weakness in many big city law firms, especially among the managing partners. Those lawyers frequently succumb to the twin temptations of greed and one-upmanship. As time passes, they let their better instincts petrify and crumble to dust.

At their best, lawyers do magnificent work that helps to support Michael and his angels in maintaining the integrity of society. But they often forget that human law is always trumped by Divine law. The first law of Heaven, in any century, language, or religious tradition, is to do unto others as you would have them do unto you. If Roy Blackwell thought he would have wanted anybody to berate him that way after an honest mistake, he allowed his pride to deceive him far more profoundly than Kate ever could.

The Creator chose to give humanity the perilous and beautiful gift of free will, and who am I to argue? I've lost count of the times that I've seen human beings freely choose kindness and decency even in the most oppressive circumstances. When they do, free will is a glorious thing, and the angels dance with joy. When they choose to be vindictive, cruel, and hateful, though, free will loses a lot of its luster. We aren't so exultant then.

Kate freely chose to lie about the files, and that was wrong. But Roy Blackwell's free choice to vilify her on the day of her father's death was pretty darned dreadful, too. It might not be entirely angelic of me, but I sincerely hope that Azrael won't rush through that particular conversation when Roy Blackwell passes over and conducts his life review. In fact, I hope he gets to hear himself screaming at Kate again and again and again. Kate was beginning to understand the consequences of her poor decisions. To my mind, Roy Blackwell deserves the same opportunity.

By the time Blackwell was done with her, Kate was devastated. Fortunately, one of Raphael's angels whispered into Bella's ear, suggesting just the right remedy for Kate's distress. Raphael always says that healing comes in the simplest things–good, plain food, a favorite story, a comfortable place to sleep, the loving attention of familiar friends. Kate needed rest, relief from the stresses of her life, and time to come to terms with her father's death. She wouldn't have found those things in Manhattan, but with a little angelic assistance, Bella was able to give Kate exactly what she needed. Thank Heaven for Raphael and his talented, compassionate team.

CHAPTER SIX

The next morning, I woke to the sun streaming in my bedroom window and Honoré snoring softly under my chin. Feeling better rested than I had in ages, I set *The Once and Future King* on my bedside table, stretched, and wandered downstairs to see what time it was, still dressed in my sweater and jeans from the day before.

The clock in the parlor struck ten as my feet crossed the threshold. When had I last slept that late on a weekday? Bella came bustling in.

"Good, you're up! I was going to come get you in a minute. Pastor St. James is coming by at 10:30," she said. "Do you want breakfast?"

"Maybe just some coffee," I replied. "Is what I'm wearing OK? I don't have a lot of clothes with me."

"You look fine," Bella assured me. "Nobody is going to expect you to dress up like Mrs. Astor's pet horse here."

I smiled at Bella's choice of expression. "Does anybody even know who Mrs. Astor was anymore?" Somehow, I doubted it. The reigning diva of Gilded Age high society wasn't likely to be much of a celebrity in the twenty-first century.

"Probably not," Bella said, smiling back. "All the more reason for you not to worry about dressing like her, or like her pet horse, either."

Pastor St. James arrived at 10:30 sharp. He was younger than I had expected, well under forty, a tall, lithe, light-skinned black man with an engaging, crooked grin and cheeks dusted with freckles. Bella brought him into the parlor, where she had set out coffee, tea, and a plate of snickerdoodle cookies. He bit into one of them and smiled delightedly.

"Bella," he said, "when it comes to baking, those hands of yours are truly blessed."

Bella blushed as she thanked him, then excused herself and left the room.

Pastor St. James turned to me. "We have not met before, Ms. Cunningham. Let me begin by telling you how much I admired your father," he said. "Christopher gave so generously of his time and treasure. He will be sorely missed in this community."

"Please, call me Kate," I replied, trying to keep my eyebrows from lifting in surprise. The last thing I expected was to hear my brooding, ambitious father praised for his generosity. "My father never said anything about your church, Pastor St. James. I didn't even know he had started attending services again. We didn't go much as a family after he left public life."

"Then let me be the bearer of good tidings, Kate," the rector said with a winning smile. "Your father was among the strongest pillars of our church community. He tithed generously, tutored underprivileged children in English and mathematics, helped several of our senior members fill out their tax returns each year, organized the annual silent auction to fund our outreach program in Africa, cooked in our soup kitchen every Tuesday, and served on the grounds committee. You should have seen him out pruning the forsythia and planting daffodils every spring. That man could work in the flowerbeds for days on end. Our meditation garden is entirely his creation."

"*Really?*" If my eyebrows were in danger of vanishing into my hairline, my jaw was in immediate peril of crashing down onto my chest. Had Pastor St. James claimed to have seen my father sprout wings one fine summer morning and fly to the top of the church steeple, I might have been less shocked. "Respectfully, that hardly sounds like my father," I replied.

The rector smiled again, somewhat cryptically, I thought. "Children rarely know everything about their parents, Kate, and you have been very busy with your own career. Yes, I know all about your job at the law firm," he said, raising a slender hand to keep me from interrupting. "Quite the accomplishment, attaining partnership at such a prestigious firm when you were still so young. Your father often told me that he was very proud of your achievements, though I think he wished you had been able to come visit him more often." He graciously looked away as I felt my cheeks flush with embarrassment—or was it guilt?

"In any event," he went on, "there are a great many people who will want the opportunity to honor your father's memory at the memorial service." The rector opened his prayer book and pulled out a folded sheaf of pages. Even reading upside down, I instantly recognized my father's sharp, distinctive handwriting. "Your father was as meticulous as ever, Kate. He left detailed instructions with me about how he would like the service to be conducted. But did you have any thoughts about it?"

Truthfully, I didn't. My father had always been such a force of nature that, even knowing he had cancer, I had never admitted to myself that he would eventually die. "Whatever my father told you is fine with me," I told him. "It's his service—it should be the way he wanted it."

Within half an hour, we had agreed to hold the memorial service in two days, and Pastor St. James had explained exactly how it would be conducted. He helped himself to one more cookie, finished his tea, and was headed for the door when Honoré sashayed down the staircase and into the front hall.

"My, what a handsome cat," Pastor St. James said. He squatted down to offer his hand to Honoré, who contemplated the rector's outstretched fingers for a moment before delicately rubbing his cheek against them. "What is his name?"

"Honoré," I said. "I named him for a character in my mother's favorite movie when I was still a girl. He has been part of the family for a very long time."

Pastor St. James gently ruffled the top of Honoré's head and stood. "Ah, yes, your mother. Do you have any idea how we might let her know that your father has passed away?"

I shook my head. "She disappeared when I was thirteen. I haven't seen or spoken to her since. I thought perhaps she had been in touch with my father at some point, but he never said anything about it to me."

The rector's expression turned grave. "Unless your father misled me, Kate, he was never able to find out where your mother went or why she left. He hoped that perhaps she had been in contact with you. I am sorry if that news is a disappointment."

It was, but I wasn't going to admit that to a man I had met less than two hours earlier, minister or not. "It's nothing new," I said. "Thanks, anyway. I appreciate your letting me know." I picked up Honoré and opened the front door.

Pastor St. James took his overcoat from the hall coat tree and slung it over his shoulders. "As I said, Kate, children rarely know everything about their parents. I am sorry to have raised a troubling subject. Please give me a call if there is anything I can do for you between now and the memorial service. I am very sorry for your loss." He pressed my hand, ruffled Honoré's ears, and left. I pulled the door closed, still holding Honoré close to my chest.

The rest of the day passed quietly, as far as I can recall. Bella, Andrew, and I must have talked a little, eaten dinner, found other ways to pass the time. I probably spent an hour or two with Honoré planted in my lap. The only thing I really remember is that Pastor St. James's questions revived the old ache of missing my mother. Perhaps if she had been there when my father died, she would have known what to do.

Or maybe, if she hadn't left, he wouldn't have died at all. The idea was ridiculous, I knew. Broken hearts don't cause cancer. Still, I wondered whether my father might have been different if my mother had stayed with us. The rector's description of my father's recent, saintly behavior had been a little disturbing. It didn't add up with my memories of him at all. Perhaps I had misjudged him, and he had only wanted to help his headstrong daughter grow into a successful woman. If I had found his methods to be harsh and overly demanding, the fault might lie in me. Maybe, if I had been more cooperative, he would have been kinder.

Then again, maybe not.

That night I dreamed of monstrous sharks circling furiously in stormy seas. The wind whistled under blackened skies, and a cold, salty spray dampened my cheeks. The sharks swam around and around, searching madly for something to kill. Occasionally, one would leap from the water and land with a massive splash before resuming its relentless hunt.

To my horror, I saw that all the sharks' eyes had been gouged out, leaving bloodied scars. Maybe that should have made them less terrifying, but the effect was just the opposite. I was certain that they were in agony and that, despite their blindness, they could still smell and sense the presence of prey. Given an opportunity, those sightless, pain-maddened creatures would instantly rip apart and devour anybody foolish enough to dip so much as a single toe in the turbulent waters.

In the dream I stood barefoot on the doorsill of my father's house, which bobbed uneasily on the surface of the storm-tossed waters like an unanchored ship at sea. Waves lapped at the front stoop, the water getting deeper and deeper, and the rising wind dampened my hair. My father stood behind me, big, bony hands on my shoulders, urging me to step out into the gale and cross to another, unidentified building across a partially submerged wooden boardwalk. I knew that if I so much as set foot on the planks the sharks would attack and kill me. But my father insisted, pushing against my shoulders and the small of my back until I stepped forward to avoid losing my balance and falling into the churning surf.

My foot slipped into the icy water, and the largest shark lunged... I woke up shaking all over.

With a dry mouth and trembling hands, I reached over to check the time on my cell phone. It was 4:44 a.m. The silence in my darkened bedroom was so complete that I could hear the black-lacquered grandfather clock in the parlor downstairs dutifully ticking away. Honoré murmured a little from his place on the pillow, deep in his own feline dreams. I sat up slowly, still shaken from the nightmare.

The symbolism of the dream was far from subtle. Blind, vicious sharks, frigid, roiling waters, a perilous crossing from the safety of home to an unknown destination—the dream was a pretty accurate portrayal, all told, of life in a prestigious Manhattan law firm.

Even the image of my father pushing me into those stormy waters when I wanted so badly to hold back was probably closer to truth than either of us would have admitted. Had my father been anyone other than the illustrious Christopher J. Cunningham, had my mother been around to temper his expectations, had there been a son or a second daughter to absorb at least some of his ambition, would I have felt compelled to follow him into the law? Probably not. No, assuredly not.

Pastor St. James's description of my father's recent good deeds at the church was so at odds with my memories of him that I could not reconcile the two no matter how hard I tried. My stern, demanding father tutoring small children? Filling out tax returns for dotty old ladies? *Designing and planting a beautiful meditation garden*? Impossible.

Still, the rector had seemed a decent sort, and there was no reason to doubt his account. My father simply must have been a very different person around the church than he had been when I still lived at home. That thought revived the question of why the differences were so extreme, but my head ached and I was still shaken from the nightmare. No real insight was likely to come while I was half-asleep and emotionally off-balance in the middle of the night.

The cell phone was still in my hands. Looking down, I noticed that one new e-mail message had posted earlier in the day. Ruth Martingale, the law firm's human resources director, had written asking me to meet with her to discuss my severance benefits. That surprised me. After the dressing down from Roy Blackwell, I hadn't expected to receive anything more from the firm than a reference so harsh I would never work in New York again. But she had asked politely whether I would be available for a meeting in her office the next afternoon. There was no real reason to turn her down.

I wrote back and said I would be there at two o'clock, as requested, then rolled over and tried to go back to sleep. Honoré settled down on my shoulder and fell asleep instantly, as only cats can. Stroking his fur, I eventually calmed down enough to close my eyes and doze off, and I slept without dreaming until morning.

Archangel Gabriel speaks:

Dreams, portents, visions, premonitions—my angels and I use them all to speak to the people in our care. Sometimes, when the truth is too hard to bear in daylight, a dream can introduce it in a way that the dreamer finds easier to accept. After that, the dreamer usually makes a smoother adjustment to the painful reality in the waking world.

It takes a lot of time and effort to create a dream filled with symbols that are meaningful to an individual dreamer. Different people view images differently—for instance, a lit candle can symbolize faith to one person and steadfastness to another. We have to look into the subconscious mind of each dreamer to find the images that will speak most clearly and then weave them together into the message we want to send. We do that kind of detailed work only on the dreams that people are supposed to remember and act upon. If we had to handcraft every dream every person on Earth had, it would be a nightmare—no pun intended.

So if you suddenly wake up from an especially powerful dream, please don't just dismiss it and go back to sleep. We're trying very hard to get through to you. Pay attention, OK?

In this case, we were definitely trying to get a point across, so Kate's dream was a doozy. Ravenous sharks, rising waves, hurricane-force winds... That girl certainly had a flair for drama! Still, she got our message the first time. It was a distinct improvement over her stubborn refusal even to acknowledge the note and the hints I had sent her just a few days before. She was finally starting to listen to her inner voice. It was all very encouraging! Sure, we went a little over budget on the special effects, but that's nothing when the soul of a beloved child of the Creator is at stake. Archangel Metatron would just have to understand.

Those blind, vicious sharks were especially effective, something that would speak to almost any dreamer. I'll have to remember to ask my angels to find space for them in the prop closet. We never know when we might need them again, and it will be cheaper to reuse them than to build a whole new set.

CHAPTER SEVEN

The next day dawned cool and clear, brilliant sunshine glowing through every autumn leaf. If there's anything prettier than early fall in the Hudson Valley, I can't imagine what it might be. I woke to the trill of birdsong and the sweet, haunting aroma of burning leaves.

There was no need to check my bag or closet—I knew I had nothing with me that would be suitable to wear to my exit interview at the firm. But I'd be damned if I was going to give Roy Blackwell, Mark Davenport, or anyone of the other predators there the satisfaction of seeing me drag in wearing my law school jeans. I had been fired, but that didn't mean I had to *look* defeated. I would get an early train, and there would be plenty of time to stop by my apartment and change into one of my several lawyer suits, uniformly dark, starkly tailored, and expensive. If they sound a lot like armor, what can I say? They probably were.

I took a quick shower, told Honoré to behave himself for Bella, and on a whim, threw the battered copy of *The Once and Future King* into my purse for entertainment on the train. Andrew drove me to the station and dropped me off. Ready or not, I was on my way back to Manhattan.

Inside of half an hour, I had bought my ticket and boarded the train. I looked around for the kindly *Harry Potter* lady, but of course she was nowhere to be seen. I picked out an empty seat by the window, settling in just before the train began to move.

The Once and Future King sat unopened in my purse as I watched the landscape roll by my window. The mighty Hudson River flowed past, vividly indigo under the autumn sky. We passed massive boulders, tiny, half-hidden coves, and mile after mile of woodlands cloaked in auburn, russet, scarlet, and bronze fall foliage, streaked with the silver-white bark of birch trees and randomly dotted with dark green stands of pine. It was a breathtaking view, and I watched, enthralled, trying to soak up its beauty as if it could fortify me for the challenges awaiting me in Manhattan.

All too soon, we arrived at Penn Station. Within seconds of stepping off the train, I was engulfed by the frenetic energy of New York City. The blare and bustle of New York usually enchanted me, but not that day. Nervous about my upcoming meeting, I felt almost physically assaulted by it all.

Unencumbered by luggage (and, let's not forget, unexpectedly unemployed), I had no need to splurge on a taxi. I walked down to the subway, crammed myself into one of the packed cars, and rode north to 79th Street, my hand firmly on my purse to keep it safe from the wandering fingers of a pickpocket. For an instant, a memory of the raspberry-dreadlocked busker flashed into my head. Tense though I was, the memory made me smile.

Emerging from the subway station, I noticed how hot the city still felt and how little evidence there was of the changing seasons. No russet leaves or ripening apples here, unless you counted the ones that were neatly stacked in bins outside the greengrocers on Broadway. I walked quickly to my building, got the mail from my box in the lobby, and took the rattletrap elevator to the tenth floor.

My apartment was startlingly still, the blaring car horns and sirens of the streets below muffled by ten stories of brickwork. Although I had left only days ago, it smelled dusty and uninhabited, as if no one had been there in months. I was struck by how empty the apartment seemed without Honoré, and by how little there was to tell any casual observer about the woman who lived there. There were only a few pieces of stylishly stark modern furniture, plain curtains, and a rug or two. There wasn't even any art to speak of. Apart from the freshly washed cat food and water dishes sitting primly on a towel next to the kitchen sink, the apartment might as well have been in one of those anonymous rental buildings with which Manhattan abounds. It might have been my apartment, but it sure didn't look like anybody's home.

I added the mail to the stack piled on my tiny kitchen table. Most of it was likely bills and circulars—I would come back and look through it later. Having made the trip to Manhattan, there was no sense in turning around and going straight back to Angel Falls. I would return to the apartment after my meeting with Ruth. That would give me time to pack enough clothes to last for a week or so and allow me to appear decently dressed at my father's funeral.

I quickly changed into one of my favorite suits: a pencil skirt and Chanel-style jacket in charcoal wool. Worn with oxblood pumps, an unadorned ivory silk blouse, a gold necklace, and pearl button earrings, it was the perfect professional uniform. I added neutral makeup, gelled my hair to coerce it into a smooth, straight pageboy, and stepped back from the mirror to check out the overall effect.

There I stood, Kate Cunningham, Esquire, the brilliant, accomplished daughter of an important man. The image was absolutely perfect, and I could walk into the firm with my head held high. So why did I feel like an utter fraud beneath that sophisticated facade?

I shook my head. No time for self-defeating thoughts now. I grabbed a carton of lemon yogurt out of the almost empty fridge—dinner was Chinese takeout delivered to my desk at work more often than not—and ate it standing up at the kitchen sink. I rinsed the spoon, dumped the carton in the trash, and headed off to my meeting with Ruth Martingale.

Riding downtown, I sat on the subway with every muscle tightly clenched, trying to manage my nerves. There had been so many times since moving to Manhattan that I had cursed the infernal slowness of the subway. Now, when a little delay allowing me time to compose myself would actually have been welcome, the train banged and rattled along at full speed, reaching Wall Street in what felt like record time. Go figure.

I left the station and crossed the street to enter the massive skyscraper that had been my workplace for over eight years. The firm had started out on the fifty-fourth floor when it opened its doors, but had grown over the years to occupy the three floors above and the six below. My office had been on the fifty-sixth floor—I wondered whether there was someone else in it already—and Ruth Martingale's was on the floor below. I punched the button on the express elevator and was rapidly lifted to my destination.

The elevator compartment was paneled in mirrors and polished mahogany, complemented by a dark green marble floor and brass light fixtures. At the fifty-fifth floor, the doors slid smoothly open to reveal an elegant lobby furnished with leather club chairs, polished occasional tables, thick carpets, and overpriced art. Nothing says "preeminent Manhattan law firm" like expensive furnishings, and the firm's interior decorator had been the best in New York. The main lobby was two floors down and made this display look downright modest. Still, there was no question that anyone who set foot in the firm's offices on any floor was entering a world of wealth, prestige, and power.

Ruth was waiting in the lobby as I stepped off the elevator five minutes early for our appointment. It was considerate of her to be there. Her presence meant that I didn't have to announce myself to the receptionist and wait like an outsider as my erstwhile colleagues strolled by snickering. "Come with me, Kate," Ruth said, all business. I followed her down the hall and into her office.

Ruth Martingale was what an uncharitable person might have called a battle-ax. She looked to be about sixty, but could have been anywhere from forty-five to seventy-five years old. She wore her dyed brown hair in an unflattering bob, her face was reddened with rosacea, and her wardrobe consisted entirely of dumpy shirtwaist dresses and sensible pumps. Anyone who made the mistake of underestimating her would soon regret it, though. Ruth might not have had Margaret Thatcher's classy British accent, but she was every inch the Iron Lady that the former British prime minister had been. Nobody liked Ruth, but everyone respected her, and throughout the firm her word was law. Even the most senior, successful partners treated her with deference and shuddered at her frown.

She waved me into the seat in front of her immaculate desk, gracelessly plunking herself behind it. "Sit down, Kate. I was sorry to hear about your father. Are you all right?"

"Well enough," I replied. "He had been sick for a while. It was probably a blessing that he finally passed."

"Are you going to stay up there?" she asked.

I paused. "Probably not. I still have my apartment here in Manhattan. If I can find a job with another firm…"

"About that," she said, cutting me off. "Mr. Blackwell and I have had words. He was dead set against giving you a decent reference, but I have persuaded him to see reason." She handed me a manila folder filled with papers. "There is an excellent letter of reference in there, along with your termination paperwork and information about extending your benefits. If anyone wants a reference, have them call me, and I will corroborate what the letter says."

I was shocked. A good reference might make all the difference in my being able to find another legal job. "Thanks, Ruth. That's very generous. I really don't know what to say."

"A week ago, I would not have done it," she retorted. She leaned forward across her desk and looked me dead in the eye. "To be honest, Kate, I never liked you much," she said, in a low voice. "I thought you were a spoiled little rich girl who only cared about getting ahead, no matter who you hurt. But that fight you had with Blackwell over the Grandy transaction really impressed me."

Ruth's voice got even lower. "Rumor has it that you took those files so they couldn't close the deal. Is it true? A lot of us were mighty impressed. It takes guts to protect a naïve client from a vampire like Blackwell."

It would have been so easy to say yes! I wanted more than anything to be able to tell Ruth that I had made off with the files to protect Dr. Grandy. I even wanted it to be true. But I couldn't bring myself to lie to Ruth when she was looking at me with so much admiration.

"Honestly, Ruth, I wish I had been that smart," I admitted. "When I took the files home that evening, I was hoping to find something in them that would let us negotiate a better deal for Dr. Grandy. But it never occurred to me to try to stop the closing. In fact, I never had a chance to look at the files at all. The call came in about my father and I headed straight for the train. I just left my briefcase in the cab, period. It was careless and unprofessional. Mr. Blackwell was right to fire me. I deserved it."

Ruth leaned back in her chair, looking less disappointed than I had expected. "Not necessarily," she said, smiling a little. "I would have known if you lied to me, and *then* you would have deserved it. But you didn't, and I respect that. So, here's the thing."

She leaned forward again, beckoning me closer. Her voice had dropped so low I could barely make out what she was saying, so I leaned in until we were almost touching noses. "I really can't help you, Kate," Ruth whispered. "I can't tell you that three of the male junior partners have made bigger mistakes than this in the past six months, and Blackwell papered over them all. I can't tell you that I overheard two of the senior partners talking about how Blackwell never would have fired you if you hadn't been a woman and wondering whether you would figure it out and sue. I can't tell you that, over the years, I have had to settle several discrimination claims from young female lawyers because of things Blackwell did to them when they worked here. And I *certainly* can't tell you that if you filed a sex-discrimination lawsuit against the firm and Blackwell, I would be compelled to tell the truth, the whole truth, and nothing but the truth about all the lousy things Blackwell has done to the women in this firm, if you called me as a witness and put me under oath. *Got it?*"

I was absolutely stunned. Of all the people I might have looked to for help, Iron Lady Martingale would have been last on my list. "Thank you, Ruth," I stammered back. "I don't know what to say."

"Don't say anything, except that you won't sign the damned severance agreement in that file without talking to a lawyer first," she whispered back fiercely. "I am sick to *death* of watching that son-of-a-bitch Blackwell ruin the professional lives of talented young women while his partners look the other way in the name of the almighty dollar. Somebody needs to take him down, Kate, and nobody will ever be better equipped to do it than you."

Ruth abruptly sat back up and resumed speaking in her normal voice. "Look over those papers and get back to me if you have any questions. You have four weeks to get the signed agreement back to me. Oh, there is one more thing." She reached back and pulled out my briefcase from behind her chair. "I imagine you will want this back."

It was only a briefcase. Just an empty briefcase made of fine black leather, with my initials embossed in gold under the handle. I could barely bring myself to touch it, and had to force myself to take it from her. "Thanks, Ruth, I'd forgotten all about it."

Ruth noticed my hesitation. "Your dad gave it to you, didn't he? I remember you mentioning that once," she said.

"He did." I tightened my grip on the handle and tried to force a smile. "Thanks."

"Come on," she said. "I'll walk you to the elevator."

We left her office, Ruth striding ahead while I followed, down the hall and back to the lobby. Word of my presence in the office must have gotten around. Several of my former colleagues, Mark Davenport prominent among them, had stationed themselves along my route, pretending to look at files or engage in conversation so they could watch me pass by. Head held high, I ignored them all and marched to the lobby, clutching my empty briefcase in one white-knuckled hand.

Ruth pushed the elevator button for me and leaned in close. "Lousy little cannibals," she muttered. "Can't wait to gloat over the fallen. Think about what I said, Kate. And God bless."

"Thanks, Ruth," I replied. "I will."

The elevator door opened and I stepped inside, leaving the law firm and the Kate Cunningham who had once worked there behind me forever.

Archangel Jophiel speaks:

As our beloved Azrael has already told you, each of the archangels serves the Creator best according to his own nature. Michael is our warrior hero, Gabriel our master communicator, Metatron our director of administration—no one can coordinate a Divine intercession or apocalypse like our Metatron—and Raziel is the keeper of all of the Creator's best-kept secrets. My particular gift is Beauty. Aren't I just the luckiest archangel in Heaven?

Beauty being our particular passion, my angels and I are simply mad about women. Why wouldn't we be? You women are the culmination of Creation, the last and best thing crafted after Adam, and you embody the Creator's finest ideas about loveliness. From infancy to old age every last one of you is breathtakingly beautiful, no matter what color your hair and complexion are, how tall you are, or how much you weigh. Little girls look different from teenagers look different from their mothers look different from their grandmothers, and every stage is just delightful. It's an absolute joy to contemplate the miracle that is every single one of you.

But, oh, you ladies make me want to wring my hands and pluck my wings sometimes! If despair weren't absolutely forbidden here in Heaven, there are days when I just might succumb. Women were created to be intelligent, competent, talented, personable, and lovely. So why do you insist on trying to turn yourselves into mirror images of men? It tells the world that you believe you have to be masculine to be successful. Then, you ask why men continue to treat you like second-class citizens when you so clearly aren't male. Why should they respect you when you're so disrespectful of yourselves?

Kate wore those horrid dark suits to shield herself in a nasty, cutthroat profession. Ruth deliberately drabbed herself down, the better to be "taken seriously" by her employers. They both succeeded to a point, but at what cost? Our Michael positively dotes on Ruth—he says he would rather have her at his side in the Last Battle than any of the high-priced ambulance chasers she works for. "Give her a sword and permission to use it and Ruth Martingale could conquer the world," he always says. Can you imagine what Ruth might have accomplished if she had ditched those dowdy dresses and hideous shoes and allowed her inner warrior queen to shine through? She wouldn't have had to settle for being the terror of some ugly little law office, that's for sure.

Consider Eleanor of Aquitaine, Mary, Queen of Scots, and the Mona Lisa. (Raziel knows who she was, of course, but he isn't telling. Typical.) Not one of them would have succumbed to the self-loathing in which modern women constantly indulge! They knew better than to torture their bodies and stifle their souls trying to be anything other than their own exquisite, very feminine selves.

Reclaim your natural loveliness and you will be shocked by how quickly your genuine power will follow. Celebrate your Heaven-sent beauty, ladies! The Creator adores every last gorgeous one of you, and so do we angels. Honestly, darlings, couldn't you find it in your hearts to be a little more accepting of yourselves?

CHAPTER EIGHT

The subway trip uptown to my apartment was as quick as my earlier trip to Wall Street had been. Good thing. I was on the edge of tears, overwhelmed not only by the reality of having lost a job I had slaved for years to get, but also by Ruth's unexpected support. With the information she had given me, I could sue the firm and Roy Blackwell for sex discrimination and probably win. The question was, though, whether filing a lawsuit was something I wanted to do. The idea of having anything more to do with Roy Blackwell, even beating his socks off in court, was enough to turn my stomach. I decided to get through my father's funeral and then decide.

Arriving back at the apartment, I quickly changed out of my power suit and into a light sweater and a fresh pair of jeans. I packed my big suitcase with a black silk suit for the funeral, several days' worth of more casual clothing, and all the shoes, accessories, and toiletries I could possibly need.

At the back of my closet, I found a simple, rose-colored dress I had bought on impulse from the sale rack at Bloomingdale's. It had a flowing skirt, a gracefully draped neckline, and full sleeves gathered into pearl-buttoned cuffs. It looked nothing whatsoever like the suits I had worn to work at the firm. The dress had been an impractical purchase, and I'd had no idea where I might wear it. Still, the price was right, it fit, and I loved it, so I bought it anyway. On a whim, I decided to bring it back to Angel Falls with me.

Finished packing, I unlocked the door, propping it open a few inches with the bag to make it easier to lug it out to the hallway when I was ready to go.

But first, better deal with the mail. I stood over the kitchen table and went quickly through the stack, tossing advertising flyers, charitable appeals, and catalogs straight into the trash. Until I found another job, I wasn't going to be in any position to spend discretionary money no matter how tempting the ads were or how urgently the charities begged.

Buried toward the bottom of a pile of bills, I found a letter from the apartment building management. That warranted attention. I carried the letter over to the couch, sat down, tore open the envelope, and started to read.

The letter was written in the nicest possible language, but its message was crystal clear. The building was being sold, and my lovely, affordable little apartment was about to be converted into a condominium unit. I would be allowed to buy it at an attractively discounted price. If I didn't agree to purchase my apartment, however, it would be sold to someone else.

As a junior partner at a Wall Street law firm, I could have bought the place in a heartbeat, keeping my home and enjoying the tax advantages. Unemployed and with no immediate prospect of a new job, I couldn't do anything of the kind. My apartment was about to be sold out from under me, and I had no idea of where I would go. Honoré and I would be forced out on the street.

The strain of the past few days suddenly proved to be too much. I started to cry and couldn't stop. I cried and cried, clutching one of the sofa pillows in lieu of Honoré.

At some point, I slid off the sofa and onto the floor, still in tears. That's where Jack found me when he tapped on my open apartment door and, hearing no reply, walked in.

"Hey, Katie," Jack said. "What's wrong?" He knelt down next to me and helped me back to the sofa, hugging me with one arm and rocking me gently as I sobbed.

Jack Reilly was my oldest friend—well, my oldest *human* friend, not to insult Honoré. We met in college, where Jack was a drama major and I was pre-law. He was a tall, good-looking, broad-shouldered guy with bright blue eyes, brown curls, and an incredible baritone voice. But Jack wasn't just a pretty face. His good looks were matched by a warm smile, a generous heart, and a God-given talent for enjoying life, no matter what it threw his way.

Jack had been one of the few straight guys in the drama program, and had never lacked for gorgeous, aspiring-actress girlfriends. They came and went, and Jack always seemed to enjoy their company, though he never settled down with any of them for very long. I took the hint, concluding that Jack just wasn't the settling-down type, and never tried to date him. It had been easier to stay friends that way.

In college, Jack and I had lived just a couple of doors down the hall from one another in the dorm. We struck up a friendship at an end-of-semester party in freshman year, and hung out regularly through college. After graduation, I went on to Columbia Law School and Jack started trying to make it on Broadway. We were both in New York, so it was easy to keep in touch. We would get together for Chinese or Italian takeout once in a while, catch the odd movie, or buy twofer tickets for Broadway shows if Jack's finances and my work schedule permitted.

As embarrassing as it is to admit, I never treated Jack especially well. He was just an actor, hardly in the same class as my peers in the law. He made a modest living doing commercials and industrial-training films, but he wasn't a Broadway star. In other words, Jack wasn't the high-powered, financially successful alpha male my father would have insisted upon for my husband, assuming work ever eased up enough to allow me to marry at all. I liked Jack a lot, but I never really took him seriously. Jack was, however, one of the nicest people I knew, and a far better friend than I deserved.

At that particular moment, my very good friend was hunting around my apartment for a box of Kleenex. He found one in the bathroom and helped me mop up my face, gently wiping away the smeared remnants of the lipstick and mascara I had applied so carefully before my meeting with Ruth.

"Jack, what are you doing here?" I asked between sobs. "How did you even get in?"

"I charmed one of your neighbors into opening the door by carrying her groceries to the seventh floor," he replied. "Good thing for her, I'm harmless. But what happened to you, Katie? You never cry like this. You want to talk about it?"

My breath coming in staggering gulps, I poured out the whole story. The fight with Roy Blackwell, the note on my desk, the singer on the subway, the note turning up again when I got home, the call from Nurse Paula, my hurried trip upstate, the missing files, my father greeting me so coldly and then dying almost as soon as I arrived, getting fired the very same day, hearing from the rector that my father had secretly been some kind of saint, and now learning that my apartment was about to be sold right out from under me. The only thing I kept back was Ruth Martingale's offer to help me sue the law firm. I hadn't yet decided what to do, and it would have betrayed Ruth's trust to tell even Jack about her clearly confidential promise of support before I had chosen to take her up on it.

After I finished talking, Jack leaned back and stared at the ceiling for what felt like a long time, giving me a few moments to pull myself together. When he finally spoke, his words surprised me. "Can I see the note?" he asked.

"What note?" With everything else that my outpouring had revived in my mind, I had forgotten about it.

"The one that said your dad was dying and you should go home. It sounds important," he replied.

I found the crumpled note on my bedside table, where I had left it just days before. Jack took it from me, placed it reverently on his lap, and gently smoothed it out. "Wow, Katie," he said. "This is *amazing*."

His fascination with the note irritated me. "Jack, it's just a piece of paper. It doesn't mean anything."

"Sure it does," he replied. "Come on, Katie, don't you see how fantastic this is? A mysterious note appears not once but twice, first on your desk, then at your apartment after you threw it out at the other end of town? It's downright magical. This note *means* something. No disrespect to your job or anything, but this note might be the most important part of your story."

"Come on, Jack," I replied. "There is nothing magical about it. I must have stuffed it in my purse instead of throwing it away at the office like I thought. It fell out of my bag when I came home, and Honoré found it. Stop trying to turn that note into a movie prop, OK? It's nothing special."

"But Katie, who would leave you an anonymous note like that? '*Your father is dying, come home at once*,'" Jack intoned in an exaggerated British accent. "It's like something out of a Dickens novel."

"Dickens would never have written anything that shamelessly melodramatic," I retorted.

Jack was utterly unperturbed. Well acquainted with my temper, he knew that the best way to handle me when I got testy was to ignore my tone. "Are you kidding?" he asked. "Are we talking about the same Charles Dickens here? What could be more shamelessly melodramatic than Jacob Marley in *A*

Christmas Carol, wandering through eternity dragging miles of chains behind him? Or what about Miss Havisham in *Great Expectations,* lurking alone in her cobwebbed mansion in a mildewed wedding gown? Or Sydney Carton in *A Tale of Two Cities,* nobly sacrificing his own life on the guillotine so the woman he loved could be reunited with her wrongfully imprisoned husband?

"You were summoned to your dying father's bedside in a mysterious note left for you by an anonymous messenger, for Pete's sake," Jack continued. "How is that not melodramatic? Dickens knew shameless melodrama, and I'm telling you, Katie, he would have *loved* this!"

"That note was just some jackass at the firm amusing himself at my expense, all right?" I shot back. "I had to tell Roy Blackwell that my father had cancer in case something happened while we were working on the Grandy deal. Blackwell could have told half the firm, for all I know. Maybe Mark Davenport thought it would be funny to leave that note on my desk as some kind of sick joke. Or maybe he hoped I'd go rushing off and leave him in charge of the closing.

"Either way, it worked. I'm out of a job, Davenport will take over all of Dr. Grandy's legal work, the firm will make a ton of money, and everybody wins but me. Well, and maybe Dr. Grandy," I grudgingly admitted. "So maybe you can understand why I'm not in the mood for a lecture on Charles Dickens right now. What are you doing here anyway?"

"Whoa," Jack exclaimed. "Remind me never to make the lady lawyer *really* mad. I just happened to be uptown for an audition and thought I'd stop by to see if you were here and wanted to go grab some dinner. You up for Italian? I got paid this week, so it's my treat."

"I can't," I replied sulkily. "My father's funeral is tomorrow. I have to get back tonight."

"Jeez, Katie, I'm sorry," Jack said, instantly contrite. "I got so excited about the note that I forgot all about your dad for a second. What an awful thing to have him die like that, especially when you got all that other rotten news on top of it. Do you want me to come up to Angel Falls with you for the funeral? I don't have anything much to do tomorrow."

In a better frame of mind, I would have accepted. My father's house had plenty of empty bedrooms, and it would have been nice to travel with a friend. But losing my father, my job, and my apartment all at once had put me in a foul, self-pitying mood, and I took it out on Jack.

"Thanks, but I'd rather travel alone. I'll call you when I get back, OK?" Jack's eyes widened for a moment and then he nodded. I had hurt his feelings for sure, but I was too engrossed in my own concerns to care very much.

Ever the loyal friend, Jack insisted on hauling my suitcase downstairs and hailing me a cab. As I was about to climb in, he kissed me on the cheek. "Take care, Katie," he said. "Things will get better, I promise. Scratch behind Honoré's ears for me, OK? See you when you get back." He was still standing on the curb watching me as the cab pulled away.

There was no effusive Russian driver at the wheel of my taxi this time. The cabbie was a nondescript man in a beige jacket who drove me to Penn Station and collected his fare without a superfluous word. I bought a one-way ticket back to Angel Falls, wrestled my suitcase onto the train, and settled into an empty window seat. If there were any other passengers in the car with me, I didn't notice them. I just stared out the window, brooding, as the landscape slid past. Anyone watching me at that moment would have said that I looked exactly like my father.

Archangel Gabriel speaks:

"Just a piece of paper"?

My angels and I moved Heaven and Earth to put an authentic, hand-crafted, miraculous portent into her hands, and Kate dismissed it as "just a piece of paper"?

Ouch.

Kate wasn't uniquely ungrateful. Most people don't appreciate all the things that we angels do for them. The human race has been complaining night and day since before we had to kick them out of Eden. You can bless them with the downright impossible—manna from Heaven, parted seas, wine that used to be water, even the revival of a guy who has been dead for days—and somebody will find something to grouse about. Mostly, my angels and I have learned to shrug off the complaints and take satisfaction in a job miraculously done.

Still, the note we left for Kate was the culmination of an awful lot of time, thought, effort, and administrivia. It would have been nice to get thanked for a change.

At least Jack understood. I love actors, especially actors like Jack, who realize that all the world is a stage and that life is bursting with hidden magic. What a talent that young man has! I really must introduce Jack to Charles Dickens when he gets to Heaven. The two of them will get along famously.

Jack would have known exactly what to do with my note, and working with him would have been an absolute joy. But then, Jack didn't need me. Kate did.

Jack was right. Things were going to get better for Kate. Lots better. Just not necessarily right away.

CHAPTER NINE

The morning of my father's funeral dawned as depressingly as the previous day had been glorious. The leaves that had glowed so brightly the morning before hung dank and wet from the trees, dripping with the cold drizzle that fell from low, leaden clouds. Everything was murky and unpleasant. It suited my mood to a tee.

Andrew had picked me up at the train station the previous evening, quickly gathering from my terse responses to his questions that I didn't want to talk about how things had gone in New York. I had declined Bella's homemade chicken potpie and gone straight to bed. Even Honoré had barely gotten a pat on the head before I had rolled over and away from him, facing the wall. I had felt miserable, bitter, and disinclined to accept comfort of any sort, even the feline variety.

My sleep was troubled that night. There were no dramatic visions of blind sharks and raging storms at sea, but a parade of seemingly random images instead that refused to resolve into anything comprehensible. I dreamed of walking down a darkened, empty hall, searching for something I desperately needed but couldn't find. Then I found myself sitting on the ground under a dead tree, clumps of its dry, crumbling leaves around me. The next instant, I was staring at a pile of letters addressed in a language I couldn't decipher. Voices from some unseen source whispered nearby in worried conversation, their words indistinct and incoherent. The dreams weren't nightmares, exactly, but they disturbed me all night long, leaving me exhausted and ill-tempered when I finally awoke the next morning.

I rolled out of bed, showered, styled my hair, and applied minimal makeup, and then dressed in the severe, black silk-shantung suit I had brought from New York. After adding pearl stud earrings and unadorned black pumps, I looked every inch the grieving daughter of a successful man. My reflection stared grimly back at me from the mirror of my childhood dresser. At some point, I thought, I would really need to give this old bedroom furniture away.

Bella offered me breakfast, but I declined, accepting a cup of coffee and then leaving it untouched after a sip or two. She and Andrew were already dressed for the funeral, and they watched me worriedly as I stared into space at nothing in particular. Honoré sat next to me on the sofa, close enough to be companionable but not so close as to demand attention. He too seemed a little concerned.

The clock struck nine. It was time to go.

Andrew drove us to Pastor St. James's church in the old black Lincoln. The church was a massive stone edifice built in the Gothic Revival style, all lancet arches and narrow spires. It might have seemed welcoming on a sunny afternoon, but that grim, drizzly morning, the church looked like something out of an old horror movie. I half-expected a bolt of lightning to sear across the sky, accompanied by a melodramatic crash of thunder, as we drove up to the heavy, dark front doors.

That unsettling image dissolved as I stepped out of the car and into the vestibule. Organ music was playing quietly from inside the church, and a lovely older woman in a tweed suit and pearls greeted me at the door. It took me a moment to recognize my old kindergarten teacher, Mrs. Braun, but she knew me immediately and gently clasped me by the shoulders.

"I'm so sorry for your loss, Katie," she said. "Your father was such a wonderful man. I know you're going to miss him terribly."

"Thanks, Mrs. Braun. You're kind to say so," I replied. It would never have occurred to me to refer to my father as a "wonderful man." Mrs. Braun had always been a softie, though, with a kind word for everyone she met. It was no surprise that she found a few for my father.

"Come this way, dear," she said, taking me by the elbow. "We have a place reserved for you right in the front pew."

If the outside of the church had seemed grim and foreboding, the nave was something else entirely. Despite the miserable weather, stained glass windows glowed brilliantly from all sides. Flowers crowded the altar and spilled onto the floor, enormous beeswax candles blazed, and organ music drifted sweetly over the people already seated inside. My father's casket, sleek and black, sat closed before the altar. I could have reached out and touched it from where Mrs. Braun sat me in the front pew, but I didn't.

I was too busy marveling at the size of the crowd.

If the first pew hadn't been reserved, there would have been nowhere for Bella, Andrew, and me to sit. Every remaining pew was crammed, and well-wishers stood shoulder to shoulder in the aisles, gently jostling one another for an unobstructed view. The church was packed to the rafters with people who had come to pay their last respects to my father. I recognized only a handful of them.

The music ended, and Pastor St. James stepped to the pulpit to begin my father's funeral mass. I can't remember much of what he said. My late father had left explicit instructions for the service, selecting his own music, readings, and prayers. Since I had been at a loss to provide any suggestions of my own, the rector simply followed my father's instructions to the letter. Christopher Cunningham remained the captain of his own destiny even after he died, just as he had planned.

When the time came, Pastor St. James delivered a short sermon, praising my father for his generosity, his kindness, and his many contributions to the community. Then he invited anyone who wished to speak to do so.

And they did. Boy, did they ever speak.

One after another, people rose from the pews or stepped forward in the aisles to lavish praise on my late father. They spoke of his charitable contributions, his invaluable service on volunteer boards, the positive difference he had made in the lives of the children he had tutored and the aging widows he had helped to file their taxes. They praised his work in the church, the beautiful meditation garden he had built, his volunteer work at the local hospital, his kindness, his patience, his generosity. People raved about my father, one after another, for over two hours, as I sat there in complete, deepening shock. The Christopher Cunningham they described, a pillar of his community and unimpeachable role model for small children, was a total stranger to me.

Apparently, I hadn't known my father at all.

The testimonials eventually tapered off, and the service concluded with a beautiful arrangement of "Going Home." It was, I dimly remembered, my father's favorite hymn. Perhaps he wasn't a complete stranger to me after all. It was a comforting thought.

The casket was lifted by six men and carried toward a waiting hearse.

My father had specified that he be cremated rather than buried. He had selected the crematorium, prepaid for its services, and even selected a handsome urn to hold his ashes.

He had thought of everything.

As the service ended, I stood and turned to walk up the aisle, when a man stepped into my path. He was about my age, tall and a little gawky, with wavy, reddish hair and round spectacles. They should have looked silly on him but somehow didn't. Instead, they put me in mind of a college English professor. "Ms. Cunningham?" he asked.

"Yes," I replied, a trifle annoyed to be accosted when I should have been following my father's casket. Surely, whatever this man wanted to say to me could wait.

"Ms. Cunningham, my name is Richard Helmsworth. I was your father's attorney." He reached into the inside pocket of his brown tweed jacket and pulled out a thick, letter-size envelope. I would have instantly recognized my father's pearl-gray stationery even if the single word "Kate" hadn't been written on it in his sharp black cursive. "I'm sorry to intrude at a difficult moment, but your father specifically instructed me to deliver this to you at the end of his funeral service," Mr. Helmsworth stuttered. Why did he seem so nervous?

He extended the envelope to me, nearly dropping it as I reached for it. He caught it in midair and pressed it into my hand. His face was flushed crimson, presumably because he was embarrassed that he had nearly fumbled his mission.

The envelope was heavy, seemingly holding several pages. I tucked it into my bag, intending to read it later. "Thank you, Mr. Helmsworth. You're very kind."

"No, I'm really not," he replied miserably. It wasn't quite what I would have expected a lawyer carrying out his client's last wishes to say, but perhaps he was being self-deprecating because he had admired my father. A lot of people had, it seemed. "I'm terribly sorry, Ms. Cunningham," he said.

"Thank you, Mr. Helmsworth. I appreciate your condolences."

"No, that's not what I mean," he stammered. "Of course I'm sorry for your loss, but it's not only that. What I mean is, well, I'm just very, very sorry. That's really all I can say." He turned on his heel and practically bolted out of the church.

I exchanged looks with Bella and Andrew, who had witnessed the odd exchange. They seemed as puzzled as I was.

Andrew went out to get the car, so Bella and I wouldn't ruin our clothes in the rain. As we waited for him to pull up, Bella asked if I was all right.

"I'm fine," I told her. "Just a little shocked at how much my father did in the community after he retired. He certainly wasn't like that when I was a kid."

"He changed a lot after your mother disappeared, Katie," Bella said. "He had to finish raising you by himself, and then there was that whole nasty business with his political career going up in smoke. I think he lost his way for a while. That happens to people, you know, when they suffer a sudden shock or grief. Andrew and I were just glad to see him turn things around in the last little while so he was more like his old self.

"It's a shame they always kept you so busy at that horrible law firm," Bella continued. "It would have done your heart good to see how many fine things he did in his last years. You would have been proud of him. So would your mother, I think."

My mother again. Somehow, no matter where things started in my father's house, they always seemed to come back to her terrible, unexplained absence. "Bella," I asked, "do you know what happened to her? My mother, I mean—" But then Andrew drove up in the Lincoln, we got in, and the moment passed with my question unanswered.

No one said a word as we drove behind the hearse to the crematorium, where the casket containing the body of the late Christopher Cunningham was respectfully received by a team of men in somber black. Condolences were expressed, hands were shaken, and then I was walking with Andrew and Bella to the car. As the crematorium doors closed, we drove back to my father's house, shrouded in silence.

The funeral service behind me, I found myself with nothing to do. I hung up my black silk suit, kicked off my pumps, changed into jeans and a sweater, and then wandered back to the living room. Bella and Andrew had disappeared, and Honoré was nowhere to be seen.

My purse was sitting on the floor next to the sofa. The pearl-gray envelope stuck out of it, silently demanding my attention. I pulled the envelope out of my purse and sat down on the sofa, holding my father's letter in both hands but not quite ready to open it.

I can't claim to have been filled with dread or anything else so dramatic. It was more that I felt chilled and a little queasy while holding the envelope in my hands. That heavy gray packet, with my name written so starkly, carried a finality that I wasn't entirely ready to accept. Whatever it contained would be my father's last words to me, and there would be no way to change them once the envelope had been opened and its contents revealed.

Perhaps there are adult children who eagerly tear into their parents' deathbed letters, knowing they will receive a final blessing, a last expression of love and pride to cherish for decades to come. Not me. The father I knew wasn't the sort of man to write such a letter. The best I could hope for was a grudging expression of satisfaction that my career had come out more or less the way he had always insisted it should.

Still, the funeral service had revealed a Christopher Cunningham very different from the father I had once known. The man described in that service had been generous, patient, kindly, and committed to good works. Perhaps, just perhaps, some of his charitable impulses had been extended to his prodigal daughter. Perhaps my father had come to regret our chilly relationship and left me a final blessing, in hope of making things right between us from beyond the grave.

Hoping for the best, I slowly tore open the envelope and unfolded its contents. There was a copy of my father's will, accompanied by a handwritten letter. In sharp, black letters, my father had recorded his final words to me.

Kate,

If you are reading this, it means that I am dead and Helmsworth has followed my instructions. He has the original of my will and has been instructed to execute it <u>exactly</u> as written. Do not even think about trying to break it. I spent months working on that will, and it is absolutely airtight. There is nothing you can do to change it now.

You are not getting a dime of my money. I worked hard for it and I am leaving it to people who will be thankful for it, which is more than I could ever say for you. If you wanted to inherit anything from me, you should have been a better daughter. But then, you were

not my daughter in the first place, so maybe I should have expected you to turn out as selfish and ungrateful as you are.

That's right—you are not my daughter and you never were. Your mother was pregnant when I married her, and God only knows who your father was. She never told me and I never asked. But I married her anyway, gave her my good name and a home, and raised you as my own child. She repaid me by walking out without so much as telling me what was wrong or giving me a chance to fix whatever it was she was unhappy about. She ruined my career and my life, and she did not even take you with her. She just dumped you on me and took off, even though we both knew you were not even mine.

And did it ever even occur to you to wonder what it was like for me, losing my wife and having to raise a teenaged girl by myself? Did you ever think about how it felt to be investigated by the police for maybe murdering your mother, when I did not know myself what had happened to her? Did you ever consider, even for a minute, what it felt like to lose my Senate seat because people were sure I must have done something terrible to her? Did you ever realize how humiliating it was to know that everyone in town was whispering behind my back, wondering if I had beaten her or if she had run off with some other man? Did you ever think to thank me for giving you a home, an education, and Bella to look after you, so I could make the money it took to support you?

Hell, no! All you did was whine about missing your mother, complain mightily whenever I tried to instill a little discipline into you, and run away just like her the minute you graduated from high school. You have not been back to visit more than a dozen times since then. But you have always had some glib excuse for why you could not be bothered to come home. Even when you knew I was dying of cancer you stayed away. You thought you were being so clever, all that cheap talk about making partner and making me proud. I am a lawyer too, Kate, and I know it is possible to get away for a weekend now and then if you really want to.

Obviously, you did not.

So, this is where it ends. I am leaving you the house and everything in it. I bought and furnished the damned place for your mother, the best money could buy and more than I could afford. Even so, it was too damned much trouble for her to stay here and live in it with me. There is nothing in the house that means anything to me now. Keep it, sell it, burn it to the ground for all I care. It is all you are getting from me, and it is more than you deserve.

Enjoy your fancy Wall Street law practice. I hope it is worth the price you paid for it.

Sincerely,

Christopher J. Cunningham

The will slipped off my lap and fell to the floor, unread. My mouth had gone dry, and my whole body was shaking, but I could not let go of the letter. My eyes went back again and again to the furious words my father had unleashed on the page, words far angrier than any he had ever spoken to me in my entire life. I had suspected that he was disappointed in me, but I'd had no idea how profoundly enraged he was. For that matter, I'd had no inkling that he wasn't really my father.

In less than a dozen paragraphs, Christopher Cunningham had up-ended everything I had thought I knew about our family history and forced me to see it from a different perspective. It was his perspective and clearly not unbiased. Still, no matter how much I would have liked to defend myself, facts are facts, as any decent lawyer can tell you. The man had raised me after my own mother had abandoned me, and I had never thanked him. Instead, I had rejected him even in his final illness. Based on those facts, Christopher Cunningham had judged and condemned me for being selfish and ungrateful. In that horrible moment, I believed he was absolutely right.

Archangel Azrael speaks:

Our beloved Raphael often observes that emotional hurts are much more difficult to heal than physical injuries are. Rejection, abandonment, betrayal, lies, and broken promises can leave scars on the heart that decades will not heal. Pain festers, turns to rage, and creates a compulsion for revenge. Abused children grow up to become abusive parents, betrayed lovers betray others in turn, and the agony gets passed along from heart to heart, leaving a trail of emotional wreckage.

Raphael says that those injuries present the toughest challenges he and his angels face. It is not that Raphael cannot heal them. It is that the injured person often clings to the hurt for one reason or another and will not let the angels come close enough to make things better. In those situations, all we angels can do is watch, wait, and pray.

Take Kate's father, for example. Christopher Cunningham was a proud man who had suffered many losses. Over time, his hurt feelings soured into self-righteous indignation. He clung to his injuries as stubbornly as a barnacle clings to a rock.

With time, though, even Christopher mellowed to a degree. Toward the end of his life he began reaching out to help others. At first he just wanted to regain the admiration of his neighbors and, if he had been honest with himself, to escape the deathly silence in his house. Later, he began to enjoy his community service. He even started to realize that other people had suffered more than he had. By then, though, the cancer in his body had taken a deep and permanent hold. Raphael and his angels were able to hold the disease back for a while, but not quite long enough. Despite his good works, Christopher died with profound, unresolved anger and bitterness in his soul. And he focused it all on Kate.

Oh, the things people do when they are close to death! A precious few rise to the occasion and deliver the most loving last words, forgiving, blessing, and leaving behind the best possible memories for their loved ones to cherish. Most do not do quite that well, but they manage to say at least some of their good-byes and reconcile a few old hurts before they pass over. But then there are the ones who cannot resist taking one last angry swipe or two at someone who cannot challenge them before departing the mortal coil forever.

Christopher Cunningham was definitely in the latter category. He was also what youngsters now call a "hot mess" when he first arrived in Heaven. He strutted and crowed with triumph over coldly rebuffing Kate's tentative efforts to reconcile with him the night before he died, punishing her for what he saw as years of neglect. Better still, he had successfully condensed decades of anger and hurt feelings into one tight, excruciatingly well-written letter bomb, then left it behind to explode all over her. How puffed up with pride he was!

We stood back and let him blow off as much steam as possible. It is usually the most efficient way.

After his first burst of triumph, Christopher was eager to see firsthand just how much damage he had inflicted. At his request, we escorted him to his funeral, where he had what you might call a ringside seat, right at the head of his own casket. He was thrilled, determined not to miss a thing. (We do our best to be patient when people expose the worst of themselves, but it is not always easy.)

When Kate came in, she looked so wan and exhausted that the sight of her distracted him from his incessant gloating, thank the Creator. He tried to talk to her, but of course she could not hear him. That might have been the point when it began to dawn on Christopher not only that he really was dead, but that any hope of reconciliation with Kate had died when he did. He was not so triumphant after that.

The service began, and Christopher listened as his neighbors sang his praises for over two hours. It would have been a sweet moment for him if his conscience had been clear. As it was, though, his pleasure was spoiled by the guilty expectation of what would happen when Kate (whom, he abruptly remembered, he had loved very much, even when he was angry and frustrated with her) read the horrible letter that he had left behind. As his anticipation grew, he became so intent on watching Kate that he missed half of the glowing things people said about him. Such a shame.

When Richard Helmsworth approached Kate after the funeral to deliver the letter, Christopher lunged at him. We think he hoped to retrieve the letter before Kate could see it, but it was much too late for that. There was enough emotional power in Christopher's lunge to knock the letter out of the attorney's hand for an instant, but Richard caught it and gave it to Kate, just as Christopher had repeatedly ordered him to do. You should have seen Christopher's face when Kate tucked it into her bag! That was the moment when he realized exactly what he had done. Unfortunately, there was nothing he could do to take it back.

Again at his request, we escorted Christopher back to what had once been his home. There he watched, unable to intervene, as Kate opened and read the letter he had left for her. He began to weep then, and continued for a very long time.

There are many painful things in Heaven and Earth. The remorse of the dead is among the worst.

CHAPTER TEN

The next three days and nights passed as days and nights do, but I will probably never really remember them. At some point Bella came, gently took the letter out of my hand, picked the will up off the floor, and removed them both from my sight. She and Andrew tucked a blanket around me, brought me soup and tea that I left untouched, and quietly urged me now and then to go to bed, never pressing when I ignored them.

Honoré came and went, but mostly stayed with me. Sometimes he sat on my lap, other times he just snuggled up next to me, occasionally butting me with his head, wanting to be petted. I ignored him, too.

It was not that I wanted to rebuff their gentle efforts to rouse me. It was just that I had no attention left for anything but the condemnation in that dark, dreadful letter. My father's angry words—*no,* I kept having to remind myself, *he was never really my father*—swirled like the blackest tornado in my mind. He had judged me guilty beyond any hope of forgiveness. Worst of all, I couldn't even disagree with what he had said.

After my mother's disappearance, Christopher Cunningham had been the only parent I had. Our relationship had been complex and thorny, but I had devoted most of my life to seeking his grudging approval. Now, he had irrevocably rejected me, and there would be no more chances to bring him around.

It seemed all too much to take in, especially on top of the losses I had already suffered. In a matter of days I had lost my job, my home, the only father I had ever known, and any sense of who I was or where I belonged in the world.

Maybe I didn't belong anywhere. I wasn't thinking about suicide—I didn't have the energy. But if a burglar had pointed a gun at me and threatened to pull the trigger, I would not have lifted a finger to stop him. Why bother? From the contents of that letter, it was clear that I was totally worthless. What would be the point of saving someone like me?

An ocean of guilt and pain roiled inside me, as dark and dangerous as the shark-ridden seas of my nightmare. I couldn't bear to feel it for more than a moment or two, so I mostly felt nothing at all. I just sat, suspended in a shadowy twilight of stifled emotion, staring straight ahead and essentially motionless as the days and nights crept by.

On the morning of the fourth day, Bella came in. She had a big glass of ice water in one hand and a small silver tray in the other. After looking me up and down, she pressed her lips together into a tight, determined line, unhappy with what she saw.

"Katie," she said firmly, "this cannot go on any longer. You're going to make yourself sick. I want you to drink this whole glass of water right now, and then you absolutely must look at what came for you." She set down the tray, shoved the glass of water into my hands and stepped back, hands on hips, watching me intently. From her posture and her tone, it was clear that she would not take no for an answer.

I looked up at her from my stupor, momentarily called back from oblivion by her loving, insistent voice. It was the same voice that had sent me to bed when I hadn't wanted to go, made me finish my math homework when my favorite shows were on TV, and ordered me off to school when I pretended to be sick. Bella wasn't my mother, but she was the closest thing I had. Devastated or not, I loved her enough not to want to disappoint her.

Licking my lips, I found them cracked and dry, and discovered that I was desperately thirsty. I drained the glass in three big gulps. Bella smiled.

"That's better," she said, relieved. "You can have another one in a minute. Now, though, I want you to have a look at this, Katie." She held out the little silver tray as if she were offering me a very special canapé.

Dashing Bella's hopes, I took one glance at the hand-addressed, ivory parchment envelope, centered prettily on the tray, and instantly recoiled. The last thing I ever wanted to see again in my life was a letter. "Take it away, Bella," I whispered. "Whatever it is, I don't want it. Please, just take it away."

Bella's lips thinned again, and she shook her head. "Yes, you do, Katie," she insisted. "You don't know it yet, but you really, really want this note. Now open it, honey."

My hand trembled as I reached out and took the envelope off the tray. The cream-colored paper seemed to glow softly with a golden light that I almost recognized but could not quite place. Both my hands shook as I clumsily ripped open the envelope and pulled out the notecard inside. In elegant, handwritten script it said:

> *My dear Miss Cunningham,*
> *Please accept my heartfelt condolences on the losses that you have so recently suffered. This must be a very difficult time for you. I hope that you are surrounded with friends who will care for and comfort you.*
>
> *If your schedule permits and you feel up to it, would you be so kind as to come for a visit tomorrow afternoon? I have heard a great deal about you and am eager to make your acquaintance. Andrew is an old friend and would be happy to bring you by, I am sure. No need to reply—I will expect you at four o'clock. Looking forward to meeting you at last.*
>
> *Best wishes,*
> *Lucina des Anges*

Blame it on three days of fasting and sleeplessness if you will, but that graciously phrased, elegant invitation upset me enormously. I had never heard of, much less met, Lucina des Anges. I was in mourning for my father—*no,* I reminded myself again, *not my father*—and hardly in a position to accept social invitations. Her blithe assumption that I would cheerfully drop everything to scurry over to her home on no notice at all bordered on being downright offensive.

I looked up from the note, ready to refuse in a huff, when my eyes met Bella's. She was watching me with so much love and expectation that my annoyance melted away, leaving me feeling childish and a little silly.

"Who is this woman?" I asked, trying to keep the irritation out of my voice.

"Oh, you'll love her!" Bella replied, clearly enthused but not exactly answering my question. "Andrew and I have known her for years, and we both think the world of her. Lucina des Anges is a very special person, Katie. I am so glad that you're *finally* going to get to meet her!"

"Did my father—I mean, did *he* know her? Was she friends with him, too?" I was beginning to accept that Christopher Cunningham hadn't actually been my father, but that acceptance left me without a clue about how to refer to him. Quickly, I retreated to—somewhat—safer ground. "Did she know my mother?"

"Just go see her, Katie." Bella's sweet voice was tinged with exasperation. "I promise you will be glad you did."

At that moment, Honoré hopped up onto the couch beside me. He delicately rubbed his cheek and whiskers against the note, still clutched in my hand, then looked at me and meowed. Apparently, he was in full agreement with Bella.

Sighing, I ran my fingers through my hair. I was surprised to find it greasy and lank, but then again, it had gone unwashed for three days, so maybe its neglected condition wasn't so surprising. Bella stood by patiently for my response.

"OK, I'll go," I finally said. It wasn't as if I had any other pressing engagements, after all. "But let me take a shower and get a decent night's sleep first. I wouldn't want to offend your friend by dozing off in the middle of my visit. What do we have to eat around here?"

Bella's smile widened into a lovely grin. "Come with me, Katie. I'll fix you some scrambled eggs and buttered toast, and then you can take a nice long shower." Her mission accomplished, Bella bustled off to the kitchen, Honoré trotting along behind her. After a moment's hesitation I followed, leaving Lucina des Anges's note behind on the couch.

It seemed I was about to return to the land of the living, like it or not.

Bella's good cooking and a leisurely hot shower proved to be the best possible medicine. While a nap would have been welcome, I didn't want to risk a bout of insomnia later that night. Instead, I decided to spend the rest of the afternoon in my room, going through and clearing out all the things that hadn't been touched or thought about in years. Honoré kept me company, sprawling in a wide, golden sunbeam that made its way across my bed.

First, I went through my bookshelves. My interests had been remarkably varied when I was younger. The shelves contained everything from historical fiction to Elizabethan poetry; there was even a book on how to draw unicorns. What a romantic I had been! I put aside a few high school

English texts to donate later, but was reluctant to part with the remaining books. There might actually be something good about unemployment. For the first time in years, I would have time to read just for pleasure. Why not revisit some of the books I used to love?

The next job was clearing out my old desk, its ivory paint yellowed and chipped. The drawers were crammed with a jumble of odds and ends. Bottles of congealed nail polish, their caps stuck tight, mingled with pencils, tarnished charms suspended from a thin chain, dusty paper clips, a button or two, an old wooden ruler, a small Super Ball that had lost most of its bounce, petrified erasers, some dried-out ballpoint pens, and a calculator whose batteries had long since died. There were pads of notebook paper, faded and fragile, dingy index cards covered with notes from a forgotten social studies project, even an empty Cheetos snack bag. Roy Blackwell had complained more than once about my messy office at the firm. Evidently, that messiness had become a habit long before I went into law.

There didn't seem to be much in the desk worth keeping, so I started emptying the drawers straight into the trash, one at a time. The last drawer, though, held some items that made me pause. Inside were two spiral notebooks containing poetry I had written in high school and college. How long had it been since I had even read a poem, much less tried to write one? I couldn't recall.

I leafed through the notebooks, quickly concluding that my younger self had been more ambitious than skilled when it came to writing poetry. Still, I couldn't quite bring myself to throw the notebooks away. I set them aside to read later.

That last drawer yielded additional treasures. There was a box of colored pencils, another box filled with pastel chalks in shades of terra-cotta, black, and gray, and a thick notebook of heavy artist's paper. Opening it, I found sketch after sketch of Honoré in various poses, some funny, some dignified, all beautifully rendered. I sat down on the bed to look at them, each different pose making me smile. "See what a handsome boy you are?" I asked, showing one of the sketches to Honoré. He looked up, yawned widely at me, and rolled over onto his back so the sun could warm his tummy.

Flipping to the end of the sketchbook, I discovered a yellowed manila folder tucked inside the back cover. There were several drawings of a woman's face inside. They were in different poses, the proportions varied and the expressions uneven, some seemingly completed, others just a handful of strokes. Unlike the drawings of Honoré, these pictures were awkward, unbalanced; a few of them were even scribbled over, as if the artist had been frustrated by being unable to properly capture the woman's features. Inexpert as those drawings were, though, there was no question about who the model had been.

These were drawings of my mother. I had done them myself from memory in the months after she disappeared.

Notwithstanding Pastor St. James's questions, people rarely asked about my mother anymore. It had been a long time since she had disappeared, and I had pretty much stopped talking about her once I graduated from high school. When people did ask, I always told them that we never found out where she went, assured them that I was fine, and quickly changed the subject before they could pry any further.

If anyone could actually have told me where my mother was or why she had left, I would cheerfully have given my right arm for the information. Nobody could, though. By that time I wasn't at all interested in idle speculation or uneasy sympathy, having suffered through too much of both over the years. People meant well, but they didn't know what to say, any more than I knew what to tell them. My mother's departure remained a mystery, and over the years I had inured myself to the loss. Or so I thought.

The sight of those drawings forcibly reminded me of how horrible the weeks following her disappearance had been. I remembered my confusion, my sorrow, my fear, and my loneliness when she vanished. Worst of all, I remembered my terrible certainty that I must have done something unforgivable to make my own mother run away from me. All of those feelings came bursting off the pages, and soon I was crying so hard I could barely breathe.

Honoré got up out of his sunbeam and came over to me, gently bumping his head against my arm. He always knew when I was upset, and always did his best to make things better.

The sketches of my missing mother cascaded out of my hands and down onto the bed. I picked up the cat who was my closest friend and buried my face in his fur, drenching him in tears as he cuddled comfortingly in my arms.

I hadn't cried for Christopher Cunningham. But for my mother? I wept inconsolably for her.

Archangel Gabriel speaks:

What a relief! We all watched Kate as she sat almost completely motionless for three days, uncertain whether she would choose to come back to her life or not. It was her choice, of course—another of the infinite aspects of free will—but we were praying for her nonetheless. Kate is very special, and it would have made us very sad if she had chosen to leave her life behind before experiencing all the blessings she still has in store.

The Creator can have the most wonderful plans in the world for people, but that doesn't mean they will go along with them, even if they are Divine will. We angels can nudge, suggest, inspire, and pray, but the choice is always theirs—that's what free will is about. Too often, our charges' desires are distorted by other people's opinions and social pressures, not to mention their own failure to commit to their dreams. And then, of course, there's the active interference of the Adversary (whom I mostly choose to ignore because it so thoroughly infuriates him). Bad choices can lead to lost opportunities and delayed happiness, always a shame as far as we're concerned.

Fortunately, when people's plans depart dramatically from Heaven's design, they don't tend to hold up very well. It can seem catastrophic to those who think they have lost everything when their choices fall apart. If they can just be patient, though, they usually learn that their drab little dreams weren't anywhere near as splendid as the lives the Creator designed for them.

Take Kate, for instance. Her choices had been dictated largely by her own insecurities, her father's punishing expectations, and the lingering pain of her mother's unexplained disappearance (another example of an unfortunate choice). Those choices drove Kate into a career she hated, working for people she disliked to achieve goals she rightly thought were unethical. They alienated her from her family, distanced her from her friends, and ultimately deposited her in an empty apartment in an enormous, anonymous city, leaving her with little to do except to work herself into an early grave. Her cat was her closest companion. While we all loved the old boy dearly, that's not exactly the recipe for a life well lived.

So when Kate agreed to visit Lucina, we were very happy. And when she actually started to cry, we positively rejoiced. Please don't think we were being unkind! We were just glad to see her defenses start to break down, because it meant we could finally get to work on healing her heart. As Raphael likes to say, tears are the most miraculous healing potion in the world. It always puzzles my gentle brother that people struggle most mightily not to cry when crying is the thing they most need to do.

We had so many blessings in store for Kate! My angels and I couldn't wait to shower them down. With a healing heart, Kate could finally begin the journey toward her best Divine destiny. We were determined to dance beside her every glorious step of the way.

CHAPTER ELEVEN

Someone once told me that tears are good for the soul. That may or may not be true, but they certainly were good for me. I woke the next day feeling lighter and more relaxed than I had in years.

I spent the next morning and early afternoon helping Bella around the house. Like or detest the place, it was mine, after all, so I might as well get used to taking care of it. It wasn't clear how I was going to maintain that drafty old pile without any income, but there would be plenty of time to worry about that later. I could always sell it, if nothing else. For now, though, just having a roof over my head was a blessing.

We hadn't talked about what Bella and Andrew would do now that my ex-father was dead. I didn't want to think about that, much less discuss it. Bella, bless her heart, never said a word, undoubtedly sensing that I wasn't ready to deal with such a sensitive topic. We just washed dishes, folded laundry, dusted, vacuumed, and talked about trivial things when we talked at all.

As we worked companionably together, I tried not to think too much about my upcoming visit to the mysterious Lucina des Anges. I had reread the invitation she had sent the day before and was a little annoyed with myself. She hadn't written anything offensive—I had just been in a mood to take offense when her note arrived. The fact that Bella and Andrew liked her so much spoke volumes in her favor. I resolved to receive her invitation in as kindly a manner as she had extended it.

Bella and I stopped working at around noon, and headed into the kitchen for lunch. "So, Bella," I asked, "what does somebody wear to go visiting this Ms. des Anges? Is this a jeans-and-a-sweater visit, or is something more formal in order?"

I had been half-kidding, but Bella took my question very seriously. "Oh, no, don't wear jeans the first time you meet her, Katie," she replied. "Especially when she went out of her way to send you a personal invitation! That's rare for her, and quite an honor. She deserves more respect than an old sweater and raggedy jeans. Didn't you bring home anything better to wear?"

I decided to disregard Bella's commentary on my leisure wear. "There's the black suit I wore to the funeral," I replied. "But that's pretty severe."

"Too mannish. This isn't a business meeting," Bella said. "Let's go see what we can find. I wish you had asked me yesterday—we could have gone shopping for something suitable." She bustled away before I could object, and there was nothing for me to do but follow.

Bella was already rummaging vigorously through my closet when I caught up with her, and she pulled out the rose silk dress I had packed on a last-minute whim.

"Perfect!" she exclaimed triumphantly. "This is exactly right, Katie. Now, go take a shower and get ready. You don't want to be late." I resisted the urge to yes-ma'am her, and went off to wash up.

As I showered, I pondered Bella's sudden, intense interest in my wardrobe selection. Who was this des Anges woman to inspire such deference from the normally pragmatic Bella? I started to get peeved again but stopped myself. After all, I was the one who had asked Bella what to wear. It would hardly be fair to blame Lucina des Anges for Bella's recommendation, nor would it be wise to go against Bella's advice. The rose dress was very pretty, a welcome departure from my somber professional wardrobe. Why not wear it?

I stepped out of the shower, toweled off, and promptly hit another speed bump. My tube of hair-straightening gel was empty, producing only a pathetic sputter no matter how vigorously I squeezed. Aggressively straightening my hair had been part of my grooming regime ever since my first year of law school. That was when my Contracts professor, Ms. Curtis, had warned me that curls looked unprofessional and would cost me job opportunities. After striking out on a couple of early interviews, I had decided she was right and started conforming my hair to big-firm style by burying it in straightener. Without the gel, however, there was no way to force my hair to lie straight, and there was no time to run out for another tube. Like it or not, Lucina des Anges was going to have to see my hair in its natural state.

Trivial as it might seem, going out in public without straightening my hair felt like a major—and risky—departure from the way I normally presented myself to the world. All of a sudden, I was nervous. Lucina des Anges would undoubtedly judge me by my appearance. Could I pull myself together enough to impress this woman? And apart from Bella's obvious admiration for her, did I even care?

Ignoring the flutter of butterflies in my stomach, I pressed forward, determined to do the best I could with what I had. I put on a little makeup, blew my hair dry without gel and pulled on the rose silk dress. I added neutral pumps and pearl earrings, then looked in the mirror and was amazed by what I saw.

The woman who gazed back at me bore so little resemblance to Kate Cunningham, Esquire, powerhouse junior partner, that the lawyers who had worked with me at the firm wouldn't have recognized me on the street. I looked more like that Kate Cunningham's younger, prettier sister. The woman in the mirror had wide blue eyes, wavy hair the color of butterscotch, and a dusting of freckles across the bridge of her nose, softened but not entirely concealed by a light coat of powder.

Those sketches of my mother that I had drawn so long ago popped into my head. Stripped of my professional persona, I looked just like her.

I walked out of my room, feeling almost shy, to where Bella was waiting. Her eyes widened first, followed by her smile. "OK?" I asked.

"Now, *that's* my Katie," she replied, and hugged me. "You look beautiful, sweetheart, and so like your mother. Andrew's gone to get the car. It's a little chilly outside, though. You're going to need this."

She handed me a light shawl. It was crocheted from soft yarn the color of pink champagne, with the tiniest hint of sparkle, and it complemented my dress perfectly. "That was your mother's favorite," she said. "You should wear it today. Oh, and you'll need these." She handed me half a dozen roses, cream-colored with a hint of pink at the tips of their petals, tied in a sheer ribbon of a deeper pink. "You can't go visit the Lady for the first time without bringing a little gift."

The Lady? I wondered. What was that all about? I was about to ask, when Andrew came in, bringing a breath of chilly autumn air behind him. "Time to go, Miss Kate," he said. "You don't want to be late."

Bella hugged me again. "Have a wonderful time, Katie! You're going to love her, and I know she's going to love you." If I hadn't known better, I could have sworn she was on the edge of happy tears as Andrew hustled me off to the car.

We drove through a brilliant autumn afternoon, the sun setting every tree ablaze with golden fire. "Nervous, Miss Kate?" Andrew asked, his eyes crinkling in a half smile.

I was, a little, but I shook my head. "You don't have to call me 'Miss Kate,' Andrew," I replied, avoiding his question. "It's not like you and Bella are my servants or anything like that."

Andrew pulled up to a red light and turned to look straight at me, his expression puzzled. "You don't remember?" he asked.

"Remember what?"

Andrew sighed. The light turned green and he resumed driving, his eyes fixed firmly on the road. "When you were really little, I used to call you Princess Katydid. You liked it a lot until you were seven or so. Then one day, you informed me in no uncertain terms that you were too old to be a princess anymore and that I was to stop calling you Princess Katydid *that very minute*. You were so indignant, scowling up at me, that it was downright funny. I started to laugh, which made you start to cry. So then I started making faces and saying I was sorry, which eventually made you laugh. We finally agreed that I would stop calling you Princess Katydid, but you would let me call you Miss Kate." Andrew smiled fondly at his memory of an opinionated little girl ferociously insisting on being addressed as she chose. "So 'Miss Kate' is kind of a nickname. We can change it again if you want, though." His tone was light, but somehow it seemed that my answer might be more important to him than he was letting on.

"Not a chance," I retorted, and watched him relax. I had been right—he would have been disappointed if I had said anything else. "Now that you've reminded me, I wouldn't let you change it if you wanted to. 'Miss Kate' it is!"

Andrew seemed reassured, and I was relieved by his explanation. Since coming home, I had become increasingly uncomfortable about treating Bella and Andrew like staff. Christopher Cunningham might have hired them as servants years before, but since his death they felt more like family to me than he ever had. It was reassuring to think that Andrew felt the same way.

We drove on, and my thoughts returned to the mysterious Lucina des

Anges. I was about to ask Andrew why everyone seemed to think I should be nervous about my impending visit to her. Then, Andrew swung the car to the left and I saw the reason for myself.

Wide emerald lawns stretched in front of us, bordered by an immaculately painted white rail fence. A driveway paved in tiny, sand-colored stones that crunched under our tires cut into the sea of green. Massive trees, their leaves burnished autumn bronze, lined the drive on either side, forming a canopy overhead. Even with the car windows closed, I could smell fresh grass, herbs, and a hint of roses.

At the end of the drive stood an enormous old farmhouse painted the color of fresh cream. It had copper roofs and shutters painted deep, sepia brown. There was a wide, welcoming front porch, dripping with Victorian gingerbread and surrounded by deep gardens. There were clusters of coppery chrysanthemums, apricot astilbes, clumps of ornamental foliage, and drifts of late roses in shades of peach, russet, and ivory. Behind the house was an unruly ramble of wings and extensions facing this way and that, each presumably added over the years by various different owners. A glassed-in conservatory angled off the end of a long gallery of Palladian windows on the right side, and a tall tower soared behind the porch on the left. At the right, the stone driveway ended in a generous parking area. A pretty, cream-colored carriage house faced the main house from the right across a swath of manicured grass and still more gardens bursting with flowers. A huge barn painted the same creamy white sat welcomingly behind, its doors thrown open.

That odd architectural muddle should have seemed disorderly, but somehow the house presented a welcoming whole, the afternoon sun glinting off the shining glass of its countless windows and French doors. At the very top of the barn, a brass weather vane in the shape of an angel turned lazily in the wind. Despite the distance, it was easy see that the angel was beautifully crafted. Its hair glowed a brilliant copper, and both its robes and the enormous trumpet it blew straight to Heaven were exquisitely embellished. For just an instant it occurred to me that I should recognize the angel, but then the thought slipped away.

Andrew pulled into the parking lot and turned to me, grinning as broadly as I had ever seen him. "We're here, Miss Kate," he said. "Welcome to Angel Abbey."

Archangel Metatron speaks:

There is always a great deal to do in Heaven, and as I am the Creator's chief administrator, much of the responsibility for running everything smoothly falls to me. It is not easy keeping planets in their orbits, ensuring that the galaxies expand and separate at an orderly rate, preventing black holes from encroaching where they do not belong, maintaining time at a steady pace, and otherwise making sure that Creation does not tear itself apart in an excessively enthusiastic moment.

And then there is all the celestial work! Polishing halos, pressing robes, straightening feathers, burnishing trumpets... Just restoring all of the Cherubim's harps to perfect tune can take the better part of a day. Heaven's streets of gold must be swept daily, and the gems that decorate the foundations of every building must always be polished to a perfect gleam. The Pearly Gates in particular are in constant need of attention. For some reason, every new arrival in Heaven seems to feel compelled to touch them when crossing through, invariably leaving smudgy fingerprints behind. What with one thing and another, the to-do lists that my angels and I complete in one morning alone could wallpaper your little planet six times over.

Still, I am one of only two archangels who were once human—my brother Sandalphon, who conducts the Heavenly choir, is the other—so I continue to take an interest in Earthly affairs from time to time. The project that Gabriel had been working on with such passionate intensity (and with such characteristic disdain for perfectly reasonable administrative and budgeting requirements) had most of the archangels positively mesmerized. Raphael, Azrael, and Jophiel talked of nothing else. Michael, distractible as he is, could hardly turn away. Even our secretive friend Raziel took an unusual interest. We can all attend to an almost infinite number of matters at a time, but it is rare to see so much angelic attention riveted on a single situation.

Personally, I thought it all a trifle unseemly. The Creator loves everyone, and I, for one, try to emulate my Master and avoid playing favorites. It was not as though there was only one person on Earth needing our help and attention at that time. With more than seven billion people to look after, surely there were at least a few others deserving of equal angelic support.

Nonetheless, I will admit to glancing over for a moment as Gabriel's young protégée finally arrived at Angel Abbey. Favoritism may be in questionable taste, but when history is about to be made, even I will concede that due attention must be paid.

CHAPTER TWELVE

As Andrew leapt from the car and hurried to open my door, I found myself almost paralyzed with stage fright. "Andrew, would you like to come in with me?" I tried to keep the quaver out of my voice as I stood up, clutching the roses in one hand and holding my shawl closed with the other. "Her note said you two are old friends. She might like to say hello or something."

Andrew grinned even more widely, something I would have thought impossible before that moment. "Not a chance, Miss Kate," he replied, his eyes twinkling. "This is your debut, not mine. I'll be back to pick you up later." He jumped back into the car and sped off, the Lincoln's tires sending up a spray of golden gravel.

Unless I was going to walk home alone, there was no alternative but to stifle my nerves and go knock on the door.

As I walked up the steps, delicious aromas drifted up from the gardens, calming me a little. Soon, I stood on the front porch. It was comfortably furnished with off-white wicker chairs and loveseats, all cushioned in cream-and-cocoa-striped fabric. Pots of flowering plants hung overhead, trailing variegated green vines and lush cascades of blooms. The porch ceiling had been painted to look like the sky at dawn, soft turquoise blurring into shades of peach and rose, dotted here and there with clouds and hints of stars. A brass door knocker in the shape of an angel brandishing a trumpet, again exquisitely crafted, decorated the front door.

Swallowing hard, I reached out for the knocker, but the door opened before my fingers could connect. A petite, pretty woman of twenty or so looked up at me shyly from the doorway, her heart-shaped face nestled in a tumble of dark ringlets. I need not have worried about straightening my hair. Curls seemed to be welcome at Angel Abbey.

"Miss Cunningham?" she asked, in a voice so soft that I had to strain a bit to hear her.

Surely, this couldn't be the fabled Lucina. "Yes, that's me," I replied. "I'm here to see Ms. des Anges. She's expecting me, I think."

The girl nodded. "She is. Please come with me, and I'll take you to her." She scurried away before I could reply, and I followed.

My young guide led me down a long hallway, passing a wide staircase and several doorways. Curious, I glanced from one side to another, but we were moving too quickly for me to get a good look into any of the rooms beyond.

Eventually, we emerged into a spacious sitting room. The walls were covered in ivory-colored damask wallpaper. Oriental rugs in soft shades of sage and cocoa covered the gleaming hardwood floors. An impressionistic painting of a summer landscape hung over the fireplace between two enormous shelves crammed with books. A baby grand piano stood in one corner, draped in a green paisley shawl. Atop it, russet-colored roses cascaded from a huge crystal vase, delicately scenting the air.

A sofa, several chairs, and a number of occasional tables were scattered artfully here and there around the room. Between two lushly upholstered club chairs, a low table had been set with a tea and coffee set and a tiered tray of bite-size sandwiches and pastries. Everything in the room was as bright, warm, and welcoming as my father's house was dark and forbidding.

At the far side of the room, a woman who could only be my hostess stood with her back to me, gazing out a wide picture window that framed a courtyard and the barn. Hearing us enter, she turned around and smiled.

Lucina des Anges carried herself with the grace of a retired ballerina or, perhaps, a displaced Russian countess. She had large, dark eyes under arched brows, a daintily pointed chin, and high cheekbones. Her lips were full, her nose broad and slightly aquiline. It was impossible to guess her age—though she was clearly several years older than me, her face was unlined, and her hair fell to her shoulders in a thick, rippling auburn cascade. She wore a simple, scoop-necked dress with elbow-length sleeves. The dress draped to her ankles in flowing folds, its color changing from jade to copper whenever she shifted. Crystal drops glittered at her ears, a stack of bangles glimmered on her left wrist, and her feet were clad in flat bronze sandals that laced at her ankles. She wasn't conventionally pretty, but she presented a striking package.

"Kate, thank you so much for coming," Lucina said, crossing to me with her arms outstretched. She took my hands in both of hers and kissed me on the cheek in a slightly affected gesture that struck me as calculated to charm. Her voice was pitched lower than I might have expected—another affectation?—and she wore a touch of spicy fragrance. "You have met our Amy, I see. Good!" The girl blushed to the roots of her hair, then quickly nodded to me and all but ran out of the room.

"Amy is a little shy at first, but she'll warm up to you with time," Lucina observed. "I don't know what we would do around here without her. But enough about us. I was so very sorry to hear about your father's passing," she continued, easily changing the subject. "How are you doing, dear?" she asked, her beautiful voice touched with concern.

"Fine, thanks," I replied, falling back on a polite half-truth. I wasn't fine by any means, but I wasn't ready to admit it. "He'd been sick with cancer for a long time. It's a blessing that he isn't in pain anymore."

My hostess cocked her head to one side for an instant, as if listening to a voice I couldn't hear. Then she focused her gaze on me again, with just the hint of a smile. It was a gesture I would come to know well in the months ahead, but it never failed to strike me as a odd when I saw it. "I'm glad you're able to be so much at peace," Lucina said. "Still, it's never easy to lose someone you've loved, and I'm very sorry for it."

Lucina beckoned me to one of the two chairs where tea had been laid. "Please, come have a seat," she said. "I am so looking forward to getting to know you. Our mutual friends have nothing but wonderful things to say about you."

"Mutual friends?" Now, I was curious.

She smiled again. "Bella and Andrew, among others. Those two absolutely adore you, you know. You're like the daughter they never had. I don't think they could stop bragging about you if they tried."

That was news to me, though perhaps it shouldn't have been. "They've been very good to me," I replied, embarrassed to realize that I was actually blushing a little. "I don't know how I would have gotten through the last few days without them."

"They were glad to do whatever they could for you, I'm sure," Lucina answered. "Bella and Andrew are among the most generous people I know. There's certainly no one they would rather look after than their 'Katie.' Or, should I say, their 'Princess Katydid'?" Her smile grew impish.

I forced myself to smile back, blushing harder now. "Sounds like Andrew's been telling tales about me."

"He has, and they're all delightful, I assure you," she said. "But we're getting ahead of ourselves, don't you think? Tea first, then gossip. Or would you prefer coffee? From what I understand, you lawyers live on the stuff."

She was right about that. "Coffee, thanks," I replied. "Just black."

Lucina poured steaming coffee into a delicate porcelain cup, creamy white with a gold-patterned rim, and passed it to me. Then, she placed a selection of tidbits on a matching plate and passed that to me as well. My hostess had prepared a veritable feast. There was curried chicken in puff pastry shells, glistening smoked salmon and cucumber on rounds of toast, pickled ham salad tucked into hollowed cherry tomatoes, deviled eggs, and a mushroom pâté, rich and earthy, spread over toasted triangles of pumpernickel bread. There were sweets, too: tiny squares of pecan shortbread, tarts filled with custard and topped with glazed apricot slices, strawberries dipped in chocolate, and miniature cream puffs dusted with confectioners' sugar. Everything was simple, fresh, and so beautifully prepared that I had to resist the temptation to have a taste before Lucina filled her own plate and poured herself a cup of tea.

Again, my hostess paused momentarily as if listening to that inner voice, then looked at me, picked up a deviled egg, and took a dainty bite. I followed suit, and quickly discovered that everything was perfectly delicious.

"Now," Lucina said, dimpling, "we can gossip. What was it like, growing up in Angel Falls?"

Initially, I intended to tell Lucina as little as possible about myself. Yes, Bella and Andrew both liked and trusted her. She was still a stranger to me, however, and life in Manhattan had taught me to be wary of strangers, no matter how charming they seemed.

Under Lucina's sympathetic gaze, though, my self-protective instincts evaporated. I found myself telling her about my childhood (touching only briefly on the sore subject of my mother's disappearance), college and law school, life at the firm. Finally, I described the string of misadventures that had left me living in what used to be my father's house, unemployed and soon to be evicted from my apartment. The only thing I left out was the letter informing me that my father really wasn't my father. That seemed too private to discuss with anyone.

I had meant to be more circumspect, but it was impossible to resist Lucina des Anges. She wasn't at all motherly—that was Bella's territory—but she had an air of kindly authority, rather like a favorite teacher or the glamorous aunt you idolized as a child but hadn't seen in years. Telling her my story felt like the most natural thing in the world. Time passed without my noticing, as I talked and talked. The setting sun was slanting through the windows when I finally finished, stretching its fingers of golden light across the oriental rugs and hardwood floors.

Throughout, Lucina listened attentively, asking the occasional sympathetic question, refilling my coffee cup when it went dry, and nodding at my responses as if confirming something to herself. She had been the perfect audience.

"It sounds as though you have had a pretty difficult time, Kate," my hostess said, when I finally stopped talking. "Have you thought at all about what you're going to do next?"

"Not really," I admitted. "I'd been putting that off until after the funeral. It's probably time for me to focus on it, though."

"Will you go back to Manhattan?" she asked.

"Hard to say," I replied. "It won't be easy for me to get another legal job in the city after getting fired from my old firm. There's really nothing else for me to do, though. Law is all I know."

Lucina looked at me thoughtfully. "You're awfully young to limit yourself like that, Kate," she said. "There are undoubtedly many things you know in addition to the law. Perhaps your legal practice has been so consuming that you just haven't had much opportunity to think about anything else." She certainly had a point there.

"Unless you have to go back to Manhattan immediately, why not stay here for a while?" Lucina continued, with a graceful wave of one hand. "It sounds as though you have a lot to mull over, and this can be a beautiful place to relax and think things through."

I wasn't sure whether she meant the town in general or Angel Abbey. Before I could ask her, though, Amy hurried into the room. "Excuse me, Lady," she said to my hostess, ignoring me completely. "Mr. Andrew is here for Miss Kate. Should I ask him to come in?" It was hard to say whether the young woman was painfully shy or just in utter awe of my hostess, but either way, she was so deferential that she seemed to be suppressing the urge to curtsey. Then again, thinking of how readily I had spilled my own story under Lucina's kindly attentions, I could relate.

Lucina's smile widened. "Of course, Amy! Please bring him right in." Amy nodded enthusiastically and bustled away.

A few moments later, Amy came bounding back with Andrew in tow. Lucina greeted him as she had me, taking both of his hands in hers and kissing him on the cheek. Andrew positively beamed.

"So, how have the two of you been getting along?" he asked.

"She's everything you said, Andrew," Lucina replied. "I'm confident that we're going to be great friends. Thank you so much for bringing her to visit. And, of course, it's always good to see you, my dear. Do you have time for a cup of coffee?"

Andrew shook his head. "Wish I could, but we need to be getting back. Bella will be finished cooking dinner soon, and you know how she hates to let good food get cold."

Lucina smiled. "I do indeed. Please tell Bella I said hello. Oh, and ask her when she'll be by for a visit. We haven't seen each other in far too long, and you are both always welcome at Angel Abbey."

Andrew grinned back. "I'll tell her, thanks." He turned to me. "Time to go, Miss Kate."

Ordinarily, I would have been more than a little put out by their exchange. After all, I was hardly a child to be shuttled about at the whim of the grown-ups around me. For some reason, though, I felt protected rather than insulted and was glad to see Andrew happy that my visit had gone well. "Thank you, Lucina," I said to my hostess. "This has been a lovely afternoon. I really appreciate your invitation."

She took my hands in both of hers and kissed me on the cheek as she had Andrew. Again, I smelled her spicy perfume. "It was my pleasure, Kate. I very much enjoyed meeting you. Thank you for coming." She smiled almost as though she were blessing me somehow.

Then, Amy was leading us out the front door and waving good-bye. Andrew quickly bustled me to the car. The air outside was crisp and chill. The angel weather vane on top of the barn was silhouetted against a darkening sky. For just an instant, the setting sun flashed golden on the edge of the angel's trumpet. Without meaning to, I had been there all afternoon, and I probably would have stayed still longer if Andrew hadn't come to collect me.

The gravel crunched under the Lincoln's tires as we drove away. My visit to Angel Abbey had come to an end.

Archangel Gabriel speaks:

We had done it! We had finally done it! After months of planning, preparation, hinting, and herding, with the occasional bout of frustration—OK, maybe more than occasional—we had finally gotten Kate to Angel Abbey. She had gone to the Abbey of her own free will, she had met the Lady, and it looked as though they even liked each other. It was more than I would have dared to hope for. Oh, the high-fiving that went on in Heaven that day!

Metatron thought we had all gone a bit mad. But then, he has never fully appreciated the importance of this particular project. Angel Abbey is tiny compared to most of what Metatron and his angels do. An archangel who oversees the orderly movements of the celestial spheres and the maintenance of Heaven itself probably can't be expected to think too much of the goings-on in one small American town. For someone who prides himself on his attention to detail, however, the Administrator could have shown a little more enthusiasm for what was really a remarkable achievement. Every soul counts, after all.

Then again, maybe I'm expecting too much from our Administrator. Raziel told me later that he thought Metatron had actually been quite pleased with the day's events, though Heaven itself could freeze over before he would ever admit it. That was a major concession coming from Raziel, the archangel who thinks he is personally responsible for keeping every secret in Creation. Raziel must have been pretty impressed too, now that I think about it.

Getting Kate to the Abbey was only the first step in a long journey, and we all knew there would be plenty of challenges still to come. Nonetheless, I felt entirely justified in pulling out my trumpet and treating all of Heaven to a concert that lasted for a good long while. I just love it when a plan starts coming together!

CHAPTER THIRTEEN

Andrew was quiet as we drove home through the deepening twilight. But he kept glancing over at me with twinkling eyes and a barely suppressed grin every few minutes, as if waiting for me to tell him how spectacularly well the afternoon had gone. He used to do that exact same thing whenever he drove me home from winning a debate tournament or acing an exam in high school, giving me an opportunity to describe every aspect of my latest triumph. As a kid, I had loved that little game we played together. As an adult, I found it to be remarkably irritating. I wasn't a boastful child anymore, no matter what Andrew might think.

Despite Andrew's obvious eagerness for a full report of my visit to the Abbey, I was reluctant to talk about it. While in Lucina's presence, I had been all too ready to spill my life story. Having left her, though, I was mortified to have been so indiscreet with a total stranger. Disarming as Lucina might have been, I was suddenly sure that I had told her far too much.

In the back of my mind, an ugly little voice insisted that my hostess had tricked me into embarrassing myself that afternoon. What did I really know of Lucina des Anges? Sure, Andrew and Bella liked her, but they could be far too trusting. Who was the woman, really, and why was she so curious about me? What was her interest in the personal details of my past? Could I trust her not to gossip about me with everyone who walked into Angel Abbey? I didn't know, but if she was so inclined, there was nothing I could do to stop her. She knew almost every awkward detail of my life, because I had been too stupid to keep my big mouth shut.

For that matter, the ugly little voice observed, what kind of egomaniac names her property something as pretentious as "Angel Abbey"? The place was a farmhouse, not a palace. I had always been contemptuous of people who gave their homes romanticized names, as if they were ancestral estates in a Charlotte Brontë novel. We were in upstate New York, for Heaven's sake, not the Yorkshire moors. Instead of letting Lucina beguile me into spilling my life story, I should have laughed at her overblown airs.

What a credulous idiot I had been.

Andrew, of course, had no idea of the storm that was gathering in my mind. We rode in silence, Andrew continuing to steal looks at me as I stared resolutely out the car window, my face turned away from him. He may have chuckled once or twice, but I chose not to listen.

Bella, by contrast, was as relentlessly inquisitive when we got home as Andrew had been circumspect. We had barely set foot inside the front door when she pounced, peppering me with questions about my visit to Lucina des Anges. How had it gone? Was anyone else there? What had we talked about? What had she asked me? What had I said? Did I like her? Did she like me? Most important, *had she invited me back to the Abbey?*

Honoré sat on the stairs a few feet away, washing one paw, as Bella grilled me with the intensity of a military interrogator. Although he seemed engrossed in his bath, I had this irrational sense that Honoré, too, was listening intently. Even my cat seemed insatiably curious about the afternoon's events.

I would love to be able to say that I answered Bella fully and fondly, because that is what she deserved. Unfortunately, her torrent of questions unnerved me, and her obvious reverence for Lucina des Anges annoyed me even more than Andrew's barely suppressed enthusiasm had. So, like a sullen little girl, I responded in flat, uncommunicative monosyllables.

The visit was fine. We made small talk over tea sandwiches and pastries. I liked Lucina. She seemed to like me well enough. Some girl named Amy met me at the door, but she left as soon as she handed me off to Lucina. No, Amy didn't stay for tea. Didn't I already tell you that?

I wasn't sure what we talked about. Just stuff, all right? She asked me about growing up in Angel Falls, so I told her. It wasn't any big deal. (I didn't mention the other things I had told Lucina. No need to embarrass myself twice.) Yes, Lucina said she enjoyed meeting me. No, she hadn't invited me to come back.

Yes, Bella, I was sure. Lucina had not invited me to come back to Angel

Abbey. How many times did I have to say it, for pity's sake? Don't badger me, Bella, *OK?*

I didn't realize how sharp my voice had gotten until Bella suddenly retreated a step or two, visibly disappointed. "Well, that's that," she said to Andrew, sighing and shaking her head. "I had so hoped..."

All of a sudden, she rounded about, facing me. "Honestly, Katie, couldn't you have made *some* effort to be pleasant, just this once?"

That hurt. It was especially hurtful coming from Bella, who rarely had a cross word to say to me. Andrew, ever the peacemaker, leaned forward as if he were about to intervene, but I cut him off.

"What does *that* mean?" I demanded. "I was perfectly 'pleasant,' Bella! I drank her coffee, I answered all of her questions—and she had plenty, believe me—I thanked her for the visit and, frankly, let her talk me into telling her a heck of a lot more than I wish I had. What is the big deal about this woman, anyway? She has a nice house. The food was good. Is that supposed to make me fall down and worship her? What's so important about Lucina des Anges, that you're all of a sudden grilling me like this? What does she *do*, anyway?"

Bella shook her head again, visibly distressed. "She does far more than you can possibly imagine, Katie," she told me. "I'm just very disappointed that you didn't take better advantage of this opportunity."

"Well," I fired back, "maybe I might have, if someone had had the decency to explain to me what the heck was going on! Are you going to tell me now, or do I have to wait until you and Andrew and the great Lucina decide that it's finally time to let me in on whatever little secret it is that you're keeping? Why is all of this such a big deal? You're acting like she's some kind of goddess or something!"

When Bella was silent, I went on. "If you wanted me to do something while I was at Lucina's house, Bella, you should have just told me. I'm not a child anymore."

Bella's eyes grew sad. "No, you're not," she answered. "But this isn't something you would appreciate if I just told you about it. You would understand a lot better if you figured it out for yourself. I was afraid she had invited you too soon, and it looks like I was right." She looked as if she were about to say more, but Andrew put a calming hand on her arm and she quieted.

It would have been smart of me to take a step back then, but the lawyer in me wouldn't let the argument go. "You know, Bella, you're probably right," I snapped. "It's probably too soon for me to be accepting invitations from the high society of Angel Falls. After all, I've only just lost my father, my job, *and* my apartment. But what difference does any of that make, compared with keeping the almighty Lucina happy? Heaven forbid that I should ever allow anything to make me *unpleasant*."

Bella sighed again. "All right, Katie, you've made your point," she conceded, turning toward the kitchen. "What's done is done, and there's no sense in us continuing to quarrel about it. Dinner's been ready and waiting in the oven for almost half an hour. Come and eat before it's completely ruined."

"Lucina the Great served up way too much food, but I thought I'd better eat it to be polite," I retorted. It was a blatant lie, but I wasn't going to admit it. "I'm not hungry. Eat dinner without me."

In Bella's mind, rejecting her cooking was the same as rejecting her. I had known that since childhood, and had always managed to swallow at least a few bites of whatever she put in front of me to avoid hurting her feelings. This was the first time I had ever outright refused to eat a meal she had gone to the trouble of cooking. It was tantamount to an act of war.

Bella spun back toward me, tears springing to her eyes. Andrew tried again to intervene before things got even worse, but I cut them off before either of them could say a word. "This whole thing is a ridiculous fuss over nothing, and I'm sick of talking about it. If Lucina des Anges doesn't think I'm good enough company for a return visit, it's her loss, not mine. And if you don't like it, Bella, that's just too bad. I'm going to bed. Good night." I stormed upstairs to my room, trying to pretend that I wasn't acting like a rebellious schoolgirl.

Later, I overheard Bella and Andrew talking long into the night, her voice distressed, his soothing and conciliatory. I couldn't hear their words and didn't want to. My anger was evolving into shame at my childish behavior, but I wasn't yet ready to apologize. The obvious and sensible thing to do would have been to go downstairs and make peace with them both. Instead, stubbornly, I rolled over and tried to sleep.

My room was unpleasantly cold and seemed even chillier because, for once, Honoré had not cuddled up in his usual position on my shoulder. He sat primly at the foot of my bed, his back turned to me in an unmistakable display of feline disapproval. He too had taken sides against me with the mysterious Lucina des Anges. Or maybe he thought I should have shut my mouth and eaten Bella's dinner. Either way, he clearly wasn't going to be much company.

I lay awake in the cold and dark for hours. Every little while I would shift in search of a more tolerable position under my chilly blankets, willing myself to sleep, without much success. It was going to be a long, comfortless night.

When I finally dozed off, I dreamed of wandering through an abandoned old house at twilight. The place smelled of dust and decaying flowers, and my footsteps echoed eerily off the scuffed wood floors and dingy, distressed walls. Several rooms away, someone was quietly laughing at me. With the dim logic that applies only in dreams, I recognized the ugly little voice in my head that had taunted me on the drive home. For the life of me, though, I couldn't figure out who its owner might be.

Archangel Michael speaks:

Poor Gabe! There he was, blowing his heart out in a triumphant trumpet riff, when his little protégée turned around and blew up all over her friends. Everyone who had been watching her debut at Angel Abbey and slapping Gabe on the back not an hour before heard every nasty word she said. Boy, was she ever obnoxious!

None of us knew what to say to Gabe. We all know that people are unpredictable, but this particular gal could be a real brat. There was one heck of a silence in Heaven after she turned down dinner, stomped off upstairs, and slammed her bedroom door.

Eventually, Raphael spoke up in his gentle way. He pointed out that we all knew Kate had understandable issues with trust. She had been under a lot of stress, and of course we couldn't expect her to appreciate what was happening. (Just like a human, to be given a fantastic opportunity and then immediately back away from it looking for the catch. I really wish you guys would trust us sometimes! If you would just relax and let us help you, your lives would be a whole lot easier. Angel's honor!)

Once Raphael was finished, Jophiel piped up, saying that Kate had looked lovely when she went to the Abbey. He's got a real eye for fashion, our Josie. Then Chamuel, who's all about relationships of every kind, reminded Gabe that Kate had made a great first impression during her interview with the Lady, so no real harm was done. It was beautiful, all of our brothers doing their best to prop up Gabe's spirits.

What nobody said, even though we all were thinking it, was that the Adversary had gotten to Kate on her way home. He doesn't need much, just a little chink in a person's confidence, to dig in and ruin a good thing. Kate's confidence was already in tatters. That gave him plenty of ways to get into her head and rough her up.

It's always frustrating when the Adversary manages to mess with somebody's head. We can't stop him when you guys decide to let the demons in. My angels and I are right there to evict them the instant you ask us for help, but we're not like the Adversary, who forces people to do what he wants. We always respect your free will, even when it's tough to watch you use it.

Luckily, the Adversary's intervention didn't accomplish much. Kate wasn't evil. She was a confused but decent person who would be fine once she settled down and got some sleep. Andrew and Bella were going to be OK, too—they never held a grudge, especially not against Kate. Nobody died, and nothing happened that couldn't be set right pretty fast. We all knew, though, that Kate's little hissy fit had to feel like a serious setback to Gabe after all the time and effort he had put into bringing her along.

When Kate finally fell asleep, we all heard the dark laughter in her dreams. Seems the Adversary was mighty pleased with himself. That probably hurt Gabe most of all. Me, I just wanted to grab my sword and go beat the living daylights out of the son-of-a-gun, but Uriel reminded me that it wasn't time yet. There's no hurrying the Apocalypse, no matter how much I would love to wipe the arrogant smirk off my fallen brother's face. It will be one more whack he'll have to take on Judgment Day. Let's see how smug he is then.

Gabe was quiet for a long time after the laughter subsided. When he finally picked up his trumpet and started playing again, he had switched from jazz to the blues. It was sweet, sweet music, but I hated to see my brother so sad.

CHAPTER FOURTEEN

The next morning, I woke up to birdsong, bright sunshine, a mild headache, and the certainty that I had behaved very badly the previous evening. I had two choices: I could hide in my room all day pretending that I hadn't made a complete fool of myself, or I could get up, go downstairs, and apologize to Bella.

In other words, there really was no choice at all.

Sighing, I hauled myself out of bed, threw a robe over my pajamas, and tromped downstairs to start mending fences. It didn't take me long to find Bella, sitting at the kitchen table with an untouched cup of coffee steaming in front of her. There was an empty place set across the table from her. A freshly baked streusel cake and a coffee pot sat at her elbow. Andrew was nowhere to be seen, but Honoré was perched expectantly on the kitchen counter, where he would have an unobstructed view of the table. It was obvious that he and Bella had heard me get up and stationed themselves strategically where I would be sure to find them. The battle lines had been drawn.

I sat down across from Bella and cleared my throat. "Good morning."

"Good morning," she replied, in a carefully neutral tone of voice. Honoré glanced at me and then looked away, as if I were beneath his notice. I was in trouble for sure.

Time to bite the bullet. "Look, Bella, I'm really sorry that I lost my temper with you yesterday," I told her. "I was way out of line."

"Yes, you were," she said crisply, but she filled my coffee cup anyway. Maybe this wasn't going to be quite as bad as I feared. "I was wrong too, though, Katie, so you deserve an apology as well. I shouldn't have pushed you so hard to go to the Abbey. As you say, you're not a child any more. You have every right to choose your own friends. If you didn't like Lucina, it's not my place to force her on you."

So much for my hope that the discussion was going to be easy. When Bella started talking about her "place," it meant I had really hurt her feelings. Better tell the whole, ugly truth if I wanted to make amends.

"It's not that I didn't like her," I replied, choosing my words carefully. "You were right, Bella. Lucina is lovely. If anything, I probably liked her too much. She asked me a ton of questions and I answered them in more detail than I should have. By the time we got home I started thinking that I had told her too much. Then I started worrying that she was going to start gossiping about me with other people who came to see her. It was crazy, I know, but that's why I got so mad at you. I'm sorry, Bella."

"Now, *that* makes sense," Bella said. She leaned forward a little, the dark cloud starting to lift from her face. "If you were already feeling like you had answered too many questions, it's no wonder you felt like I was grilling you when you got home."

"Well, Bella, you kind of were," I answered, trying not to sound too defensive. All we needed was to go another round about Lucina des Anges.

Bella paused for a moment, then smiled ruefully, much to my relief. "Yes, I suppose I was," she admitted. "I was just so anxious for the two of you to like each other, my eagerness got away from me. I apologize, Katie."

"No need," I told her, meaning it. "But Bella, you've never been so concerned about me making friends with somebody before. If it was that important to you for me to make a good impression on Lucina, why didn't you just say so before I went up there? It's not like I couldn't tell there was something going on, but you being so secretive about it made the whole experience pretty stressful. Why was it such a big deal?"

"You're right, Katie," Bella agreed. "I should have told you more about Lucina and the Abbey before you went to see her. I just thought it would be better, instead of me trying to explain things that you might find hard to understand, if you figured it out for yourself."

"Figured *what* out?" I was starting to get annoyed again, but stifled my irritation before it could erupt into another spat. "Bella, maybe I'm blind or stupid, but none of this makes any sense to me. I don't understand what the big deal is about some woman who lives in an old farmhouse, no matter how nice she is. Please, just tell me what's going on."

Bella sighed. "That's not going to be as easy as you think, Katie, but I'll try." She took a sip of coffee and then carefully set the cup back on the table before she spoke.

"Angel Abbey is a very special place, Katie," Bella began. "All kinds of people go to the Abbey, and they know they'll always find what they need when they get there. It's almost like magic. The reason I can't explain it to you is that I don't really understand myself how it works, and I don't know of any other place that's quite like it."

Now I was more puzzled than annoyed. "Is it like a community center or something?"

"In a way, maybe, but it's much more than that," Bella replied. "The Abbey is very old, and people have been going there for decades. It's big, and there are a lot of rooms, and somehow it seems to change so that no matter what you need, you can find it if you go there."

"You're making it sound like the 'Room of Requirements' in *Harry Potter*," I joked. Maybe I hadn't taken time to read the books but, thanks to Jack, I had seen all eight of the movies.

Bella sighed again, more deeply this time. "I knew it would be hard to explain it to you. The Abbey is sort of like that room in *Harry Potter*, I guess, but it's more complicated than that.

"People go to Angel Abbey for healing, for companionship, for learning, to find what they have lost and to get what they need," Bella continued. "They also go there to make a difference, to contribute their talents, and to donate whatever they have to give away. Sometimes, the thing people need most is to give of themselves to someone else. Angel Abbey is the one place where they can always do that, no matter what.

"The Abbey is important to a lot of people in Angel Falls, including Andrew and me. Lucina is in charge of it all. She's the Lady of Angel Abbey," Bella finished, her voice tinged with awe.

My eyebrows lifted, but I quickly forced them down. No need to offend Bella with skepticism when she was so obviously sincere. "You're making Lucina sound like an abbess or something," I said, trying to keep any sarcasm from creeping into my voice. "What do you mean, she's 'the Lady'? Is that her title or something?"

"I've never once heard her refer to herself as 'the Lady,' but everyone else calls her that," Bella replied slowly. "It suits her, somehow. I guess Lucina *is* sort of like an abbess, or maybe a noblewoman in one of the old stories. She's certainly the face of the Abbey to the people who come there."

"But what does she *do*, exactly?" I asked.

Bella thought for a moment. "It all depends, Katie. I don't mean to be mysterious, but it's hard to describe. It's like Lucina has some kind of inner wisdom guiding her. As big as the Abbey is, she always seems to know exactly what's going on and what needs doing, even if nobody else has noticed it yet. Somehow, Lucina always makes sure it gets done.

"Lucina encourages the volunteers when they come in to package up food and donations for the homeless shelters and soup kitchens. She hosts parties and concerts, drops in on classes, that kind of thing," Bella went on. "But she's not just a social butterfly. I've seen her perform weddings, baptisms, and memorial services, too. And if somebody needs food or clothing, Lucina somehow makes sure the perfect things are waiting when they arrive at the Abbey. If someone needs space for a group or class, or even just room to work on a project, Lucina always manages to find the perfect place, and it's always clean and ready to use.

"But it's not just logistics," Bella went on. "Lucina is better than anybody I've ever met at keeping everyone happy. If there's a meeting going on and people start to argue, she'll just appear out of nowhere and settle things right down. People who would bite your head off anywhere else in town turn downright affable around her. Somehow, she walks through the Abbey spreading goodwill wherever she goes, and people love her for it.

"Sometimes the Lady meets with people one-on-one, but it's rare," Bella continued. "That's why I was so thrilled that she asked you to visit. It's quite an honor to receive a personal, handwritten invitation from her."

"And that's why you were so upset that she didn't invite me back," I said, the light belatedly dawning. "You thought she was going to ask me to help out at the Abbey somehow."

Bella nodded, visibly struggling not to let her disappointment show on her face. "Well, I had hoped she would. You've had so much bad luck lately, Katie, and it has been so hard for you. It just breaks my heart. When you went away into yourself those days right after the funeral, Andrew and I were so worried! We didn't know what to do for you or how to bring you back.

"But then the Lady's invitation came, and the timing was so perfect that it felt almost like a miracle," Bella went on. "We thought that getting to know Lucina and helping out at the Abbey might be the best thing in the world for you. There's nothing better to help you get over your own troubles than to do something for somebody else."

Bella took another sip of coffee and looked down at her hands, worn and reddened from a lifetime of taking care of other people, myself included. "Andrew and I started going there to help out after you left for college. There wasn't much to do here without you around, just taking care of the house and yard and the few things your father asked us to do. We wanted to feel like we were doing something worthwhile with our extra time."

By then I was thoroughly ashamed of myself. Bella had just been concerned for me, wanting something for me that I hadn't known enough to want for myself. "And you think Lucina's not inviting me back to the Abbey means I messed up somehow?"

"It might mean that," Bella replied slowly, "but I don't really know. When the Lady hears about somebody who might have something worthwhile to contribute, she invites them up to the Abbey. It's not usually for a personal meeting like she did with you, though. Ordinarily, it will be for a community event, where she can watch them interact with the folks who volunteer there on a regular basis. If she likes what she sees, she encourages them to come back. But I've never heard of her telling anyone they were not welcome at the Abbey. So I have always assumed that when she doesn't invite people to return, it means they aren't ready or able to be part of the work there."

Things were finally starting to make sense. "So that's what you meant when you said you were worried that she had invited me too soon," I said. "You thought I must have offended her somehow, so Lucina decided that I wasn't ready to help out at the Abbey." Bella nodded again, a little shamefaced, though whether for herself or for me I couldn't say.

Thinking back over my visit to the Abbey, I realized belatedly that Bella might have been right. I had talked about myself all afternoon. True, it had been in response to Lucina's questions, but maybe my hostess had decided that such a self-centered person wouldn't have much interest in helping anyone else. It was a sobering thought.

"OK, I get it," I said. "No wonder you were so upset with me, when you think so much of Lucina. But Bella," I asked in a voice so small it surprised me, "what did you mean when you asked me why I couldn't 'just be pleasant for once'?"

It would have been nice if she had said she hadn't meant it, but Bella has always been too honest to soothe me with a comforting white lie. Instead she sat silently for a moment, seemingly measuring her words. Finally, she looked me in the eye and spoke.

"You've always been touchy, Katie," Bella said, "ever since you were a girl. Always so concerned about your dignity! Andrew and I figured it had to do with your mother disappearing the way she did. How could anybody expect you to relax and trust people after that? But you've always had a good heart, too, and you used to care a lot about doing what was right. You seemed to be fond of us, too, and we have always been as proud of you as if you were our own daughter.

"But then you went to law school and onto that horrible job, and it changed you," Bella continued, sadly shaking her head. "You never came home anymore, and you used to lie about how busy you were at work to avoid calling." She put up a hand to stop me before I could protest. Somehow, it came as no surprise that Bella had known all along about the little lies I had told to maintain my distance. It was only surprising that her loving acceptance of me had never wavered despite those lies. I was suddenly terribly ashamed.

"I know he was difficult, especially toward the end," Bella continued, presumably referring to Christopher Cunningham. "But he did the best he could, Katie, and so did we. We knew you had to grow up, but that didn't mean you had to grow so far away from us."

Bella sighed. "You've turned so cold, Katie! You seem determined to keep everyone at arm's length now, even Andrew and me. Sometimes I think Honoré is the only thing in the world you still love." She quickly looked down at her hands again, but not before I saw that her eyes were reddening, damp with unshed tears. I glanced over at Honoré, but he had turned his back and was studiously ignoring me. There would be no help from him.

I sat beside Bella for a long, silent moment. Part of me wanted to defend myself, deny it, insist that she was wrong. Another part wanted to be very, very angry with her. But the bigger, better part of me had to admit that Bella had gently put her finger smack dab on the truth. I could hardly blame her for that, or for the waves of shame that were washing over me.

"I'm so sorry, Bella," I finally said. "You're absolutely right. Working in the law can change people, and I've let it change me. Not for the better, either." All of a sudden, Bella wasn't the only one forcing back unshed tears.

Bella put her hand over mine and squeezed it reassuringly. "It's OK, Katie. Andrew and I figured that out, and we understood. But you might want to think a little about how working in law might have changed your father, too. Law and politics can be dirty business, Katie, plus he suffered some pretty heavy personal losses. He was never the same after your mother left. Watching you run as far away from him as you could just made him that much worse. I never understood how he survived so long, with so much bitterness in his heart."

I looked up at her. "You know he wasn't really my father, right?"

"Yes, I know," Bella replied, squeezing my hand again. "When you went all quiet on us for days on end after the funeral, we finally decided that we had better read that letter he left for you. We didn't want to violate your privacy, but we didn't know what was wrong or how to help. I'm so sorry, Katie—the things he wrote in that letter were just plain awful."

"From what you're saying, I probably deserved every word of it."

"Nobody deserves to be attacked like that." Bella disagreed with a vigorous shake of her head. "Especially not by their father. He was sick and unhappy, or he never would have done such a thing. You weren't perfect, Katie, but you weren't anywhere near as bad as he made out."

"Maybe not, but I sure could have been better," I admitted. "Thank you for telling me all this, Bella. I'm really, really sorry."

She smiled gently. "It's all right, honey. I was too hard on you last night. You're still our Katie, no matter what. I don't think there's anything you could do that would change that for Andrew and me."

"Let's not test that, OK?" I smiled ruefully. "But here's an idea about how I can start making it all up to you." Bella started to protest, but I pressed on. "Maybe Lucina didn't invite me back to the Abbey, but I distinctly remember her telling Andrew that it had been far too long since she'd had a visit from *you*. Is there anything going on up there that you'd like to get involved in? What if you went back to the Abbey and took me with you? Lucina doesn't strike me as the type to turn away a willing volunteer."

Bella positively beamed. "That's a great idea, Katie! After you left for the Abbey yesterday, I got to thinking that I hadn't been up there myself in quite a while. And you're right—the Lady would never turn you away if you came along to help out. I know just what we can do for starters."

"That's great," I smiled back, reaching out and catching her by the wrist as she started to get up. "But can I get a piece of that streusel first? I didn't eat dinner, last night, remember, and I'm starved."

Bella laughed and cut me a generous piece. As she did, Honoré jumped down from the counter and started twining around my ankles, purring as loudly as he could. I picked him up, and he lovingly licked my cheek before settling down into my arms. It seemed I had succeeded in mending fences with him, too.

Archangel Chamuel speaks:

Lovely, loving Bella! She has always been a particular favorite of mine. She may not be a great beauty, though that is certainly a matter of opinion–Jophiel insists that she would have been a sensation in the sixteenth century–and perhaps she is not as book smart as some. But Bella has a huge, open heart, and she is always ready to forgive and move on. If more people could do that, the world would be a much happier place.

My angels and I are responsible for building and sustaining all kinds of benevolent relationships on Earth. We handle romantic love, of course. But unlike humans, we are not obsessed with it to the exclusion of all the other loves that make life worth living. Yes, love between young lovers is a beautiful thing. So are the platonic love between friends, the complex bonds of love between family members, and the supportive, respectful love between a mentor and mentee–or, in this case, the love between an unhappy little girl and the childless couple who generously took her into their hearts even before her mother disappeared.

Raphael teases me once in a while about recruiting Bella to work with the healing angels, but I keep telling him that he is only allowed to borrow her. We need the help of as many tenderhearted souls as we can find to strengthen the loving relationships on Earth, and no one is more loving and accepting than Bella. Raphael and I are on the same team, of course–all the archangels are–but I am very glad that Bella chooses again and again to contribute her good works to my particular sphere.

Azrael reported that Christopher Cunningham watched the entire conversation as Bella worked her magic on Kate. He seemed a little calmer afterward, Azrael said. Hearing Bella talk about how his life experiences had changed him may have helped that poor, tortured man begin to forgive and make peace with himself. Once again, Bella did more good than she intended or even knew. Marvelous!

Bella may be a servant on Earth, but when her time comes to join us here, she will be welcomed as a queen in Heaven by my angels and me. That will be a glorious day indeed.

CHAPTER FIFTEEN

Forgiven by Bella and fortified by a second cup of coffee and her delicious streusel cake, I began my campaign to win the good opinion of Lucina des Anges. I was still embarrassed to have spilled so much of my story the first time I met Lucina, especially since I had apparently come off as too self-involved to be of much use at the Abbey. That stung. But it was important to me to mend fences with Bella. Bella loved Lucina, so I couldn't pretend I didn't care what Lucina thought of me. I swallowed my discomfort and got to work.

Bella reminded me that unless one was coming to the Abbey for help, it was customary to bring a gift on a first visit. The idea was to offer something that would demonstrate a sincere desire to contribute to the greater good. The roses from my first visit were an appropriate present for the Lady. (Despite Bella's obvious admiration for her, I couldn't bring myself to refer to Lucina as "the Lady." Not wanting to antagonize Bella, though, I bit my tongue.) To demonstrate my value to the Abbey and the larger community, however, a more practical gift would be better.

Fortunately, I had no shortage of available donations. The house was crammed from basement to attic with things I didn't need, so it was simply a matter of sorting through them to see what might be useful to somebody else. The house and its contents were mine, after all. It was time to find out what my erstwhile father had bequeathed me. There wasn't likely to be much that I wanted, but maybe some of it might do someone else some good. When I described my plan to Bella, she said she knew exactly where to start and dragged me off to the master bedroom.

It had been over a decade since I had set foot in what had once been my parents' room. Christopher Cunningham had abandoned it two or three years before, moving to a first-floor bedroom off the parlor when the cancer made it difficult for him to climb the stairs. He had died there, on the first floor. The master bedroom upstairs remained unused and closed off.

Creaking open the heavy oak door and stepping into the room felt like taking a step back into my childhood. It was a mild shock to realize that nothing had changed. The massive, four-poster brass bed was still there, along with the dark navy wallpaper, the looming mahogany dresser, the thick, plum-colored velvet drapes. Tea-dyed lace curtains behind them provided the only feminine touch in what was otherwise a very masculine decor.

The room was a perfect reflection of my parents' marriage. Looking around, I could see the force of Christopher Cunningham's personality overwhelming my mother's more sensitive nature. Dark colors and weighty furniture were not her taste, but they were definitely his. He would have insisted on this decor and she, either wanting to please him or exhausted from arguing, would have yielded to his insistence, as she always did. The furnishings were luxurious, to be sure, but the room was so dark, so confining. My mother must have felt like a trapped bird every time she went to sleep in the enormous cage of that brass bed.

For the first time, I began to have some inkling of why she left.

But there would be plenty of time later to ruminate on the mystery of my mother's disappearance. Right now, Bella and I had a job to do. It was a relief to focus on something practical.

We began going through the late Christopher Cunningham's clothes and personal effects. He had left behind a handsome camel hair overcoat and a Burberry raincoat with the signature plaid lining. There were two big closets full of expensive, classic suits, jackets, pants, shirts, and ties, along with several pairs of beautifully made, all but unused dress shoes. There was even a tuxedo, pristine on its cedar hanger in a separate garment bag.

I was taken aback at first by how many clothes my former father had left behind, but upon closer inspection, I could see that nearly everything was at least twenty years old. That made sense. A state senator needs an extensive wardrobe, and Christopher Cunningham would have made sure that his clothes stood up to scrutiny. He was never one to let a detail like an unfashionable suit stand between him and his ambitions.

None of my mother's clothes remained in either closet. It was disappointing, but I hadn't really expected to find them. Her angry, abandoned husband would have discarded them long ago.

Still, the closets yielded an unexpected bounty. Christopher Cunningham's clothes were not the height of fashion, perhaps, but they were of the classic quality that never goes out of style. They would be a godsend for an unemployed man who needed a decent outfit for a job interview. Bella pronounced them a perfect gift for my next visit to the Abbey, just the sort of thing that would demonstrate my interest in helping my neighbors.

"But are these clothes likely to fit anyone?" I asked her. "He was a pretty big man before he got sick."

"It will be fine, Katie," Bella assured me. "We'll just drop everything off at the Abbey and Mr. Moskowitz will make alterations, at no cost, for anyone who needs them." Mr. Moskowitz, I dimly remembered, had been my erstwhile father's tailor. So, he volunteered at the Abbey, too. Interesting.

"I've never heard of anything like that before," I said. "I always thought you just dropped things off at Goodwill, and people who needed clothes rummaged through until they found something that sort of fit." Until that moment, I had never really thought about what happened to used-clothing donations. It occurred to me that I had lived a remarkably privileged life.

"See?" Bella responded. "That's what I meant when I said there is nowhere else quite like the Abbey. People who volunteer there go out of their way to help others. The Lady sees to that."

"The Lady," indeed. Could anyone be that saintly? I resisted the urge to roll my eyes or say something sarcastic as we emptied the closets and packed up all the clothes. Whatever private misgivings I might have about Bella's hero-worship of Lucina des Anges, it felt good to be doing something practical that might benefit someone I didn't know. I hoped that the clothes would do some real good for their new owners, whoever they might be.

The heavy mahogany dresser was immaculately organized. Even when terminally ill, Christopher Cunningham liked everything to be just so. There were several pairs of unused socks and pajamas—we added those to the donation pile—and used underwear that we threw away. Soon, the big brass bed was covered in a satisfying heap of giveaways.

Again, though, there was nothing that had belonged to my mother. It seemed he had been remarkably thorough in rooting out anything that might remind him of her.

In the top dresser drawer, I found some beautiful English hairbrushes and shaving tools. Bella initially wanted to donate those, too, but readily agreed when I suggested setting them aside for Andrew instead. Then, I found a box tucked away at the very back of the drawer, and carefully drew it out.

The box was made of oxblood leather, with an elaborate clasp and an ivy border tooled on the top in gold. It was small enough to fit comfortably in my hand and remarkably heavy for its size. It looked and smelled antique, a charming trinket that some Victorian dandy might once have owned. It didn't seem to fit with my erstwhile father's other handsome, plain belongings.

Pushing a pile of shirts aside, I sat down on the bed, opened the box, and found Christopher Cunningham's treasure hidden inside.

There was a mirror inside the lid of the box, its silver back tarnished just enough to soften the image of whatever it reflected. The box itself was lined in dove-gray silk that had yellowed a bit. The interior was divided into three compartments, one large, two smaller. Out of the first, largest compartment I drew an antique pocket watch, engraved with a C. It played "Greensleeves" when I gently wound and opened it. Inside the cover was a tiny enameled portrait—it seemed to be eighteenth century—of a lady who was not my mother but looked remarkably like her. She had the same lovely blue eyes, the same delicate profile and mass of butterscotch curls. Was the resemblance a coincidence, or was this lady a distant ancestor? With Christopher Cunningham dead and my mother missing, there was no way to know.

In the second, smaller compartment sat a complete set of classic, gold-rimmed onyx tuxedo studs. There were matching cuff links, diamonds set in their shiny black faces. They looked expensive, better quality than anything you would find at a tuxedo-rental store.

A second set of cuff links, heavy gold squares, each engraved with the letter C and studded with a ruby, nestled beside the stud set in the second compartment. The ruby had been Christopher Cunningham's birthstone, I remembered. Perhaps they had been a birthday gift.

The last compartment held a woman's ring. It was set with a large oval diamond surrounded by pearls, its shoulders embellished with interlocking swirls of gold. The ring was accompanied by two matching wedding bands, one large, one small, each set with a row of tiny diamonds. When she left us, apparently my mother had also left her engagement and wedding rings behind. My ex-father had kept them—along with his own ring—ever since. I picked the rings out of the box, arranging them in a triangle on the palm of my hand.

I sat for a long time staring silently at those three rings. They stared back up at me, inscrutable. Whatever secrets they knew, they were not telling. Eventually, I felt Bella's hands rest on my shoulders. "He loved her very much, you know," she said from behind me.

"Maybe," I replied, not turning around. "I don't really remember. Funny, that he got rid of all her clothes and jewelry but he kept her wedding rings. Bella, what happened? Do you know why she left?"

Bella came around, sat down next to me on the bed, and put her arm around my shoulders. "Honey, I don't," she assured me. "If I knew what happened, I would have told you a long time ago.

"All I've ever been able to guess is that he loved her, but not in the way she wanted," Bella went on. "I know she tried. She gave him every single piece of jewelry in that box, except the rings he gave to her. She gave him that pocket watch as a wedding gift, and surprised him with the onyx studs and cuff links when he was first elected to office. I think the ruby cuff links were a birthday present.

"He just loved all of them, I remember that," Bella continued. "He wore those cuff links and carried that pocket watch every day when he was in the senate, even when the other men kidded him about wearing a woman's music box instead of a man's wristwatch. And he wore the onyx studs and cuff links whenever he could come up with an excuse to put on a tuxedo. They were such a handsome couple, your mother and father! When they were dressed up for a fancy political affair, you couldn't keep your eyes off them."

Unbidden, a vision flashed into my mind of my mother, hair piled high on her head, dressed for an evening out. Aqua chiffon swirled around her ankles and silver dancing shoes gleamed on her feet as she turned in a graceful circle, showing off her evening gown to her dazzled little girl. Christopher Cunningham hovered in the background, dark as a crow in his black tuxedo, a rare, proprietary smile on his usually stern face. Had they ever been happy together? Why couldn't I recall?

"He wasn't my father, remember?" I was surprised at the bitterness in my voice.

Bella was quiet for a moment. "No, it seems he wasn't," she finally admitted. "But he was your mother's husband, and he loved both of you as well as he could. Maybe someday you will find it in your heart to forgive him for not being able to do better." She gave my shoulders a gentle squeeze, got up, and went downstairs, leaving me alone with my parents' wedding rings and too many unanswered questions.

Archangel Raziel speaks:

In Heaven, I am known as the Keeper of the Secrets. Throughout Eternity I have labored at the Creator's side, chronicling every glorious aspect of how the Universe came into being. I recorded how Creation grew into what it is now, and I know what it will become. I am the Creator's scribe, and I am very good at my job.

What I record, I remember, and I record everything. My memory is boundless. I could tell you the number of stars in the sky, the dreams of wild horses as they run, the titles of the melodies played by the Seraphim who sing ceaselessly around the Holy Throne. I really could. But I will not, because they are secret.

Heaven's secrets are always mysterious and unfathomably lovely. They nestle within the heart like the most sacred, golden flames, echo in the mind like the songs of the rarest, most beautiful birds. To know Heaven's secrets is to smile softly, always and forever.

Humanity's secrets? Not so much. I know those secrets, too, and sometimes ache to reveal them before they cause too much hurt and harm. But I am the Keeper of Secrets. It is in my nature to protect even the darkest of skeletons in every human closet, no matter how much I might long to throw open the doors and let the light of Heaven pour in.

Rings, cuff links, and watches in antique boxes—what mysterious secrets they kept! I remember when Kate's mother gave each of those treasures to Christopher Cunningham, and the secrets she withheld even as she presented every gift. But then, I also remember the secrets he kept from her even as he placed his rings on her finger. Secrets and silences—does anything murder love faster?

There were so many things that those two sad, sorry people never told one another. In Heaven, however, we can hear every word, no matter how deeply it might be buried in the depths of the human heart.

I know where Kate's mother went. I also know why she left. Such a pity, but I cannot tell Kate—or you. It is a secret, and I must keep it.

Sorry.

CHAPTER SIXTEEN

Eventually I put the rings back and returned the box to the dresser drawer. My family's mysteries had haunted me for years. They were not going to be dispelled by a handful of trinkets.

The room suddenly felt chilly, too quiet, and a little grimy, even though Bella had undoubtedly cleaned it every week without fail. Gloom left its shadow no matter how often it was waxed and dusted away. Suddenly, I felt an intense need to shower, to wash away my unhappy past and try to move toward a better future. It was time to get ready for my return visit to the Abbey anyway.

Bella had decreed, "just this once," that I could wear jeans and a sweater to take our donation to the Abbey. She also pointed out, though, that I really needed something to wear besides outdated denim and power suits. What could I say? Bella was never wrong about things like that. Life at the law firm had rarely afforded me the luxury of time to shop. Now that I had plenty of time on my hands, though, I would need to diversify my wardrobe to the extent that my finances would permit.

By the time I got out of the shower and dressed, Andrew had loaded most of the clothes into the car. Bella and I helped him finish, but there were a lot of them, and it took us almost half an hour to get the job done. Andrew assured me that we would not need to call ahead. "There's always someone at the Abbey," he said. "If worse comes to worse, we can leave everything in the barn. Nobody steals from the Lady." Again, I suppressed the urge to roll my eyes.

The three of us made pleasant, inconsequential conversation as we drove to the Abbey. We had definitely made peace, but the goodwill between us felt fragile. Nobody wanted to break it. Driving up the long, tree-lined avenue to the Abbey, I felt a flutter of worry that I would somehow manage to step in it with Lucina again. It was good to have Bella and Andrew with me.

Andrew was right—there was definitely someone at the Abbey when we arrived. There was a small army of someones, in fact. The barn door was open, and what looked to be some kind of dance or martial arts class was in full swing inside. A dozen youngsters were parading around in a circle in front of the barn, leading what looked like a herd of small white llamas by their halters. (I later learned that they were a local 4-H group, training their pet alpacas for the show ring.) Several elderly ladies were seated on the front porch when we arrived, drinking iced tea and engrossed in a vigorous discussion of when and where to hold some kind of art show. They looked up and smiled as we came up the walk and then returned to their debate.

Meanwhile, I noticed that another gaggle of kids had taken up residence on the front lawn. They were building vividly colorful kites under the direction of a tall man with rumpled, reddish hair and glasses. Something about him looked familiar, but his back was turned to me. Try as I might, I couldn't place him.

Andrew strode up the front steps and across the porch and knocked on the front door. Amy quickly answered. She smiled brilliantly when she saw Andrew and Bella, clearly more comfortable with them than she had been with me. "The Lady will be so glad to see you," she exclaimed. "She's with someone right now, but I can go tell her you're here."

"Don't disturb her if she's busy," Bella said. "We just came by to do a quick drop-off. Kate has been going through her late father's clothes, and there were some nice things she wanted to donate."

"That's right," I quickly added, smiling. It was important for me to look both earnest and eager. Whatever gaffe I had committed, Lucina des Anges wouldn't think any better of me if it looked as if Bella had forced me to make amends.

"That's very kind of you," Amy said, "and your timing is perfect. We have a group of unemployed men from the south side coming tomorrow. They'll be looking for clothes for job interviews. Let's go put your donations in the Green Room, so everything will be there when they arrive in the morning."

The trunk of the old Lincoln was crammed with men's clothes, and I wondered how long it would take us to haul everything inside. I need not have worried. Before any of us could say a word, the youngsters dropped their kites on the lawn and trooped over to help. Bella and Andrew loaded them up. Arms full to overflowing with Christopher Cunningham's clothes, the kids followed Amy into the Abbey like baby geese trailing after their mother.

The man who had been helping them came too. Seeing his face, I recognized him instantly as Richard Helmsworth, the lawyer who had handed me that hateful letter at the funeral. He blushed redder than his hair when he saw me, but didn't walk away. If nothing else, I had to give him credit for sheer nerve.

"Ms. Cunningham," he said, "I don't know if you remember me, but I'm—"

"Richard Helmsworth," I interrupted tartly. "Yes, I know who you are. You're the attorney who gave me that *remarkable* letter from my late, well… father. Can I assume you're aware of its contents?" Bella and Andrew, I noticed, had moved a polite distance away. Apparently, they intended to let me fight this battle on my own.

The lawyer sighed and ran his fingers through his hair, rumpling it even further. "I am and you can," he said. "You have every right to be angry with me, Ms. Cunningham. Giving you that letter was one of the most disagreeable things I've ever done for a client. If you'll remember, though, I did tell you I was very sorry when I handed it to you. Mr. Cunningham was adamant about where and how you were to receive that letter. You're an attorney yourself, I believe. Certainly you understand that clients sometimes require you to do things for them that you'd never dream of doing on your own."

All things considered, it wasn't a bad excuse. I would have loved to tell the man that I had no idea what he was talking about, but I couldn't. There had been far too many times when I had done uncomfortable things just to please the firm's clients or, more accurately, to appease Roy Blackwell.

"Yes, I understand," I muttered, somewhat ungraciously. "You only followed your client's instructions. If I'm going to be mad at anyone, I should be mad at myself for making him so angry. If we'd had a better relationship, he would have told me that he wasn't my father himself, while he was still alive."

"Then I'm forgiven?" the lawyer asked, visibly relieved.

"There's nothing to forgive. But sure, you're forgiven if it's important to you," I replied. "And please call me Kate. 'Ms. Cunningham' makes me sound like a Sunday school teacher."

"Great! Then call me Richard," he said. He had, I noticed, a disarmingly crooked grin, and the eyes behind his horn-rimmed glasses were velvet brown. "I'd still like to make it up to you, though. Can I at least help you carry these things into the Abbey?"

"That," I replied, with a smile of my own, "you can definitely do."

We each grabbed a hefty stack of clothes, clearing out the trunk of the car, and started walking together toward the Abbey door. Bella and Andrew followed several long steps behind us. I had the distinct impression that they were exchanging significant looks and smiles of their own, but didn't look back to see.

Amy and the kids had vanished. I didn't know where the Green Room was, but Richard proceeded with no hesitation. "This way," he said, starting down a long hall. "Follow me." Hoisting my awkward armload of clothes, I followed.

If the outside of the Abbey had seemed busy, the inside was downright bustling. Every room we passed was crammed full of people, and all of them were intently occupied. One room housed a book discussion group, another held a small choir in mid-rehearsal, and the next was filled with attendees of what looked to be an AA meeting. We passed an industrial-size kitchen, where a pretty brunette in a chef's coat was barking directions at a group of men and women as they divided steaming piles of food into enormous metal trays. "Who's she?" I asked, struggling to keep up with Richard as he surged ahead.

"Oh, that's Violet Markham," he answered over his shoulder, not bothering to slow down. "She's a professional pastry chef. She teaches at the community college and runs the food pantry projects here at the Abbey. Every restaurant in town brings its leftover food here, and she works with volunteers to repackage and distribute it on the south side of town. Don't ever make her mad," he added, grinning archly. "She's been known to use her ladle to whack people who annoy her." I couldn't tell if he was joking, but decided it would be better not to find out.

Just as my arms were starting to ache under the weight of the clothes,

Richard ducked into a room on his left. I followed him in, stopped, and looked around. Richard had led me to what could only be the Green Room.

The walls of the room were painted the color of spring moss, but that clearly wasn't where the room got its name. As if backstage at a television studio or theater, the Green Room was set up as a communal dressing room. There were Formica counters and folding chairs, big mirrors surrounded by naked light bulbs, a whole wall of closets, a couple of couches, and several movable clothing racks. The other clothes we had brought were already hanging neatly on two of them—the kids had hung them up in a hurry—but there were at least ten additional racks loaded with men's clothes in an array of colors and sizes. Any man who came looking for something to wear would be able to find whatever he needed.

"This is incredible," I said. "Is it always like this?"

"The Abbey, you mean?" I nodded. "Actually, this is a fairly slow day," Richard said. "I've seen it a lot busier than this."

"That's hard to imagine," I replied. "But why is there a dressing room here? Do they put on plays at the Abbey?"

"Plays, concerts, ballets, you name it," he answered. "Lucina loves the performing arts and especially performing artists. There are always actors, singers, and dancers trooping through the Abbey. The Green Room is a place for them to prepare for performances and hang out when they're not onstage. But it gets put to other uses when there are no shows going on."

"Amazing," I said, shaking my head. "I have an actor friend in New York who would go nuts over this."

Richard treated me to another of his crooked grins. "You ain't seen nothin' yet, lady. This is just the tip of the iceberg." He took the clothes out of my aching arms and started hanging them up.

"Bella told me that people who come to the Abbey always find what they need here," I said, grabbing back a few of the shirts and hanging them up myself. "Is that true?"

Richard considered a moment. "Probably, but I'd wager they don't always know what they're looking for when they first start coming here. I sure didn't."

"OK, I'll bite," I said. "What were you looking for?"

Richard grinned again. "Well, I thought I was looking for networking opportunities to build my legal practice. The first time I came, my pockets were crammed with business cards, but I left without handing out a single one. I've gotten some clients from the Abbey since then, and that was great. But I didn't understand what I *needed* when I first started coming here."

"Which was what, exactly?" I was getting impatient.

"To work with kids," Richard replied. "I make a decent living as a lawyer, and the work is fine, but I'm really more of a teacher at heart. The Abbey gives me a venue to exercise that talent. I've got a group of middle-schoolers who meet me here once a week. We make stuff, we talk, and we hang out. They seem to like it, and it's a lot of fun for me."

"Incredible. You make it sound so simple," I said.

"That's because it is. Couldn't be simpler," he replied. "They enjoy it, I enjoy it, and their parents enjoy getting a break for a couple of hours every week. Everybody wins."

"Well, what do you know? A lawyer with a social conscience," I joked. "Apparently it's possible, no matter what the skeptics say. Do you get as sick of nasty lawyer jokes as I do?"

Richard shook his head ruefully. "You have no idea. And I'm not even with a big New York City firm. You could probably wallpaper your office in nasty lawyer jokes."

"My turn to say 'you have no idea,'" I retorted playfully. It didn't seem like a great time to confess that I had lost my fancy Wall Street office. "You've given me a lot to think about, though. Thank you, Richard," I said.

"My pleasure," he replied, "though if I had succeeded only in getting you to forgive me, I would count that as a victory."

We left the Green Room and walked back up the hall together. Voices echoed softly from the various rooms, interspersed now and then with snatches of music from the choir. It was a comforting sound, and I found myself wishing that I was in one of those rooms, engaged in something enjoyable with friends who shared my interests. Even those few minutes in the Abbey had made me realize how isolated I had been in Manhattan. I'd had plenty of work and lots of coworkers, but little playtime and few genuine friends.

Richard must have taken an unexpected turn as we walked back, because instead of ending up in the foyer, we suddenly came upon the room where Lucina had hosted me for tea. She was seated on a low sofa next to Bella, Andrew was lounging in a big club chair across from them, and all three of them were laughing. For just an instant I wondered whether they were laughing about me, but the ugly thought vanished as soon as I realized that it wouldn't bother me if they were.

Lucina rose gracefully and came straight to me, arms outstretched as if she were greeting a long-lost friend. She took my hands in hers and kissed me on the cheek in a gesture that was already becoming familiar.

"Kate, thank you for coming, and thank you so much for your contribution," she said, smiling warmly. "Those clothes will make a huge difference in a lot of lives. You were so generous to bring them!"

Lucina paused for a moment, her eyes unfocused, as if listening to that inner voice, and then looked back at me with a brilliant smile. "And I hope you can forgive me," she added. "I was so engrossed in our conversation last time you were here that I neglected to invite you back. Please, consider the Abbey your second home. We will be delighted to see you whenever you would like to come by." She kissed me on the cheek again. As I glanced over her shoulder, Bella looked up, caught my eye, and winked.

I turned around to look for Richard, but he had quietly disappeared while I was occupied with Lucina. Oh, well. There would be other opportunities to talk with him. Bella was visibly delighted, and Andrew was grinning from ear to ear. For the moment, that was all that mattered.

Archangel Raphael speaks:

As part of our healing work for the Creator, my angels and I often help human doctors when they're faced with medical crises. They don't realize that angelic hands are guiding their own. But our assistance can make the difference between life and death.

So, I happened to be helping a brain surgeon with a tricky operation on a little boy named Saakaar, when I noticed that Kate had gone back to Angel Abbey. It wasn't a distraction for me. Archangels can concentrate on about a million things all at once, because we don't experience time the way people do.

Creation seems a lot more complicated to you folks, I know. Your physicists are just beginning to understand how time and space really work. Until Einstein, only the mystics even had a glimmer. Just trust me when I say that I could easily hold the surgeon's blade steady, listen to Kate's conversations, and tell Gabriel to stop moping around and pay attention to what she was doing, all at the same time. Easy as pie, and I was glad to do it. Watching Kate go back to the Abbey made my brother happier than I had seen him since her little meltdown the day before. Besides, it was in everybody's interest to cheer him up. Heaven is always a happier place when Gabriel is in a good mood.

You might wonder why so many of God's archangels were engrossed in the escapades of one self-centered, moody young lawyer, and I can see why you would. There wasn't anything all that special about Kate herself, other than the uniqueness that is the birthright of every soul. Every person on Earth is an irreplaceable masterpiece, crafted with infinite Love by the hand of the Great Artist. Unique, exquisite individuality is the only trait that everyone alive has in common. It's an interesting paradox, don't you think?

So, yes, the archangels could have been focusing elsewhere, and a lot of us were. But there were at least two reasons several of us were keeping an eye on Kate, and a few of us had even more. Jophiel, for instance, never misses a chance to steer women away from what he likes to call "the miserable travesties of modern Western fashion." When Kate gave up her business suits, Jophiel took it as a personal victory. Chamuel has doted on Bella since she was a little girl, so he's always looking out for her no matter what else he's doing. Kate was important to Bella, so Chamuel took a special interest in her too.

Most of us, though, kept an eye on Kate because Gabriel had thrown his entire heart into helping her. We're all devoted to our glorious, golden brother, with his quick wit and incredible music. If something is a big deal to Gabriel, it's a big deal to all of us, period.

But there's one more secret I'll share with you, since Raziel never will. The truth is that we archangels love humanity every bit as much as our Master does. We delight in studying you and we're always looking for ways to help you grow into the incredible beings that the Creator intended you to be. Don't worry –we don't spy on you! But whenever you take even the smallest step in the right direction, there are always flights of us cheering you on. In fact, there is a host of angels lovingly watching over you now.

That operation turned out fine, by the way. Little Saakaar woke up clear-minded and cheerful, much to his parents' relief. If he continues on the path that our Creator has set for him, that boy could turn out to be the hope of the world. And if you found and continued on your ordained path, so could you.

Isn't that just fantastic?

CHAPTER SEVENTEEN

From then on, I divided my days between cleaning out my house—I was finally starting to think of it as mine—and visiting the Abbey. Every day, Bella and I would tackle a different room, and each one yielded a welter of fascinating items.

The library was crammed with an eclectic mix of books ranging from leather-bound classics to paperback novels. Christopher Cunningham seemingly had been willing to read almost anything. It took me more than a week to get through the stacks, partly because I kept getting engrossed in one book or another and partly because there were just so many of them.

I kept some of the better volumes. There was a first edition of Dickens's *Bleak House* that I couldn't bear to part with and a beautifully bound collection of Shakespeare's plays that I set aside for Jack. But more than half of the books ended up at the Abbey. I even gave away my erstwhile father's law books. I had plenty of my own and no desire to hold onto his. Amy told me later that they had been picked up from the Abbey by a professor who was planning to start an English-speaking law school in Kazakhstan. I smiled at the thought of those old books being used to train law students in a developing country.

The music room proved to be another gold mine of treasures and memories. I had forgotten that my mother used to sing and play the piano, and her old upright remained exactly where it had been when she disappeared. I had probably never known that she also played classical guitar, recorder, and Celtic harp, but she had a fine collection of those instruments, too. There were shelves and shelves of sheet music, collections of everything from art songs to show tunes. I paged through each of them, hoping to find something that my mother had left behind—a note, perhaps, or even a list of songs she especially liked—but there was nothing of the sort.

Music had been my mother's passion. She played the piano beautifully and sang like an angel in a sweet, contralto voice. Undoubtedly hoping that I would follow in her footsteps, she had enrolled me in piano lessons when I was young. My teacher said I had some talent and could probably play well if I practiced. However, I quickly developed the unfortunate habit of practicing the same mistakes over and over, much to Christopher Cunningham's irritation. Whenever I hit the same sour note three or four times in a row, he would lose patience and roar at me to stop practicing and go do something useful. My mother would tell him not to shout at me, he would shout back at her that I was a musical idiot, and I would run from the room before things got any worse. It was a relief to all of us, I think, when I gave up music in favor of other pursuits.

If there had been any hope of my mother coming home, I would have kept that piano forever. But she was gone, and I had long since surrendered my childhood dream of someday opening the front door to find her standing there. She would have wanted someone to play her instruments, I thought. That someone was not going to be me, so I donated them to the Abbey. Richard kindly came over with a small truck to transport them, along with the boxes of sheet music that she had left behind.

It turned out that Mrs. Braun, the kindergarten teacher who had greeted me so fondly at the funeral, moonlighted as a music teacher. She promptly started signing up students for lessons at the Abbey on my mother's instruments. Mrs. Braun also set up a lending library of the sheet music so her students could borrow and learn the pieces in my mother's collection. It wasn't as good as getting her back, but it was comforting to know that my mother's music was still being played on the instruments she once had loved. Whenever I walked past a music lesson at the Abbey and heard a struggling student hit a sour note on my mother's piano, I smiled.

The music room emptied, Bella and I continued to search my house for donations. The big linen closet on the second floor gave up a dozen sturdy wool blankets and several beautiful old quilts. The blankets went from the Abbey to a homeless shelter on the south side of town. Violet Markham made a donation to the Abbey and claimed the quilts to decorate her new pastry shop on the town green, which she had whimsically named "Violet's

Angel Cakes." Having enjoyed Violet's confections on my first trip to the Abbey, I was delighted to see her put the quilts to such artistic use.

In the basement, we found cartons of empty canning jars and stacks of old board games. The jars went to the Abbey and were assigned to Violet's cooking classes. Lucina kept a few of the board games to entertain visitors—she was rumored to be a fiend for Monopoly—and shipped off the rest to the children's ward at the local hospital.

In the guest room, I discovered an old brass bed, a massive mahogany wardrobe, and a matching, marble-topped dresser. They were not my taste, but an antiques dealer I met at a potluck dinner at the Abbey came over, examined them, and offered me $10,000 cash for the lot. He toted them off the next day, and I donated half the money to the Abbey for Lucina to distribute as she saw fit.

I gave the rest to Bella to cover household expenses. She had put me off when I first asked how much she and Andrew had spent since I came back, but all of that good food had to be coming from somewhere. We still had not discussed what would happen in the future—neither Bella nor I was eager to raise the question of whether she and Andrew would stay on or whether I would go back to Manhattan—but I certainly wasn't going to let the two of them pay to feed me and maintain my residence.

As Bella and I cleared out the clutter and emptied closets, the house almost seemed to take a deep breath, then let it out in a sigh of relief. It was still old and unattractively furnished, but the rooms felt a little lighter, the windows a bit brighter. Even though we were getting well into autumn and the outdoor air was chill, the house grew warmer and more cheerful daily, as Christopher Cunningham's dark, bitter ghost faded away.

Looking back on those days, it still amazes me that I gave so little thought to what was going on in Manhattan. I had no job. My apartment was being sold out from under me. I had not given any real consideration to Ruth Martingale's advice to file a formal complaint against Roy Blackwell, and I had absolutely no idea where I would go or what I would do next.

I needed to resolve my housing situation, find work, and either challenge Roy Blackwell or consciously choose to move on. But the idea of rebuilding my entire life from the ground up was too daunting. It was easier and more immediately rewarding to sort through heaps of household items, box up donations, and pass almost everything on to Angel Abbey, where people who genuinely needed the things could find them and put them to use. Maybe I wasn't making much progress on solving my own problems, but I was doing my best to help out with everybody else's.

Meanwhile, Bella took it upon herself to refurbish my wardrobe, using some of the money I had given her from the antiques dealer. She insisted that I needed to be properly dressed for social events at the Abbey and made it very clear that neither my jeans nor my "lawyer clothes" would do. Bags and boxes began to appear on my bed from time to time, filled with soft sweaters, embroidered flats, arty dresses, and long, embellished skirts that swished when I walked. Everything was in shades of blue, turquoise, sage, gold, and sand, a welcome change from my dark power suits. The jewelry Bella bought looked as though she had stolen it from a Gypsy's treasure chest: dangling earrings, long beaded necklaces, and stacks of glittery enameled bracelets. I felt a little silly in the new things at first, but they were pretty, distinctive, and so supremely comfortable that I soon came to enjoy looking more like an escapee from an artists' colony than a high-powered attorney.

The new clothes came in handy. Life at the Abbey was an endless whirl of work parties, potlucks, performances, and get-togethers. I came to know the Abbey's facilities well. The seemingly numberless rooms in the main house were used for meetings, classes, and work groups. The barn had been refurbished as a party space. It could seat more than two hundred guests and was the perfect setting for dinners, concerts, plays, and receptions.

Only the carriage house went largely unoccupied. It was a charming place that had served as the groundkeeper's quarters for many years. Now it was used only occasionally, mostly for extra storage. Amy told me that Lucina had "never gotten around" to repurposing it. That struck me as odd, but it was her house, to use—or not—however she saw fit.

To Bella's delight, Lucina was as good as her word. Whenever I arrived she would welcome me warmly, taking my hands in both of hers and kissing me on the cheek. Over the course of several visits I heard more than one person refer to that distinctive gesture as "the Lady's blessing," and it disturbed me. Lucina was a gracious hostess with a positive genius for keeping polite social chitchat humming along, but from what I could see she didn't seem to have any special power to bless anyone or anything. The little pause that she often took, looking away as if listening to some inner wisdom before returning to the conversation at hand, struck me as eccentric and even pretentious. Still, these gestures were harmless, I supposed. On the plus side, Lucina appeared to be genuinely concerned for the comfort of her guests. I could not deny that she provided an incredible venue for community service and artistic expression at the Abbey. Eventually I concluded that she was pleasant enough, if a trifle affected, and tried not to let other peoples' blatant adoration of her get under my skin too much.

It soon became obvious why her home was called "Angel" Abbey. I had presumed the place was named after the village of Angel Falls, but the Abbey's decor lent independent credence to the name. There were flocks of angels on display in every room, though they were not always easy to spot. Angels hovered in the backgrounds of paintings, murals, and tapestries. They looked up from illustrations on the pages of the books that lay scattered and open around the library. Statues of angels rested unobtrusively on shelves, peeked out from behind vases and lamps, danced among the flowers in the gardens. There were angels carved into the woodwork in some rooms, and angels woven into drapery fabrics or wallpaper patterns in others. The Abbey's dishes were creamy white with a gold border that, carefully examined, was made up of pairs of tiny, outstretched wings, connected at the tips like the joined hands in paper-doll chains. Some of the lampshades were edged with similar winged borders, and wings appeared in the corners of most of the mirror and picture frames. Even the crystal chandelier in the dining room incorporated the angel theme, its many arms gracefully curved like stylized, glittering wings.

If the angel-saturated decor of the Abbey suggests a toddler's nursery or a New Age gift shop, though, think again. The angels whose images decorated the Abbey weren't chubby little cherubs. In whatever media they were depicted, the denizens of Angel Abbey were uniformly tall, gorgeous, and powerfully built. Several of them carried jeweled books or artistically embellished musical instruments. One in particular, the trumpet-carrying, copper-haired angel featured on the Abbey's weather vane and door knocker, appeared in one pose or another all over the house. I wondered now and then who that angel was supposed to be but never got around to asking Lucina.

None of the Abbey's angels was overtly threatening, but the idea of actually encountering one of those imposing messengers was a little unsettling. And they were *everywhere*. If you looked carefully for them, you would soon become convinced that dozens of angels were watching over you at the Abbey no matter where you stood or sat. I couldn't quite decide whether the entire effect was comforting or unnerving, and I began to have a new sympathy for Jacob Wittesteen. It must have been quite a shock for the founding father of Angel Falls to awaken from a drunken stupor and see such a magnificent creature looming over him. A sight like that would make me reconsider my own sinful ways for sure. I was confident, however, that such an encounter would never happen to me.

Determined to keep the peace with Bella and Andrew, I resolved my discomfort with Angel Abbey and its Lady by focusing on getting to know the people I met there. Pastor St. James, the minister who had conducted my former father's funeral service, was a frequent guest and an engrossing conversationalist. He always had a heartwarming story to tell, and his smile was positively infectious. Chef Violet went out of her way to befriend me, and we quickly became good buddies despite my utter inability to prepare anything more complicated than a cup of tea or instant soup. Over time, I came to know the gaggle of elderly ladies who ran the art shows, the members of the book club and the various choirs (there were three), and the kids from the 4-H club. I even made it a point to learn the name of each of the kids' pet alpacas.

Like me, Richard Helmsworth was often at the Abbey. We spent a lot of time together, chatting about anything and everything except the law. I wasn't sure whether he was flirting with me or not. He was far less aggressive than the men I had dated in Manhattan and had not even asked me out. Still, I always enjoyed our conversations, and began to look forward to running into him at one Abbey social function or another.

Days turned into weeks, and the fine autumn weather turned chilly as winter approached. I spent my time socializing, clearing out the house, donating whatever I could find to give away, and otherwise ignoring the troubles that were still brewing in New York City. I told myself that I needed time to rest, heal, and plan what to do next. The resting was easy and the healing appeared to be coming along. Somehow, though, the planning never quite came together.

Honoré continued to sleep on my shoulder at night and follow me around during the day, but I came to rely less on his company as I became more involved in the community at the Abbey. Occasionally he would look at me with what might have been a hint of reproach, but that was easy to overlook. I loved him dearly, but he was just a cat, after all.

What I have learned since then is, if you do not attend to your problems, your problems will come looking for you. One late autumn afternoon, Bella and I were in the parlor going through stacks of paintings that we had collected around the house, deciding what to keep and what to give away. Andrew was off having the car serviced, and Honoré was sprawled on the sofa, watching us with half-closed, drowsy eyes. We were talking companionably about nothing in particular when the doorbell rang.

Bella started to get up, but I beat her to it, hurrying to the door. I was half-hoping it would be Richard, who had taken to dropping in on occasion when he could come up with a credible excuse to do so. I still wasn't sure whether I was interested in dating him, but he was funny and charming, good company when he happened to come by.

When I opened the door, though, Richard was not on the other side. A big man in jeans, worn leather boots, and a dark pea coat stood on the stoop. His lower lip was pierced and he carried a toothpick in the corner of his mouth. Half of his head was shaved and tattooed with an enormous, indigo-winged bird. What remained of his dark hair was braided at the front, and a second braid ran down the center of his ragged black goatee. I took an involuntary step back. The man was just standing there, not doing anything particularly menacing, but I was suddenly, acutely aware that Bella and I were alone in the house.

"Katherine Patricia Cunningham?" he asked in a hoarse whisper. The toothpick in the corner of his mouth bobbed up and down as he spoke.

"Yes," I managed. "That's me."

The man shoved a heavy manila envelope into my hands. "You've been served," he said. "Have a nice day." He grinned, revealing gorgeous white teeth, and I caught an incongruous whiff of peppermint on his breath. Then he turned, walked down the path to a muddy Jeep that was waiting in the driveway, got in, and drove away.

My hands were trembling and my mouth was dry as I carried the manila envelope back to the living room. Smudged with dark finger marks from the big man's hands, the envelope was addressed to me and sent by the law firm where I used to work. I sat down on the couch to open it. Honoré settled into my lap, presumably for moral support, as Bella sat down next to me, her sweet face the picture of motherly concern.

The envelope was made of thick, sturdy paper, glued securely shut and then taped for good measure. It was difficult to open neatly, but, for whatever reason, I was reluctant to tear it apart. It took me several minutes to work open one corner and then carefully rip across the fold at the top. Honoré and Bella watched intently as I slowly reached inside.

The first document I pulled out of the envelope was a neatly typed court filing. It was more than twenty pages long, but I had to read only a few paragraphs to recognize it as a complaint in a civil lawsuit, accusing me of professional malpractice. My hands shook as I read.

My former law firm was suing me on behalf of Dr. Grandy for three million dollars. They claimed that I had conspired with seller's counsel to cheat Dr. Grandy in the same shady real estate deal I had so vehemently opposed. They then accused me of disclosing confidential documents in violation of my professional responsibilities, thereby giving the seller an unfair advantage in the negotiations.

The complaint droned on for pages, written in a ponderous style that I instantly recognized as that of my old nemesis, Mark Davenport. Twenty-odd pages later, it ended in a lengthy list of reasons the court should rule against me. It came as no shock, though, that Davenport was not serving as lead counsel on the suit. That role had been claimed by Roy Blackwell, who had signed the complaint on Dr. Grandy's behalf with a bold, vindictive flourish.

By the time I finished reading the complaint, my hands were shaking so badly that I could scarcely hold onto the pages. My heart was pounding, and my breath came in shallow, ragged gasps. Life in Manhattan was expensive, and I had had to pay off tens of thousands of dollars in law school loans. I not only didn't have three million dollars, I didn't have a hundredth of that amount in ready cash. The costs of defending a lawsuit alone could bankrupt me. Regardless of whether my opponents won or lost, I might well spend the rest of my life paying off my legal fees, assuming I could ever find another decent job.

Visions of an impoverished life in some back-alley tenement flashed through my head. I even imagined myself dressed in rags and begging for change on the street corner outside the law firm office, shivering with cold and hunger as Davenport and Blackwell sauntered past, sneering. It was a laughable cliché, but it proved remarkably difficult to drive out of my mind.

The lawsuit itself was bad enough, and the thought of losing everything I had worked so hard to build was worse. Tough as my situation was, though, it seemed Roy Blackwell was not done with me. Even with the lengthy complaint removed, the dirty manila envelope was still too heavy to be empty. Something else had to be inside.

I reached in again and pulled out another sealed envelope. This one was from the New York State bar, sent by certified mail to my old law firm address. How ironic that they should have written to me there.

Ripping open the second envelope, I discovered that Roy Blackwell and Mark Davenport had not been content to sue me for every nickel I could ever make and more. They had also reported me to the New York bar for discipline, accusing me of breaching my professional duty of confidentiality to Dr. Grandy.

It seemed like a lifetime since I had left my briefcase full of Dr. Grandy's papers in the taxi, but I remembered it as a simple mistake. I had been careless, but not deliberately dishonest. That's not the way my accusers presented my actions, though. They twisted the story, claiming that I had stolen the documents for the seller's negotiating team, then lied about the theft when confronted by my noble managing partner. They asserted that as a result of my vile deception and thievery, Dr. Grandy had lost a unique opportunity to purchase a property that he intended to convert into a hospital for the underprivileged children of New York City. (Dr. Grandy had had no such plans as far as I knew, but the assertion added an artful touch of pathos to their lies.)

Blackwell's story was as happy a crock of horse manure as I have ever seen before or since, but the bar counsel seemed to buy it. I was charged with professional misconduct and directed to show cause why I should not be disbarred. Unless I successfully fought the charges, I would lose my right to practice law forever.

The letter slipped from my fingers, and Bella caught it before it could flutter all the way to the floor. I buried my hands and face in Honoré's fur and felt the same dark, despairing nothingness that had claimed three days of my life after the funeral start to creep over me again. It would have been easy to drown in that darkness, and I almost let it take me.

Just at that moment, though, I heard a blast of trumpet music from very far away. It didn't last long, it was barely audible and I had no idea where it came from, but it was enough to bring me back to myself. I sat up, shook my head to clear it, and turned to Bella. She had read the bar's letter over my shoulder and had tears in her eyes. Honoré looked up at me as well, his sapphire eyes mirroring her concern.

"Katie, honey, I don't understand. What does this mean?" Bella asked. Her voice was shaking almost as badly as my hands were.

"It means," I told her, "that I'm going to need a lawyer."

Archangel Gabriel speaks:

You know, I really had done my very best not to meddle. I let Kate make her own choices, bit my tongue and sat on my hands whenever she lost her way, hinted and coaxed her from a seemly distance, and generally tried to behave like an archangel should. As Metatron keeps reminding me, we're Divine messengers, not movie directors. It's not our place to tell the people in our charge what to do or how to do it. Free will is important. I can respect that, I honestly can.

The thing is, though, Kate was finally starting to get it! She had humbled herself, done good works, donated her time and treasure, and begun making friends with the people around her. For the first time in her life, she was starting to fully appreciate Bella and Andrew. She was even making an effort to put aside some of her cynicism around the Lady and the Abbey. Maybe she wasn't fully facing her situation, but she was making incredible progress. It wouldn't have been even remotely fair to let the Adversary knock her off kilter again without giving her at least some support.

So, yes, I played one tiny little riff on my trumpet. It was a minor fanfare that lasted only a few seconds. Kate could barely even hear it. I admit that it broke some rules, but I didn't care as long as it helped her. If it meant that I had to polish halos for the Administrator for a week, well, so be it.

Archangels can humble themselves too.

CHAPTER EIGHTEEN

Roy Blackwell probably intended to incapacitate me with the ugly contents of that manila envelope. He galvanized me instead. That trumpet blast became a call to battle. Even though I could not have told you where it came from, it was just what I needed.

Suddenly, I was wide awake and ready for a fight. It was long past time for me to resolve my problems. There was an unoccupied apartment waiting in Manhattan for me, and if I wasn't careful, a legal battle that would destroy my finances and ruin my future. Both had to be dealt with. It was late enough in the day that I couldn't do a whole lot until the next morning, but there was no excuse to put off the little that could be done right then.

Honoré jumped off my lap just in time to avoid being dumped off, as I stood and went hunting for my cell phone. After several minutes of rummaging I found it in my bedroom, half-hidden under an open copy of *Harry Potter and the Sorcerer's Stone*, which I had started reading as a first step toward catching up on all the fiction I had missed while buried under in my legal practice. No service—the law firm had wasted no time cutting me off. Undeterred, I marched downstairs and used the kitchen phone to book a ride to Manhattan the next afternoon. On a whim, I called Jack, too. When he didn't pick up, I left a message inviting him to meet me for dinner that evening. As long as I was going to be in the city, it wouldn't hurt to spend some time with a friend. Besides, I still felt a little guilty for having been so rude to Jack the last time we saw each other.

While making my travel arrangements, I pondered what to do about my legal problems. I was definitely going to need a lawyer. I couldn't afford to pay top dollar, though, and wouldn't know whom to hire even if I could.

None of the lawyers at the firm could represent me, of course—it would be a blatant conflict of interest—and no one else came immediately to mind.

To be honest, I had not made many friends among my opponents when practicing in Manhattan. My professional style at the time, inspired by my demanding father and reinforced by the hard-hitting culture of my firm, was so aggressive that it shames me to think back on it. To other lawyers, business was just business, and it ended at the close of the day. Attorneys who had ferociously attacked each other for hours at a time in court or at the bargaining table often went out together afterward for drinks. It kept the practice of law at least marginally civilized for them, and sometimes provided opportunities for quiet compromise.

Not Kate Cunningham, though. To me, opposing counsel had never been anything more than someone to beat, and maybe humiliate for good measure. I had refused invitations and rebuffed friendly overtures, focusing only on the win, not on the impression I was making or the potential friends and allies I was losing along the way.

In hindsight, I admit that I had even looked down on the other young lawyers in my firm, sneering at their shortcomings and competing viciously against them for partnership. Mark Davenport, for example, might have been the jackass I believed him to be, or he might have been a decent guy. But I had made no secret of my disdain for him when we first started working together. He must have relished the opportunity to take me down a peg or two. If I had been nicer to him at first, perhaps he would not have attacked me quite so eagerly later.

In need of help and with no idea where to get it, I wondered how I could have been so arrogant and so blind.

I considered hiring an inexpensive ambulance chaser, one of the cut-rate lawyers who charge next to nothing for their legal work and still cheat their clients. I hadn't often run into attorneys of that ilk, because I had worked almost exclusively on high-end projects, crossing swords with talented, pricey opponents. Still, I had heard the horror stories about lawyers who charged rock-bottom prices but then missed filing deadlines, failed to appear on hearing dates, or worse, showed up drunk to argue on behalf of their pitiable clients. They were the dregs of the legal profession, and those of us at the top used to sneer at them every chance we got.

The idea of hiring one of those hacks made me sick to my stomach, but

I couldn't afford better. In fact, I probably couldn't afford even as much as a hack would charge. Even the worst Manhattan lawyers charge an hourly rate for their services, and legal fees run up fast when clients get billed by the minute. I had Dr. Grandy's civil lawsuit and Blackwell's bar complaint pending against me, and both would need to be defended. The facts might be essentially the same, but defense lawyers don't bill two legal proceedings for the price of one. The cheapest shyster I could find in Manhattan would probably bankrupt me long before clearing my name.

I also thought about handling the cases myself, but quickly rejected the idea. There is good reason for the saying "the lawyer who represents himself has a fool for a client." I had been foolish enough to get myself into this mess. It would be even more foolish to try to get myself out of it without another attorney's help.

It abruptly occurred to me, however, that there was one lawyer who might be willing to help me without charging an arm and a leg for his services. He wasn't in Manhattan but he *was* a New York State attorney. That meant he could represent me in court and before the bar.

Better still, I knew this lawyer had to be capable. Christopher Cunningham was nothing if not demanding, and he had trusted Richard Helmsworth to write a will so airtight that even his talented attorney stepdaughter could not break it. If Richard's legal work had been good enough for my erstwhile father, it certainly should be good enough for me.

Richard might not be able or willing to represent me himself. But even if he were not, he might know someone who would take my case. Unlike me, Richard had been smart enough to build a network of friends in his community. I just hoped that by now he counted me as one of them.

Richard was out of his office when I called. I left a message asking whether I could come by to see him the next morning. If he couldn't see me or wouldn't represent me, I didn't know what I would do. There would be plenty of time to worry about that when he called me back, though. Meanwhile, the situation with my apartment still had to be settled, and I needed to get ready for my trip to Manhattan. I pulled out my overnight bag and was just beginning to pack when Honoré jumped up on the bed and climbed inside.

"Not this time, big guy," I said, rumpling his ears. "Stay here and take care of Bella and Andrew, OK? I'm only going to be gone overnight."

Honoré looked solemnly at me, uttering the little cry that meant he was concerned. "Everything's going to be OK," I promised him, hoping it was true. As I lifted him out of the bag, Bella called up to say that dinner was ready. I gently set Honoré down, pushed the bag aside, and headed downstairs. Honoré jumped off the bed and followed me, a supportive shadow.

When we got downstairs, Andrew had returned from the garage. He looked worried. "Bella told me about the package that arrived today, Miss Kate," he said. "I can't believe they're really suing you over that fiasco with the briefcase. Is there anything we can do to help you? Do you need money or anything?"

My eyes misted with unshed tears. What had I ever done to deserve the kindness that Andrew and Bella continued to shower on me? "Andrew, you're incredibly generous to offer, but I couldn't possibly take your money. Besides, this is my problem. I created it, and it's my job to solve it. Thank you, though. It means the world to me that you'd even offer."

Andrew shook his head, smiling sadly. "You have never been one to accept help, have you? We won't push you—we know better—but we are here for you if you need us. Just remember, Miss Kate, nobody makes it all on their own."

"I will, Andrew. Thank you." I leaned over and kissed him on the cheek, then followed him into the kitchen.

Bella had roasted a chicken, surrounding it on a platter with heaps of mashed potatoes and seasoned vegetables. Everything was homey and delicious, but I couldn't eat much. Honoré got more than his share of my dinner that night, licking shreds of chicken from my fingers with more eagerness than I could muster.

Later, I lay in bed in the dark, staring up at the ceiling. Honoré snored softly on my shoulder, but sleep eluded me. It amazed me to realize that my father's gloomy house had become a haven. Bella and Andrew had proven to be far more caring, supportive companions than I ever expected or deserved. Angel Abbey had provided me with opportunities to make new friends and contribute in ways that I would never have imagined. Once, I couldn't wait to get to New York City and make my mark on the world. Now, all I wanted was to get myself there, settle my unfinished business, and come back home as quickly as possible.

The irony of it all made me smile. At that moment, I realized that I was much more grateful for the blessings of the past few weeks than nervous about what lay waiting for me in Manhattan. That unexpected, happy thought finally relaxed me enough that I could rest.

Asleep at last, I dreamed of walking through the woods in winter. The path under my feet was narrow and only dimly lit by the crescent moon overhead. Dead leaves crunched under snow with my every step, eerily loud in the otherwise unbroken silence. Trees stood in looming clusters to either side, their branches drooping down to tangle in my hair as I walked. Something, or things, lurked in the shadows beneath, and they meant me no good.

If I stepped off the path, I knew, those things would attack like rabid animals, enveloping me in darkness. So long as I continued on the path, though, I was safe. Whatever lurked beneath the trees could threaten and inspire fear but could do me no genuine harm.

Far off in the distance, a light flickered, beckoning me to safety. One careful step after another, I walked through my dream toward the light, trying to ignore the mutters and growls from beneath the trees. Whether I ever arrived to a place of safety, though, I cannot recall.

Archangel Michael speaks:

So, there I was, putting the Legions of Heaven through practice maneuvers, when I heard this trumpet blast from somewhere near the Pearly Gates. It had to be Gabe, and he had to be upset about something. I was busy with my own projects, though, and really didn't have time to check it out.

Not to worry you or anything, but there's a lot going on in Heaven right now. The Adversary knows he's down to the wire, cosmically speaking, so he's been pulling out all the stops lately. It really keeps my legions on their toes. We can't afford any unwanted visitors from the Adversary's army, if you know what I mean.

We welcome defectors, though. The Adversary's minions have been coming back for centuries, limping in one or two at a time, almost as sorry for what they've done to Creation as they are for what they've done to themselves. The Creator always forgives them, and we always take them back.

Nobody works harder to be good than a repentant angel. Metatron never runs out of stuff for them to do. Stained glass windows to wash, streets of gold to sweep clean… You get the idea. It's hard, dirty work, but they all swear it's better to serve in Heaven than to reign in Hell. They would know better than anybody, I guess.

As much as I love a good battle, there's a lot to be said for this war of attrition we're waging. By my count, over three-quarters of the Adversary's army have come back to our side without any of my angels having to swing a single sword. Hold him off long enough, and at this rate the Adversary will soon be the only demon left in Hell. Won't that be something? It cracks me up every time I think about it. Maybe then he'll stop being an idiot, put his stupid pride down the sinkhole where it belongs, repent, and come home.

He'll be welcome, believe it or not. The Creator is amazingly forgiving about such things. We'll have one heck of a party when our arrogant prodigal brother finally figures out that he never should have left Heaven in the first place.

Anyway, once we finished our maneuvers, we stored our gear and went back to HQ. Couldn't believe what we saw when we got there! Half the archangels in Heaven were sitting around, polishing stacks of halos as if the Second Coming had been rescheduled for tomorrow and we all had to be spiffed up and ready for the big finale. (No, I'm not going to tell you when it'll be. Go ask Raziel if you can't take the suspense any more. Good luck getting an answer out of him, though!)

Seems that trumpet blast I heard was Gabe, like I thought, calling out to his little protégée, so she wouldn't sink headfirst into another one of the Adversary's depression pits. That broke about a gazillion of Metatron's rules, so Gabe got stuck on halo duty. Raphael and Jophiel decided he shouldn't have to do the whole thing alone–I guess they thought Metatron was being a little too hard-nosed–so they started helping Gabe with the job. Then Chamuel and Azrael decided they might as well help too, and pretty soon there was a major polishing party going on.

Metatron stood above the whole thing scowling so hard I thought his eyebrows were going to grow together into one big, black thundercloud, but he didn't say a word. So, I thought, what the heck? I picked up a cloth and a halo and got to work myself. Didn't quite know what it was Gabe saw in that kid, but if he was ready to polish a roomful of halos just to get a chance to help her, I figured I might as well pitch in too.

CHAPTER NINETEEN

Richard called me back promptly the next morning. When I told him I needed his help with a legal problem, he invited me to come straight over. I grabbed my overnight bag, along with the manila envelope and its horrible contents. Then I hugged Bella, ruffled Honoré's fur, and followed Andrew out to the Lincoln. I climbed in and let him drive me to Richard's office.

It was silly to have Andrew driving me everywhere. I was an adult, after all, not a child or an invalid, and certainly not some *grande dame* who needed to be chauffeured from pillar to post. But Andrew seemed to enjoy driving me, and I was grateful to be driven. With Andrew in charge, my worries wouldn't distract me to the point where I might cause an accident. Besides, I couldn't bring myself to get behind the wheel of Christopher Cunningham's old black Lincoln. He had never allowed me to touch it during his lifetime, and I was half-afraid that if I drove it now, his furious ghost would rise up and protest from the grave.

The green Ford Mustang that had gotten me through college and law school was still in the garage, but I wasn't eager to drive that, either. The events of the past few months had really shaken my confidence. I trusted Andrew behind the wheel a whole lot more than I trusted myself.

We rode quietly, Andrew's eyes on the road, mine on the late autumn landscape that rolled past the passenger-side window, a study in faded gold and deepening shades of brown. I was anxious about how Richard would react when he saw the complaints. We had started to be friends and I didn't want him to lose whatever respect he might be developing for me. If he believed the lies in those court documents, I didn't know how I would handle it.

Richard's office turned out to be in a lovely old farmhouse. The clapboard was stained rust red and the shutters and trim were painted tan. The front door was a dark, almost nautical blue, and it featured a round brass knocker instead of a bell. A milk can full of dried autumn grasses and wildflowers stood next to a wooden rocker on the small front porch. It couldn't have been less like my lavish Manhattan office, but it gave a respectable and trustworthy impression. All told, I thought the contrast between our two offices spoke better of Richard than it did of me.

Richard opened the door himself and ushered me inside. Andrew had insisted on waiting in the car. He said he had some reading to catch up on, so I went in alone.

Richard's office was the perfect picture of a country lawyer's place of business. The furniture was simple and well made, and the walls were covered floor to ceiling with leather-bound law books arranged neatly on deep shelves. A seascape hung over the credenza behind the antique Shaker desk, where a handful of files sat in a tidy stack next to a coffeepot and a tray of stoneware mugs. There were a few knickknacks on the shelves—a brass clock, a couple of duck decoys, and one well-tended philodendron in a hand-thrown pot. All he needed was a Labrador retriever snoozing on the rug to complete the picture.

This was a space for calm reflection and careful decision-making, and it spoke volumes about Richard's professional style. I thought back again to my own cluttered office and was suddenly grateful that Richard had never seen it. It might have given him an insight into my character that I would rather keep to myself.

"Your office is really handsome, Richard," I said. "I keep expecting Gregory Peck to walk in and sit down."

"Yes, well, who didn't want to be Atticus Finch back in law school?" Richard smiled. "I have never had a case as high-profile as the one in *To Kill a Mockingbird,* but that hasn't kept me from dreaming." Richard handed me a mug filled with excellent coffee, motioned me over to a comfortable wing chair in front of his desk, and then sat down and asked me what had happened and how he could help.

I didn't know quite where to begin. I had attended many initial conferences before, but always as the attorney, never as the client. It was one thing to sit calmly behind an imposing cherrywood desk radiating competence and professional concern while the client fumbled for words, and quite another to be the fumbler whose life had abruptly fallen apart. After a couple of false starts, I stopped talking and just shoved the manila envelope across the desk and into Richard's hands.

Richard pulled out both documents and read them silently, as I sipped my coffee and watched. He was careful to control his facial expressions, but his eyebrows quirked a couple of times, and once I thought I heard him chuckle. When he finally finished reading and looked up, it was clearly all he could do to keep from laughing out loud.

"You're quite the conspirator," he said, his face twitching with the effort it took to suppress a grin. "Did you bury Jimmy Hoffa, too? Are you the shooter on the knoll who took out President Kennedy? Or did you just engineer the fall of the Soviet Union?" And then he did start laughing, shaking his head as though the two documents he held were the funniest things he had ever seen.

My first reaction was to be absolutely furious. I was being sued for millions, my career was over, I would be bankrupted for life, and he was *laughing?* I wanted to reach across his desk and slap him. But then, suddenly, I started giggling myself, and soon the two of us were laughing together.

When we finally stopped, I sighed weakly. "You've got one heck of a bedside manner, Richard," I said. "My father was always so serious. How could he stand you?"

"He couldn't," Richard replied, still panting with laughter. "I think that's why he hired me. He figured I was the only lawyer he'd ever met who might actually be able to handle you." That started him off again, and soon we were both laughing even harder than before.

That laughter washed away weeks of tension for me. It erased the shame I felt over Christopher Cunningham, my fear of the lawsuit, and my uncertainty about what the future might bring. It wasn't that my problems had disappeared. But after laughing with Richard, they seemed more manageable.

My sides aching, I finally put up one hand in a gesture of surrender. "OK, I get it. Maybe these complaints aren't as serious as I thought. But all kidding aside, Richard: what am I going to do? They're a lot of nonsense, but I still have to respond to them."

Richard grinned. "Of course we have to respond to them, but that doesn't mean we have to act as though *we* believe them. These accusations aren't true, are they? You didn't really steal a bunch of confidential documents from a vulnerable old man and sell them to the enemy, did you? If you did, I would hope you at least would have gotten enough money that you wouldn't need legal help from a country hack like me. Anybody that evil should be able to afford the best that money can buy."

It was my turn to grin. "You know, I'm starting to think that you might actually *be* the best that money can buy. I certainly like your approach better than the one I was taught in Manhattan. But no, I didn't steal Dr. Grandy's documents so his sellers could fleece him. In fact, I got myself in pretty serious trouble by trying to derail the deal. Losing those files was just a stupid mistake. I got distracted and left my briefcase in the cab when I caught the train up here." And then I told him the whole story, from the anonymous note on my desk right up to the point when the grubby process server shoved the envelope into my hands.

Richard thought for a moment, his elbows on the desk and his fingers steepled in front of him. I noticed that he was awfully good-looking, but then forced myself to focus on my legal troubles instead. Flirtation would have to wait.

"Do you have any idea who left that note on your desk?" Richard finally asked.

"Oh, for pity's sake, what is it about that note?" I asked, though there was no real heat behind the question. "My friend Jack was totally obsessed with it too. He thought it was downright mystical. But I don't know anything about it. The note just appeared on my desk out of nowhere, and then reappeared when I got home that night. I probably jammed it into my purse without thinking when I left the office and then dropped it when I walked into the apartment that evening. Why does everybody seem to think that note is so important?"

Richard smiled mysteriously. "Ah. *That*, Kate, is the three-million-dollar question! Don't worry, though, I don't ascribe to your friend's belief that there was anything supernatural about the note. I'm more inclined to think someone put it on your desk to rattle you. They may even have snuck another copy into your apartment somehow, so you would think it was the same note magically reappearing under your feet. Would it be difficult to convince, or even bribe, your superintendent to get access to your apartment? Do you have any enemies at work who might do something like that?"

"At least two, and their names are on the complaints," I replied, referring to Blackwell and Davenport. "But to tell you the truth, there were probably at least half a dozen others, too. I wasn't the best coworker in the world. My competitive instinct got away from me sometimes."

Richard chuckled. "Why does that not surprise me? Whatever Christopher Cunningham might have believed, you're more his daughter than he thought. So, there were people in your law firm who had access to your desk and who might have disliked you enough to play a nasty prank on you?"

I nodded.

"And might any of those people have thought that if they worried you enough, you'd go rushing out of the office and leave the files behind?"

After thinking for a moment, I nodded again. "You know, it's possible," I told him. "I almost did exactly that, in fact. If I hadn't been so angry about what Blackwell was doing to Dr. Grandy, I probably would have left the files on my desk when I went home. I took them only to see whether there was anything in them that might help me persuade Dr. Grandy to walk away from the deal. He's such a sweet old guy; he didn't deserve to be cheated out of any more money.

"Then again, maybe he isn't such a sweetheart," I corrected myself. "He is suing me, after all."

"True, but that doesn't mean he isn't a sweetheart. We don't know what Blackwell has told him about you," Richard reminded me. "Maybe there was something in those files that Blackwell didn't want you or your friend Dr. Grandy to see. Blackwell knew your father was dying. Maybe he slipped that note onto your desk so you'd take off and leave the files where he could get at them and remove anything incriminating."

"And now they're back in his miserable clutches," I groaned, frowning. "If that cabbie had just kept my briefcase, Blackwell would never have known I'd lost the files, and I'd still have my job."

Richard leaned forward across his desk and looked me in the eye, suddenly all business. "Kate," he asked, "do you still even *want* that job?"

His question startled me. "Well... I guess... No, probably not," I slowly replied. "Not really. I guess I just kind of got used to it, you know? The money was great, and it certainly gave me something to occupy every waking minute of my life. But now that it's gone, I'm starting to realize how unhealthy that job was for me. I was turning into a pretty awful person."

Richard relaxed and smiled. "Great. I can do a better job with this case knowing that you're willing to walk away from the firm for good. Is there anyone there who might be willing to help us with this? Or were you such a dragon lady that even the janitor despises you?"

"You know, there is, or at least there was," I answered. "Ruth Martingale from HR actually encouraged me to sue Blackwell for discrimination when I came in for my exit interview. She said he had ruined the careers of a lot of young female attorneys and deserved to be brought down. I don't know whether she'd help us now that Dr. Grandy is suing me, though. Ruth may not like Blackwell, but she's incredibly loyal to the clients. If Ruth thought I'd hurt Dr. Grandy, she'd be first in line to help Blackwell beat me up."

"She still could be useful," Richard said. "Maybe she wouldn't volunteer to help you, but would she lie under oath to protect the firm?"

"Not in a million years," I replied with perfect certainty. "Ruth prides herself on her ironclad integrity even more than her loyalty. If you could get her on the stand, she'd tell the whole truth and damn the consequences for anybody who didn't like what she said."

"Do you know how to get in touch with her?"

I thought for a moment. "We shouldn't call Ruth at the office, but I still have a copy of the law firm's directory at my apartment. I used to refer to it once in a while when I had to get hold of the other lawyers after hours. Her home phone number should be in it. There might be a personal e-mail address, too."

Richard shook his head. "Even if there is, we shouldn't use e-mail unless there's no other choice. She'll probably be a lot more willing to talk off the record than to put something in print. Grab the directory on your next trip to the city, OK? We can look through it and see if there's anybody else who might be helpful."

"I'm headed down there this afternoon," I replied. "Among other things, I have to figure out how to get my stuff out of my apartment. There's no way I can afford to buy it at this point, so it looks as if Angel Falls is going to be stuck with me, at least for a while. I'll bring the directory back with me."

I paused for a moment, then pressed on. "Richard, speaking of not being able to afford things, how much will you charge to represent me? I've got only a little money left, and I've given away a lot of things in the house that I could have sold to pay for my defense. Can we agree on installment payments or something?"

Richard smiled. "Do you have a dollar on you?" he asked.

"Of course."

"Give it to me."

"But Richard—"

"No buts, Kate," he interrupted. "Just give me the dollar."

Richard's request for me to give him a dollar as his retainer was a cliché that novelists and screenwriters have used a thousand times. Like many clichés, though, it had a grain of truth behind it. I reached into my bag, fished out my wallet, and removed a one-dollar bill. As I handed it to Richard, I noticed a little red smudge on its top left corner.

"There," Richard said, smiling, as he tucked the dollar into his desk drawer. "You have asked me to represent you, I have agreed, and you've paid me. You're officially my client, and I'm officially your lawyer. It's all nice and legal.

"Honestly, Kate," he continued, "I'm sorry all this has happened, but I'm glad to be able to help you out. Maybe now I can stop kicking myself for giving you that letter at the funeral. It's the first time in my entire career that I've done something so shameful, and it has been haunting me." He shook his head with a rueful grimace.

"You don't need to be ashamed of anything. I'm just grateful for your help." I glanced down at my watch and realized that we had been talking for over two hours. "Listen, Richard, I really need to go or I'm going to miss my train to the city. I'll bring the firm directory back with me. Do you need anything else?"

"Not right now," he replied. "I'm going to reread these complaints and start figuring out our strategy. You just get your business in town straightened out and get back here." He stood up and walked me to the door. "And Kate," he added, "don't let this worry you too much. It's scary, I know, but everything's going to be all right."

I shook my head, forcing a smile. "Hope you're right, counsel. Remember, though, I've said the same thing myself to a lot of clients with tough cases. You're talking to somebody who knows just how bad lawsuits can get."

"Yes, but have you ever lost one?" he asked.

"Now that you mention it, no."

"Why does that not surprise me, either?" Richard chuckled. "This case won't be your first loss, Kate. That's where faith comes in. See you when you get back." He ushered me out the door, where Andrew was waiting patiently in the car.

As we drove to the train station, I reflected on Richard's final words to me. Faith was all well and good, I decided, but it was no substitute for a solid strategy and hard work. Luckily, having Richard as my lawyer might just give me both.

Archangel Metatron speaks:

Please understand that I am not by any means the unbending tyrant that I am sometimes represented to be. I enjoy a good joke as well as the next Heavenly being. It is simply that a certain level of decorum is essential to the smooth functioning of the Universe. Rules must be followed or chaos will ensue. The Adversary would just love that, would he not?

So, when Archangel Gabriel insisted on directly interfering in the choices of the young woman he had selected to mentor, I really had no alternative but to impose a penalty for his infraction. We take free will very seriously in Heaven. Angels are not permitted to force our preferences on human souls, no matter how dearly we would love to do so or how self-destructive those souls might be. Gentle guidance is one thing, coercion quite another.

Gabriel had what he perceived to be a very good argument for bending the rules in this instance, as he always does. What astonished me, however, was his ready agreement to polish as many halos as I put in front of him to make amends for his infraction. He must have been quite devoted to the young lady in question to willingly perform such a menial task without complaint. Such devotion is worthy of admiration, as it mirrors our Creator's devotion to each and every one of us.

And so, when his fellow archangels turned Gabriel's punishment into a party, I was disinclined to stop them. I maintained a disapproving mien, of course—Heaven's high standards must be maintained—but in my heart

I was glad to see it. Harmony among the archangels is a truly beautiful thing.

Perhaps Gabriel's project was more deserving of my attention than I had previously thought.

CHAPTER TWENTY

My train trip to Manhattan was uneventful. I watched out the window as the scenery flew by, reflecting on the difference a few weeks had made. When I first returned to Angel Falls, my career and future had seemed secure. Now, my sense of security was gone. Oddly enough, though, I felt much calmer than I had during my mad rush upstate to see Christopher Cunningham before he passed away. The weeks of living in Angel Falls had granted me unexpected peace of mind, despite the many challenges I faced.

I found myself thinking about my erstwhile father and, in particular, about Bella's observation that he, like me, might have been changed for the worse by his legal career. It seemed unlikely—though, in fairness, I had never really known the man. By the time I had grown old enough to have some hope of understanding him, the emotional distance between us had grown too wide to cross. I thought of him mostly from a child's perspective, and children never give their parents much license to be human.

Christopher Cunningham may have been nothing more than the demanding taskmaster of my memories, the man who drove me to succeed with such intensity that he ultimately drove me away. The people who spoke at his funeral seemed to think there was more to him than that. But he was gone, and I would never know for sure. For the first time, I genuinely regretted that the opportunity to understand Christopher Cunningham had passed me by forever.

It was late afternoon by the time my train pulled into Penn Station. Manhattan remained warmer than Angel Falls, and it was balmy enough for me to walk the forty-some blocks uptown to my apartment without a coat. I slung my bag over my shoulder and started walking, gawking like a tourist as I went. I watched a busker here, a street vendor there, a gaggle of foreign students talking animatedly over one another in the crush of Times Square, and smiled at their energy and amazement. It was a sad smile, though. The noise and bustle of Manhattan charmed me as ever, but the city I loved no longer felt like home.

North of Times Square I stopped on a street corner, waiting for the light to change. A street vendor was selling roasted chestnuts from a cart nearby, a heavenly aroma rising around him. He was tall and lanky, with uplifted eyebrows and a shock of brown hair that tumbled over his high forehead. His hands and face were weathered, and his red hoodie was faded under his old denim jacket, but his eyes were brilliant green as they looked into mine and he smiled broadly. "Be brave," the chestnut seller said to me cheerfully. "No one is ever alone." Then he turned back to stirring his wares, the light changed, and the pedestrians around me pushed me across the street before I could reply. When I turned back to look for him, the vendor was gone, leaving only a whiff of roasted chestnuts that quickly dissipated in the autumn air.

New York City can be a very unsettling place.

Shaking my head, I dismissed the strange encounter from my mind and walked on. Even with luggage hoisted on my shoulder, it took me a less than an hour to get from Penn Station to my apartment building. I was pleased not to be out of breath when I arrived. All the housecleaning in Angel Falls had given me a better daily workout than I had realized. I would never have been able to walk uptown so quickly when my days were spent behind a desk.

Feeling a bit more cheerful, I took the elevator up to my floor and let myself into my apartment. Apparently, the superintendent had been bringing in my mail while I was away. A small mountain of paper was piled on my kitchen table, burying the tabletop and spilling onto the floor. The bills had multiplied, as had the ads and charitable appeals.

The most pressing correspondence, though, was a series of increasingly forceful notices about the condo conversion. The first letters were cheery invitations to buy the apartment, but the subsequent ones were less enticing and more insistent. By the time I opened and read the last notice, it had been made very clear that my failure to respond was not going over well. There were some notes from fellow tenants, too, trying to rally a response to try to bring the prices down or fight eviction. But I recognized the name of the cutthroat law firm sending the notices and knew that it would be a nasty battle—one I just did not have the heart or the money to fight.

So much for any hope I had been harboring of keeping my pied-à-terre in Manhattan.

The letters upset me less than I would have expected. Maybe there had just been so many losses that one more didn't matter very much. But, looking back, I suspect that part of me was already done with my old life. Besides, I was unemployed—why fight for an apartment I couldn't afford to keep? Like it or not, the time had come for me to let go and move on. I may as well try to accept it.

Looking around the apartment, I was forcibly struck by how little there was that I wanted to take with me. The fashionable, modern sofa looked unwelcoming, the kitchen table ridiculously small. The bedroom furniture seemed characterless compared with the antiques I had sold in Angel Falls. I would reclaim my jewelry and a few clothes, but the rest could go out on the curb as far as I was concerned.

Then I noticed my empty briefcase, sitting next to the bedroom door where I had left it on my last visit to Manhattan. I hadn't thought of it in weeks, and somehow it had lost its power to intimidate. It was just a big, black leather bag. It might have belonged to anyone, but it certainly didn't seem to belong to me. Not anymore.

The intercom buzzed Jack's customary "shave and a haircut" pattern. I let him in and listened as the elevator rattled its way up to the tenth floor. A few minutes later, he knocked twice on the apartment door.

"Katie? Is that you?" Jack's eyes widened as I let him in. He was dressed in his customary jeans and a fisherman's sweater. I had forgotten how handsome he was.

"Hey, Jack." I smiled and went to hug him.

"Gosh, for a minute I didn't even recognize you," he said, hugging me back. He pushed me to arm's length without letting go of my shoulders. "You look fantastic, Katie! You've grown your hair out, and you're actually wearing normal clothes. You haven't looked this good since college. Life upstate must really agree with you."

I looked down a little sheepishly at the embroidered blue peasant dress and low-heeled pewter pumps that Bella had picked out for me. Not exactly power-lawyer garb. "Thanks, Jack. It does, I guess. It's certainly been a wild ride, though, and it doesn't look like I'm going to be coming back here anytime soon."

I realized, all of a sudden, that I was famished. "Come on, let's go get some dinner, and I'll fill you in."

We ended up at a Thai place a few doors down the street. Over pad thai, spring rolls, and tea, I filled Jack in on what had happened since we had last seen each other, trying not to dwell too much on my legal troubles. Fortunately, Jack was mostly curious about my discoveries in the house and intrigued by every aspect of Angel Abbey. Typical Jack, he quickly honed in on my lingering discomfort with "the Lady of Angel Abbey." Clearly, he knew me too well.

Jack peppered me with questions about Lucina. How old was she? Where did she come from? And what was it about her that I disliked, anyway?

"It's hard to say," I replied to his last query. I felt uncomfortable, for some reason, gossiping about Lucina behind her back, even if it was with an old friend like Jack. "I can't claim that she's ever done anything *wrong*," I conceded. "Quite the contrary, in fact. She has always been gracious with me, and she goes out of her way to make sure that everyone feels welcome at the Abbey. It's all the reverence that gets on my nerves, I think. Lucina's fine. There's nothing wrong with her, except maybe that thing she does where she stops in the middle of a sentence and looks away, as if someone else is talking to her. That's a little creepy."

"Maybe she's having private conversations with the angels," Jack said, waving his fingers to imitate flapping wings.

I smacked him lightly on the wrist with my fork. "Very funny, Jack. You may be onto something, though. Maybe she wants people to *think* she's talking to angels. It'd be just like her. I've never heard anybody say that, though."

"So she's not a very good actress," Jack retorted. "Seriously, though, Katie, why don't you like her? It's not like you to let some New Age flake get under your skin."

I took a big swallow of jasmine tea. "You know, that's a really good question, and I haven't been able to come up with an answer," I told him. "What bugs me, I guess, is that people act like she's some kind of goddess or something. Even Bella and Andrew get all wide-eyed and worshipful when they talk about her. It's always '*the Lady* this' and '*the Lady* that,' never just 'Lucina.' It's all a bit too much for me."

Jack's blue eyes twinkled. "No chance you could be a little jealous of her, of course."

"Of course not!" I retorted, even as I realized that he might be right. "OK, maybe you have a point," I admitted. "Lucina always seems so sure of herself, it *is* a little enviable. She never looks unhappy or frazzled, no matter what happens at the Abbey. Even those weird pauses she takes—they freak me out, but she acts as though they're totally normal. It's like she's so supremely confident that you're dying to hear whatever she has to say, and that you'll just stand there until she comes back around to you and *then* thank her for wasting your time. She never seems to doubt herself even a little, you know?"

"And you do? Doubt yourself, I mean." Jack arched a skeptical eyebrow.

"You might be surprised." I smiled ruefully. "A lot of my 'confidence' is just smoke and mirrors, Jack. It's me putting on a good show for the clients or trying to bluff opposing counsel. Nobody realizes how scared I am a lot of the time."

"Actually, you're the one who might be surprised, Katie," Jack retorted. "You're more transparent than you think, at least to me. I'm an actor, remember? It takes one to know one, kiddo, and I've always known you were putting on one hell of a show for the firm. We've been friends long enough for me to remember what you were like before you started playing the evil witch on wheels to please the partners. Frankly, I always thought your performance was a little over the top. Nobody is as big a dragon lady as you pretended to be."

"Funny you should say that," I replied. "Richard asked me just this morning how big a dragon lady I'd been at work."

"And who is this 'Richard'?" Jack asked.

"He's my lawyer," I answered. "Well, he's actually my father's lawyer, or he would be if my father had really been my father like I thought. Sorry, that was confusing. Richard's the guy who gave me that horrible letter at the funeral."

"And you're trusting him to handle the lawsuit for you?" Jack asked. "After he messed with you like that? That doesn't sound like the Katie Cunningham I know."

"It wasn't his fault, Jack," I explained. "My father—well, my ex-father—made him do it. Richard's a great guy. He does a lot of work with kids at the Abbey, and they love him. Besides, he's got to be a terrific lawyer for the almighty Christopher J. Cunningham to trust him with his personal legal work. He was confident that Richard could write him a will I couldn't break. There aren't many attorneys he would have respected that much."

"You sound pretty high on him," Jack said. "Should I be jealous?" He winked.

I slapped him playfully on the shoulder. "Jealous of what? He and I are just friends, and nowhere near as good friends as you and me. Richard's helping me through a tough time, that's all. He says this is his way of paying me back for that stunt with the letter." Talking about Richard with Jack felt uncomfortable, too. "But enough of my drama. I'm sick of talking about it, and you must be as well. What's going on with you, Jack? Give me the latest in the life of my favorite soon-to-be Broadway star."

As it turned out, my question was right on the money. With a winning smile, Jack revealed that he had been cast as the romantic lead in a new play just that afternoon. The show was going to open in three months in a theater that wasn't quite on Broadway, but "close enough to smell the greasepaint," as Jack put it. It was a major break for him, and I was glad to have a reason to celebrate his success.

Jack insisted on picking up the dinner check. It was fair payback, he said, for all those times I had treated when he was a starving actor and I was a rich lawyer. We walked back to my apartment, stopping to pick up an oversize bottle of cold champagne from a liquor store on the way. Jack wanted to toast not only his new show but also my "liberation" from the law firm. "They say a door never closes without a window opening," he intoned with mock solemnity. "It's time to celebrate the windows that are opening in your life, Katie." He grinned impishly, and I couldn't resist grinning back.

When we got back to my apartment, Jack popped the cork while I hunted up some glasses. I had never troubled to buy champagne flutes. The kitchen cabinets were too small for them, I claimed, but Jack shook his head, pretending deepest sorrow. "There was no room in your heart for merriment, Katie," he said, his eyes dancing with amusement despite his somber tone. "Maybe now that you've been freed from indentured servitude on Wall Street you'll remember how to have a good time."

I snorted and pulled a couple of generic wineglasses out of the cupboard. Jack filled them to the brim. I reached over to turn on a lamp, but Jack turned it back off. Even though the sun had gone down hours before, the ambient city light was glowing in the tall windows; the accompanying comforting hum of traffic and passersby rose up from the streets below. New York prides itself on being the city that never sleeps, and New Yorkers quickly become accustomed to living with the background music of its perpetual bustle.

We started out sitting on the sofa, but quickly agreed that it was far too hard and sharply vertical to be comfortable. We slid down onto the rug, leaning back against the sofa, talking and sipping our champagne. Jack put an arm around my shoulders, and I let my head rest against him as we chatted. It felt almost as though we were back in college, with nothing more serious than an upcoming exam or a fleeting romantic interest to worry about. I relaxed into the familiar comfort of being with an old friend and drank deeply, letting the champagne relax me even more.

"So, Katie," Jack murmured, "as tough as it's been, you've been given a new lease on life. What are you going to do with it? Any dreams you've put on the back burner? Anywhere you've always wanted to go, but never had time? Anything you always wanted to do but couldn't because you were forever slaving away at work?" He refreshed my nearly empty glass, filling it to the brim again.

I took a big swallow and shook my head. The champagne had ignited a warm glow in my stomach, and everything in the dimly lit room was surrounded by a golden halo. "I don't know," I admitted, a little sheepishly. "Succeeding as a lawyer has been my only goal forever. Now that it's gone, I really have no idea what to do next."

"Funny," he said. "Now that you mention it, I have an idea. Something I've wanted to do for a long time, in fact." Jack's arm tightened around my shoulders as he turned, pulled me close, and kissed me.

Archangel Chamuel speaks:

Your novelist F. Scott Fitzgerald once wrote, "There are all kinds of love in the world, but never the same love twice." None of us in Heaven can applaud the way Fitzgerald managed his own love life. Still, he had a point.

There are all kinds of love in the world, each love as unique and magnificent as the souls who experience it. Many of those loves, however, are also complex, multilayered, and fragile. It is astonishing to my angels and me how quickly human love can be shattered by a simple misstep.

Take Kate and Jack, for instance. They had been friends for many years. In college, they had spent a lot of time together—"hung out," I think you would say—sharing their dreams, celebrating each other's triumphs, and consoling each other over disappointing grades and briefly broken hearts. If asked, each would freely admit to loving the other "as a friend," meaning that they shared a deep platonic love. Yes, there was attraction between them, but at the time neither of them would have dreamed of risking their cherished friendship for the sake of a short-term romance.

After college, Jack and Kate's relationship changed as they did, so slowly and subtly that neither of them noticed. They continued to relate to each other as their younger selves, not recognizing that their individual growth was bound to change the nature of their love for each other. Neither of them had ever really given much thought to their relationship. It was not until they had been apart for a significant time, each on a separate journey, that they could come back together and reconnect as the adults they had become.

Jack, ever impulsive and romantic, felt a spark upon seeing Kate again and acted on it. A handsome, charismatic man, he was accustomed to easy conquests. Not only that, he was elated by his success earlier in the day and just the tiniest bit drunk. His affection for Kate felt far less platonic than it ever had before. From Jack's perspective, why not make a leap of faith and see where it might take them?

As for Kate, well, she was always more complicated than Jack, more prone to overanalyze and to shy away from her feelings (if she could even recognize them). She had also suffered a series of recent, difficult losses. That left her vulnerable and too self-protective to risk losing one of her very few close friends. And, like him, she was more than a little drunk.

Jack and Kate loved one another—but could that love survive Jack's bold jump from the platonic to the romantic? We in Heaven could only wait and see.

CHAPTER TWENTY-ONE

Over the years, I had fantasized many times about what it might be like to kiss Jack, or even to let things go a lot farther than that. After all, he was cute, funny, smart, and a genuinely nice guy. He was also my oldest friend, apart from Honoré (who probably did not entirely count, being a cat). I loved Jack dearly.

For that reason, though, I had always firmly squelched any thought of romance between us. If I wanted a handsome playboy for some short-term fun, New York was crammed with options. But a kind, loving friend who had known me well and had had my back for over a decade? I had only one, and Jack was it. His friendship was so precious to me that the risk of losing it never seemed worth the potential rewards of a roll in the hay. Jack wasn't the kind of guy who stayed in any romance for long. Sleep with him once, and the friendship would soon vanish. Or so I had convinced myself, anyway.

Believing that friendship and desire don't mix was one thing. Explaining that belief to a good-looking, slightly intoxicated guy was another. The smart thing to do would have been to pull away gently, give Jack a big, sisterly hug, and tactfully tell him that I loved him far too much as a friend to gamble our cherished relationship on a casual fling. It would have been smart to flatter his ego, make a joke or two about having had too much wine, then plead exhaustion, send him on his way, and go off to bed alone. It would have been even smarter to invite him back for breakfast the next morning, and maybe suggest that he come upstate for a visit in a week or two if his rehearsal schedule allowed.

Whoever said I was smart?

Jack turned out to be a great kisser, even better than I had imagined. It would have been so easy to dissolve into the pleasures of the moment and let the kiss take its natural course. In just a few seconds, however, I went from shock at what was happening through a brief moment of enjoyment to absolute, mindless panic, and reacted before I could stop myself.

Instead of pulling back gently, I shoved Jack away from me and, without thinking, wiped my mouth on the back of my hand like a little girl rubbing away lollipop stains. "Jack, *what do you think you're doing?*" I demanded.

For someone who is supposed to be intelligent, I can be an absolute moron sometimes.

Jack banged the back of his head on the hard metal arm of the sofa, which must have hurt. From the confused expression on his face, however, my clumsy rejection of his advances had hurt him a whole lot more. "Jeez, Katie, what's the matter with you?" he snapped. "It was only a kiss, for crying out loud! I just thought—"

"No, you *didn't*!" I interrupted, shrieking like a schoolgirl whose pigtails had just been dipped in indelible ink. "Jack, we never, I mean, I never, I mean…" The champagne was making me stammer. "What *ever* made you think for even a second that I would ever in a million *years*—"

"Obviously, I *didn't* think," Jack snarled, suddenly as angry as I was. "If I'd given it any thought at all, I would have recognized that you are never, *ever* going to change! You are *never* going to stop being the goody-two-shoes little girl, always trying to win Daddy's favor! You are never going to grow up, and you're going to spend the rest of your life pushing away everyone who tries to get close to you! You want to be alone with your damned cat for the next fifty years, lady? Well, go ahead. Be my guest! It's perfectly fine with me.

"Don't get up." Jack sprang to his feet and stalked to the apartment door. "I'm leaving." He yanked the door open, then turned back, the picture of Rhett Butler rejecting Scarlett O'Hara, to deliver his exit line. "And tell your poor sap of a lawyer that I wish him good luck dealing with you. He's gonna need every last bit of it he can get." He sailed out the door, slamming it behind him so hard that my half-finished glass of champagne fell over, spilling onto the floor.

Jack's footsteps echoed as he stomped down the hallway. There was a pause, then a bell chimed gently as the elevator doors slid open. They closed with a soft clash, and Jack was gone.

Stunned, I picked up the empty glass and sat on the rug for a long time, rolling the stem in my fingers. It occurred to me that I probably should be crying, but the tears wouldn't come. Taxis honked, an ambulance screamed past, and the voices of pedestrians on the sidewalks below rose and fell in unintelligible, murmuring waves. Life in New York would go on just as always, heedless of the fact that my best friend had just slammed out of my apartment and perhaps my life forever.

Out of nowhere, a chuckle rose in my throat. It forced itself past my teeth and suddenly I found myself laughing so hard I could barely breathe. Eventually I fell over onto one side, still cradling the wineglass, laughing until I was gasping for air. I looked around for someone to share the joke, but of course there was no one there. Clearly, I had grown entirely too accustomed to my one-sided conversations with Honoré.

"Damnation," I muttered, still chuckling to myself as I pushed the glass aside and slowly sat back up. I was a lot drunker than I had realized. "That, Katie m'dear, has to be the single dumbest thing your ever did in your entire life."

Head spinning, I hauled myself up off the floor. I tossed the empty champagne bottle in the trash, put the glasses in the sink, and staggered off to bed. My last coherent thought before sleep overtook me was that it had been a lot more fun to share a laugh with Richard in his office that morning than it had been to laugh in the dark by myself after Jack stormed out that night.

When I woke late the next morning with a dry mouth and a champagne headache, the sun was already streaming through the windows. The traffic and pedestrians were both louder in daylight. A construction worker was running a jackhammer at full tilt somewhere nearby, and police sirens blared from a few blocks away. New York was wide-awake and well into its day. Time for me to get on with mine, hung over or not.

I tried calling Jack to apologize, but his phone was switched off and, according to the metallic female voice that picked up, his "mailbox was full." Sighing, I hung up, choked down some aspirin, showered, and started packing up to leave. My jewelry and the clothes I wanted to take filled my overnight bag to bursting, but everything just fit, and with sufficient tugging, the zipper eventually closed.

I couldn't bring myself to leave a mess behind. It took only a few minutes to wash up the wineglasses and put them away. I crammed Honoré's food and water dishes into the side pocket of my bag, which strained to the breaking point but held. He had others back in Angel Falls, but the dishes were his. It would have felt wrong to leave them behind.

After that, it was an easy task to dump nearly all of the opened mail into the kitchen trashcan. Burying the empty champagne bottle under their layers of multicolored paper filled me with relief. Somehow, the bottle didn't look so funny in the bright morning glare.

Glowering at my few pieces of uninviting furniture, I decided it was time to make a clean break with Manhattan. I fished a Goodwill flyer out of the trash, dialed the number, and persuaded the bored young man at the other end of the line to schedule a couple of guys to come over to pick up everything the following day. The super would let them in, I told him.

Setting the phone down, I remembered to look for my old law firm directory. Sure enough, it was in the kitchen under a stack of takeout menus, a thin, comb-bound binder with a clear plastic cover, printed out on plain white paper. Ruth Martingale's home address and unlisted home number were prominently recorded. That was a relief.

My overnight bag was too full to hold the directory, and it would not fit inside my purse. Losing that directory could cost me the chance to seek Ruth's help, something I was not willing to risk. Then I noticed my briefcase, standing empty by the bedroom door and ready to safeguard the contact information for the one person at the law firm who might be willing to help me. It seemed fitting, somehow. I dropped the directory into the briefcase and latched it closed.

I tried one more time to reach Jack, but he didn't pick up, and his voicemail remained stubbornly full. There was no more reason to linger. I dialed the super, and left a message telling him that I was leaving. The keys would be on the kitchen table, I said. The movers from Goodwill would be arriving the next day and had my full permission to take everything they could lay their hands on. They didn't even need to mail me a tax receipt. I scribbled a short note confirming that I was leaving the apartment and would not be coming back, and included the address and phone number of my house in Angel Falls in case they needed to contact me. There was a chance that the building management would want more official confirmation of my decision to leave, but I decided to make them come get it from me if they did. Jack's comment about me being a goody-two-shoes little girl had stung. I pulled the keys to my apartment door and the mailbox off my key ring and placed them on top of the note.

I grabbed my purse, overnight bag, and briefcase. For the first time ever, the briefcase felt light as a feather. Looking down, I noticed the handwritten parchment note that had sent me tearing off to Angel Falls what seemed like a lifetime ago lying on the floor. Somehow, it had gotten under my briefcase. Setting down my luggage, I leaned over and picked it up.

"*Your father is dying,*" the note read. "*Come home at once.*" Thanks to Richard's prompting, I wondered who had written it and why. For that matter, how had it gotten under my briefcase? If asked, I would have sworn that I had thrown it out on my last trip into the city. Somehow, though, the note had escaped the trash again. I must have set the briefcase down on it myself sometime after my meeting with Ruth Martingale.

For the first time, I looked at the note carefully. It was on expensive, cream-colored paper that seemed to glow in the morning light. The paper was familiar, though I couldn't quite place it. The handwriting, a graceful black cursive, also looked puzzlingly like something I had seen before.

Someone I knew had written the note, but I could not imagine who it might be. Was it someone at the firm, perhaps? It seemed unlikely. Mark Davenport was too cloddish to create something so elegant, and Roy Blackwell's handwriting was nothing like this. Perhaps they had had one of the female associates write it. That would be something for Richard to consider.

Whatever else it might be, the note was potential evidence. Richard would want to see it. I opened the briefcase and dropped the note inside, right next to the firm directory. Then I closed the briefcase again, carefully latching both locks. I slung my purse over my shoulder and picked up my briefcase and overnight bag, one in each hand.

I looked around the apartment one last time, trying to figure out how the eager, ambitious young woman who had rented it years before had changed so much. Tears stung my eyes, but I held them back. Nostalgia for that young woman was a luxury I could not afford. With a sad smile, I stepped out of the apartment and closed the door, locking the keys inside.

Archangel Barachiel speaks:

As the archangel whose duties include distributing the Creator's blessings, I am one of the happiest beings in Heaven. There are so many divine things to do! So much joy to spread, so many miracles to foster, so much delight to distribute! My angels and I spend every day and night circling the globe, looking for people who are ready to receive our Master's blessings and delivering them in style. What a joy our service is, and how much we love to bless you!

It had been years since I had paid much attention to Kate. It was not that we did not love her, you understand. Heavens, no! She had once been a beautiful, sensitive child, with a clever mind that my angels and I loved to tickle with puzzles and jokes. But she had grown so self-conscious and serious over the years! We kept trying to bless her, but she managed to brush off almost every smile we sent her way.

Nothing satisfied Kate for long. In school, a good grade on a test only made her worry more about the next one. Victory in court left her triumphant but concerned about losing should her opponent file an appeal. She drove most of her potential friends away, and even a pleasant evening with Jack rarely lifted her spirits for long. Eventually, we just decided to wait and see if she would ever come around.

We cannot force people to enjoy life, you know.

Luckily, Gabriel caught up with me just as I was heading out to scatter laughter all over Broadway. He asked me to check in on Kate. I agreed and took an extra pocketful with me, just in case.

I had meant to get there sooner, but the theater audiences were having such a good time that it took me a little longer than expected to get to Kate's apartment. I was just in time to see Jack make his grand exit. What flair that boy had! He could have a tremendous career in the theater, provided he did not give up too soon. The Creator's blessings have to ripen before they are fit for enjoyment, and Jack was not quite ready to be a Broadway star.

Anyway, I was too late to help Kate and Jack work their argument through to the point of forgiveness and hugs. We would have to address that later. Still, laughter is always best when it is fresh, so I poured two hefty handfuls of giggles all over Kate. It dissolved her upset and defensiveness in seconds, letting her sleep for a bit and then finish her work in the apartment. Nothing like laughter to lighten the heart and speed a task along!

Gabriel said Kate needed to get back to Angel Abbey as quickly as possible. He can be just the teensiest bit impatient when he is working on an important project, so I was glad to be able to pitch in. It occurred to me later that it was probably time to start planning for the first snow of the season to fall on Manhattan. There is nothing like a few fresh snowflakes to get even the most hardened New Yorkers looking up and smiling.

What a wonderful job I have!

CHAPTER TWENTY-TWO

My trip back to Angel Falls passed in a haze. The aspirin I had swallowed took enough of the edge off of my headache that I was able to doze a little. By the time I got off the train, I was feeling considerably better.

I thought about calling Jack again, but decided it might be a good idea to give him time to cool off. Dear friend though he was, Jack had an actor's powerful ego, and I had undoubtedly bruised it. For some reason, that thought nearly sent me into another hysterical fit of giggles. I suppressed them, but not without some effort. It was all very strange.

Andrew picked me up at the station and drove me home to a warm welcome from Bella and Honoré. I told the three of them about my success in retrieving the directory, but left out the parts about the note and Jack. For some reason, I was reluctant to discuss the note with them. My reasons for omitting a blow-by-blow description of my disastrous evening with Jack should be obvious. Just thinking about it was enough to make me wince.

Richard was not in his office when I called, so I left a message saying that I had located Ruth Martingale's contact information and asked him to get back to me. After that, there wasn't much to do but wait. Telling Andrew and Bella that the trip had left me tired, I excused myself and went up to my room to nap. No need to mention the last vestiges of my hangover.

Honoré followed me upstairs, jumped up on the bed, and looked at me expectantly. I stretched out next to him and tried to doze off. But now that I was back home, worries about my legal problems started swirling through my brain again. My body might be still, and my eyes closed, but my thoughts were racing in circles. Sleep was simply not an option.

The bed shifted a little, and something tickled my nose. Opening my eyes, I saw Honoré standing right above me, staring directly into my face.

"OK, OK," I grumbled, rumpling his ears. "You're right, this isn't working. Let's try something else."

Sitting up, I noticed my old sketchbook and pastels sitting on the corner of my desk. Honoré rolled over on his back, tail stretched out behind him, and swatted delicately at the air with one sable paw. Grinning, I reached over and grabbed the pad and pastels. "You asked for it," I told him. "Just don't come crying if you don't like how you look in pictures. We haven't done this in a while."

I opened the book to a blank page, selected a dark brown pastel, and started to sketch. My first several attempts were awful. It had been years since I had even touched a pencil, much less tried to draw anything. In one drawing Honoré's head was too small, in another too large; in a third, his legs were of visibly different lengths. Slowly, though, I began to get back into the rhythm of drawing, relaxing my fingers and letting the pastel skim lightly across the page.

Honoré was very cooperative, flowing from one pose to another with Zen-like grace. I soon remembered that when it comes to sketching cats, less is often more. That started me drawing less for detail than for impression. My seventh attempt, a minimalist outline of Honoré looking at me over his shoulder, was credible enough that I decided to finish it, coloring the eyes a brilliant blue. It was no Michelangelo, but it wasn't bad.

Just then, Bella called up the stairs. "Katie, Richard's on the phone. Do you want me to tell him you'll call him back?"

So much for my brief artistic reprieve. "No," I called back. "Ask him to hang on, please. I'll be right down." I set the sketchbook aside and hurried downstairs to take Richard's call.

Richard's voice on the phone was solid and reassuring, just what I wanted to hear. "Welcome back," he said. "You found Ruth Martingale's phone number?"

"Yes, and I found the note, too," I replied. "It's the weirdest thing. I could swear I've seen the paper and handwriting before, but I can't remember where. Do you want to see it?"

"Absolutely," Richard said. "Who knows? If we can figure out who wrote it, maybe it'll help us with your defense. Do you have time to come over now?"

"Sure—it's not like I can't get away from the office," I joked, trying to keep the bitterness out of my voice. "See you in a few."

Andrew offered to drive me to Richard's office. It might have been a little self-indulgent, but I gratefully accepted. I grabbed my briefcase and purse, threw on my coat and a pair of comfortable flats, and we headed over. Andrew, saying he had a few errands to take care of, promised to be back in an hour or so to pick me up.

When he answered the door, Richard was dressed in a casual plaid shirt and jeans. "Not exactly senior partner attire," I teased him.

He smiled back. "One of the few benefits of being a solo practitioner," he said. "I get to ignore the dress code whenever I want. Come on in."

Richard's office was as welcoming as I had remembered. After handing him my coat and the briefcase, I sank comfortably into one of the wing chairs. Richard set the briefcase on his desk, unlatched it, pulled out the directory, and sat down across from me.

"Ruth Martingale's contact information is in here, right?" he asked, opening the directory.

"Yep. It's right on the first page," I answered. "It was a hard and fast rule at the firm. We all had to know how to reach Ruth at any hour, day or night, in case there was an emergency. That way, she could storm the battlements and set everything to rights."

He smiled. "And to think I called *you* a dragon lady. She sounds pretty formidable."

"Oh, she definitely is," I agreed. "It still amazes me that she offered to help me. I always figured her for the quintessential company woman, loyal to the death."

"Maybe she got sick of watching Roy Blackwell trash the careers of young women, just like she said," Richard mused. "Then again, Kate, we can't ignore the possibility that she lied to you. Maybe everything she said was just to trick you into to saying something against your own best interests. It's good that we have her contact information, but we need to think carefully about whether and how to approach her. We don't want to give Blackwell any more advantage than he already has."

Richard set the directory aside and then reached into the briefcase again. He felt around inside with a puzzled look on his face, then stood up and peered in. "I thought you said you found the note."

"I did." My stomach, still a little queasy from the night before, began to roil.

"It's not in here, Kate," Richard replied. "Are you sure you didn't leave it in your apartment?"

"It's in there, Richard. It has to be!" I quickly stood up and looked in the briefcase myself. Richard was right—the note was nowhere to be seen. I checked the inside zippered compartment, but that was empty too. "It was in here, I swear! I put it inside myself and latched the briefcase. There's nowhere it could have gone!" My breath started coming in short bursts.

"Slow down, Kate. Maybe it just got stuck in the directory. Let's look," Richard said soothingly. He opened the directory again and started turning its pages, one by one. About two-thirds of the way through, he stopped and triumphantly pulled out the note. "See? False alarm. Nothing to worry about." He left the directory open on the desk.

My breathing started to settle. The thought of losing the note had upset me more than I would have expected. "Sorry. Guess I'm a little nervous."

"Perfectly understandable, after everything you've been through." Richard sat down again, holding the note in both hands, and carefully examined it. "There's not much here," he finally said. "Still, whoever wrote it had to know that it would elicit some kind of reaction from you. How many people at the firm knew about your father?"

"It's hard to say," I told him. "I didn't talk about it much, but I had to tell Blackwell that my father was terminally ill in case there was an emergency while I was working on the Grandy transaction. He was supposed to keep it confidential, but who knows how many people he told? The person who wrote that note could have been anyone, I guess."

"Interesting," Richard said thoughtfully. "As terse as it is, this note contains just enough information to be upsetting, to make you at least call home and maybe even leave town. Then there's the way it appeared on your desk like it had dropped out of the sky. Did you see anybody go into or leave your office that afternoon who wasn't supposed to be there?"

I shook my head. "No, but that doesn't prove a thing. I was in meetings at the other end of the office all day. They could have led the Macy's Thanksgiving Day parade through my office, and I wouldn't have noticed."

Richard chuckled and then placed the note in a folder marked "Kate Cunningham Matter." It was disconcerting to see my own name on a case file—that was something that happened to my clients, not to me. "Somehow, I don't think the Rockettes danced out of rehearsal at Radio City to plant this on your desk," he quipped. "If you do remember where you saw this paper or the handwriting before, let me know right away. It's probably nothing, but it looks to me as if somebody was trying to upset you. It might just have been petty malice, or it might have something to do with the case. We won't know unless we can figure out where the note came from." He reached over to close the directory, but I grabbed his wrist to stop him.

"Richard, wait a minute." I snatched up the firm directory, still opened to the page where the note had been, and pointed to a name halfway down. "Jeanine Powell! I'd forgotten all about her. She was three years behind me on the partnership track, but she left the firm very abruptly a couple of months before I got fired. No one ever explained why she left. Maybe Blackwell got to her, too, somehow."

Richard's eyes lit up. "Now, *that* could be useful. Were you friends? Could you call her?"

"You're kidding, right?" I asked. "Nobody stays friends with the junior lawyers after they make partner, Richard. Once they let you into the partnership, you're supposed to spend all of your time cultivating new clients and massaging the egos of senior partners like Blackwell. Junior partners who continue to hang out with the associates get labeled as juvenile and unfocused. You don't lose your partnership, but they don't let you near the plum assignments."

Richard looked at me and sighed. "If I ever start to wonder why I didn't go for the big firm partnership track, kick me, will you? Sorry, Kate, but that's about the sorriest excuse for snubbing somebody I've ever heard." Shaking his head, he stuck a Post-it note on the page next to Jeanine's name, closed the directory, and stuck it in my file. "We don't need to contact Jeanine immediately, but I'm going to hang onto this just in case. Maybe Blackwell soured her on the firm enough that she'd be willing to tell us what he did to her. If it turns out that we need her, though, we'd better hope she'll forgive you for treating her like a second-class citizen."

He wasn't wrong, but that was the first time Richard had criticized me, and it hurt. I almost snapped back at him to defend myself, but what was there to say? I *had* treated Jeanine like a second-class citizen, and she would have every reason to hang up on me if I called her. I bit my lower lip and said nothing.

Richard looked up at me, aware that he had been too blunt. "Look, Kate, I'm sorry—" he began, but I interrupted him.

"No need to be. You're absolutely right. I deserved that, just like I've deserved every other lousy thing that's happened to me since that damned note turned up on my desk." I stood up and headed for the coatrack.

"Richard, I hope you won't take this wrong, but that's about as much as I can handle for one day," I said. "You've got the court papers, the bar complaint, the note, and the directory. That's everything I've got at this point. Rotten human being or no, I'm worn out with all this. You've been nice enough to offer to help me, and I'm going to take you up on it. Please just take everything, do whatever seems best to you as my lawyer, and let me know if you need me to get anything else for you. Right now, I'm going home."

Richard looked alarmed. "Kate, I really didn't mean to upset you. Please, won't you at least wait until your ride shows up? It's gotten dark outside, and it'll probably be cold."

I shook my head. "If you want to do me a favor, Richard, when Andrew gets here please just tell him that I needed some time to think, so I decided to go for a walk. I'll be home in a little while." I pulled on my coat, buttoned it up, and slung my purse over my shoulder. "It'll be good to get some fresh air."

"Don't you want to take your briefcase?" he asked, clearly distressed.

I gave him a bitter little smile. "Richard, believe me, if I never saw that briefcase again, it would be too soon. Hang onto that note, though. It likes to wander. Talk to you later." I stepped out of his office and into the blue chill of the late-autumn twilight.

Richard had been right—it was cold out, and my coat wasn't a heavy one. Still, it felt good to walk, to breathe in fresh air and breathe out my fears. I strode along, letting the simple act of walking down the road from Richard's office calm my nerves. It wasn't long before I arrived at the town square. On impulse, I climbed a few of the library's wide granite steps and sat down, ignoring the chill of the stone beneath me.

The town square was as picturesque as ever. Its charm made little impact on me that evening, though, preoccupied as I was with my troubles. Through a series of bad breaks and worse choices I had lost my parents, my oldest friend, my apartment, my job, and quite possibly my professional future. Bella and Andrew had been incredibly kind, but sooner or later they would have to find another place. Then I would lose them, too. Honoré had been my devoted companion for years, but he wasn't going to live forever. I could sell the house and get by for a while, but I didn't know what I could do to support myself once that money ran out.

Worst, I had lost whatever pride I had once taken in my professional accomplishments, along with any sense of myself as a decent person. It was time to admit that I was totally worthless. I had heard of people hitting rock bottom. Now, I experienced it for myself.

Tears began to trickle slowly down my cheeks as I sat, silent, on the library steps. I was so immersed in misery that it took me a moment to register the quiet rustle of someone sitting down next to me, and yet another moment to turn and see who that someone might be.

The man seated on the step next to me was a stranger. He was very tall, and looked to be about thirty-five years old. His sleek, dark hair fell to his broad shoulders. It complemented his chiseled features, high, patrician forehead, and the gray eyes that he fixed on me with just the hint of a smile. He was dressed in jeans, hiking boots, and a dark red cable-knit sweater under an olive-green military jacket that he had left open, notwithstanding the deepening cold. Despite his informal attire, there was an air of solemnity about him. If someone had told me that he was a Renaissance scholar or a foreign duke in disguise, it would not have surprised me at all.

"Are you lost, miss?" he asked, in a rich, melodious voice that reminded me of a viola. He had a trace of an accent, nothing I could place. "It's getting cold and dark for you to be out here alone."

"I'm fine, thanks," I replied, brushing one last tear away. Strange, but the sudden appearance of this stranger in the dark felt comforting rather than frightening. "I guess I might be lost, though not in the way you meant. I've just been going through a tough time and needed to think things out, so I decided to take the long way home."

"Odd, how often people do that," the stranger said. "Take the long way home, I mean. Somehow, though, they always seem to get there, and just at the right time, no matter how long it takes. Perhaps if you went too quickly, you might not recognize your home when you arrived."

It was a strange thing to say, but somehow I felt as though I knew what he meant. "You might be right about that," I said ruefully. "I have an incredible gift for overlooking the things around me that are most important."

The man seemed to consider what I had said. "That might be because you have been looking too hard for the wrong things," he finally replied. "Or perhaps it is because you have been focusing too much on the things you think are wrong with you, instead of the things that are right. Nobody is perfect, Kate, but nobody is perfectly awful, either. You have virtues you have never explored, and friends who love you far more than you can even begin to imagine."

"Wait," I said, puzzled. "How do you know my name? Have we met?"

"Not that you would remember," the man said kindly, "but we have mutual friends. It was not hard to figure out who you were from all the wonderful things they say about you."

I shook my head. "It's hard to believe that anyone would have wonderful things to say about me. I've messed up everything I have ever touched."

"Hardly that," he replied. "You have done more good than you know, and it is nothing compared to the good you will do in the years to come."

The man stood up, brushed his hands against his jeans, and walked down the library steps. "Do not be so hard on yourself, Kate. Remorse can be a good thing if it inspires you to do better, but letting it grow out of proportion is just another form of pride." He nodded in farewell, and started walking across the square.

"Wait," I called after him, standing up myself. "You didn't tell me your name."

The man turned around and smiled. "You are right," he replied cheerfully. "I did not. Have a pleasant evening, Kate." He waved once and then turned and walked away, vanishing into the darkness as completely as if he had become a shadow himself.

I watched him go, amazed. I still felt cold and tired, but the despair that had overwhelmed me as I sat on the library steps had disappeared. Whoever the stranger had been, he had inexplicably lifted my spirits.

I felt a little tingle on my face and then another. Flakes of snow were just beginning to fall, and they landed on my upturned face like fairy kisses. I walked home in the dark, enjoying their tingle, feeling lighter and more hopeful than I had in a long time.

Archangel Uriel speaks:

So, that was Gabriel's protégée. A few of my angels and I had been nearby in Albany, helping several members of the state legislature resolve their disagreements over a controversial but important education bill that needed to pass. By the time Kate's distress caught my attention, my angels had things well in hand. It was only a minor detour for me to swing by Angel Falls and spend a few minutes with her before heading back to Heaven.

Kate was far more approachable than I had expected, based on the things Michael and Metatron had said about her. Then again, the poor child had dropped nearly all of her defenses. It might have been more difficult for me to appear to her if she had not finally been ready to see.

People sometimes refer to me as the Archangel of Wisdom, a rather overstated title that I rarely use myself. I appreciate the sentiment behind it, however, and endeavor to spread wisdom and good sense wherever I go to any soul who is open enough to accept them.

Do let me know when you are ready, will you?

In Kate's case, it was just a matter of blessing her with a little perspective, disguised as snowflakes. Every touch lifted her mood and helped her to take a more balanced view of her forgivable human frailties. Simple enough, really.

Having met Kate, I could see why Gabriel was so taken with her. Behind all that self-protective bluster was a lucid mind and a gentle, sensitive spirit. Her biggest mistakes were, as I said, focusing on her shortcomings to the exclusion of her virtues and trying much too hard to be who she thought other people wanted her to be, instead of just being herself. It is a common, if somewhat puzzling, mistake. Why would anyone want to be other than the person the Creator made her, or him, to be?

It occurred to me that Kate had been very like an angry kitten for most of her life, puffed up to twice her size and spitting at anything she thought might hurt her. No wonder she got along so well with Honoré! The thought made me smile all the way back to Heaven.

CHAPTER TWENTY-THREE

By the time I got home, Bella was frantic with worry, and Andrew was putting on his coat to go out looking for me. Richard had called three times to apologize for upsetting me and to make sure I had gotten home in one piece. Even Honoré was hovering around Bella, looking anxious. The stranger had been right—I had more and better friends than I realized.

After hugging Bella, kissing Andrew on the cheek, and giving Honoré's back a thorough scratching, I calmly apologized for worrying them, explaining that I had needed some time alone to process everything that had happened to me in the past few weeks. The brief solitude, I assured them, had been very beneficial. I was fine. If they were taken aback by my composure, they didn't say so.

Then I called Richard back and apologized for taking his very legitimate observations too hard. He apologized in turn for having been tactless. I insisted he had nothing to apologize for, and in minutes we were laughing together. We ended the call on a positive note, with Richard agreeing to let me know if there was anything I could do to help him or if he had any news about the lawsuit or the bar complaint.

Having represented many worried clients myself, I knew that it would take months, perhaps even years, for the lawsuit and the bar complaint to be resolved. Fretting constantly and calling Richard every day would be pointless. The best strategy for me would be to trust him and get out of his way while he worked.

The only problem with that strategy was that it left me with time on my hands and precious little to do. Bella and I had already cleaned out most of the house, and the last few rooms could be done in a week or less. I could have looked for a job, but given my circumstances, it would hardly be realistic to expect a local law firm to hire me. Besides, the thought of returning to legal practice tied my stomach in anxious knots. The events of the past weeks had traumatized me so badly that practicing law just was not an option. Unfortunately, though, I couldn't think of any other way to make a living.

I was lucky to have a little money left from my time in Manhattan and a roof over my head. Those small advantages gave me the luxury of time to decide what to do next. I didn't want to go back to drifting along as I had before Roy Blackwell's envelope so rudely shook me awake, but I didn't want to rush down the wrong road, either.

After a little mulling, I decided it was time to focus on my interpersonal skills. There had been plenty of recent suggestions from people whose opinions mattered to me that life at the law firm had changed me for the worse. It might be time to make a conscious effort to become a nicer person. And where better to do that than Angel Abbey?

So, as weeks passed and autumn gave way to winter, I spent every free moment at the Abbey. Deciding it was time for Andrew to stop playing chauffeur, I drove myself, putting more miles on my old green Mustang than I had since law school. It felt good to have somewhere to go and something useful to do with my time.

The steady stream of donations that I had previously made ensured my welcome at the Abbey. There wasn't much left in the house to give away, though, so I donated my time instead. I packed care boxes for Africa, tutored children in English and social studies, helped Violet repackage her contributions to the local food pantries. I applauded at performances, sat in on book clubs, and hauled baskets full of Bella's casseroles and cakes to potlucks and bake sales at every opportunity.

Not all of my efforts were successful. There was one unfortunate incident where I mistook a bin of sugar for salt and ruined a batch of stew, prompting Chef Violet to banish me from the kitchen unless she had time to watch me herself. A couple of the kids who came to me initially for tutoring dropped out, complaining to their mothers that I scared them.

Worse still, at one book-club meeting, I disagreed with an elderly lady about the actions of a character in the novel we were reading. She liked the character despite his flaws; point by point, I built a devastating case against him. It wasn't until I looked around and saw everyone else in the room staring at me, silent and motionless, that it occurred to me that I had been arguing like a prosecutor, not engaging in polite discussion. And over a fictional character to boot.

I stopped, mortified, and kept my mouth shut for the rest of the session. My opponent gently patted my hand as she left the room at the end of the meeting. For some reason, that cheered me a little.

Despite some initial awkwardness, though, my behavior improved considerably over time, and with it, my confidence. The more people at Angel Abbey warmed up to me, the more I realized how lonely my time in Manhattan had been. Increasingly, my life revolved around the Abbey, and it felt good to relax into the company of the neighbors and friends I encountered there.

Richard and I ran into each other from time to time, and occasionally he would call with some bit of news about the lawsuit or the bar complaint. He had entered his appearance as my counsel in both proceedings, filing the necessary papers and engaging in preliminary discussions with the law firm and the bar. Predictably, Blackwell rebuffed all of Richard's efforts to settle the lawsuit, claiming that Dr. Grandy had insisted on taking the matter all the way to the Supreme Court if necessary. That hurt, but I should have expected it. Dr. Grandy had always said there was no sense in hiring attorneys if you were not going to take their advice. Blackwell was almost certainly advising him to fight me to the death—*my* death, if Blackwell had anything to say about it.

Thankfully, the attorney for the New York bar was less confrontational. Richard persuaded her to hold off on processing the ethics charges against me while the lawsuit was pending. Blackwell's accusations were essentially identical in both proceedings. If the court upheld my version of events, the bar would have no real reason to discipline me, though I might still have to answer for my carelessness in leaving my briefcase behind.

My own emotions were mixed. On the one hand, it was a relief to know that my eligibility to practice law was not in imminent peril. On the other hand, it made the lawsuit that much more ominous. If Blackwell won, the bar would expel me from the legal profession. It was a sobering thought.

Richard decided that it would be worth the risk to call Ruth Martingale. He left a couple of messages for her, but she never responded. Too loyal to the firm, he surmised. Personally, I concluded that she had only feigned concern for me the day we met, hoping to sniff out more incriminating information for Roy Blackwell to use against me. Then again, maybe I had disappointed her by not filing a complaint against Blackwell when she had told me he had abused other women. Either way, it seemed unlikely that she would be willing to help with my defense. That made me sad. Ruth's good opinion mattered more to me than I had realized.

Richard's news about Jeanine Powell was no better. She had left New York the week I was fired, and Richard had no idea where to find her. She might still turn up, but without more information, the odds of our being able to locate her were infinitesimally small. Still, I answered his questions about her as best I could. Jeanine was a petite, pretty black woman with pixie-cut hair, a few years younger than me. She had a trace of a Southern accent, and I vaguely remembered that she came from Louisiana—or was it Mississippi? Richard sighed and promised to do his best, but warned me not to be too disappointed if he could not track her down.

Once again, I was paying a price for my lack of interest in the people around me. If I had been friendlier to Jeanine when we worked together, she might have been able to help me now. That was depressing. Whenever I started to sink too low, however, the memory of the stranger on the library steps would come to mind. Then, instead of punishing myself for my past mistakes, I would redouble my efforts to do better in the future.

It was about two weeks after my faux pas at the book club that I ran into the elderly lady with whom I had had the argument—and I mean literally. I was carrying a box of sheet music I was donating, so intent on getting to the music room that I neglected to watch where I was going. She stepped out of a side room right into my path, and we collided. Thankfully, I didn't actually mow her down, but she bumped against the wall and nearly dropped her cane.

"I am so *sorry*!" I gasped, dropping the box and reaching for her elbow. "I was in such a hurry, I didn't notice you in the doorway. Are you all right?"

The lady looked up at me from under the wide brim of her periwinkle-blue hat. She might have been eighty or older, and her eyes were framed in a network of wrinkles and creases. But they were a lovely shade of blue, and they twinkled as she reached out to pat me on the cheek. "Heavens, child, you worry so! I'm fine, dear," she assured me. "Don't give it another thought."

"Listen," I said, "I'm really sorry to have run into you that way, but at least it gives me the opportunity to apologize for what happened at our last book-club meeting. I let my mouth run away with me, and it was terribly rude. I'm so sorry, ma'am."

She chuckled, her eyes dancing merrily. "You're Kate Cunningham, aren't you? Christopher's little girl?"

I had no idea how she had known Christopher Cunningham, but I was not going to ruin a promising conversation by correcting her about my parentage. "That's right, ma'am."

"Well, Kate, it's very nice to meet you. I've heard lovely things about you from so many of the people here at the Abbey. My name is Florence Stanley, but everybody just calls me Miss Flo." She reached out and patted my cheek again.

"It's very nice to meet you, too, Miss Flo." All the pats on the cheek were making me feel about five years old.

"You know, Kate, before you brought it up, I had forgotten all about our little disagreement at book club," she told me. "You're entirely forgiven, dear. We all step on one another's toes once in a while. Don't give it another thought."

Miss Flo gave my cheek a final pat and then continued down the hall, leaving me to pick up the music I had dropped. The conversation left me happily amazed that people at the Abbey all seemed to be so forgiving. That's not a trait I had often encountered at the law firm. It made for a refreshing change.

October gave way to November, and Thanksgiving provided new opportunities for the Abbey's volunteers to shine. Under Violet's supervision, I joined a team of workers who filled massive stainless-steel trays with sweet potatoes, sage dressing, green beans, and carrots, and prepared about fifteen turkeys and three dozen pies for delivery to the homeless shelter on the south side of town. It took us the better part of a day to make all the preparations, but by the time we were done, we had a veritable feast ready to load into waiting vans.

Violet invited me to help her cook and serve dinner at the shelter on Thanksgiving, but I turned her down. It took me a while to realize it, but I was ashamed that I had never gone out of my way for the homeless during my years in Manhattan, when I had had so much. I felt that showing up at the shelter with Thanksgiving dinner like some kind of rescuing angel, after I had done so little for so long, would have been hypocritical. Still, when Bella, Andrew, Honoré, and I sat down to our own turkey, I was genuinely thankful to have done a bit better.

The next couple of weeks flew by, and before I knew it, the winter holidays were right around the corner. The customary bustle at Angel Abbey ramped up into a joyful frenzy. Every one of the Abbey's innumerable rooms had to be decorated. Gifts for needy families, including plenty of toys for children who might not get presents otherwise, had to be collected, wrapped, and packaged for delivery. On top of all the volunteer work, there was an endless round of concerts, plays, caroling parties, dinners, and get-togethers. I pitched in wherever possible, attended every event, and worked hard to be as nice as I could to everyone whose path crossed mine.

Lucina des Anges was constantly at the Abbey, of course, and we often ran into one another. She was always gracious, but something about her still put my teeth just slightly on edge. Jack's pointed observation that I was jealous of her stayed with me, and I had to admit that he was probably right. That should have made dealing with her easier, but it did not. Still, I learned to put on a friendly face, make polite small talk with her, and escape whenever her adoring fans got on my nerves.

Lucina didn't seem to realize that I did not like her, and there wasn't any reason for me to tell her so. Call it petty, but my distaste for her came to feel like a nasty, precious little secret, sort of like a tiny black mouse I could conceal in my pocket and caress while no one was looking. That the mouse might eventually bite me was something I never even considered.

The holiday festivities at Angel Abbey culminated with the decorating of an enormous Scotch pine on Christmas Eve. The tree grew in the courtyard near the barn, and was home to birds and squirrels throughout the year. On Christmas Eve, the Abbey regulars got together and strung it with endless garlands of popcorn and cranberries. We then added hundreds of edible ornaments, all shaped, of course, like angels. My favorites were donated by a local scout troop, silhouettes of angels made of seeds and peanut butter for the birds to enjoy. There were angel-shaped molasses cookies that would be safe for raccoons and deer to eat, angel corn dollies for the mice and rabbits, and even strips of dried jerky, carefully woven into the shape of angel wings, for the foxes and crows. Winters in the Hudson Valley can be hard on wildlife. The decorated tree would give them sustenance for weeks.

Angel Abbey being what it was, we didn't just decorate the tree and call it a night. While some volunteers worked on the tree, others set up long tables decorated with pine boughs and dozens of heavy candles in tall glass chimneys. The tables were loaded to groaning with cakes, cookies, sandwiches, apples, doughnuts, cider, hot chocolate for the children, and mulled wine for the adults.

Several of the musicians who frequently performed at the Abbey brought their instruments. They accompanied us as we sang carols, laughing at ourselves when we couldn't remember the lyrics. Then, when the last angel had been hung on the tree, one of the fiddlers started playing a Celtic reel, and almost everyone at the party started to dance.

Richard had arrived sometime during the festivities, and he came over to me with a cup of mulled wine steaming in his hand. "Care to dance, counsel?" he asked, smiling.

I smiled back, but shook my head. "I've never had any talent for dancing, Richard. I'm a complete clod. You'd be putting your toes at mortal risk."

Richard took a generous swallow of wine, then grinned at me. "Suit yourself, Kate, but have a cup or two of wine for courage and then come find me. You never want to miss a chance to dance at Angel Abbey."

Looking over my shoulder, Richard's eye lit on something, and I turned to look. Lucina, exquisitely dressed in a caramel-colored jacket trimmed with creamy faux fur, was standing not far away with a couple I didn't recognize. Her wardrobe was incredible—I had to give her that. As we watched, Lucina tipped her head back, laughing. "I'll catch up with you later," Richard said to me. "Have fun, OK?" He brushed past me and went over to Lucina, easily joining the conversation. I couldn't hear what he said, but she burst into delighted laughter and so did her companions.

"You're just jealous, remember?" I muttered to myself, and went off to look for the wine.

The evening wore on, and the dancing became the focal point of the festivities. Everyone danced, young and old, sometimes in pairs, sometimes in long lines that snaked around the courtyard in graceful spirals. Everyone, that is, except me.

The thing is, I never danced, because I never really could. Oh, I had tried when I was younger. My parents paid for ballet lessons, but I never overcame my fundamental awkwardness. I was always trying too hard and thinking too much, tripping over my feet and flinging my arms in the wrong direction. Eventually, my ballet teacher flatly informed my mother that I was hopeless and demanded that she remove me from class before one of the other students got hurt.

I overheard their conversation at the ripe old age of seven, and it stayed with me for years. My mother told me not to take Madame's hurtful comments too seriously and encouraged me to keep trying. But then she made the mistake of telling Christopher Cunningham what Madame had said. He absolutely refused to pay for any more ballet lessons or, as he put it, "to continue throwing good money at a lost cause." There was no point in arguing with him. He wouldn't change his mind, I knew even then. He never did.

After that, I never tried to dance again. Even the free-form wiggling that passed for dancing during my high school and college years seemed fraught with opportunities for embarrassment, so I turned my attention to my schoolwork. I was irredeemably clumsy—no need for the world to know.

When my debate partner haltingly asked me to the high school prom I refused him, pretending that my family was going out of town for the weekend. Then, when Bella asked if I wanted to go shopping for a gown, I lied, telling her that no one had invited me to the dance. It was just as well, I told myself. My father would not have wanted pictures of me in a prom dress anyway.

Now, looking around on Christmas Eve and listening to the music, I found my feet *itching* to move. But even three cups of mulled wine didn't give me enough courage to join in the dancing. Instead, I stood in the shadows beside the huge, decorated tree, watching my new friends enjoy themselves, as they turned and skipped to the music, their features aglow with candlelight and wine.

Now and then I would spot Bella and Andrew, their faces flushed with pleasure, dancing together as if they were young lovers again. Richard repeatedly swung past me with one partner or another, but I always looked away before he could catch my eye, and eventually he stopped trying. I noticed Amy, her dark hair falling loose in a cascade of curls, dancing with a handsome young man I had never seen before. She was smiling as beautifully as a Broadway ingénue, her chronic shyness gone.

There was no missing Lucina, who always seemed to be leading the dance. That figured, I thought sourly, but as I watched her, my envy started to fade. Despite the admiration of the people around her, and even in the center of a crowd, Lucina des Anges was always alone. In all my time at the Abbey, I had never seen her with a husband or sweetheart, and she never spoke of her family or having a child of her own. Solitude was something we had in common, I suddenly realized. I tucked that realization securely in the back of my mind, to ponder later in the privacy of my room.

It was long after midnight, and the candles had guttered down to puddles of wax on the tables, when Bella, Andrew, and I finally drove home from Angel Abbey. Across Angel Falls, children would be dreaming of visits from Santa and presents in the morning. Thanks to the good work of the Abbey volunteers, a lot of kids from the south side of town would enjoy a happier Christmas than their parents could possibly have provided alone. The fact that I had been one of those volunteers made me quietly glad, even if I couldn't imagine ever being brave enough to join the dance.

Archangel Gabriel speaks:

People around the world and throughout time have created many beautiful holidays, and I love them all. Christmas will always be my favorite, though. It's not just that I remember that first night, millennia ago, when the miracle was shining new and everyone from impoverished shepherds to wise kings paused to wonder and to worship. I have loved every Christmas since then, and the myriad ways that people from century to century have celebrated the momentous birth of one small, miraculous child. From Charles Dickens to José Feliciano, I've cherished every artist who produced even a scrap of holiday magic for people to enjoy.

Celebration is, in my opinion, the finest form of worship.

There were many reasons for me to drop by Angel Abbey that Christmas Eve, and I certainly wasn't the only archangel there. You may believe we're a solemn bunch, but the truth is that angels, apart from a few sticklers like Metatron, are mad about parties. We'll eagerly attend any gathering of two or more that's joyous enough to make us feel welcome. Lucina knows that, and she makes sure that all of her get-togethers are festive enough to satisfy flights of angels. We, in turn, show up and shower the partygoers with blessings and good cheer. It's a happy arrangement that makes for memorable celebrations even though the human guests don't recognize the angels among them.

When I got to the party that night and looked around, Ariel and her angels had already arrived. They were clustered around the tree, a beautiful gift to the wild creatures under Ariel's care. I could tell she took particular pleasure in blessing it. Sandalphon and several of his angels had brought their instruments along, and were merrily enhancing every tune the human musicians played. What a joyful noise they made! Chamuel and his angels made their way through the crowd, scattering fistfuls of love wherever they went. More than a few marriages were rejuvenated that night, and there would be a bevy of new romances and engagements come spring. Barachiel was there too, tossing fistfuls of gleaming white rose petals into clusters of partygoers and grinning with satisfaction when Lucina's guests exploded into laughter each time he released them.

It made perfect sense for me to make an appearance, too. Dropping by the party gave me a chance to bless the people who gave so generously to make Christmas festive for their neighbors. It allowed me to spend a few quiet moments with Lucina, the visible heart of the Abbey.

It also gave me a chance to check on Kate.

Uriel had told me about his brief encounter with Kate a few weeks before. It was generous of my brilliant brother to share a little perspective with her. I was glad that Kate seemed to have taken his wisdom to heart. Overall, she looked pale and reserved but more grounded than she had since I first left that note on her desk months before.

Kate seemed to have ingratiated herself at the Abbey. When people at the party spoke about her, they had good things to say, and Lucina seemed to like her. Kate wasn't happy yet, but at least she was happier.

It was progress, of a sort. Still, Kate looked like a sad little orphan at somebody else's birthday party that night, standing alone while everyone else was dancing. In a sense, I suppose that's what she was.

I remember the day Kate's ballet teacher dismissed her from class, perhaps even more vividly than Kate does herself. Little Katie had trouble learning ballet at first, but she was slowly improving. If Kate's instructor hadn't been such a perfectionist, she might have spoken more kindly. Better yet, she might have held her tongue and reserved judgment, letting Kate continue to study. As it was, though, that overbearing woman inflicted a scar on Kate's seven-year-old heart that lasted for decades. Children are so easily wounded! It's a shame more adults don't remember that.

It had been a long time since Kate left ballet class, and it was her choice to let that one bad memory ruin dancing for her. By the time Kate got to Angel Abbey, she'd had many years and dozens of opportunities to laugh off the hurt. She didn't have to dance like a prima ballerina to have fun, but she couldn't see that.

It broke my heart to see her standing alone at the party. But Kate's isolation that Christmas Eve was entirely her own doing. Had she stretched out her hand to anyone there, they would have welcomed her into the dance and she would have had a wonderful time. No one would have watched Kate's dancing, or criticized her even if they had. She just didn't know that yet.

It was good that Kate was finally willing to work at the Abbey. I could only hope that, given time, her heart would heal enough to let her dance there, too.

CHAPTER TWENTY-FOUR

There being no small children in our house, nobody was inclined to get up at the crack of dawn on Christmas morning to see what Santa had left under the tree. It was nearly eleven o'clock before I dragged myself downstairs, still clad in my pajamas and robe, Honoré padding quietly behind me. Bella and Andrew were nowhere to be seen. They must have been utterly exhausted by the party the night before. I was glad for the quiet—it gave me a chance to take care of them for a change. I put on a fresh pot of coffee, opened a can of food for Honoré, and even managed to throw together a cinnamon coffee cake for breakfast. It wasn't as good as what Bella would have made, but I still felt a surge of pride when I pulled it hot out of the oven and it hadn't fallen. My long hours in the Abbey kitchen with Violet had improved my baking ability.

The scents of coffee and cinnamon must have roused Bella and Andrew. They appeared in the kitchen a few minutes later, dressed in their night-clothes, robes, and slippers. Bella praised my coffee cake as lavishly as if I had prepared a seven-course meal, much to Andrew's amusement and my own embarrassed pleasure. We cut and buttered generous pieces, poured ourselves coffee, and headed into the parlor for presents.

Busy as we had been at the Abbey, Bella and I had still found time to decorate a small tree a few days before Christmas, using ornaments we had found in the attic. There were strings of lights, garlands of old silver beads that had tarnished to a lovely, soft patina, and dozens of gleaming glass globes in shades of ruby, sapphire, emerald, and gold. There was a handful of ornaments I had made as a child, clothespins decorated with felt and rickrack to look like reindeer, yarn woven around crossed popsicle sticks forming little kite shapes. "God's eyes," I remembered they were called.

One special ornament was a tiny Siamese kitten, proudly bought with my allowance when Honoré first arrived. There were other ornaments marking milestones in my childhood, too: a tiny two-wheeler bike, a wooden boat to represent the sailing lessons I took one summer, a little brass trophy to commemorate my first debate club win.

But the most treasured item on the tree was the topper. Unlike the stars that crowned the Christmas trees in so many of my friends' homes, our tree topper was a handsome, auburn-haired angel, with enormous wings and embroidered white robes, who brandished a golden trumpet. Taking it out of the box, I had noticed that the topper looked almost exactly like the angel whose face appeared again and again at the Abbey. No wonder he had seemed familiar when I saw his likeness flying over the barn—funny not to have noticed that before.

"Bella," I had asked, carefully unwrapping it, "do you know which angel this is supposed to be? I see him everywhere at the Abbey."

Bella had set down the string of beads she was untangling and come over, looking down at the angel in my hands. "That's supposed to be Archangel Gabriel, I think," she had said. "The story goes that he was the angel who told Mary she was expecting, and who told the shepherds not to be afraid when the baby Jesus was born. You can tell it's Gabriel by the trumpet in his hands. They say he'll blow it at the end of the world."

The face of the angel in my hands had almost seemed to shift a little, as if he were eavesdropping on our conversation. "Interesting," I had murmured, though not really meaning it. I was far more curious about where the tree topper had come from than in old fables. "Bella, do you remember when we got this? It has to have been when I was really little—it has been at the top of our tree every year for as long as I can remember."

Bella had thought for a moment, then her face had brightened. "As a matter of fact, Katie, I do," she had replied. "Your father told me once that he bought that tree topper for your mother the first Christmas after your family moved to Angel Falls. He said the artist who made the angel told him that, according to local legend, it was Archangel Gabriel himself who stepped out of the waterfall and told Jacob Wittesteen to build a town here. Can you imagine how terrifying that must have been?"

The story of the angel's appearance to Jacob Wittesteen had always seemed pretty far-fetched to me. More likely, I thought, Wittesteen had suffered a drunken hallucination and created an elaborate fiction around it later. I had never revealed what I really thought about it to Bella, though. She had always loved magical stories—no point in throwing cold water on her dreams.

What mattered more to me was that Christopher Cunningham had purchased the angel tree topper as a gift to my mother. It was beautifully sculpted, and the angel's face and wings almost seemed to glow. "Whichever angel this is, it's certainly a pretty thing. My father—well, *he*—he must have wanted her to love living here."

Bella's face had softened, and she had looked at me with what might have been a hint of pity. "You can still call him your father, Katie." She had started to say more, but stopped herself. Her comment had seemed to be a clear invitation to respond, but I hadn't been able to think of anything more to say. Christopher Cunningham was not my father. Pretending that he was wouldn't do anybody any good.

Sighing a little, Bella had picked up the beads again and resumed working on untangling them. Carefully setting the angel aside, I had helped her cover the tree with ornaments. When every last branch was decorated, I had climbed up on the arm of the couch to gently place the angel on the very top of our tree.

Now, sitting in the parlor with coffee and cake on Christmas morning, I looked up at the angel perched over our heads. "Merry Christmas, Gabriel," I murmured, toasting him with my coffee cup. For just an instant, his sculpted lips seemed to curve into a hint of a smile. I blinked, and the smile was gone. There was just a beautiful, motionless statue of an angel topping our Christmas tree.

Bella, Andrew, and I had only a few presents for one another piled under the tree that morning, but we had a lot of fun opening them nonetheless. For Andrew, I had bought a set of leather driving gloves to thank him for all the time he had spent squiring me around. For Bella, I had found a baking book, with hundreds of recipes and color photos. She was so tickled with it she could barely put it down.

Bella and Andrew gave me a deliciously soft, fluffy beret, with matching gloves and a long scarf, all in pale pink shot through with rose-gold thread. From the quality of the knitting, I guessed (correctly) that Bella had made them herself. She seemed even happier than I was that I liked them so much.

Honoré made out like a bandit. He got a big bag of his favorite kitty treats and a toy dragon made of red pom-poms from me. When I tossed the dragon into the air, he caught it with one paw and chased it all over the parlor, still kittenish despite his years. From Bella and Andrew, Honoré received a plump cushion, exactly matching the blue of his eyes, to lounge on when he wasn't sleeping on my bed. He sprawled across it with ease, the king of all he surveyed.

Bella and Andrew exchanged the same gifts they had every year for as long as I could remember—a little bottle of Bella's favorite perfume from Andrew, and a little bottle of Andrew's favorite brandy from Bella. They would nurse those two bottles all year long, making them last until the next Christmas Eve. We all knew what those presents would be, but the two of them pretended to be surprised by them, just as they always did. Watching them flirt and tease each other, I wondered if my parents had ever been that happy together. Somehow, I thought not.

As the remnants of the morning wore on, we laughed and talked and admired one another's presents. Nothing was expensive, and nobody minded. Every gift had been chosen with care and given with enormous love. Andrew pronounced my coffee cake excellent. Bella dove happily back into her recipe book. We all lingered over second cups of coffee, enjoying a rare, leisurely day.

All too soon, it was early afternoon. I went up to take a shower and was just getting dressed when the doorbell rang. "Katie," Bella called, "come on down. There's somebody here to see you."

Thinking that Richard might have dropped by, I yanked a sweater over my head, dragged my fingers through my still-damp hair, and ran downstairs in my stocking feet. But it wasn't Richard at the door. Jack stood in the foyer in his coat, hat, and gloves, looking handsome and a little sheepish. He had a duffel bag thrown over one shoulder, like a sailor on leave, and a big bag from Zabar's, one of New York's best delicatessens, in his other hand. "Merry Christmas, Katie," he said. "Thought I'd come up and surprise you."

Despite his big smile, Jack seemed nervous, as if he was not quite sure whether I would be glad to see him or not. He held out the Zabar's bag. "Peace offering?"

I ran over and threw my arms around his neck, grateful beyond words to have my friend back. "Merry Christmas, yourself," I murmured into his ear. "I am *so* glad to see you! I thought you would never talk to me again. Jack, I'm truly sorry about what happened!"

"Yeah, listen, don't worry about that, OK? It was really my fault," he insisted. "After you left town, I got to thinking about what an idiot I had been. I shouldn't have grabbed at you like that, and I *really* shouldn't have been such an obnoxious jerk when you stopped me. I feel awful about the things I said to you. I mean, there are plenty of available girls in New York, but I've only got one Katie.

"Can we be friends again?" he asked. His tone was nonchalant, but I could sense real apprehension underneath.

"You bet!" I grinned, hugging him hard. "Thanks for coming, Jack. You being here is the best Christmas present you could possibly give me! Now, let's see what's in that bag."

It looked as though Jack had bought out Zabar's. There was champagne, smoked salmon, a big box of chocolate truffles, several containers of fancy salads, stuffed grape leaves, three kinds of cheese, two types of salami, jams, pickles, and a cheesecake. He had even remembered to buy a few cans of upscale cat food for Honoré.

"Wow, this is amazing!" I said, rummaging through the plunder. "Who knew you had such great taste in food when you feel guilty? I should let you make passes at me more often."

Jack recoiled in mock horror. "Never again, Katie! I can't afford to do this more than once. Not on an actor's salary." We laughed together, relieved to be best buddies again. Out of the corner of my eye, I saw Bella and Andrew standing in the doorway, watching us and smiling.

We put Jack's duffel bag up in the guest bedroom and then rejoined the others downstairs. He was the perfect guest, joking with Andrew and charming Bella with a steady stream of compliments. Jack had been to the house often when we were in college together, and it felt like old times to have him back again. Out of nowhere, it occurred to me that it was too bad my ex-father wasn't still alive to see him there. The thought felt good but strange. Then Bella herded us into the kitchen to help her make Christmas dinner, and I forgot all about it.

Earlier, Bella had set a turkey with stuffing roasting in the oven. We prepared mashed potatoes and roasted vegetables to accompany it. Jack proved to be a dab-hand in the kitchen, scrubbing vegetables and peeling potatoes like a professional sous chef. We dished up several of the salads that he had brought from New York, an added treat we had not expected. Everybody drank a little wine and nibbled on Jack's goodies, joking and horsing around as we prepared our bounteous feast, all the happier because we were together.

Carrying a bowl of steaming mashed potatoes to the dining room, I noticed that Bella had set an extra place at the table. I was about to ask her why when the doorbell rang again. "I'll get it," I called, in the general direction of the kitchen, and went to answer the bell.

A burst of clean, cold air tingled on my face when I opened the front door. Night comes early to the Hudson Valley in late December, and beyond the circle of light from the carriage lamp above the door, the winter darkness was lit by only silvery moonlight and a handful of stars. A few snowflakes swirled in the air, glistening in the lamplight like flecks of molten gold.

Lucina des Anges stood alone on my doorstep, the creamy fur collar of her caramel-colored jacket framing her lovely face.

"Merry Christmas, Kate," she said. It struck me again, how melodious her voice was. "May I come in?" she asked.

Was she a little nervous? Perhaps. I felt a sudden, intense desire to put her at ease. "Yes, please, come in and join us, Lucina," I replied at once. "I have a friend who came up from New York who's been dying to meet you. It'll be such fun to introduce you both. Merry Christmas, Lucina! We're all very glad you're here," I said, and I meant every last word.

Though Lucina's visit was unexpected, the nasty little black mouse in my pocket was quiet. I was genuinely happy to see her. Closing the door, I ushered her out of the cold and into our Christmas celebration.

Archangel Azrael speaks:

We angels adore Christmas! Every year, all of Heaven celebrates, and it is even more glorious on that blessed day than it is the rest of the year. The streets of gold shine more brightly, the celestial choir sings more sweetly, the Divine light shimmers more luminously, and every angel gleefully commemorates the joyous anniversary of that miraculous morning.

Sadly, some of the departed souls who dwell among us have a more complicated reaction to Christmas when it comes around. Those who passed away at peace with their loved ones and the world are happy to join in the angels' celebrations, singing and dancing as joyously as the innocent children of God that they are. But there are others who are less fortunate. Souls who died in sorrow, guilt, or shame, those who left important business unfinished or words of love unspoken, and especially those who pine for something or someone they left behind... Well, they suffer at the holidays. My angels and I try to be particularly gentle with them, but there is not much we can do until they finally relinquish their regrets and reconcile themselves to the mistakes they made in life.

Christopher Cunningham continued to torture himself, consumed with regret for the things he had done on Earth. His self-loathing was so profound that it was almost absurd. No mortal soul can be perfect as the Creator is perfect, but Christopher was prideful enough to think he should have been the single exception to that universal rule. I declined Uriel's perfectly reasonable offer to point that out to him, though. Uriel was right—he always is—but poor Christopher was not ready to hear it.

It was late Christmas afternoon when Gabriel came by. I was surprised but very pleased to see him. Gabriel's work with signs, portents, and Divine messages frequently takes him among the living, but he is rarely inclined to converse with souls who have left the mortal world. (I sometimes think he believes that they ought to be able to figure things out for themselves once they get to Heaven.)

At any rate, I was sitting with Christopher, holding his hand as he wept and mourned, when I looked up and saw my beautiful brother. Gabriel looked uncharacteristically tired, and his wings were a trifle frayed, unexpected when you consider that Christmas is usually his favorite holiday. Nonetheless, he strode purposefully over to us, stood in front of Christopher, and loudly cleared his throat.

Christopher looked up, startled. It is impossible to ignore Gabriel when he is determined to get your attention, and my brother seemed very determined indeed.

But when he spoke to Christopher his voice was gentle, and his hand on Christopher's arm rested as lightly as a feather. "Mr. Cunningham, I believe? My name is Gabriel. It would be a kindness if you would come with me, sir. There is something that I think you might like to see." He gave Christopher's arm a little tug. "This way, please."

Amazed, Christopher stood up and meekly permitted Gabriel to steer him over to one of our windows to Earth. Looking down, he saw Kate, busily preparing Christmas dinner with Bella, Andrew, and Jack, as Honoré lounged, watching, on his new cushion, one paw pinning down his dragon toy. Kate was laughing, teasing her friends, and clearly having a terrific time. She seemed to be happier than she had been in years.

Christopher watched her for a long time, motionless. His stillness worried me a little—had his soul entirely fled? Two fat tears rolled slowly down his cheeks, but there was no sobbing, no spasms of grief. He turned to Gabriel, and for the first time since his arrival in Heaven, cracked the merest ghost of a smile.

"Thank you," he said.

Gabriel smiled back, glowing as brilliantly as the rising sun on Christmas morning. "You're welcome, Christopher. Merry Christmas!"

All of the angels who had tended Christopher Cunningham since his death subtly exchanged relieved glances. My brother Gabriel had worked a Christmas miracle indeed.

CHAPTER TWENTY-FIVE

That Christmas dinner marked a turning point in my relationship with Lucina des Anges. Bella, I later learned, had invited Lucina to dinner without really expecting her to come. She had nevertheless added that extra place setting at the dinner table. Shocked at Lucina's actual arrival, Bella greeted our newest guest as if she were a visiting empress and we were honored by the company of such an eminent visitor.

Astonishingly, Bella's hero-worship of Lucina didn't bother me a bit. Maybe it was my relief at being back on good terms with Jack, maybe it was Christmas spirit run riot, or maybe it was something in the wine. But whatever the cause, my heart was filled with holiday cheer. I would have welcomed Roy Blackwell himself if he had shown up on my doorstep that day.

Well, maybe not.

Fortunately, Lucina was no Roy Blackwell. Andrew greeted her with the casual good humor he shows to everyone. Jack was instantly taken with Lucina, surprising all of us when he recognized her. Lucina des Anges had a past, it seemed, and Jack knew about it.

Before she became the so-called Lady of Angel Abbey, Lucina had enjoyed some minor success as a movie actress in the 1980s. Jack had seen her in a grade-B space opera that became something of a cult classic among sci-fi nerds. Although not widely applauded, the film had garnered Lucina some attention at the time as an up-and-coming talent.

Jack's story explained a lot. A trained actress could easily present herself as a mystical wise woman, I thought, a little smugly. But there wasn't anything truly mystical about Lucina at all. The Lady was just her latest role, and one that she had learned to play well.

"But you were working under another name then, weren't you?" Jack asked her. "What was it? Lucia, Lucy—"

"Lucy Stevens," Lucina replied. She seemed calm enough, but I sensed a touch of unease under her poised demeanor. "It was a stage name, and that was a long time ago. You're kind to remember me so generously, Jack. To be honest, I never really was very good. I'll bet you're a marvelous actor, though," she said, deftly steering Jack onto safer conversational ground. "Are you working on anything right now?"

"As a matter of fact, I am," Jack said, eager to impress our lovely guest. He launched into a description of the new play he was rehearsing. He regaled us with plot summaries, punch lines, and funny stories about rehearsal mishaps. Enjoying himself, Jack treated us to wicked impersonations of his anorexic leading lady, the crazy Hungarian director, and the scowling, dark-suited producer. He had us all roaring in minutes, and Lucina was visibly charmed.

Away from her crowd of devotees at the Abbey, Lucina proved a lot easier to like. Instead of showing up in one of the long, floaty dresses she typically wore at Angel Abbey, she had come to our house in slacks, a green pullover, and subdued earrings. Her outfit was attractive, but no one could fairly call it an attention-grabber. She had abstained from her usual spicy perfume, perhaps to avoid clashing with the aromas of Christmas dinner. It was a considerate thing to do.

Lucina turned out to be an attentive listener and a skilled conversationalist, though she said relatively little. She was low-key and almost humble, very different from my previous perception of her as an overconfident prima donna. She praised the meal and the beauty of our holiday decorations, especially the Christmas tree. She even refrained from taking her odd little pauses from the conversation, though I thought I saw her smile once or twice as if enjoying some private joke. I also noticed that she didn't touch her wine, and I wondered whether her abstinence had something to do with her work at the Abbey. Maybe she was a method actress who thought mystics should not imbibe.

As we ate and talked, my attention was definitely divided. Part of me laughed at Jack's antics, enjoyed Bella's excellent meal, and joined in the celebration. But another part watched Lucina, carefully appraising all she said and did. By the time we had finished our turkey, I had to admit that there was nothing about her to dislike. Jack was right—I had just been jealous of her.

In hindsight, it surprises me a little that I liked Lucina better once I found out she was an actress. Many people dismiss actors as phonies. Jack and I had been friends for a long time, though, so I knew from personal experience that actors could be wonderful people.

More important, I vaguely understood even then that there was something special about the Abbey. The place had a spiritual undertone that encouraged its guests to be their most generous selves. They responded immediately and wholeheartedly to Lucina, eager to impress their charming hostess. If interacting with the "Lady" inspired people to do and give more to the community, where was the harm? She was just a performer playing an unusual role, I thought.

Lucina had brought a couple of pounds of coffee as a house gift, saying it was a Christmas tradition where she grew up. That suggested to me that she might have come from the Pacific Northwest. I was about to ask her, when Bella called from the kitchen, asking me to help her serve dessert.

By the time I got back with dessert plates and forks, the conversation had moved on. Lucina was telling Jack and Andrew a funny story about a choir practice at the Abbey. There was no gracious way to go back and ask Lucina about her upbringing, so I decided to let my curiosity go unsatisfied for the time being. We ate Jack's cheesecake with cups of Lucina's superb coffee, and everyone agreed it had been a marvelous Christmas dinner.

Lucina left shortly after we finished, gratefully accepting Andrew's offer to drive her back to the Abbey. I wasn't sure how she had gotten to the house in the first place, but decided it would be rude to ask. She had been an exemplary guest, and if she didn't care to mention who had dropped her off it was none of my business. She hugged Jack and Bella, stroke Honoré's cheek, and then turned to me, taking both of my hands in hers.

"Thank you so much for having me, Kate," she said warmly. "This was the nicest Christmas I've had in a long time." It occurred to me again that Lucina seemed always to be set apart, even when she was surrounded by adoring fans. Could the Lady of Angel Abbey actually be lonely? For the first time, I started to think that we might just grow to be friends someday.

I squeezed her hands and smiled. "Thank you so much for coming,

Lucina. I'm really glad you did. Are you still planning a party for New Year's Eve? I can drop by and help with the preparations if you'd like."

Lucina smiled back. "That would be great. Heaven knows we can't ever miss an opportunity to dance at the Abbey." Did she seem just the slightest bit sad? "Come by at any time that's convenient for you. I'll look forward to it."

Before I could answer, something very odd happened. The Christmas tree appeared to shiver slightly, and its lights flashed. For an instant, it was as though the entire house was ablaze with radiance. The fragrance of lilies wafted through the room, dissipating almost as quickly as it came. The angel at the top of the Christmas tree raised the trumpet to his lips, and I thought I heard a fanfare, like something out of a medieval fantasy movie.

The moment passed. The lights returned to normal, the scent of lilies was gone, the last echo of the music disappeared, and the angel was just a motionless tree topper once again.

I looked around, frankly spooked. "What the heck? Did you see that? Did you *smell* that?" Jack, Bella, and Andrew all gaped back at me, equally perplexed. Only Lucina seemed unperturbed. I thought I saw her wink at the angel, but it happened so quickly I couldn't be sure.

"Must have been a short in the wiring somewhere," Andrew said. "I'll check it out as soon as I get back. Come on, Lucina, let me drive you home." He led her out the door, leaving the rest of us to stare at one another, nonplussed.

"Jack, have you ever seen anything like that in your life?" I asked. He shook his head, dumbfounded. "Bella, what about you?"

"Not that I can remember, Katie," she replied, her voice unsteady. "We'll have Andrew check the wiring the minute he gets back. This house is so old, I guess anything could happen." She shook herself like a duck shedding water. "Who would like some more coffee, or maybe more wine? After that little display, I don't want to go to bed until Andrew tells me the wiring is all right. Some Christmas it would be if the house burned down around us while we slept."

"Damaged wiring doesn't smell like lilies," I pointed out, but Bella had already headed off to the kitchen. Jack and I followed, and we spent the next hour washing dishes and putting leftovers away. When Andrew got back, he went down to the basement with a flashlight and checked the fuse box, and then inspected the lights and the receptacle they were plugged into. He assured us that the wiring was just fine.

"Maybe it was a *sign*, Katie," Jack joked, wiggling his fingers and widening his eyes.

"Sure, Jack, it must have been the Archangel Gabriel, sending us a Christmas greeting," I rejoined. "Lucina probably set it up somehow to make herself seem more mystical." Even as I said those words, I felt petty and small. Lucina had been lovely all evening—it was downright nasty of me to snipe at her that way.

Jack rolled his eyes. "Jeez, Katie, what it is with you? I watched Lucina carefully all evening, and she didn't put a foot wrong. If I didn't know better..."

"You'd say I was just jealous," I sighed. "You're probably right. Don't you ever get tired of being perfect, Jack?"

"Yeah, like that's ever gonna happen," he shot back. "Perfection is nothing to which I aspire, Katie. I just want to be a billionaire, superstar acting phenomenon!" He favored me with a practiced, satirical grin. There was nothing I could do but grin right back at him.

Jack spent the night in the guest room, and I was grateful that he didn't even joke about spending it with me. It was great to be friends again, and I didn't want to risk our friendship for anything. I was grateful that he had figured that out.

Still, sleep eluded me, perhaps because I had gotten up so late that morning. I lay in bed in the dark, watching the starlight glimmer through my window, edging the furniture in silver. Honoré slept, curled up on my shoulder. Once in a while he would twitch a little, or let out the ghost of a cry. I imagined him dreaming of slaying real dragons instead of the pom-pom toy I had given him, and smiled.

My thoughts kept returning to Lucina des Anges. So, she had been an actress. That explained why she always seemed so poised. She was just "in character," so to speak. Even her little pauses might just be a performance, designed to suggest that she was conversing with spirits or something.

I realized that Lucina had told us next to nothing about herself over dinner, deftly redirecting our questions and encouraging us to talk about ourselves instead. And if "Lucy Stevens" was a stage name, was "Lucina des Anges" her real name? Or had she just taken it on with the role of the Lady of Angel Abbey? The name certainly had a theatrical ring to it. Who was Lucina, anyway?

And then there was that weird business with the lights when she was leaving. No matter what the rest of them said, I knew that what we had all experienced was no surge in the wiring. Something strange had definitely happened.

But despite the wisecrack I had made to Jack, I could not imagine how Lucina could have arranged it herself. Then again, she had arrived on my doorstep without any visible means of transportation. Who knew how long she had been there, or whether she had somehow managed to sneak something into the house to make the lights flicker? And what about the lily fragrance, or the music I had heard? The angel had sat at the top of our Christmas tree for as long as I could remember, and I had never heard it play music. It was just a figurine, silent and inert.

The whole thing was very mysterious, and unlike Jack, I don't much care for mysteries.

Finally, still wide-awake at two o'clock, I eased Honoré off my shoulder, careful not to wake him. Throwing on my robe, I tiptoed downstairs to the parlor. The house was hushed; everyone else was asleep.

Given Andrew's assurance that the wiring was just fine, we had left the tree plugged in. It cast a steady glow around the room. I looked under the tree skirt, but there was nothing amiss. I glanced out the windows, but didn't see anything out of the ordinary outside, either. The room was quiet—there was no hint of trumpet music. I sniffed but could not smell even a trace of lilies. No matter how unblinkingly I stared at it, the angel at the top of the tree didn't move so much as an eyelid. It was a beautiful tree topper, and nothing more.

Defeated, I started to go back upstairs but then stopped. I turned back and walked right up to the tree. If I stood on tiptoe, the angel and I were almost eye to eye.

"Gabriel," I whispered, staring into the angel's painted eyes, "if you have anything to say to me, now would be a really good time."

Nothing happened, of course. The angel remained motionless. Sighing, I turned away and went back up to bed.

Archangel Gabriel speaks:

What a Christmas it was! I've seen a lot of Christmases, but that one just might be my favorite since the very first. What a change from the night before! Kate had seemed so subdued at the Abbey party, and while she thought she was being discreet about disliking Lucina, anyone watching would have recognized her distaste in an instant. I was starting to think she might never come around.

It took a little persuading to get Lucina to show up for Christmas dinner. She was well aware that Kate didn't like her, and Lucina hates being around anyone who doesn't enjoy her company. She finally relented, though, and handled herself beautifully throughout the evening. She even took Jack's questions about her acting career in stride. That was hard for her—Lucina never wants to think about her past, much less discuss it with people she doesn't know.

So, yes, the plan for the evening was touch and go for a while. Until the doorbell rang, I wasn't sure Lucina would actually go through with it, or how she would manage if Kate was openly hostile. It was an incredible relief to see everything go so well. My two ladies together, enjoying each other's company and starting to be friends—it was the best Christmas gift I could possibly have gotten! That's why I threw in a few pyrotechnics of my own at the end. Kate wasn't quite ready for a full-blown angel encounter, but it was time to remind her that Creation is far more mysterious and beautiful than she has allowed herself to believe.

As an added bonus, seeing Kate with her friends, happy and having fun, seemed to do her erstwhile father some good. Azrael had told me that Christopher wasn't making much progress. He isn't one of my favorites, and it's hard for me to forget what the man did in life, no matter how much he regretted it later. Still, he was important to Kate, whether she wanted to admit it or not. Besides, what's Christmas without a few good works?

Anyway, once Christopher had taken a good look at the festivities in what had once been his kitchen, I handed him off to Azrael, who was so grateful for what I had done that it was almost embarrassing. What a sweet, generous soul my brother is, and how deeply misunderstood. All of that nonsense about judgment and eternal damnation! Truly, I don't know where you people come up with this stuff.

The Angel of Death is a forgiving spirit, every inch the embodiment of the Creator's love. When he comes for you he'll cradle your soul in infinitely tender hands. So stop worrying about eternal damnation, OK? The only condemnation you need to fear in Heaven is the condemnation you impose on yourselves.

CHAPTER TWENTY-SIX

Jack took the train back to New York the next morning, loaded down with books from Christopher Cunningham's library and enough leftovers to feed him for days. Bella had even gotten up early and baked a Bundt cake for Jack. She said it was to fatten up his leading lady, but I think she just wanted to send a gift back home with him. Bella has always been generous, and Jack has always been one of her favorites.

Christmas had no sooner ended than it was time to start getting the Abbey ready for New Year's Eve. It has always struck me as unfortunate that the holidays come one right after the other that way. It would be better, I thought, if the New Year began in autumn, when everybody goes back to school and work after summer vacation. The start of the school year always felt more "new" to me than January first.

And if the new year started in September, nobody would have to waste the days right after Christmas worrying about whether they had a date for New Year's Eve.

I knew it was silly for a grown woman to feel left out because she didn't have a New Year's Eve date lined up. That's the sort of thing you're supposed to outgrow. I had done plenty of New Year's Eve celebrating in Manhattan, seeing the different years in with various men, none of whom had stuck around for an entire year despite traditional kisses at midnight. And the invitations to end-of-year parties had dwindled to nothing as I allowed work to dominate my life more and more. A couple of times, Jack and I had braved the crowds in Times Square together. It was raucous and crazy, and my wallet had nearly been stolen once, but those New Year's eves had been the most fun of any, and certainly the least pressured. I had pretty much decided to stop going out on New Year's Eve dates even before my life in Manhattan imploded.

So why was I so unhappy that this New Year's Eve nobody was going to take me out?

Maybe it was seeing Jack clowning around the house on Christmas Day and realizing how much I had missed him. More likely, it was my growing suspicion that Richard didn't like me much now that he had really gotten to know me. He remained as cordial as ever, and was certainly too much of a gentleman to withdraw as my lawyer. But he still hadn't suggested dinner or a movie, and I was starting to think he never would.

Then again, maybe it was just disappointing that although people at the Abbey were uniformly welcoming, no one had moved from being a casual acquaintance to a real friend. No one had dropped by on Christmas to say hello; only Lucina had come over, and only because Bella had invited her. Triggered by New Year's Eve's approach, I began to realize that my life was uncomfortably solitary. Bella and Andrew were wonderful company, but they felt more like parents than friends. Honoré was my rock, but if it's ridiculous for a grown woman to pine for a New Year's Eve date, it's downright ludicrous for that same woman's best friend to be a cat.

Truly, there is nothing like an impending New Year's Eve with no specific plans to make you confront your social inadequacies.

It would have been easy to spend the next few days curled up with Honoré and a good book or two, waiting for New Year's Eve to come and go. Oddly, though, it was the thought of spending time with Lucina that kept me off the couch. Whoever she was, I was starting to like her a little. Maybe if we spent more time together, that tentative liking would grow. Besides, I had promised to help with the New Year's Eve party preparations, and as Bella had reminded me dozens of times as I was growing up, a promise is a promise.

So, a couple of days after Christmas, I threw on some clothes and went up to the Abbey, driving my little Mustang. The winter air was crisp, and it smelled like snow was on the way. Silver birch trees stretched bare limbs toward a sky that was shading to pewter. At one point I noticed a cardinal, its crimson feathers vivid against the dark green pine bough where it perched.

Pulling into the Abbey, I discovered that the cardinal had plenty of company. Our Christmas tree was covered in birds, greedily pecking away at the edible ornaments we had hung on Christmas Eve. It looked as though the foxes, mice, and other wild creatures had been busy too—the branches were noticeably barer than they had been. Our offerings, it seemed, had been gratefully accepted.

I walked up the front porch steps. Someone had replaced the striped cushions on the wicker furniture with others covered in a heavy emerald and ruby jacquard. It was Christmas fabric, and it featured an angel pattern, of course. A wide evergreen wreath hung on the door, the angel knocker carefully centered. I had stopped using the knocker long before—none of the regulars at the Abbey ever knocked—but on impulse, I took a moment to examine it.

The knocker was all brass, so there was no way to know what color the angel's robes might be. Still, it would have been impossible not to recognize that face. The angel on the knocker looked exactly like our tree topper, and I would have been willing to bet that the angel on the weather vane did, too, if you could get close enough to see.

Someone had decided that Archangel Gabriel should occupy a place of special honor at the Abbey. It made sense, given his reputed role in the spiritual conversion of our town father, but the thought made me uneasy. Archangel Gabriel was a mythical character. Why did all the renditions of him look the same? And how could anybody possibly know what an archangel looked like, anyway?

Pondering these mysteries, I was a little startled when the door was yanked opened. Amy stood there, wreathed in smiles. "Oh, good, you're here!" she said. "I'll go tell the Lady. She's been hoping you'd come by." Before I could ask if she'd had a good Christmas, Amy had scampered away.

Now that the knocker had piqued my curiosity, I decided to see whether there were any other recognizable angels around the Abbey. Wandering from room to room, I quickly identified several. There was a tall, muscular angel with piercing eyes and a strong jaw. When rendered in color, his clothes were brilliant blue. He wore armor over them, and he carried a massive sword. He had to be Archangel Michael. My religious education had effectively ended when my mother disappeared. But I vaguely remembered her telling me stories when I was small about a great battle in Heaven, and the mighty warrior angel who led the celestial armies to victory. Archangel

Michael had also, according to legend, played a role in European history, communing with Joan of Arc and, later, flying to the aid of British forces in the Battle of Mons at the outset of World War I. With such feats he had inspired the construction of the cathedral on Mont Saint-Michel, the French island that bears his name. Gazing on the determined, intelligent features depicted in the many portraits of Michael around Angel Abbey, I could almost believe the legends were true.

Michael and Gabriel weren't the only angels whose figures graced the Abbey, though. A few other faces quickly became familiar. There was an angel in green robes with golden curls and an open, friendly expression. Another angel had a slim, aristocratic face; dressed in heavily embroidered gold or yellow robes, he managed to convey an air of amused sophistication.

One broad-built angel was always portrayed in orange and carried a weight of no-nonsense authority. There was a female angel with a feline face, dressed in green or brown and always accompanied by a deer, rabbit, or other wild animal. A second female angel, all in twinkling blue, conveyed flawless grace with every tilt of her head or curve of her arm.

One male angel looked to be African or Native American. He wore pink robes that should have seemed effeminate but somehow did not. His face radiated love. There was also an angel in cream-colored robes, usually standing some distance from the others. His expression was so patient and accepting that it was humbling to look at him.

Once I had figured out who to look for, though, it became obvious that Archangel Gabriel was the star of Angel Abbey. The image was everywhere of the tall, handsome angel wearing white robes embroidered in gold. He had spectacular wings, hazel eyes, and waves of copper-colored hair that tumbled to his shoulders. He usually carried a golden trumpet, deeply chased with copper, though I saw a few renditions of him presenting a lily to a young girl. But his face was always the same—its expression clever, kind, and just the tiniest bit mischievous. Looking at him, I instantly thought of Jack, and decided that Gabriel must be a bit of a showman. No wonder Lucina kept him around.

Again and again, I was struck by how individualized the renditions of the angels were. It unnerved me. I had seen plenty of angels in museums and galleries, but most of them were forgettably pretty, with interchangeable faces that could not possibly represent anything real.

But that was not true of the angels who appeared all over the Abbey. These angels had distinctive faces and, more important, *personalities*. Michael looked powerful and trustworthy, the protective big brother every kid longs for on the playground. Gabriel seemed clever and charming. The angel in the yellow robes looked as though he would be a witty conversationalist. The blond male angel in the green robes came across as an approachable, friendly companion. The darker female angel had a wild beauty that reminded me of the Greek goddess Diana, while the blonde angel looked for all the world like somebody's fairy godmother. They were each so individual, it was hard to dismiss them as mere fantasy.

I assumed that the angel art at the Abbey had been collected over years, even decades. The various pieces had probably been created by many different artists, with unique talents and artistic styles. How was it that all of their models looked so much the same, from one rendering to the next?

An answer suggested itself when I wandered into the library. An oil painting of a dark-haired angel in ruby-red robes, his snowy wings gilt-edged, hung over the fireplace. The angel stood in what looked like the shadowed library of an old European castle. The darkness of his surroundings made the angel, who seemed incandescent, gleam even more brightly. He held an enormous book and appeared to be studying it. The painting looked hundreds of years old, as though it had been created by one of the Old Masters. Nonetheless, and even though his face was lowered toward the page, I instantly recognized the model. The angel in the painting was, without a doubt, the man I had met a few weeks before on the library steps.

All of a sudden, I thought I understood why so many of the angels in the Abbey had such distinctive appearances. They must have been modeled on real people. That theory comforted me enormously for some reason, though it did not begin to explain how those same people could have modeled for so many different artists or, for that matter, for more than a few years without aging. Not one of the angels depicted around the Abbey had a single wrinkle or gray hair.

Maybe it was a matter of artistic convention. I knew that artists often relied on conventional symbols to tell their viewers what they were seeing. So, for instance, ancient Greek sculptors almost always portrayed Aphrodite, the goddess of love and beauty, with a hand mirror. Athena, the goddess of war, wore a helmet and breastplate and often carried a spear.

Maybe there were artistic conventions about what each of the archangels was supposed to look like, and I just did not know what they were. The idea seemed improbable, but it was the best explanation that came to mind.

"Ah, you have met Uriel, I see!" Lucina had come into the library behind me. It looked as though she had resumed her role as the Lady. She was dressed in a floor-length gown of Christmassy green velvet, worn with bronze flats. Angel-shaped earrings dangled beside her face, and crystal bracelets clattered on her arm. Her mystical attire no longer irritated me, though. Jack goes to work in costumes too.

Lucina took both of my hands in hers and gave me a kiss on the cheek. I could smell her spicy fragrance—which she had not worn to Christmas dinner—and wondered what perfume was standard issue for an angel lady. The thought almost made me giggle, but I stifled the impulse. If I was going to make friends with Lucina, laughing at her was no way to begin.

"As a matter of fact, I think I have." I told her about my conversation with the man on the library steps. "He looked exactly like this. He could have modeled for this painting, in fact."

"That painting is over three hundred years old, Kate," Lucina replied lightly. "One of our wealthier benefactors donated it to the Abbey decades ago. It hangs in the library because Archangel Uriel is the Angel of Wisdom. Did this man tell you his name?"

"No," I replied, puzzled. "He knew my name, though. He said we had mutual friends. When I asked his name, he wouldn't tell me. It was strange."

"Ah, life's little mysteries," Lucina said, with a smile. "Angel Falls is a small town, Kate. You will run into him again at some point, I am sure. Maybe he won't be so secretive next time." She looped her arm through mine as if we had been best friends forever. "Come down to the kitchen with me. Violet would like us to help her with the food for New Year's Eve."

I let Lucina lead me down to the kitchen, putting aside my questions about the mysterious painting. Violet greeted me warmly, and soon she, Lucina, and I were up to our elbows in food. My culinary skills were still rudimentary enough that Violet didn't trust me to mix or cook anything, so I volunteered to wash and peel the mountains of vegetables that she needed for her various creations. Parties at the Abbey drew big crowds, and it took a lot of food to feed them.

We talked as we worked, and Violet asked us how we had spent

Christmas Day. She had spent the afternoon serving dinner at the same homeless shelter on the south side of town where we had delivered all the food for Thanksgiving. Listening to her, I felt a bit guilty to have done so little for anyone else on Christmas Day.

But before I could say a thing, Lucina started describing her visit to our house, sounding grateful beyond words to have been invited. My guilt evaporated, as it occurred to me that welcoming Lucina might have been all the generosity that had been required of me that Christmas. Having focused for so long on getting the big win every time, I had forgotten that small kindnesses are often sufficient.

Lucina also told Violet about Jack, managing to describe his charm, good looks, and humor, while subtly making it clear that she was not romantically interested in him. That eased a concern I had not realized that I'd had. While it was impossible to guess her exact age, I was pretty sure that Lucina was at least fifteen years older than Jack. The idea of her becoming romantically involved with him troubled me, though it was really none of my business. If she wasn't interested, though, there was no reason for me to worry.

Violet, on the other hand, seemed to find Lucina's description of my handsome friend very appealing indeed. Unlike Lucina, Violet was about my age, and she was remarkably attractive when she wasn't barking orders in the kitchen. I quietly resolved not to bring Jack to the Abbey anytime soon, telling myself that he didn't need an upstate romance distracting him while he was working on his new play. If there were other reasons I didn't want Jack to meet Violet, I was not prepared to acknowledge them.

By the end of the afternoon, the three of us had piles of ingredients prepped and ready to be combined into a dozen delicious dishes. Despite my misgivings about Violet's interest in Jack and my lingering doubts about the angels, it had been a lovely afternoon. Clearly, I needed to get out more. I hugged Violet and Lucina before leaving, effectively co-opting any administration of "the Lady's blessing." I had pretty much come to terms with the notion that Lucina had a role to play, but that didn't mean I had to be her unthinking audience.

Driving home from the Abbey, I noticed that a few flakes of snow were starting to fall. Despite the cold, I rolled down my window. The evening was utterly still, hushed but for the low hum of my tires on the road. It felt as though I had stepped out of time into an eternal forest, like one in a fairy tale. Quietly, I hummed "Silent Night" as I drove.

When I got home, Andrew had lit a fire in the parlor fireplace. It was warm and inviting, and when I sat down on the couch to enjoy it, Honoré appeared out of nowhere and settled onto my lap. I found myself thinking of Christopher Cunningham and discovered, for the first time, that I was able to take Bella's advice and recall him as "my father" without too much bitterness. As she had said, he had not been the perfect parent, but I had not been the perfect daughter, either. Maybe it was time to lay my resentments to rest with his ghost.

Bella came out of the kitchen wiping her hands on a dish towel. "Richard called while you were out, Katie," she said. "He told me to tell you that he's out in Minnesota visiting his grandmother, and he couldn't call on Christmas Day because they had a major storm. The phone lines were down all over, and he couldn't charge his cell phone because the power was out. He said to say 'Merry Christmas,' and that he hopes you're coming to the Abbey for New Year's Eve so he can see you."

My heart fluttered just a little. Ridiculous, really.

Half-hiding a smile, Bella started back to the kitchen. "Come help me finish putting dinner together, Katie. Oh, and one more thing," she said, turning back. "Richard said to tell you that he thinks he might have found someone you were looking for. Judy, or Janet… Oh, golly, what was it? I knew I should have written it down."

"Was it Jeanine? Jeanine Powell?" I asked, my heart quickly switching from a delicate flutter to out-and-out pounding.

"That's it," Bella said, relieved. "He said he would tell you all about it at the New Year's Eve party. You *are* going, aren't you, Katie? I told him I thought you were, but I wasn't sure."

"Wild horses couldn't keep me away," I assured her.

Archangel Uriel speaks:

In hindsight, I probably should have disguised myself before engaging Kate in conversation on the library steps. She was Gabriel's project, not mine, after all. We rarely interfere in one another's work without an express invitation.

But Kate seemed so lost that night, and Gabriel was so disappointed that she kept resisting his efforts. Offering her a little perspective simply seemed like the right thing to do. I acted on impulse, a rare occurrence for me. Fleetingly, I wondered whether I might have cause to regret it.

You see, it never occurred to me that Kate might recognize me from the portrait in the Abbey library. My good friend Rembrandt van Rijn had persuaded me to sit for him in Holland more than three hundred years before. He and everyone else who knew me at the time had long since passed on and come home to Heaven. Honestly, I had not given the painting a passing thought in centuries.

Thankfully, my intervention did no harm. Lucina distracted Kate well enough. The whole incident was an excellent reminder to me to be more careful if and when I talk with Kate again, however. Despite her endless preoccupation with herself and her own problems, Kate was proving to be remarkably perceptive. It was Gabriel's job to guide Kate to her destiny, not mine. He wouldn't thank me if I tipped her off too soon.

Gabriel likes to say that the whole purpose of Angel Abbey is to provide a place where anyone can come to get what he or she most needs. It struck me that Kate might be exactly what Gabriel needed himself. I just wondered whether he was ready for her.

CHAPTER TWENTY-SEVEN

Maybe wild horses could not have kept me away from Angel Abbey on New Year's Eve, but the two feet of snow that fell overnight and through the next morning kept me housebound for two days. Our power went out, for real this time, and the roads were a mess. There wasn't much to do but read and drowse by the fire. Honoré loved it, luxuriating in the heat, as he sprawled across my lap or stretched out at my side. Sometimes it seems to me that no one can relax more extravagantly than a well-loved Siamese cat. "Lazy bum," I mock scolded him, rumpling his ears. He looked up at me, closed his eyes in utter contentment, and purred.

Richard didn't call again, and I decided against calling him. If our relationship had been strictly business I would have been on the phone with him in a heartbeat, but there were personal undertones between us that I did not quite understand or, more likely, was not prepared to address. That disastrous kiss with Jack had left me wary of taking up with anybody else. After all the recent changes in my life, I clearly was not ready for a romantic relationship. I liked Richard, though, and he seemingly liked me better than I had feared. I didn't want to lose the opportunity to date him if I ever managed to get my act together.

I spent a few hours going through the last of the closets and drawers in the house, looking for anything that might still be worth keeping or giving away. There wasn't much. Bella and I had done a pretty thorough job of digging out already. Still, it was something to do.

In the room where my father had slept during his last months, I found an empty prescription bottle, half-hidden under the bed. It reminded me that I had never contacted his nurse, Paula, to thank her for taking such good care of him before he died. It was an embarrassing oversight, but one that could still be rectified if I called her right away.

Despite the power outage, we still had phone service. But when I tried to reach Paula at the last number she had given me, a woman who identified herself as Paula's former roommate informed me that Paula had moved back to Utica. No, she had not left a forwarding number. Yes, if she heard from Paula, she would have her get in touch with me. The woman was polite enough, but her brisk tone made it clear that the conversation was at an end.

Hanging up, I had the distinct sense that I had dropped an important ball. In many ways, Paula had been more like a dutiful daughter to my father than I had been. I regretted having lost the opportunity to thank her for her kindness to him.

It was late afternoon on the second day after the snowstorm when our power finally came back on, much to Bella's relief. Checking the perishables in the refrigerator, she happily proclaimed them fit to eat, and went off to take a shower now that the water heater was working again. Andrew said he would finish shoveling out our drive and then get cleaned up himself.

Alone in the parlor, I was busy sketching Honoré when there was a quiet knock on the front door. I quickly drew in a last whisker, put down my pad, and went to see who had come to visit. Thinking it might be Richard back from his trip or even Lucina, I was surprised to see Amy on my doorstep, bundled up in a parka and scarf, her hands tucked into her pockets.

"Amy, come on in," I said, waving her inside. "It's nice of you to drop by. Let me take your coat."

Amy gave me her things and let me hustle her into the living room, where Honoré was sprawled in front of the fire. "Ooh, what a beautiful cat!" she said eagerly. "May I pet him?"

"He'll never forgive you if you don't," I answered, smiling. "This is Honoré. Honoré, meet Amy." Honoré inclined his head in a lordly manner, and Amy gently stroked his fur.

"This is a nice surprise, Amy. Things have been too quiet around here since the snowstorm. Can I get you anything? A cup of tea or something?" I had no idea why she had come by, but it seemed rude just to flat-out ask why she was there.

"No, I'm fine," she quickly said. "I just wanted to ask you something." Amy paused as if searching for just the right words, and I forced myself to hold still.

"I was going to talk to you when you next came to the Abbey, but you always seem so busy when you're there, and I didn't want to disturb you," she began.

"The thing is, I'll be finishing my junior year in college in the spring, and my parents want me to decide now what to do when I graduate," Amy continued. "My father's pushing me to apply to law school. He says practicing law is steady work for good money, but nobody in my family has ever been a lawyer before, and I'm not sure it's the right career for me. I asked the Lady about it, and she told me to come talk with you."

"So you came over here in two feet of snow to ask me *that?*" I asked.

Amy shrank back against the couch. My tone had been too harsh. "I thought about just calling you instead," she explained, apologetically. "I live pretty close, though, and my dad's SUV has four-wheel drive, so I decided to just come over and see if you were home. Should I come back another day? Is this a bad time?"

"Not at all," I said quickly, kicking myself for coming on too strong. "Your question just surprised me, that's all. Let me think for a second."

Amy *had* surprised me. Her innocent question about going to law school because her father thought she should landed on me like a ton of bricks. For an instant, I flashed back to my dream of my own father forcing me to step out onto a boardwalk over roiling seas filled with blind, ravenous sharks. That was what my subconscious mind thought of the practice of law. How could I recommend that anyone else risk those dangerous waters?

In that moment, it was as though my nineteen-year-old self had appeared out of the past to ask whether she should go to law school. I wanted to tell her *no*, don't do it, do *anything* else, but don't let your future be destroyed by the bitter ambitions of an angry old man! Amy was not my nineteen-year-old self, though. The career choice that had worked out so badly for me might be perfect for her. I forced myself to focus on her face and speak as calmly as I could.

"Amy, tell me what you like to do," I began. "How are your grades? What's your major? What are your favorite subjects?"

"Well, I'm majoring in computer tech, plus I really enjoy art and music," Amy replied. She quickly rattled off a long list of favorite topics and hobbies, all related to computers and the arts. She created and managed the website for her college theater troupe, designed all the show posters, and maintained what she called the "social media."

"Facebook, Twitter, Pinterest, Instagram, YouTube, all of those," she summarized. "You know what I mean."

Actually, I had only the barest notion. Busy lawyers do not have a lot of time to play online. Not wanting to distract her, though, I just nodded as she went on. She belonged to a couple of computer clubs, she played virtual games online, she performed in college plays and sang soprano in the choir. She had an A-minus average, and her SAT scores had been high enough to be the envy of any aspiring college applicant. If she wanted to go to law school, she certainly had the academic credentials to succeed.

"Oh, and I maintain the event schedule and handle all the e-mails and other online contacts for Angel Abbey," she added. "The Lady doesn't like computers. She leaves everything like that to me."

Interesting, I thought. It was not inconsistent with Lucina's public persona—too otherworldly to bother with anything as practical as managing a calendar—but it told me that Amy had to be pretty capable. Angel Abbey could be a madhouse of activity, but it was always so perfectly choreographed that you could imagine the invisible hands of angels nudging everyone into their proper places at the perfect time. Lucina would never leave something so important to someone who was not supremely competent. It was almost funny to think that those angelic hands hung from the wrists of a pretty, self-effacing college student.

"Amy, have you ever done anything with student government? What about Model UN or the debate club? Do you like to argue?" I asked.

"Oh no," she answered, clearly aghast. "Those things scare me to death. I hate fighting. I like to do research, though. Maybe that would be useful in law school."

A would-be lawyer who hated to argue? It wasn't promising, but it wasn't a deal-breaker, either. Again, I forced myself to stop and think. "It could be," I said, careful to keep my tone neutral. "Research can be very important in law. And you don't have to love fighting to be a lawyer, though it helps in court. There are lots of different ways to practice law.

"I have to ask you, though," I continued, leaning closer to her. "Amy, do you *want* to be a lawyer? If you could do anything in the world, would you go to law school? Somehow, I don't think you'd be asking me if you did. If you really wanted to be a lawyer, you'd just do it. So what is it that you'd rather do instead?"

Amy's eyes filled with tears, but she forced them back. It was something I had done countless times myself. Watching her, I began to get angry on her behalf. Why should this lovely young woman have to suppress her feelings that way? Why shouldn't she do exactly what she wanted for a living?

"I'd rather work at Angel Abbey," Amy admitted. "The Lady wouldn't have to pay me much. I could be the manager or the IT specialist or something. I could keep everything running smoothly, so she could concentrate on other things, and the people who came to the Abbey could just relax and enjoy themselves without worrying about whether there would be somewhere for them to get together.

"I'm good at that," Amy insisted, "but my dad says it wouldn't be a real job. He doesn't trust the Lady. He says she would just take advantage of me. He thinks she's some kind of phony or something."

I suppressed a wry smile. "He's not the only person who ever thought that," I replied. "But this isn't about Lucina. It's about you. Have you asked her for a job after graduation?"

"Not yet," Amy said. "The Lady told me to talk to you, so I thought I'd do that first. So you don't think I should go to law school?" She was visibly relieved.

"Not unless you really, really want to," I replied. "There are an awful lot of lawyers already, so it's hard to find work even if you ace law school. Besides, you strike me as a very nice person, and the law isn't a profession for nice people anymore, if it ever was." The image of a smirking Roy Blackwell flashed into my mind, and I shook my head to drive it away.

"There are many ways to practice law, though," I continued, "and some of them are nicer than others. I didn't choose a very nice path, and my choices got me in trouble later. You might have a different experience. You know Richard Helmsworth, right?"

"Sure," Amy said eagerly. "He works with the middle-school group. Is he a lawyer too?"

"He is, and he's a good one," I replied. "You didn't know that about him?"

"No," Amy said. "He never talks about work when he's at the Abbey. I thought he was a schoolteacher or something."

"No, Richard's a lawyer," I assured her. "In fact, he's my lawyer. Like I said, my choices have gotten me in some pretty serious trouble, and Richard's helping me to straighten things out. Helping people work through their problems is the best part of being a lawyer," I went on, wishing I had figured that out before accepting a partnership-track position in Manhattan. "His practice is very different than mine was. You should talk with Richard, too."

"Different than your practice 'was'?" Amy asked. "Aren't you a lawyer anymore?"

I sighed, a little sorry not to have chosen my words with more care. "Yes, I am still a lawyer, but I'm not practicing at the moment. I lost my job a few months ago, and I'm taking a break to figure out what to do next."

"I'm so sorry," Amy replied. She shyly put her hand on my arm but pulled it right back, as if afraid she had been too forward. "You'll figure it out, though. You're the most dynamic woman I've ever met. Everyone at the Abbey thinks you're absolutely amazing."

Really? That was news to me. "Thanks, Amy. You're nice to say so. Just promise me you'll talk to Richard before you make a final decision about going to law school."

It may have seemed as if I were passing the buck by steering Amy toward Richard. But he appeared to be content as a country lawyer. Shy, sensitive Amy would not last a year on Wall Street, but a practice like Richard's might suit her fine. And given that my high-powered Wall Street practice had blown up in my face, I wondered whether I was really qualified to advise anybody about going into law.

Then another thought occurred to me. "You know, there would be nothing wrong with taking a year off after college to work at the Abbey and see how you like being there full-time," I suggested. "When I was in law school, the students who had taken time off to work after graduation tended to do better than the ones who came straight out of college anyway. You could tell your dad that, or I will, if you'd like. He might not push you so hard if you promise to reconsider law school after a year of working at the Abbey."

"That's a great idea!" Amy beamed. "Do you think the Lady would hire me?"

"From what I've seen, Lucina would be crazy *not* to hire you," I assured her. "Anybody who can keep the Abbey calendar running so smoothly has to be a genius." Amy smiled, and I noticed again how pretty she was. "Now, how about a cup of tea? I'm sure Honoré would love a little of your undivided attention." She nodded eagerly, and I went off to the kitchen to put the kettle on.

When I came back a few minutes later with two mugs of tea, Honoré had rolled over onto his back, and Amy was softly stroking his tummy. "He's a beautiful kitty," she breathed. "Have you had him long?"

"Most of my life," I replied, setting down the mugs. "He must really like you. Honoré's usually a lot more reserved with people he doesn't know."

"Have you ever thought about putting him on the Internet?"

"No," I answered, mystified. "Why would I?"

"Cat videos are the most popular things online," she said, amazed that I didn't know. "They get more hits than practically anything. He'd be a star in no time."

Honoré flipped onto his side, blinked at me, and yawned theatrically.

"I don't think he wants to be a star," I smiled.

"Could I just take a video of him anyway?" she persisted.

"Sure, I guess. What harm could it do?"

Instantly all business, Amy whipped out her cell phone and motioned for me to move back from the couch. She looked around and turned on a couple of lamps, evidently having decided that firelight alone was not bright enough for what she had in mind. "Does he have any toys?" she asked.

"Yeah, he does," I replied, looking around. The red pom-pom dragon peeked out from under the skirt of Bella's favorite chair. "Here," I said, pulling it out and holding it up for her to see. "He just got this one for Christmas. Will it be OK?"

"Perfect!" she exclaimed, pointing her phone at Honoré. He looked up at her, curious. "Now, when I motion to you, just toss it to him gently, OK?"

Bemused, I nodded. She pushed a button, mouthed a silent countdown—"Three, two, one..."—and pointed one finger at me.

I tossed the dragon to Honoré. He caught it neatly in one paw and then astonished me by attacking it with all four. Any thought I'd had that he might be getting old vanished in an instant. My normally dignified companion assaulted that toy with the passionate intensity of a six-week-old kitten, throwing it into the air and slamming it onto the couch. Then, just as abruptly, he reverted to his usual stately self. Placing one paw on the vanquished dragon, he looked up at Amy's camera for a moment or two, striking a pose like a conquering hero.

I was amazed. "What in Heaven's name was *that?*" I demanded. He favored me with a lofty stare, then rolled over and pretended to go to sleep.

Amy was as elated as I was astonished. "That was *awesome*!" she cried. "And I caught every bit of it. Would it be OK if I put him up online? *Please?*"

I thought for a moment, but there seemed no reason to refuse. "Oh, heck, why not?" I finally said. "I haven't seen him play like that in a long time. Might as well let the big guy have his fifteen minutes of fame."

"Fantastic!" Amy said. "Let me work with the recording a little bit first. I'll send you the link when it's done. What's your e-mail address?"

"You know, I don't think I have one anymore," I answered. "I always used my e-mail at the office, but they've undoubtedly taken that down. To be honest with you, Amy, I never really used e-mail except for work."

"I'm starting to understand why I might not want to be a lawyer," Amy replied. "You don't get much time to have a life, do you?"

"No, you really don't. Or at least I didn't. Richard might tell you something else."

"OK, then, I'll set you up a personal e-mail account," she said. "It's easy, and you'll need it to get around the Internet. How have you managed since you lost your e-mail at work?"

Embarrassed, I admitted that I hadn't been near the Internet since coming back to Angel Falls. Amy's eyes widened, but she was too tactful to say anything critical. "OK, then. I'll have everything ready for you by New Year's Eve. You're coming to the party, aren't you?"

"Wild horses couldn't keep me away," I said, for the second time in three days.

"Great! I'll bring you everything then." Amy quickly hugged me, then pulled back as if afraid she had overstepped. "I need to get home. Dad is going to want to know what you said. Thanks for helping me hold him off."

Amy leaned over and petted Honoré, who stretched and purred at her touch. "Can't wait to get Honoré online. People are just going to *love* him! Thanks for the tea and advice. See you at the party!" She hurried out the front door, and I waved as her SUV pulled away.

Walking back into the parlor, I picked up the red pom-pom dragon from where Honoré had left it on the couch. "OK, big guy, comin' at ya," I said, and tossed the toy to him. He ignored it, gazing at me with the contemptuous expression of an offended emperor. The dragon landed on the floor and lay there, untouched.

"Crazy cat," I muttered, and went off to take a shower.

Archangel Ariel speaks:

As the angel in charge of Nature, I am especially interested in the nonhuman souls who share your world. The birds, the beasts, the fish, the insects, everything that walks or crawls or swims or flies in the natural world is my special concern. I know the dreams of dolphins in the depths of the Atlantic, the worries of ants when no food can be found, and the ecstasies of hippopotami as they wallow in the mud of the Nile.

My angels and I watch over domesticated animals as well. The loyalty of dogs to their human companions, the ways they seek constantly to please, endear them to my heart. The gentle generosity of cattle, the inquisitive intelligence of pigs, the dignity of turkeys, the power and nobility of horses… I know them, and I love them all.

Like humans, though, we angels have our preferences. In Heaven I am known as the Lion of God, and all felines, large and small, are my special favorites. It grieves me every time a great cat is killed for sport in the jungles or on the African plains. Likewise, it delights me whenever anyone is astute enough to form a special friendship with a cat of any kind, from the mightiest lion to the tiniest kitten.

Honoré was a remarkable cat, a wise and sensitive soul. He had all but raised Kate, and she loved him as dearly as he did her. They were such a blessing to one another! It gladdened my heart to see them together.

The ancient Egyptians worshipped cats as gods. While that might have been a trifle excessive, it was preferable to the violence that too many of you visit on my beautiful little friends. Understand this: cats are the visible embodiment of the grace of God. Their love cannot be demanded, but it is a sublime gift when freely given to someone who appreciates their beauty and takes pleasure in their company.

The Creator blesses all souls who have the wisdom to treat cats kindly. So, for that matter, do my angels and I.

CHAPTER TWENTY-EIGHT

By New Year's Eve the roads were clear, and we were all eager to get out of the house. My biggest problem was deciding what to wear. In Manhattan, the mandatory wardrobe choice for New Year's Eve was a little black dress and skyscraper heels. Unfortunately, though, the little black dress I had brought home from the city had grown unflatteringly tight since I had stopped forcing myself to starve for the sake of my professional image.

Time was, I would have beaten myself up for gaining a couple of pounds. Now, I was glad to be rid of a dress that reminded me of the harsh, unhappy woman I had been not so long before. One more item to donate to the Abbey, I thought, tossing the offending garment into the corner and rummaging through my closet for something else to wear.

In the end, I settled on the rose silk dress I had worn for my first meeting with Lucina. It was a pretty color and still a flattering fit, so why not? Putting my hair up in a loose knot and accessorizing the dress with crystal earrings, a clutch purse, and dressy pumps made it look downright festive. I wore a little more makeup than usual and, on a whim, a spritz of the cologne that Jack had given me for my birthday.

Andrew let out a teasing wolf whistle when I came downstairs, and Bella playfully smacked his shoulder. "You look beautiful, Katie," she said, smiling.

"You look pretty spiffy yourselves," I answered. Andrew was decked out in a dark blue suit and striped red tie. Not to be outdone, Bella wore a garnet-red velvet dress that set off her dark coloring to perfection. She wore a little makeup, unusual for her, along with heavy gold hoop earrings, and she had arranged her hair in a braid that wrapped around her head like a coronet. More than ever, she looked like a Gypsy queen.

"I'll be escorting the two belles of the ball," Andrew cheerfully said, and went to warm up the car.

When we arrived at the Abbey, the festivities were already in full swing. The barn had been transformed into a welcoming party venue, lit with thousands of tiny white lights and warmed with patio heaters. Round tables, carefully arranged around a big open dance floor, had been set with white tablecloths, low bowls of flowers, and glimmering candles. The ingredients that Violet, Lucina, and I had prepared a few days before had been transformed into a huge, delectable buffet, and I wondered whether Violet had taken up residence at the Abbey and cooked her way through the snowstorm. There was a band playing Glenn Miller favorites, and the room was crammed with happy people, laughing, drinking, talking, and dancing.

We found Pastor St. James sitting at an otherwise empty table. He wished us a happy New Year and invited us to join him. The band started playing "String of Pearls," and Andrew and Bella went off to dance. I had barely set down my wrap and bag before Amy came bounding over to me, all smiles. "You're here!" she exclaimed happily. "Thank you so much for your advice—it was perfect! I talked to my dad, and he agreed to let me work at the Abbey for a year while I figure out what to do next. Now all I have to do is ask the Lady." She lowered her voice a little. "Would you put in a good word for me? She really thinks a lot of you."

That was news to me, but it was not unwelcome. "You bet," I assured her. "That's great about your dad. No sense wasting time and money on tuition if you're not sure about going into law." I glanced away from her, looking over the crowd. "Did you have a chance to talk to Richard yet? I think he's coming to the party tonight if you haven't caught up with him yet."

"He's already here," Amy replied, "and we set up an appointment to talk next week. Thanks so much for suggesting it! Oh, and I've got something for you."

Amy reached into her pocket and pulled out two small slips of paper. The first one had an e-mail address and "Password: Honore123" written on it. "Here's your new e-mail account information," she told me. "I set it all up for you, and it's free. Just log in and change your password whenever it's convenient. I used Honoré's name for now, but you can make it whatever you want."

The second piece of paper was a raffle ticket. "That's for the drawing they'll hold just before midnight," Amy explained. "We always raffle off prizes for our volunteers on New Year's Eve to thank them for their work during the year. Miss Flo and I have been working for weeks to get all the donations together. Good luck!" She bounced away as energetically as she had arrived. I smiled and tucked the pieces of paper safely away in my purse.

Without knowing it, Amy had solved one problem for me but created another. My father had not owned a computer, having declared the Internet to be the "secret weapon that would destroy civilization." I didn't agree but, relying on my computer at work and my cell phone, I had never bothered to buy a computer for personal use. When I lost my job, I lost my office computer and access to the firm's Internet account, and with them, the ability to go online. The idea of spending several hundred dollars on a new computer did not have a lot of appeal. Still, it would be almost impossible to find another job without one. I decided to look for a computer during the January sales, hoping to find something that would not be prohibitively expensive.

I headed for the bar to get a glass of wine, but people kept stopping me to ask about Christmas and wish me a happy New Year. My dress drew lots of compliments, and I found myself having a better time than expected. Who needed a date for New Year's Eve?

You never knew whom you might meet at Angel Abbey, and that evening was no exception. Halfway to the bar, I was accosted by Miss Flo, who introduced me to a small, bespectacled Asian man. "Kate, dear, this is Mr. Han," she said. "He'll be teaching art classes here starting in January. You have such an artistic eye, I thought you should meet him and maybe sign up."

An artistic eye? Me? Wondering how she had come to that conclusion, I smiled and shook hands with Mr. Han. He looked me up and down critically and asked, "Can you draw?"

"A little, just for fun," I admitted. "I mostly do sketches of my cat."

Mr. Han's face split into a wide grin. "Ah, a cat lover! So am I. So was Confucius, by the way. They say that one day, Confucius was writing at his desk in his favorite silk kimono. His cat came, curled up on his sleeve and fell asleep. When Confucius finished working and had to leave, he cut the sleeve off his kimono so he could stand up without awakening his cat."

"Really?" I replied, charmed. "I hadn't heard that story before, but I like it. My cat would definitely approve."

"Have you ever tried sculpture or pottery?" Mr. Han asked.

"Not since high school. I've been kind of busy with my career."

"Work should never take precedence over the arts," the little man declared. "Come to my art class on Wednesday night and we will see what you can do." He nodded and walked away.

I turned and nearly ran into Richard, who was standing behind me with a glass of wine in each hand. "Happy New Year," he said, grinning and offering one to me. "I've been watching you trying to get to the bar for the last half hour and decided to bring you a drink before you expire of thirst. You certainly have a lot of friends here, Kate."

"I don't know about that, but I'm grateful for the wine," I replied, smiling. "How was your Christmas? Bella said you were out in Minnesota someplace."

His grin faded. "Yeah, I was in St. Paul visiting my grandmother. I don't think she'll be with us much longer. She's nearly ninety. I'm really going to miss her when she goes. We were very close when I was little."

Before I could reply, Richard reached into his pocket and pulled out a piece of paper. "I started hunting around the Internet for you." Handing me his glass, he unfolded the paper to reveal a picture of a young black woman in a baseball cap and sweatshirt jacket. "Does this woman look familiar to you?"

The picture was a little blurry, but there was no question about who the woman was. "That's Jeanine Powell! How did you find her?" I demanded.

Richard grinned again. "Facebook, m'dear, Facebook. I just looked up all of the Jeanine Powells and then eliminated the ones who were the wrong age or who lived in the wrong parts of the country. According to her profile, she lives outside of Asheville, North Carolina, in a town called Old Fort." He cocked an eyebrow at me.

"OK, so it wasn't Louisiana or Mississippi," I admitted, handing the glass back to him. "At least I was right about it being in the South. Have you tried contacting her?"

"Not yet," he replied, tucking the picture back into his pocket. "I wanted to make sure I had the right Jeanine Powell first. Besides, it's usually impossible to reach anybody over the holidays. I'll try her next week. Have you eaten yet?" I shook my head. "Come with me, then. Violet has cooked up an incredible feast for us."

Richard took me by the elbow and steered me over to the buffet table, which was loaded down with Violet's aromatic creations. We each filled our plates and refilled our wineglasses, then headed back to my table for dinner. Pastor St. James was nowhere to be seen, and Bella and Andrew were still dancing away. That meant we had the table to ourselves, which afforded me a very welcome opportunity to have dinner alone with Richard.

I half-expected him to update me on the lawsuit as we ate, but Richard refused to talk about it until after the party. Instead, he regaled me with tales of his visit to Minnesota. The blizzard he had weathered put our little snowstorm to shame. He had been stuck for days in his grandmother's house with no power or heat.

Richard made the trip sound like a grand adventure, describing marathon card games by candlelight with his grandmother and cooking meals on top of her gas stove by lighting the burners with matches. He portrayed his grandmother as a tough, cheerful matriarch who had ruled her family with a lot of love and gumption. His grandfather had died of cancer when she was thirty, leaving her to raise his mother alone. She had gone to work as a secretary, moonlighting as a church singer when opportunities to make a little extra money arose. "She still has a terrific voice," Richard said admiringly. "Get her going, and she'll sing all of Handel's *Messiah* if you're willing to listen."

"She sounds amazing," I said. "Were your parents there with you?"

Richard's smile disappeared. "My folks divorced when I was sixteen. Dad moved to St. Paul for work a few years later and married again. His second wife was a nice enough woman, but we were never close. Dad died of a massive heart attack about six years ago. Too many Minnesota cheese curds, I guess. His widow went back to her family in St. Paul, and I kind of lost track of her.

"My mother never remarried," he continued. "She worked as an elementary school teacher when I was growing up, but she loves to paint, and she always wanted to be the next Georgia O'Keeffe. After I graduated from high school, Mom moved to Sedona because she loved the desert light. Her work has gotten better now that she's painting almost full-time, and she's been pretty successful selling her stuff to the New Age tourists. She's gotten sort of flaky since she moved out there, though. She claims to communicate with angels. Can you believe it?"

"Communicate how?" I asked. "You mean, she prays? Lights candles? Has visions or something?"

"No, she says she has actual conversations with real angels that she can physically see." Richard sounded amused and a little discomfited at the same time. "She does angel card readings for people who come to see her. It pays her rent when she hasn't sold a canvas in a while.

"But art is Mom's real passion," Richard went on. "She insists that an angel named Joe-something-or-other sits next to her easel and gives her artistic advice while she paints. It's harmless, I guess, but it freaks me out. I don't go visit her much. Either she's crazy, which isn't much fun to think about, or there's actually something supernatural hanging around her house. Whatever it is, it's a little too 'woo-woo' for me. Besides, plane tickets are expensive for a poor country lawyer," he joked.

I patted his hand. "Have you asked Lucina about it? She's the 'Lady of Angel Abbey,' after all. If anybody could tell you what's going on, it would probably be her."

"Not yet," Richard admitted. "To tell you the truth, I find the whole thing a little embarrassing. Don't get me wrong, I love hanging out at the Abbey, but it's because of the volunteer work I do here and the friends I get to see. I don't come looking for angels. And the 'Lady' stuff around Lucina, like she was a duchess or something, always struck me as a little contrived. She packages herself really well, but it's still just an act, I think."

"Richard, that may be the most perceptive thing I've ever heard you say," I replied, beaming at him. But before I could tell him about discovering at Christmas that Lucina had been an actress, a few people started tapping their glasses with spoons. Others joined in, and soon the hall was ringing with the crystalline chime of silver on glass. The band played the last few notes of "Saint Louis Blues," and the dancers all returned to their tables. Pastor St. James resumed his seat on Richard's right, while Bella and Andrew sat to my left. Soon, there were only a few whispers and a cough or two, as everyone in the room settled down to listen.

Lucina stepped out onto the dance floor, smiling brilliantly. She was dressed in a long, beaded ivory gown that left her arms bare except for strings of tiny golden beads that dangled from her shoulders, swinging as she walked. Glittery earrings and golden sandals completed her ensemble. Her auburn hair tumbled fetchingly to her shoulders, and I had no doubt that everyone near her was getting a good whiff of her spicy perfume. Miss Flo walked proudly beside her, all in periwinkle and making unobtrusive use of a brass-handled ebony cane. Amy followed behind, pushing a tea cart laden with a tower of gift-wrapped boxes and a fishbowl full of raffle tickets.

"Good evening, everyone, and happy New Year!" Lucina cried merrily, her voice pitched to the crowd. There were a few cries of "Happy New Year!" in response, but most of the guests were silent, eagerly hanging on Lucina's every word.

"We have had an incredible year at the Abbey," Lucina declared. "Thanks to your generous donations of time and treasure, we have been able to provide the less fortunate members of our community with thousands of pounds of nutritious food, tens of thousands of dollars' worth of financial and in-kind contributions, and—best of all—the love and support of every one of our dedicated Angel Abbey volunteers. We have offered almost one hundred artists the chance to showcase their talents and launch their professional careers, provided dozens of worthy organizations with meeting space free of charge, and given every one of you the opportunity to work and play together as a loving family."

Lucina certainly knew how to work a crowd, I thought, as my fellow partygoers let loose with an explosion of cheers, whistles, and applause. Glancing over at Richard, I noticed that he was clapping politely but did not seem especially dazzled by Lucina. Maybe he was even smarter than I had realized.

"Now, as is our tradition at Angel Abbey, we are going to take this opportunity to end the year by thanking all of you for your many contributions and distributing some prizes that have been donated by our local merchants," Lucina went on. "All of you have done so much that we cannot possibly decide who gets what, so we are going to raffle off the gifts and trust the good angels of the Abbey to put everything into the best possible hands." As the crowd laughed I wondered for just an instant whether Lucina, like Richard's mother, actually believed she could talk to angels. She had never said anything of the kind in my hearing, though. I decided she was just making a pun on the Abbey's name.

"But before we do that," Lucina continued, "could I please get a round of applause for our own Violet Markham, the talented chef who prepared our magnificent dinner tonight?" Violet stood and waved to thunderous applause, looking flushed and pretty in a purple gown. It occurred to me that I probably should introduce Violet to Jack at some point, but the idea was still mildly troubling. It was more comfortable to focus on Lucina instead.

When the applause died down, Lucina spoke up again. "I am going to turn the floor over to Miss Flo and Amy, who coordinated the raffle this year. Amy is going to hold the bowl while Miss Flo draws the winners, and I am going to step back so no one can say I had any influence on the results." She withdrew to the nearest table, followed by the laughter of the crowd.

Miss Flo began drawing raffle tickets from the bowl and calling out numbers. Everyone pulled out their tickets and waited to see whether their number would be called. There were a lot of prizes, more than the little tea cart could possibly hold. Many of the donated items were physically small, such as movie tickets and gift certificates from local shops and restaurants. There were larger items, too: baskets of spa items and gourmet foods, handmade jewelry, bottles of wine, various creations from the artists who worked at the Abbey, even sporting goods and tools. I could not imagine how Amy and Miss Flo had managed to cram them all onto the cart. The gifts kept coming, though, so they had clearly figured it out somehow.

"*Loaves and fishes, darling,*" an amused voice whispered from behind me. I looked around, but no one was there. I must have imagined it, I thought, turning back to the raffle.

There seemed to be something on that little tea cart for everyone in attendance, and amazingly, every item was perfectly suited to the person who won it. Bella won a garnet clip that tucked becomingly into her hair. Andrew was delighted to win a tool belt with dozens of loops and pockets, telling us that the belt he had used for a decade had finally worn through and broken. He had planned to buy another, but now there was no need. Pastor St. James received a leather-bound devotional that was exactly like one he had read every morning before it mysteriously disappeared from his office one day. Richard, one of the big winners, got a voucher for a free round-trip airline ticket.

"Now you can go visit your mother," I whispered to him. He pretended to elbow me, and we both chuckled.

The raffle drawing continued for well over an hour. Everybody won something, and everybody was delighted with what they won. There didn't seem to be any order to the prizes—something expensive might be followed by something fairly modest—but the winners were universally thrilled. Even the band got thank-you presents. I saw plenty of smiles, laughter, and some happy tears as the drawing went on and on. How were Miss Flo and Amy doing it? I wondered, but couldn't figure it out.

Although it initially seemed inexhaustible, the pile on the tea cart slowly dwindled down, until there were only three packages left. Then Miss Flo called my number, and Amy ran over to our table carrying a big, wrapped box. Opening it, I discovered a laptop computer, modem, wireless router, and a promotional coupon from the local cable service provider. It was everything I would need to set up Internet service at home, and I was stunned with gratitude. Amy threw her arms around my neck, beaming. "Everyone gets what she needs most at Angel Abbey," she whispered in my ear. Nonplussed, I hugged her back before she turned and rushed off to the dance floor.

There were two remaining boxes on the tea cart, presumably for Amy and Miss Flo. It occurred to me that, as the people responsible for running the raffle, they probably should not have participated. Everyone was so satisfied with his or her winnings, though, that it really didn't matter, and neither of them received anything expensive. Amy got a wooden box full of art supplies that could not have cost much. She looked thrilled with it. Miss Flo got a little bottle of cologne. It would not have meant a thing to me, but she cried when she opened it. "My mama used to wear this scent," she said, hugging Amy hard. "I've looked high and low but I haven't been able to find it in years. Don't know how you did, but thank you, honey."

That explained things, I thought—each must have chosen the present for the other. Then I realized that there had been no gift for Lucina. Of all the people at the party, she was the only one who had not gotten a thing. I was about to say something to Richard, when Miss Flo let go of Amy and turned back to the crowd.

"We have one more present, everybody," Miss Flo announced. "We all know a very special lady who brings us together and opens her home to all of us every day. Without her there would be no Angel Abbey, and all the good work we do here would be left undone. So to our own Lady, who makes all of this possible, we want to say a very special thank you."

Amy dragged a laughing Lucina to her feet and out onto the dance floor as the crowd applauded. As they came forward, Miss Flo reached into her pocket and pulled out a small, white silk drawstring bag. She and Amy presented it to Lucina, and the applause died down as everyone leaned forward to watch her open it.

Lucina admired the bag for a moment, clearly aware that every eye at the party was on her. Then she opened the bag, looked inside, and gasped. Slowly, she pulled out a gold necklace, and the crowd gasped back at her.

The center pendant of the necklace was about three inches long and two inches wide. A clear oval gem, roughly the size of a quail's egg, sparkled in the center, set in gold and embellished with filigree. What looked to be a ruby and an emerald, both marquise-cut, sat to either side of the crystal, and a small oval sapphire sat above it. Smaller crystals, rimmed in gold, and pearls dangled from tiny gold chains below. The gems were framed by outstretched gold wings, beautifully detailed. A gold chain extended from the tip of each wing to fasten the necklace at the nape of the wearer's neck. It was an incredible piece of handcrafted art, and I could not imagine where Amy and Miss Flo had found it, much less how they could possibly have paid for it. If the stones were real, Lucina's necklace would be worth more than a new car.

All of a sudden, my computer package didn't seem so lavish.

Amy held Lucina's hair out of the way as Miss Flo clasped the magnificent necklace around her neck. They stepped away, as the entire crowd rose to its feet in a standing ovation, roaring its approval. A tear glinted on Lucina's cheek, and she raised her hands again to silence the crowd. It took a moment or two longer for the applause to quiet, and she seemed to struggle for composure until people finally settled down.

"My dear friends," she began, "how can I possibly thank you enough? This is so beautiful, and so utterly unexpected." She turned to embrace Amy and Miss Flo, and then turned back to her audience. "I am grateful beyond words to all of you," Lucina continued. "But please remember this.

"Whatever success we have at the Abbey, whatever we are able to accomplish, whatever good we do or fun we have is all because of you," Lucina said. "Miss Flo was kind to say that I am the one who makes the work of Angel Abbey possible, but all I do each morning is open the doors. Everything else that happens here, all the good that gets done in our community, every blessing we share, every lovely memory we create comes from each and every one of you."

Her hand moved up to touch the necklace shining like a beacon at her throat. It was a pretty gesture to accompany a pretty speech, reminding me again that Lucina was nothing if not a skilled performer. "Tomorrow," she went on, "a new year begins, bringing us new opportunities to reach out and care for our community and one another. I will be honored and proud to wear this exquisite necklace as a constant reminder, to all of us, of what Angel Abbey stands for. Thank you for all the good that you have already done here, and for all the good you will do in the year to come. I am privileged to be among you. Happy New Year, everyone!"

Her guests shouted, stamped, whistled, and cheered as Lucina raised her other arm and pointed to the band. As they struck up "In the Mood," Lucina left the dance floor with Miss Flo, Amy pushing the now-empty tea cart behind them. Andrew helped Bella secure her new hair clip, and they went off to dance, along with at least a dozen other couples. Pastor St. James excused himself to thank Miss Flo and Amy for the gift. "I want to ask who donated it," he said. "Someone deserves a thank-you note for sure. I have missed my devotional, but I never quite got around to picking up another copy." He left the table, leaving Richard and me alone.

"Don't suppose you'd consider dancing with me, Kate?" Richard asked.

He looked so hopeful that I almost said yes. But the thought of making a fool of myself on the dance floor stopped me, and I shook my head. "Believe me, you'd be sorry if I did," I said, pretending to be playful. "Dancing was never my thing. Go see if Lucina or Violet will dance with you. We can catch up later tonight." Defeated, Richard walked away, and I was left alone to ponder the evening's events.

There was something about the raffle that troubled me. What kind of raffle was it, when everyone who participated was a winner? How had they managed to cram all of those gifts onto one small tea cart? And how was it that every single guest at the party had won the absolutely perfect prize?

Somebody had gone to a great deal of trouble to find the ideal gift for each recipient, pack it into an impossibly small space, and then make sure it landed in the right hands, while making the process look entirely random. That would mean keeping track of which ticket belonged to each of more than one hundred party guests, then digging out the proper gift at the proper time without slowing things down or making a single mistake. That was clearly impossible, so the raffle had to be rigged some other way. For the life of me, though, I could not figure out how it had been done.

Then there was Lucina's necklace, which was in a class by itself. Expensive as some of the raffle prizes had been—my own included—they all paled in comparison to the magnificent treasure she wore. Perhaps someone had donated a whole lot of money to buy Lucina's thank-you gift. Or maybe somebody was skimming donations to the Abbey so the "Lady" could dress up in style. Neither possibility pleased me very much.

I finished my wine and went to get another glass, working my way through the crowd of happy revelers. Richard, I noticed, had taken my suggestion and was dancing with Violet. Bella and Andrew were swing dancing as if they were teenagers again. Pastor St. James seemed to be fox-trotting with Lucina. He must have said something funny, because she tipped her head back and laughed, making the jewels in her necklace sparkle in the candlelight.

All of a sudden the party felt too hot, too frenetic, and too close. I threw back my wine and stumbled out of the barn into the courtyard. The night was icy cold and still, offering a welcome respite from the frenzied festivities in the barn. The sky was pitch black, apart from the stars that glittered across it like a million cousins to the gems at Lucina's throat. Alone, I walked around the empty courtyard, trying to make sense of my feelings.

In that moment, I missed Manhattan. I missed my little apartment, my occasional dinners with Jack, the unambiguous demands of life at the law firm. Maybe I hadn't been very happy or even very nice, but at least I'd had a clear-cut sense of who I was and what I was supposed to accomplish. That certainty had vanished with Christopher Cunningham's death, and nothing in my new life had replaced it.

There were too many mysteries at Angel Abbey, too many people I did not quite understand, too many opportunities to feel like an awkward, cynical outsider. Tears stung the base of my lashes. With no one watching, I let them quietly come.

Then I heard a bell somewhere strike twelve. The band struck up "Auld Lang Syne" amid cheers, horn toots, and cries of "Happy New Year!" The old year had passed and the new one had arrived, catching me alone in the cold and dark, while almost everyone I knew celebrated together in warmth and candlelight.

The darker part of me felt the pull of the temptation to feel sorry for myself, the sad little outcast again. But there was no denying that I was out in the cold—literally—by my own choice. Any of the people in that barn would have been happy to chat with me, and several of them had gone out of their way to befriend me even when I had not been very friendly in return.

Bella, bless her heart, had been right all along. Despite my earlier resolution to become a nicer person, I had fallen back into my bad habits of suspicion and self-isolation. The New Year had arrived though—time to try again.

I squared my shoulders and went back into the barn, grabbing a glass of champagne from a tray on a nearby table and swallowing enough of it to make anyone watching think I had participated in the midnight toast. Then I made my rounds, hugging everyone I knew at the party so each of them would think I had been occupied with someone else at the moment the clock struck twelve. I wished Richard a happy New Year, thanked Amy and Miss Flo for my new computer, tracked down Mr. Han to tell him how much I was looking forward to his art class on Wednesday, and joined in the revelry as enthusiastically as possible.

It didn't last long, of course. New Year's Eve parties usually draw to a close once midnight passes, and this one was no exception. It was about one o'clock when I thanked Lucina for a marvelous party and followed Bella and Andrew to the car. Richard insisted on carrying my new computer for me, and I let him, giving him a kiss on the cheek before climbing into the back seat. Andrew slid behind the wheel, started the engine, and before I knew it, we were safely home. After one more exchange of "Happy New Year," we headed off to our respective beds.

Honoré was curled up at the foot of my bed waiting for me. He looked up sleepily when I turned on the bedside light long enough to put my clothes away. I threw on some pajamas and climbed into bed. Honoré lumbered up, grumbling a little, and settled into his customary place on my shoulder. After I stroked his fur for a couple of minutes, he gently licked my cheek.

"Happy New Year, friend," I said. "Thanks for putting up with me." He settled his head against my neck, purring softly as we both fell asleep.

Archangel Jophiel speaks:

I will admit to being just a tad miffed by Richard's dismissive attitude toward his mother's talents and, for that matter, toward me. "Joe-something-or-other" indeed! His mother is a cherished friend of mine, and during my visits I have taught her more about color and artistic composition than she could have learned from mortal teachers in a thousand years. If that boy would ever swing by Sedona for a visit, he could see for himself. She is really very good.

Oh, well, at least Kate was beginning to get the message. Not that Gabriel was getting impatient, you understand—we angels never do—but the mortal life span is only so long. If she did not turn things around pretty quickly, Kate was not going to have time to get everything done before she had to come home to Heaven. Gabriel had been looking a little frazzled by it all, but Kate had free will. He could hint and whisper all he liked, but ultimately Gabriel could only pray that she would eventually get on board. We never force people, you know. Not like the Adversary and those drab little creatures that cater to his miserable self.

Anyway, it was a lovely party. Beautiful decorations, exquisite food, and so many gorgeous dresses! I especially enjoyed helping with the raffle, and could not resist tossing that "loaves and fishes" comment Kate's way. She was positively tying herself in knots trying to figure out how the ladies were making the impossible look easy. Silly darling!

Really, children, why are miracles so hard for you to accept? For the life of me, I will never understand why you all value cynicism so much. You have been given this lovely planet, delightful companions, and endless opportunities for joy. So why do you insist on wasting so much time sniffing suspiciously at every blessing you receive as if there must be cursed strings attached?

Some of you are so desperately proud of your intellects. It is marvelously funny, you know. Do you really imagine that you are more intelligent than the Creator? Can you possibly fool yourselves into thinking you have any hope of learning all there is to know in the short spans of your adorable little lives? It is deliciously ambitious of you, darlings, but decidedly impossible.

We do not get to create displays of infinite abundance anywhere near as often as I would like. If more of you would choose to believe in the miraculous, though, perhaps we could. Something to ponder, yes? But take your time. My angels and I will be here, patiently waiting and trying not to chuckle while you puzzle it all out.

CHAPTER TWENTY-NINE

My New Year's resolution to be a nicer person took me back to Angel Abbey again and again. Or at least that's what started my almost daily visits. In just a few weeks, the pleasure of being among friendly faces while doing real, substantial work became positively addictive. At the law firm I frequently went home after a fourteen-hour-day, having worked my brain to the point of complete exhaustion without producing anything tangible to show for it. Now, I could point to trays of food I had helped prepare for the homeless shelter on the south side of town, piles of donated clothes that I had sorted and boxed for distribution, children I had tutored, even props I had collected or sets I had helped paint for plays performed in the barn. When I fell into bed at the end of a long day at the Abbey, it was always with the sense that I had gotten my hands dirty for a good cause. I invariably slept well.

Mr. Han's art classes were frustrating at first. Among its many rooms, the Abbey had a well-equipped art studio, its shelves stacked with blank canvases and different kinds of paper, bins of paint and ink, and baskets crammed with pastels, crayons, pens, pencils, and brushes. A row of folded easels lined one wall, waiting to be set up and used. There were papier-mâché and plaster cloth for sculpting, as well as rolls of wire mesh and piles of newspaper for building armatures. There was a potter's wheel and a small mountain of clay, carefully wrapped in layers of plastic to keep it moist, along with a good-size kiln and pots of glaze.

The students put the supplies to good use. Unlike the art classes I remembered from high school, Mr. Han's class was a free-for-all, in which we each worked on the project of our choice rather than the same project all at once. Every student worked in a different medium and style, while our instructor roamed around the room, eyeing our creations and offering ideas and support.

For the first few classes I kept to what I knew, drawing still-life compositions and landscapes in charcoal or pastel. "Pretty-pretty," Mr. Han sniffed dismissively when he looked at them. It wasn't exactly encouraging, but at least it wasn't outright rejection. I kept trying.

At my fourth lesson Mr. Han pounced, grabbing me by the shoulders as I walked toward the paper bins and steering me toward the clay, despite my protestations that I had only ever drawn and painted. "Time for something new," he insisted. "If your art does not grow, it dies. Show me what you can do."

Mr. Han thunked a fist-size lump of clay on the table in front of me and walked away to help Miss Flo, who was carefully arranging crumpled sheets of hand-dyed paper, all different shades of blue, into a collage. He watched her carefully for several minutes, his eyes narrowing in concentration. "Add another color," he finally declared. "The world is never all one hue." Miss Flo, ever the blue lover, sighed in frustration. Later, though, I saw that she had added one tiny patch of yellow, carefully weathered with dry-brushed strokes of red and gray and half-hidden under a swatch of ultramarine. Mr. Han had been right—that touch of contrast brought her collage to life.

I wished fervently that my sculpture would be as cooperative. The clay felt cold and heavy in my fingers. No matter how I twisted and squeezed, it remained a lifeless, unappealing lump. I got a bowl of water and tried dampening it, but that only made the lump squishy and unworkable. Forty-five minutes into class, Mr. Han came by to check out the mess I had created. His face split in a broad grin.

"Good, good!" he exclaimed, sounding delighted. "You are already getting angry. I thought it would take many more classes than this!"

I looked up at him, annoyed, and noticed that I had managed to get clay in my hair somehow. "You're glad that I'm angry? Well, at least something's going right, but it sure isn't my sculpting. I can't do *anything* with this stuff!"

"Of course you cannot," he replied enthusiastically. "If you already knew what to do with it, the clay would be useless to you. You would just make me a pretty-pretty statue, like your pretty-pretty drawings. That would not teach you anything."

He leaned in so close that our noses were nearly touching, looking at me with absolute intensity. "Before you can be truly great at anything, you have to risk being bad," he whispered. "The clay is teaching you how to get past pretty-pretty. Go ahead and be angry. Be angry, and be frustrated, and be bored. Be a bad sculptor, and be honest about it. When you can be those things, *then* you can create." He stood up and patted my shoulder reassuringly. "Now, show me how bad you can be."

You want *bad?* I'll give you *bad,* I thought. For the rest of class, I did nothing but mess around with the clay. I squished it through my fingers, working it until it had dried out enough to retain a shape. I squeezed it, crushed it, rolled it into a ball in my palms then smashed the ball on the table. By the end of class, my hands and arms were filthy to the elbow, my section of the table looked like a mud-wrestling pit, and the clay was still a featureless lump. It didn't feel cold and stiff anymore, though. All the pounding and manipulation had warmed and elasticized it. Mr. Han came over and handed me a plastic scraper, which I used to remove most of the clay from the table and my hands. As he watched, I mashed the scrapings onto the remaining ball and dropped it into the plastic bag he held open in front of me. He closed the bag with a twist tie and then used a black Sharpie marker to write my name on it.

"Good," Mr. Han said. "Next week, you do it again." He gave me a quick nod of the head and then turned to wish Miss Flo a good night.

For the next four weeks, at Mr. Han's insistence I did nothing but mess with that same lump of clay. He would add a little more from time to time, whenever my experiments left too much on my hands or the table, keeping the amount constant. But the clay remained the same misshapen lump in the same plastic bag with my name on it, waiting for me at the studio every week, like a martyr awaiting the inquisitor's lash.

Mr. Han was right—spending ninety minutes every week wrestling with the same lump of clay made me angry, bored, and frustrated, and gave me plenty of opportunities to be a bad sculptor. I complained more than once, but he would only smile and walk away. Sometimes I had the distinct impression that it was all he could do not to laugh at me. That infuriated me all the more, and I thought seriously about quitting the class.

Mr. Han's other students were painting, drawing, and getting beautiful results. For instance, once Miss Flo's collage had dried, she had gone back with an airbrush and embellished her blue design with delicate mists of bronze and pewter. The next week, she added bits of lace and tiny beads, gluing them carefully into the paper crinkles and folds. By the end of four weeks, her collage was gorgeous. She had art; I had an ugly lump of overworked clay.

For some reason, though, pride or perhaps nothing more than sheer, cussed stubbornness, I kept going back to the studio. Despite all my recent losses, I was still the Kate Cunningham who had trounced some of the top attorneys in Manhattan. There was no way that I would let a lousy lump of damp clay get the best of me.

On the fifth week of class, I went to the shelf and got my bag of clay without being prompted by Mr. Han. After stopping at the sink for a bowl of water, I sat down at my usual place. I took the lump out of the bag—it looked like a big wad of used chewing gum—set it on the table, and glared at it. The clay seemed to stare back up at me in weary resignation, as if it were waiting for another ninety minutes of resentful abuse.

"Kate," Mr. Han asked, "what do you love?" He had slipped up behind me so quietly that I hadn't even noticed, and the sound of his voice, soft as it was, startled me.

"Excuse me?" I stammered.

"What do you love? Ultimately, art is only about love." He winked at me and walked away, leaving me alone with my nemesis.

"That's a really good question," I muttered. Tentatively, I dampened my fingers and reached out to smooth the clay. It warmed up under my fingers, stretching the way Honoré did when I petted him in long, slow strokes.

Eureka.

I broke off a piece of the clay and slowly coaxed it into a cone, then rounded off the top so it looked like an uneven barbell, one end longer and thicker than the other. I flattened the bigger end so the cone could sit upright, then rolled two slim cylinders, bent them at one end, and attached them to the larger piece to form front legs, gently stroking the clay with damp fingers to erase the visible seams. I shaped the top of the piece into a head, adding pointed ears. After using my little fingernail to make hollows for eyes, I slightly elongated the face. To either side of the base I attached smaller cones, shaped and bent, smoothing them onto what was becoming a lithe, slender torso. Rolling a final, long cylinder, I attached it to the back. I then twisted the head so it was looking back over one shoulder.

The proportions weren't perfect, but I had made a recognizable statue of Honoré.

When I looked up, the classroom was empty except for Mr. Han, who was leaning against another of the worktables, watching me with a satisfied smile. Glancing at my watch, I realized that class had ended over an hour before. I had been so intent on my work that I hadn't even noticed. "That is pretty good," he said.

"It's not quite right," I replied, "but I can stop working and finish it next time. Sorry to have kept you so late. I didn't realize that class had ended."

His smile widened. "That is how you know you are making art—when you do not even notice time going by. I am not in any hurry to leave, Kate. Take your time and finish it tonight. Even if you wrap it in plastic, it will dry out over a week and you will not like how it looks if you try to make changes later. But you said it was not quite right. What do you think should be different?"

I looked at the statue carefully. "The tail is a little long, even for a Siamese, and the front paws are a bit too big. Also, I haven't finished the eyes."

"Ah, it is a Siamese!" Mr. Han exclaimed delightedly. "Is this the cat you told me about on New Year's Eve?"

"Yes," I replied. "This is supposed to be Honoré, though I don't think he'd appreciate the mistakes I've made. I've had him for a long time. When you asked me what I loved, he was the first thing that popped into my head. I used to draw him all the time when I was a kid."

"I think he would be honored that you worked so hard to make him beautiful. Let me see if I cannot help you finish here." Mr. Han leaned over and gently wrapped the elongated tail of the statue around the oversized front paws. Suddenly, they looked just right. "Artists often make these little adjustments," he explained. "There is no such thing as 'perfect' artwork. If there was, it would be lifeless, no fun to look at. Now your statue is in balance, yes? But you do the eyes, Kate. This is your cat, not mine. I do not know his soul the way you do."

He had me there. I made two small ovals of clay, dipped them in water, and then placed them in the hollows I had made on the face, smoothing them so they would stick. I tried adding tiny balls of clay for pupils but they looked unnatural, so I scraped them away and started over, carving lids onto the eyes and cutting tiny vertical slits to represent the pupils. On a whim, I tilted the head slightly to one side, then sat back and took a look at the statue. It was as if Honoré himself was looking at back me, with the bored, lordly air he sometimes assumed. I chuckled.

"Ah, the sound of success!" Mr. Han said, smiling. "Are you finished?"

"I think so."

"Good! Let us put him aside to dry, and then we can fire him and you can glaze him."

"Do you think he needs it?" I asked, a little doubtfully. "He looks pretty good, and I'm afraid I'll ruin him if I get the glaze wrong."

Mr. Han leaned in, once again looking me dead in the eye. "If that happens, Kate, you make another statue and try again. There is no such thing as perfection, either in life or in art. But every attempt teaches you something, yes?"

I swallowed, a little uncomfortable. "I guess so. Sure, let's fire him, glaze him, and see what happens."

"Excellent!" Mr. Han grinned in triumph, picked up my little statue, and carried it over to an empty shelf by the kiln. "Good work tonight. We will let him dry until next week."

Dismissed, I gathered up my coat and purse and walked down the hall to the sitting room, where I ran into Lucina. She was alone, a rare occurrence, and for a fleeting instant I wondered whether she had been waiting for me. "You're here late, Kate," she observed. "Is everything all right?"

"Sure," I replied. "Mr. Han was nice enough to let me stay after class to finish something I was working on."

"Ah, our Zen master strikes again!" Lucina said, with a knowing smile. "Are you enjoying your classes with him?"

"Not until tonight," I admitted, "but I think that was my fault, not his. He asked me to try working with clay a few weeks ago, and I'd never done that before. It took me a while to get used to it. Why do you call him a Zen master?"

"Isn't he, though?" Lucina asked. "He says he teaches art, but I think he really teaches his students how to relax and get into the flow. The art is just the medium he uses."

Lucina paused for an instant, but it passed so quickly that for once I didn't have the impression that she had interrupted our conversation to listen to someone else. Maybe she had realized that those unnatural pauses annoyed me. "Are you in a hurry to get home, Kate, or do you have time for a cup of coffee with me?"

"Coffee would be great," I replied. It was a little late, but why not? After all, it wasn't as though I had anywhere pressing to go.

"Wonderful! Let's go have a chat in my office. I know you've been at the Abbey almost every day since New Year's, but we really haven't had much time to catch up one-on-one. Follow me."

Lucina led me out of the sitting room by a side door, then down a long corridor. There were five or six closed doors on my left and an open gallery of Palladian windows on my right, overlooking the courtyard and the barn. "I don't think you have ever come this way before, have you?" she asked, and I shook my head. "Among its many prior uses, the Abbey was a small convent for a while. These rooms were used by the sisters and by visitors who came here on spiritual retreats."

The corridor ended with a sharp turn to the right. "My office is here." Lucina pulled up a long chain around her neck that had been tucked into her dress. Three brass keys dangled from it, and she used the smallest to unlock the door. It was the first time I had ever noticed a locked door at the Abbey, and it surprised me, until she opened the door and I looked inside. Then it became clear why Lucina kept her office locked away, out of sight.

Angel Abbey was immaculate, so clean and well ordered that you might think elves—or maybe angels—worked every night until dawn to keep it spotless. Lucina's office, by contrast, was a total wreck. Her desk was covered in stacks of books and unruly heaps of paper that threatened to collapse on one another. There was a telephone, a cup full of mismatched pens, pencils, and a couple pairs of scissors, a small clock half-hidden under a stack of documents that had fallen over onto it, and a little dish of paper clips in various sizes and styles. The shelves behind the desk were cluttered too, buried in a welter of open books, files, knickknacks, and more piles of papers. A floor lamp with a glass Tiffany shade stood behind the chair, casting a golden glow and throwing circles of emerald, ruby, and sapphire light onto the shelves and walls. Set into the wall on the far side of the room, next to the bookshelves, was a closed wooden door. It was fitted with an antique brass lock and crystal doorknob and looked very, very old.

Messy as Lucina's office was, it wasn't entirely unwelcoming. In fact, it reminded me of my old office at the law firm. We shared a certain affinity for clutter; the thought made me smile.

Two wing chairs covered in amber velveteen sat in one corner, with a butler's table between them. Someone had set a coffee service on the table, along with two tan earthenware mugs. Lucina motioned me toward one of the chairs and sat down in the other. "Now you know my little secret," she said. "I need a certain amount of clutter to be entirely at ease. It's not appropriate for the public face of the Abbey, but this office gives me a place where I can hide in comfortable squalor. You take your coffee black, no sugar, correct?"

I nodded, pleased that she had remembered. "This is nothing," I confided. "You should have seen my office at the law firm. I always knew where everything was, but nobody else could find a thing on my desk. The managing partner used to threaten to take a flamethrower to it once in a while."

Lucina passed me a mug of steaming coffee, her face growing serious. "How are your legal troubles going, Kate? Is Richard giving you the help you need?"

"How do you know about that?" I asked, instantly on guard.

"There are no secrets at Angel Abbey, Kate," Lucina replied. "But please, don't worry. No one is gossiping about you. People are just concerned, myself included. You have become an important part of our little family here. No one wants to see you worried or sad."

Lucina probably meant to be reassuring, but I still wasn't comfortable talking about my legal problems. "Richard is doing a great job," I told her. "Litigation just takes a long time. It'll be months before things really get going.

"There *was* something I've been meaning to ask you about, though," I continued, deliberately changing the subject. "Amy dropped by my house a few days before New Year's to talk about her career options after college. She wants to come work here at the Abbey as a kind of schedulist-slash-manager-slash-administrative assistant. Has she talked to you about it yet?"

"Not yet, but I am not surprised. Of course I would be happy to hire her," Lucina replied. "Amy's an absolute godsend with the schedule. I could never keep everything straight on my own, and I don't know how we would keep the computers up and running without her. I am sure we could work something out. Do you want to tell Amy that, or should I talk to her myself?"

"We should probably wait until she comes to you," I said. "I don't think Amy meant for our conversation to be confidential, but it would be better if she asked you herself. Can you pay her anything?"

"Enough," Lucina said. "As I'm sure you have gathered by now, Angel Abbey has a number of benefactors who support what we do here. There is money to pay her a reasonable salary."

It occurred to me that Lucina might have invited me to her office so she could ask me to become one of those benefactors, but I quickly rejected the idea. If she knew about my legal problems, she had undoubtedly also figured out that I wasn't a rich Manhattan attorney anymore. "That's great," I replied, turning my attention back to the conversation. "Amy will be thrilled. And if she's making a living wage it might satisfy her father. He wants her to go into law, but I don't think she'd be happy as an attorney." Heaven knows I hadn't been.

Lucina was watching me closely, I realized. "You're trying to figure out why I invited you here, aren't you?" she asked. "Kate, what have I done to make you so suspicious of me? I realize that we have known each other for only a few months, but that's long enough for you to get a general sense of what I'm all about. I had hoped we could become friends, but you really don't seem to like me very much. I asked you in for coffee thinking that we might be able to work that through."

Her frankness caught me utterly off guard. "What makes you think I don't like you?" I sputtered, stalling for time to get my thoughts together.

Lucina cocked a skeptical eyebrow at me. "Come on, Kate, it's perfectly obvious to me and, for that matter, to anyone else who looks twice. You don't like me. But if you won't tell me why, maybe I can tell you."

She leaned across the table toward me, setting her coffee down. "You think I am dishonest and pretentious. You believe that I cultivate blind hero-worship from the people who come to the Abbey because I have some selfish, secret plan to take advantage of the goodwill of our volunteers. You are certain that I am not anywhere near as wonderful as I let everyone think, especially Bella and Andrew, and you are afraid you won't be able to protect them from me. Sometimes, you even ask yourself if I am some kind of deranged cult leader who is going to pour cyanide into a punchbowl full of Kool-Aid and lure everyone to their deaths. Am I getting warm?" She sat back, waiting for my reply.

It felt like an eternity before I was able to collect my thoughts enough to answer her. "Not exactly," I eventually managed to get out. "I never thought you were going to poison people."

"Well, that's a relief, at least," Lucina said tartly. "I am glad to know you don't think me capable of mass murder.

"Here's the thing, Kate," she went on. "You are right about me in some respects, but you are very wrong about the rest. I do like attention, and I appreciate how loving and supportive the regulars at the Abbey are. But it's not really me they love; it's the 'Lady of Angel Abbey.' I am just the actress who plays the role, as your friend Jack so astutely guessed at Christmas dinner.

"It's ironic, Kate," Lucina continued. "You are so protective of your own secrets that you don't even want me to know that you are being sued by your former law firm, but apparently you are not going to give me a fair chance until I show you every skeleton that lurks in the closet of my past. Still, I like you, and I would like you to trust me at least a little. So, let's get it over with, shall we?"

Lucina's voice was dead calm, as matter-of-fact as if she had been telling me what the weatherman had predicted for the following morning. "I was born in a small town near Seattle, or at least I think I was," she began. "The local authorities found me on the streets there when I was about three years old, undernourished and with hair so matted and filthy that they had to shave my head. They didn't know my name, so they named me 'Lucy,' after Lucille Ball, because I had red hair. Then, because they couldn't find my parents or figure out where I came from, they put me into the foster-care system.

"I was bounced from house to house, cared for, if you want to call it that, by people who only wanted me for the money they got from the government," Lucina continued. "That continued until I got old enough to be 'interesting' to my foster fathers and brothers. At that point it wasn't safe to stay in those houses anymore, so I ran away when I was fourteen."

The image of a young Lucina standing by the side of the road with her thumb out, skinny and terrified, flashed into my mind. "I slowly made my way south, and eventually ended up in LA," she told me. "I was dead broke, alone, and desperate. You don't want to know what I did in those days to get enough money to eat, and I wouldn't tell you if you did.

"Suffice it to say that I survived, more or less, and when I was eighteen I met a guy who played bass in a rock band. I moved in with him for a while, and he introduced me to the band's manager. She knew somebody who knew somebody who knew a talent agent, and he agreed to take me on as a client. He taught me how to dress and do my hair, and he got me several roles in some pretty bad movies, including the one Jack saw. Still, it was paying work, and it called me to the attention of people in Hollywood who liked to party with pretty young girls.

"I was pretty enough," Lucina continued, "and I started hitting the parties more and more, drinking a lot, doing drugs, and 'accommodating' anyone who promised to advance my career. Those promises were worthless, of course, but I was young and desperate for approval. I would have slept with the Devil himself for one big movie role. In hindsight, I probably did just that.

"The big parts never came, though," Lucina said matter-of-factly. "I got some auditions and came close a couple of times. But the leading roles always went to younger, prettier girls, even as the casting directors always told my agent that I was too beautiful for the character parts.

"I limped along for a few years, taking whatever roles I could get and becoming one of those girls who hang on the walls at parties, the ones that the power brokers pretty much ignore," Lucina went on. "My agent eventually dropped me, the invitations tapered off, and the little bit of money I had saved drained away until there was nothing left.

"I started walking the streets for cash, doing heavier drugs, and drinking to the point where I would have blackouts that lasted for days." Another image of Lucina, older than before but still in her twenties and scantily clad, flashed through my mind. "When the police started to hassle me, I would hitchhike to a town a few miles away and start all over again.

"I finally hit bottom in a town not far from where they first found me as a kid," Lucina said. "I hadn't eaten for days, but I had managed to scrape together enough money for a bottle of over-the-counter sleeping pills and a fifth of Jim Beam. I was twenty-six years old by then, and I was convinced that my life was so completely messed up there was no way to fix it, not ever. So I swallowed every one of those pills with sips of bourbon, then drank the rest of the bottle, and lay down on a park bench to die."

I was absolutely stunned. "Lucina, I'm really sorry," I stammered. "Look, you don't have to tell me all of this—"

"Yes, I think I do," she interrupted, her voice still deathly calm. "We have started the story, so let's see it through to the end.

"As you can see," she continued, lifting her arms as if to show me, "I didn't die that night. A police officer named Michael found me in the park, called an ambulance, and got me to a hospital in time to save my life. The social worker at the hospital found me a temporary place to stay, and the counselors there eventually talked me into joining AA. That's where I met my sponsor, who helped me pull my life together for the first time." She reached over to her desk, picked up a big, heavy coin, and showed it to me. "I have been sober ever since. I made my thirty-year anniversary this New Year's Day."

A picture of Lucina's untouched glass of wine at Christmas dinner flashed through my mind. No wonder she hadn't drunk it. "Lucina, I had no idea. I'm so very, very sorry..."

Lucina held up her hand, and I stopped. "Don't be," she said. "I am not angry and I don't blame you, Kate. You are still young enough to think that you are the only person in the world who ever had problems. I am not telling you this for sympathy, but so you will understand that I am not perfect and do not pretend to be.

"Funny thing, though. It turns out that I am pretty good at being the 'Lady of Angel Abbey,'" she continued, making air quotes with her fingers. "Yes, I am playing a character, but it is a character that people around here seem to need. Ask them to come to a big old house in the middle of nowhere to do volunteer work and maybe hang out together, and nobody will show up. Send them a special, handwritten invitation from the 'Lady of Angel Abbey,' and they will fall all over themselves to get there. Or at least the generous, good-hearted ones will."

Lucina leaned into me again, her dark eyes intent. "Do you want to know the real secret of the Abbey, Kate?" I nodded—it would have been impossible not to. "It's stone soup," she declared.

"Stone soup?" I echoed, utterly baffled.

"You must have learned the story as a child," Lucina insisted. "It's the old fairy tale about the tinker who pulled his wagon into a small village at suppertime. All the villagers were hiding in their shacks, starving to death and suspicious of one another. The tinker pulled from his wagon a big, old iron pot, filled it up with water, and then put it over a fire that he built in the town square. When the pot started to boil, he dumped a heavy stone into the water and waited.

"Curiosity overcame mistrust, and the villagers started coming out of their hovels in ones and twos to ask the tinker what he was doing," Lucina continued. "'I'm making stone soup,' he would reply, and then he would ask whether anybody had a carrot, or an onion, or a piece of potato, or a stalk of celery, or a marrow bone lying around, saying it was the one thing that would make the soup just right. Sure enough, everybody had some little bit of something, and one by one they would go get their bits and pieces, bring them back, and drop them into the pot. The tinker stirred the pot and told stories to pass the time, and soon there was enough soup to feed the entire village.

"We make stone soup here, Kate," Lucina went on. "I am just the tinker who coaxes people to bring their individual contributions. But one of the blessings of the life I have endured is that I have a pretty good eye for who is ready to be part of the work of the Abbey. Those people sense that I am able to forgive their shortcomings as soon as they are willing to forgive themselves. They come to the Abbey, they contribute whatever they have to offer, and the world is a little bit better because of it."

Lucina leaned back in her chair, looking tired. "Now, you have heard my story and you know that I am neither a saint nor a charlatan, just a fallible woman who happens to be reasonably good at her job. Can you please forgive me for that? Because I would really like to be your friend."

What was there to say after that? "Of course," I answered, deeply ashamed. "Lucina, please forgive me for being so unkind to you. This was your personal business. I never meant for you to feel as if you had to tell me all of this."

She smiled wearily. "No apology needed, Kate. Confession, they say, is good for the soul." She shifted in her chair and then stood. "I have kept you here later than I should have, though. Bella and Andrew will never forgive me if you don't get home soon. Come on, let me walk you out."

I followed Lucina to the front door, where she hugged me gently. "I am not going to inflict 'the Lady's blessing' on you," she said with a little smile. "Just drive safely and come back to us soon. Good night, Kate."

As I stepped out onto the porch and into the chill night air, Lucina closed the door behind me. Just before it swung shut, I thought I heard her ask, "Did I do all right?" But it was late, I was tired, and, of course, there was no one there.

Archangel Michael speaks:

Hard to believe it has been thirty years since I picked Lucina up off that park bench, barely breathing and about ready to drop into Azrael's hands. If Raphael hadn't stepped in to help the doctors at the hospital that night, I don't think she would have made it. That would have been a shame. Gabe would have found somebody else to be the Lady of Angel Abbey, sooner or later, but Lucina was the ideal pick. Right person, right place, right time, you know? We see a lot of that in Heaven, but it's not something people notice anywhere near often enough on Earth.

It took guts for Lucina to tell Kate her story, but then I've always admired her courage. Lucina went through hell as a kid and made a ton of lousy decisions later. But she had the humility to accept help when somebody offered it to her and the perseverance to turn her life around. Without her troubled past, Lucina might never have developed the compassion that makes her so perfect for her job. She has done a whole lot more good as the Lady of Angel Abbey than she ever could have done in Hollywood.

I'm not sure where you folks got that crazy idea that people have to be perfect to help with the Divine Plan. It must have come from the Adversary or one of his flunkies. It's clever, I'll give him that. In fact, it's almost as clever as the Adversary persuading everybody that he doesn't exist at all. That's probably the clearest example of hiding in plain sight there is. We are going to have a good, long talk about that when he finally comes limping home, believe you me.

Anyway, let's be clear about this. People who flatter themselves into thinking that they've never made a mistake usually aren't very good at forgiving the mistakes of others, so they're not as much use as they could be. Human beings aren't perfect, and nobody in Heaven expects you to be. You can accomplish a lot for the Creator if you just show up, warts and all, and do what you can. If you wait to get perfect first, you'll never get anything done.

YOU ARE GOOD ENOUGH, OK? We love you. Now, stop sitting around feeling sorry for yourself. Just get out there and do some good. It will be plenty–I promise.

CHAPTER THIRTY

Lucina's confession staggered me. I had already figured out that she was playing a role when she appeared in public at the Abbey, but I hadn't begun to imagine the pain she had suffered in the past. It had taken a lot of courage for her to be so honest with me. I was humbled by her trust, ashamed that I had effectively forced her to be so straightforward, and more than a little flattered that she had trusted me with her story.

Lucina hadn't explicitly told me not to repeat what she had said, but her sordid past certainly wasn't common knowledge among the Abbey regulars. I decided to keep it to myself. Maybe Lucina wasn't the stained-glass saint people took her for, but she had done a magnificent job of turning her life around. She deserved their admiration for that, if nothing else.

Richard called a few days later to tell me that he had managed to track down Jeanine Powell, sort of. Unfortunately, he hadn't been able to speak with her. Jeanine's mother had answered the phone and given him an earful. No, Jeanine was not home. No, he could not leave a message, and no, she was not about to let her daughter help anybody who ever had anything to do with those evil, godless monsters in New York City. They had destroyed her daughter's career and broken her heart, and nobody had tried to help *her*. Then she had hung up on him. Richard observed ruefully that the call had not been much of a success, though it certainly confirmed that Jeanine's experience at the firm had been at least as painful as mine.

Again I regretted dropping Jeanine after I made partner, but it was no longer just about losing whatever help she might have given me now. Since hearing Lucina's story, I had started to wonder how many of the other people I knew were carrying around secret, painful histories. Maybe if I had been a better friend to Jeanine, she would have come to me for help before she quit. Heck, I had been a partner, albeit it a junior one. Maybe I would have been able to protect her from whatever had driven her out of the firm. I would never know for sure, but I would always know that I had never even tried. That was something I would regret for a long time.

Meanwhile, my financial concerns had reached the point where I decided it was time to start looking for work. There was no way I could apply for a legal job with the bar complaint hanging over my head. Still, someone might be willing to hire me as an administrative assistant or a store clerk. Andrew had helped me set up my new computer after the New Year's Eve party. It was time I started using it to find a job.

When I opened my new e-mail account, I found a message from Amy titled "Check This Out." Inside, she had sent me a link, with the cryptic message, "Enjoy!" Curious, I clicked on the link.

A new window opened on my computer of a darkened video screen. I heard the first notes of "Thank Heaven for Little Girls" from *Gigi*, and up came a photo of Honoré. The photo started to move in time to the music, as Honoré madly chased his red pom-pom dragon while Maurice Chevalier sang in the background.

Amy must have spent hours editing the video. She had managed to coordinate Honoré's actions with the music, cutting in musical repeats and backtracking Honoré's movements so he seemed to be dancing. It was clever, edgy, and entirely unique. I absolutely loved it, and to judge from the number of "Likes" it had gotten, more than 250,000 other people did, too. In Amy's clever hands, Honoré had gone viral.

I called Bella and Andrew, and we watched the video together. Honoré appeared out of nowhere, jumped up next to the computer, and watched himself with a dignified stare. "You're a star, big guy," I told him, rumpling his ears. "I always knew it, but now the world does, too." He rubbed his cheek against my hand and purred.

As soon as the video ended, to Bella and Andrew's admiring applause, I sent Amy a thank-you e-mail. She replied in minutes, asking whether I had noticed the ads at the side of the screen. I had not, but she wrote back to tell me that the advertisers would pay every time someone clicked on the video. Given Honoré's popularity, it looked as though I would be getting a check pretty soon. It wouldn't be enough to put us in the lap of luxury, but it would keep food on the table and allow me to keep the house for at least a while longer.

"You're a godsend," I wrote back.

This reply came even faster: "I had fun doing it. Besides, I owe you one. The Lady offered me a job at the Abbey and my dad said it was OK!!!!!! I know you talked to her—thanks so much! P.S., when can I come over and take more videos of Honoré?"

There was only one possible reply. I wrote Amy back with an invitation to visit Honoré anytime, hit "send," closed the computer, and smiled. At least one worry was resolved for the moment.

Amy came by with her camera every afternoon for the next few days. Honoré gave her hours of footage, chasing his toy dragon, rolling in sunbeams, posing on the furniture, and otherwise acting like a trained stunt kitty. It was astounding to me and completely out of character for him. I could never quite keep his age in my head, but Honoré had not been a kitten in a long, long time. Still, he pranced and cavorted like a kitten for Amy, reverting to his adult personality the instant she turned off the camera. The change in his behavior astonished me, but I couldn't complain about it. If videos of Honoré were going to pay the bills, who was I to argue?

The afternoon of my art class, Amy seemed particularly reluctant to leave after she finished filming for the day. I had learned by then that Amy tended to drag her feet when she wanted to ask me something but wasn't sure how I would respond. I waited as patiently as I could, until she finally asked, "Are you going to fire your statue of Honoré tonight?"

"That's the plan. Why?" I had given up trying to figure out how Amy knew what I was doing when. Lucina had been right when she said there were no secrets at Angel Abbey.

"I was just wondering, if it turns out, are you going to make any more?" Amy pressed on.

"I hadn't really thought about it," I answered. "But I could. What's all this sudden interest in my artwork?"

"Well, it occurred to me, since the video is so popular, that you could make more statues and sell them online," Amy said. "People who like Honoré's videos would probably buy figurines of him, especially if they were made by his owner. Would you make a couple more and let me try selling them for you?"

"Sure, why not?" I shrugged. "If you had told me that Honoré was going to become an Internet star, I wouldn't have believed it, but here we are, thanks to you. If you could pull that off, maybe anything is possible." Amy beamed and bounced out the door, clearly delighted.

Mr. Han and I fired the sculpture that evening, and it came out of the kiln with no flaws or bubbles. I had been afraid it would shatter in the firing, but the little figurine held up without so much as a crack. Once it cooled, and with Mr. Han's help, I glazed the body a soft fawn, with seal-brown boots, mask, and tail. I glazed the eyes blue, but the paint looked dark and dull. "Do not worry," Mr. Han assured me. "Once the glaze dries we will fire it again, and then you will see the magic happen. Do you want to make another one?"

"You bet!" I smiled, and went to get a fresh lump of clay. This time, I sculpted Honoré on his back, paws bunched together and tail stretched straight out behind him as he worried his toy dragon. The statue came together in no time, and I was positively humming by the time Mr. Han took it over to the shelf by the kiln to dry.

When art class ended I walked out more slowly than usual, hoping to run into Lucina. She was nowhere to be seen, though, so I left the Abbey and drove home. In the car, it occurred to me that I was as eager to see Lucina now as I had been reluctant just a few months before. She was going to get her wish, it seemed. Whatever my initial reaction to her had been, we were well on our way to becoming good friends. It was time to bid a firm good-bye to that nasty little "black mouse" of dislike and suspicion of her that I had secretly carried around for so long.

From that evening onward, the art studio became my second home at the Abbey. True to his word, Mr. Han fired my first little statue and it came out beautifully, the fawn and seal paints clear and glossy, the eyes a shining sapphire blue. I kept that first one as a reminder not to settle for "pretty-pretty," a decision of which Mr. Han thoroughly approved. Over the next several weeks, I made half a dozen additional statues of Honoré, all in different poses. After firing and glazing them I handed them off to Amy to be posted for sale online. She made two new videos of Honoré, each more popular than the last, and my first payment arrived from his online "sponsors." I asked Amy to split it with me, but she told me to donate her half to the Abbey, which I happily did. When the six figurines sold for about ten times what I thought they were worth, I gave half of the proceeds from those sales to the Abbey, too.

I offered to pay Lucina for the art supplies I was using. She refused, telling me that I had done far more for the Abbey than I realized. "If you keep selling those statues of your cat and donating half of your takings, the Abbey will be downright rich," Lucina laughed. "Let us treat you to a little clay and paint." We were in her office having coffee, something we had done more and more often since she first told me her story.

It was a happy surprise to discover that I liked the Lucina who lived behind the scenes far more than the "Lady of the Abbey." Out of the public eye, she could be funny and spontaneous. She told outrageous, off-color jokes and loved to gossip about the celebrities who had been acting in Hollywood when she was there.

It also turned out that when she stepped out of the role of the picture-perfect Lady of Angel Abbey, Lucina had plenty of human flaws. She hated mornings and would happily sleep until noon if her duties at the Abbey didn't force her out of bed. She was disorganized and chronically forgetful. If Amy hadn't managed the calendar for her, arranging space at the Abbey would have been a nightmare. Lucina couldn't be bothered with figures, and left the administration of the Abbey's resources to the volunteers who ran programs and events there. Violet kept track of the food, Mr. Han managed the art supplies, Mrs. Braun handled the library and the sheet music, Miss Flo and Amy coordinated the in-kind donations, and there was a committee that oversaw financial contributions.

"I keep telling you, Kate, I'm just a figurehead," Lucina would say, sometimes jokingly, sometimes a little crossly if I started asking too many questions. "They handle the donations. I just write the thank-you notes. Don't cross-examine me, OK?"

I always stopped questioning when Lucina got testy. The details of the Abbey's operations were not really any of my business. Besides, I had come to value our friendship to the point where I didn't want to press her for details she did not care to disclose.

It also became obvious that some of the other regulars at the Abbey were more aware of Lucina's shortcomings than I had previously realized. Amy made sure that Lucina got plenty of advance notice of any event at which she would have to put in a public appearance. Violet brought her special tidbits and treats, coaxing Lucina to eat when she otherwise might not have. Miss Flo quietly diverted difficult people away from Lucina to spare her unnecessary upset. I remembered Richard saying that Lucina packaged herself well, but I was beginning to suspect that she was more fragile than I had grasped. Others, it seemed, had been more perceptive.

Richard would call from time to time to tell me how the lawsuit was progressing. Not much was happening, though. There were some preliminary papers he had to file, denying Roy Blackwell's version of events and setting out my own claims against the firm, minimal though they were. It would have been nice to be able to argue that I had been fired because I was female, or in retaliation for protecting a client's interests. Without Ruth Martingale's testimony, though, there would be no way to prove sex discrimination. And if I had done such a great job of protecting Dr. Grandy, why would he be suing me?

I had no real defense, apart from explaining that I had been careless but not malicious. I had not conspired with the sellers against Dr. Grandy's interests, but I *had* left a briefcase full of his confidential papers in a taxicab. That alone was more than sufficient reason for the firm to fire me and for Dr. Grandy to sue me. I finally just told Richard everything I could and let him decide how to present my side of the story.

For whatever reason, Richard seemed to have pulled back from me since New Year's Eve. We hadn't had an argument, and our conversations were always cordial. Still, there seemed to be less warmth in his voice when he called. Maybe he had decided it would be unprofessional to get romantically involved with a client, or maybe he was just preoccupied with his other work. Then again, maybe Jeanine's mother had told him nastier things about me than he had admitted to me. Whatever it was, he seemed to have lost interest in becoming closer friends. I tried not to let that upset me too much.

Winter rolled into spring, and soon the Abbey gardens were filled with crocuses and daffodils. I stopped by one bright April afternoon for a book club meeting. We had finished the last *Harry Potter* novel, and I was eager to hear Miss Flo's theories about how the story ended. She was absolutely convinced that the plot would have worked out differently if the actors in the movies, especially Alan Rickman, had not been so good. She had told me a dozen times that Professor Snape would never have been such an important character if a lesser actor had taken the role early on. I was looking forward to hearing her tell me she had been right all along.

Before I could get to book club, however, Lucina came up and pulled me aside. "Kate," she asked, "can I have a word before you head off to your book group? Something has come up, and I'd love to get your insights. The other club members can start without you, can't they?"

They could, of course, so I agreed and followed her down the long corridor. Lucina had just unlocked the door to her office when Violet came bustling up, asking Lucina to come to the kitchen at once. There was a group of volunteers there, and an argument was developing over the menu for an upcoming social event. "I've tried to straighten it out," Violet said, "but there's a new guy who insists he'll take direction only from you."

Lucina sighed. "Sorry, Kate, can you give me a minute? Go have a seat. I'll be right back." Violet shooed her off toward the kitchen, and I went into Lucina's office to wait.

Lucina's desk was as disorganized as ever, covered in piles of paper and unopened mail. Toward the center of the blotter was a list of names and addresses with a box of blank notecards on top. The cards were made of rich, antiqued ivory parchment, heavy and expensive. Even surrounded by the jumbled stacks of paper on Lucina's desk, they gleamed as if lit from within by a thousand candles. One of the cards was out on the desk, and even before I looked carefully at it, I knew that the handwriting would be an elegant, old-fashioned script. "*Dear Mrs. Harrington, Thank you so much for your generous contribution to Angel Abbey,*" the note began.

I did not need to read another word.

It felt as though a bomb had gone off in my head. My hands started trembling, my mouth went dry, and my stomach lurched so hard that I struggled not to get sick all over the desk. I had seen that graceful handwriting on that same elegant notepaper before—twice. The second time had been when Lucina sent my first invitation to Angel Abbey. But the first...

Only weeks before, I had decided to bid farewell to the "black mouse" in my pocket, to put suspicion aside and trust Lucina as a friend. But suddenly that black mouse reared its head again, turned, and bit me. Hard. And it *hurt*.

Just then, Lucina came bustling into the office, all smiles. "Sorry about that," she laughed. "That's one gentleman who won't be invited back to the Abbey anytime soon." She stopped suddenly when she saw me. "Kate, what's wrong?"

I had been leaning heavily over her desk, propped up on one arm with my other hand over my mouth, fighting back tears. I forced myself to stand and look at her. "*Why*, Lucina?" I asked, my voice hoarse and low.

"Why what, Kate?" Lucina asked. "What's the matter? Are you sick?"

"If I am, it's because of you." I wiped my mouth with the back of my hand and tried to focus. "How could you do this, Lucina? What could you possibly have gained from it? *Why did you write me that note?*"

Lucina seemed startled, almost afraid, but I could see she was struggling to stay calm. "What note? The note I wrote you when your father died? Kate, it was an invitation to visit the Abbey—"

"*Not that note*!" Realizing that I was shouting, I forced myself to lower my voice. "Not that note, Lucina." My tears were starting to flow, no matter how hard I struggled to choke them back. "I don't mean your invitation to tea. I'm talking about the other note, the one that appeared on my desk at the law firm last summer and *ruined my life*!

"How did you do it? *Why* did you do it?" I began crying in earnest, abandoning my struggle to stay calm. "You didn't even know me then. Why would you write a note like that to a perfect stranger? 'Your father is dying, come home at once.' Who put you up to it? And why? How did you even manage to get that thing on my desk?"

Lucina looked as though she was starting to panic. "Kate, I have no idea what you're talking about. I never put any note on your desk. The only note I ever wrote to you was—"

"*STOP LYING TO ME!*" I was shouting now, every few words broken up with a sob. "You've been lying to me all along! But the lies are over, Lucina. This is your stationery, and your handwriting. They're *exactly* the same as the note I found on my desk. You can't sweet talk your way around me anymore.

"God, I am such an *idiot*!" My voice cracked, but I struggled on. "I was finally starting to trust you, to like you, to think that maybe you, and this place, were actually for real. I thought you were my friend! But it was all just an act, wasn't it?"

Lucina drew herself up to her full height, but her hands were shaking and so was her voice. "Kate," she said, "I don't know what has upset you, but I won't stand here and allow you to accuse me of something I haven't done. We can talk about this after you've calmed down, but right now I need to ask you to leave."

"No, Lucina, you don't," I replied, my voice shaking as I wiped away tears. "You don't need to ask me to leave, because there is no way that I'm staying in this room with you another minute. You're a liar and a cheat, and for all I know you're part of some larger scheme to ruin my life. I don't know if someone else put you up to writing that note or if you had some twisted plan of your own, but either way, *we are done*. I'm leaving!"

I grabbed my purse and stormed out of Lucina's office, down the corridor, and out of the Abbey. It was only much later that I remembered leaving my book for the club meeting behind.

Archangel Raziel speaks:

Lies and secrets, secrets and lies. It can be so very difficult for people to distinguish between them! My angels and I always know what is true, of course. As you understand by now, however, we very rarely tell.

Secrets and lies were what got Kate into such trouble. She had tried to conceal her mistrust of Lucina, to rush into a friendship that she was not ready to embrace. Cynicism is an occupational hazard for lawyers, a natural outgrowth of hearing too many lies from witnesses, opponents, and even their own clients and business associates. Combine that with her family history, and Kate had plenty reason to be suspicious of anyone who seemed too good to be true.

Suspiciousness is not an attractive trait, however, so Kate tried to conceal hers. Then, when she felt foolishly betrayed, she lashed out at Lucina. It would have been better for Kate to be more honest about her mixed emotions in the first place.

In fairness to Kate, Lucina did have her secrets. Which one of you does not? Kate certainly did, as Lucina quite rightly pointed out to her. And, like every one of you, Kate and Lucina both lied from time to time. They could still become friends, but again, honesty between them would have gone a long way.

You all struggle so to maintain your flawless little facades! But, as my beloved brother Michael quite rightly observed, no one is perfect. No one in

Heaven expects you to be. Like our Creator, we forgive you your trespasses, accepting and loving you just as you are.

Now, if you could just learn to be more accepting of each other, my dears. That would be a very good thing indeed.

CHAPTER THIRTY-ONE

I barreled down the Abbey steps and strode toward my car. Reaching for the door handle, though, I stopped and reconsidered. My hands were shaking, my heart was pounding, and my eyes were still brimming with tears. I was too upset to be safe behind the wheel, and the last thing I needed was to get into an accident going home.

I rejected the idea of calling a cab, or of trying to get someone else at the Abbey to give me a ride. Both of those alternatives would have raised questions that I wasn't ready to answer. Instead, I decided to take a walk and try to calm down. Book club would go on for at least another hour, and I had gotten into the habit of staying late more often than not for coffee and chatter with Lucina. Bella and Andrew wouldn't worry if I didn't come home for a while. Better to take some time to get my emotions under control where none of the Abbey regulars could see me.

After locking my purse in the trunk of the Mustang, I took a deep breath and set out. I walked between the main house and the carriage house, through the courtyard, and behind the barn, headed for a footpath that led into the woods. If you followed it long enough, that path would take you through the trees and down to Angel Falls, where Jacob Wittesteen allegedly had his mystical angel encounter. It was a pretty walk on a nice day, just the right distance to take me well away from the Abbey, while still getting me back to my car before dark.

Struggling to control my tears, I stepped onto the path and strode into the woods.

It was a glorious spring afternoon, clear, cool, and fresh. The sunlight glinted brilliantly through pale new leaves, sending thin golden shafts between the branches of the trees and onto the ground below.

Wildflowers—trillium, lady's slipper, and jack-in-the-pulpit—peeked up here and there from beds of crumbled leaves or out from under the shadows of the huge stone outcroppings that dotted the landscape.

My steps crunched on the stony path. A gentle breeze murmured among the leaves. Now and then a bird would call from somewhere nearby. Behind those sounds was a profound stillness, a hush that deepened with every step I took.

Soon Angel Abbey was far enough behind me that I wouldn't have been able to see it if I looked back. I didn't look back, though, any more than I looked around to appreciate the wild, magical beauty that surrounded me. I was so obsessed with my hurt and sense of betrayal that if a live unicorn had stepped out of the trees and directly into my path, I don't think I would even have noticed.

My mind was flooded with pain at Lucina's duplicity. It occurred to me that other people had access to her notepaper. It would not be all that difficult for a clever forger to mimic her handwriting. Maybe the note on my desk had been written by somebody else...

The idea was nonsense, and I knew it. Why would some forger have gone to the trouble of creating a note from Lucina, a woman I knew nothing about at the time, and not even attach her signature to it before planting it on my desk? It was far more likely that Lucina herself had written the anonymous note warning of my father's imminent death and had arranged, somehow, to have it deposited in my office.

But if Lucina had written the note, why had she done it? How had she managed to get it into my hands? Who at the firm even knew her, or would have helped her get to me?

And why would anyone go to such strange, mysterious lengths to get me to come back to Angel Falls? My father's nurse had already asked me to come home, and I would have returned in an instant if Bella or Andrew had called me. Why take so much trouble when simpler means were readily available?

It was entirely possible, of course, that Richard had been right. Maybe the note was not intended just to send me rushing home. It could have been meant to upset me, to distract me enough to leave the Grandy files behind, where someone else could get their hands on them. But again, why go to so much trouble? We didn't lock our doors at the firm. Anyone in the office who wanted access to the files could just have slipped them off my desk after hours. No one would have been the wiser.

Then again, it was common knowledge that I often took work home. If I had taken the Grandy files with me that evening, they would have been out of easy reach. Leaving an anonymous note on my desk was a pretty far-fetched ploy, though. Besides, the person who was most likely to want the files was Roy Blackwell, and he could just have ordered me to give them to him so he could work on the closing. I would have had no choice but turn them over—Dr. Grandy was his client, after all.

Then again, maybe Blackwell's real goal was not to get his hands on the files. Maybe he had left the note hoping I would make a big enough mistake that he could fire me without having to explain himself to the other partners. Blackwell had never liked me. And with me out of the way, he would be able to squander every nickel Dr. Grandy had on bad business deals with no one around to object.

But even if Blackwell's goal had been to create an excuse to fire me, why on earth would he involve Lucina? He had no way to know that I would meet her in the days following my father's death. I seriously doubted that Blackwell had ever even heard of Angel Abbey, much less been in cahoots with its mysterious Lady. Lucina's artsy mysticism was not Blackwell's style at all.

Still, Lucina had gone out of her way to befriend me, conducting what now seemed like a determined campaign to win me over. Maybe Lucina was in league with the sellers, the people who were all set to grab Dr. Grandy's money and run? If so, Blackwell might actually have been justified in believing that I stole the files to give confidential information to the sellers through Lucina.

But that didn't make any sense, either. Blackwell would have had no reason to think I knew Lucina or that her handwriting would even be familiar to me. And why would the sellers know Lucina anyway, or think she might have some kind of influence over me…?

My racing thoughts were spinning in incoherent circles and getting me nowhere fast. I knew I should stop, take a breath, and go home. I should call Richard and tell him what I had discovered in Lucina's office. He was my lawyer, after all. Calm, rational Richard might be able to make sense of the puzzle that was confounding me.

That would have been the sensible thing to do. Instead, I kept walking.

Whatever might be going on, it felt like Lucina had lied and manipulated me to win my trust. All the while, she had been secretly conspiring with *somebody* to get me into trouble and make me lose my job. I could just imagine Richard's politely skeptical reaction if I tried to tell him that, though. True, he didn't seem starstruck by Lucina. But that didn't mean he would unquestioningly accept my assertion that she had derailed my career.

Things between Richard and me were already cooler than they had been before New Year's Eve. If I pushed too hard, he might just withdraw altogether from representing me, leaving me without a friend or a lawyer. Certainly, he wouldn't be willing to confront Lucina without more proof than I could currently provide. I didn't know how I could bear it if he sided with her against me.

Striding down the path, I worried the problem at the surface of my mind while deeper, more painful thoughts roiled underneath. All my initial misgivings about Lucina had not protected me from falling under her spell. Despite my efforts to maintain a healthy skepticism about the "Lady of Angel Abbey," I had come to think of Lucina as a good friend. I looked forward to our visits and enjoyed our conversations. But she had turned out to be the con artist I had mistrusted from the beginning. It hurt all the more that even after I thought we had become friends, she had continued to con me.

What a fool I had been.

The path began to slope gently downward under my feet as I strode along. In the distance, I could hear the tumble of falling water. The air started to soften, smelling sweetly green, and the sunlight sparkled on the occasional delicate scrap of mist. I kept walking, my feet slipping a little on the damp stone. Soon, I arrived at Angel Falls, our town's most cherished landmark.

The forty-foot waterfall spilled dramatically over a high, natural wall of weathered gray flint that was spotted with moss, lichen, and the occasional brave sapling. The water poured into a deep pool about fifteen feet across and then flowed out into a stream that babbled on in its stony bed for a quarter of a mile before disappearing underground. Beside the pool grew an ancient willow tree, surrounded by a small, mossy lawn. Years before, the town fathers had placed a stone bench under the willow, facing the falls, a memorial to Jacob Wittesteen's legendary angel encounter. The bench provided a comfortable place to sit and feel a gentle spray on your face as you watched the water spill endlessly down.

I had spent a lot of time at the falls after my mother disappeared, sitting on that bench and wondering where she had gone. It was a quiet place to grieve, as I struggled to understand why my world had been destroyed. No one had ever bothered me there that I could recall.

As I grew older and forcibly ejected the mystery of my mother's disappearance from my thoughts, my visits to Angel Falls became less and less frequent. Finally, they had stopped altogether. I had not been back in over a decade.

Nonetheless, the place was almost exactly as I remembered it. The bench was still there, looking only a little more timeworn than it had years before. The willow still grew there, too, taller than I remembered. And the waters of Angel Falls continued to pour over the gray flint wall, ceaseless and soothing as ever.

As I had so many times years ago, I settled down onto the bench to think. The willow's branches draped me in a comforting green curtain as rising mists from the pool gently kissed my face though the strands of emerging leaves. The sunlight struck gleaming rainbows across the face of the waters, and I heard a bird call once, softly, in the distance.

The voice of the waterfall seemed to fade into silence. I could feel my turbulent thoughts slow, then go still.

Slowly, almost imperceptibly, the waterfall began to brighten, as if lit from behind by a throng of religious pilgrims carrying shining candles. Somewhere in the distance, I heard the sound of a single trumpet, softly playing an impossibly beautiful melody that wove the elements of a dance, a hymn, a requiem, and a lullaby into a musical celebration of life in all its splendor, complexity, and sorrow. The scent of wet greenery sharpened, even as it mingled with an unearthly aroma that made me think of lilies, honeysuckle, roses, and herbs. Each leaf of the willow grew more vividly green, haloed in golden light. Apart from the music, the stillness intensified, as if all of existence had come to a complete halt but for the tiny, emerald space around me.

He stepped out of the waterfall without disturbing its flow, his immaculate, richly embroidered white robes gleaming in the afternoon sun. He was taller than any man and exquisitely handsome, his long, copper-colored curls falling in an artistic tumble to his broad shoulders. His hazel eyes were long-lashed and wide. His narrow feet were bare and shone like polished ivory. So did his elegant, long-fingered hands, which he stretched out to me in welcome. His head was surrounded by a radiant golden glow, finer and more beautiful than any halo in a painting. His beauty would have made Leonardo da Vinci weep.

And oh, his wings! They were even whiter and more brilliant than his robes, each feather seeming to smolder with an inner fire. They soared grandly above his head, and fell past his shoulders and down his back to train gracefully behind him without ever quite touching the ground. His wings gleamed, pristine, as though no dirt or stain could ever blemish them.

The angel turned his luminous hazel gaze on me. "Don't be afraid, Kate," he began, smiling. His voice was soothing, richly harmonic. Then he took a hasty step back and raised his beautiful hands in front of himself, startled, it seemed, by the expression on my face.

As the angel retreated, I jumped to my feet and marched out from under the willow tree, shoving its long, leafy strands aside. My eyes were narrowed to slits, my lips pulled back in an angry snarl. "I'm not *afraid*, you overgrown canary!" I hissed back at him. "I am just absolutely, completely, and totally *furious* with you! Gabriel, where on Earth did you go?"

Archangel Chamuel speaks:

With seven billion human souls on Earth alone and all of Creation to nurture, we archangels have plenty to keep us occupied. My angels and I, for instance, are constantly at work on all kinds of love, building bridges between the Creator's children and soothing hurt feelings wherever we can. It is important work, and it keeps us incredibly, happily busy.

With all that we had to do, most of us had paid scant attention to Gabriel's day-to-day efforts with Kate and Lucina. It was not that we did not care, you understand. We were just otherwise occupied and confident that Gabriel had things well in hand.

Still, nearly all of us stopped to watch Gabriel's big "reveal" that afternoon. It was the culmination of many years of hard work and planning on the part of my beautiful brother and his angels, and it was bound to be quite the event. No one can orchestrate a dramatic climax like our Gabriel.

Kate certainly appeared to be ready for a magical moment. There she sat on the bench under the willow, watching the water like an Arabian princess waiting for her genie. When Gabriel emerged, triumphant, from the waterfall, we all expected her to fall to her knees in awe, draw back in fearful amazement, or perhaps even run to her long-lost friend for a welcoming hug.

None of us expected her to puff up and hiss at Gabriel like an indignant kitten whose tail had just been stepped upon.

The silence in Heaven was nearly deafening. All of the archangels being struck speechless at once is the rarest of occurrences, something that has happened on only one other occasion in all of Eternity that I can recall. That time, we were speechless with sorrow. This time, I would say, we were all speechless with shock.

After what seemed like a century or two of silence, Raphael finally spoke up. "I did warn Gabriel that the patch he put on Kate's memories might rupture when she saw him again," Raphael said mildly, shaking his golden curls. "I wouldn't have expected her to call him an overgrown canary, though."

We all took a moment to consider Raphael's observation. Then, Michael started to laugh. His laughter boomed on the celestial walls, shaking columns and shivering windows. Metatron, usually the sternest of us all, started to chortle, Jophiel joined in, and soon, all the archangels were laughing so loudly that the halls of Heaven rang with angelic mirth.

Of all the infinite number of reasons that angels love humans, I sometimes think it is your capacity to surprise us that delights us the most.

CHAPTER THIRTY-TWO

It is hard to believe that I ever had the audacity to face down the mighty Gabriel, Archangel of the Annunciation and Chief Messenger of the Divine. But when I saw him emerge from the waterfall, it was as though a wall in my head shattered, allowing a tsunami of memories to flood my mind all at once.

Suddenly, I remembered Gabriel leaning over my cradle when I was a baby, long before I could recognize either of my parents. I remembered toddling over to him when I was learning to walk, playing games and having pretend tea parties with him, and slowly coming to the realization that no one could see him but me.

The Archangel Gabriel was my "imaginary friend" when I was little; I called him "Gabby." My parents thought their little girl just had an active imagination. They could never see Gabriel, even when he standing right beside me, holding my hand and smiling fondly at our entire family.

He stopped being "Gabby" to me when I was older, maybe seven or eight. But Gabriel did not fade away with my early childhood. He stayed a constant friend, always appearing the instant I whispered his name. By then, I had stopped talking about him with my parents, realizing that they would worry if their daughter's "imaginary friend" lingered past an appropriate age. An active imagination is one thing, hallucinations are quite another.

Still, Gabriel remained my best, most reliable companion. As soon as school let out, I would ride my bike to the waterfall and spend hours with the archangel, talking, playing games, and listening to his stories. No one thought to worry about me at home. Back then, the kids in my neighborhood rode their bikes all over the north side of town and played pretty much wherever we liked. Besides, Gabriel may well have whispered soothing messages to my parents, assuring them that I would be safe, whenever I went off to see him. And I *was* safe, as safe as any human being could be. What harm could possibly befall a child who was under the personal protection of an archangel?

Then one day I went to the waterfall to wait, and Gabriel didn't show up. I went the next day, and again the day after that, but my celestial friend never appeared. I cried myself to sleep that third night, devastated that Gabriel had abandoned me. In the morning, I had forgotten all about him. He had vanished from my mind, leaving behind only the mildest hint of loss and longing. I woke up remembering that I had gone to sleep unhappy, but without any idea why.

I avoided the waterfall after that day, though. It wasn't hard to do. I was getting older, school was growing more demanding, and the other children in my class were becoming more perceptive. They didn't know about Gabriel, but they sensed that there was something different about me, and they didn't much like it. Hanging out at Angel Falls by myself day after day would have been irrefutable proof that I was odd, a worthy target for teasing.

When my mother vanished, I instinctively started going back to the waterfall, though I couldn't have said what I hoped to find there. Gabriel didn't reappear to comfort me and my memories of him didn't return. Finally, I seemed to remember that, when I was in third grade, I had accidentally dropped a necklace I liked into the pool and had not been able to retrieve it. That unhappy "memory" was enough to keep me away from Angel Falls for years.

Or it had been until that afternoon, when hurt and confusion drove me back there. Now, my childhood friend Gabriel stood before me, and I could not have been less happy to see him.

I advanced on him, shouting, my hands clenched into fists. "Answer me, Gabriel! Where did you go? Why did you abandon me like that? I was devastated when you disappeared! *Tell me*!"

"I never abandoned you, Kate," he answered, his melodious voice colored with surprise. "It was just time for you to grow up and move into a more conventional life. You were becoming too unusual, too visibly special, and it was hurting you in other ways. But you got terribly upset whenever I tried to explain that to you. Eventually, I decided it would be best to erase your memories of me for a while. That way you could have a more normal childhood. You needed that experience to become the person you are now.

"And it wasn't as if I was really gone, Kate," Gabriel continued, almost pleading. "My angels and I always watched over you, and we helped you whenever we could without it being too obvious. How do you think you won all those debating trophies?"

"You're taking credit for my *debate* wins, now?" I demanded, with renewed fury.

"No, no, of course not!" he answered quickly, raising his lovely hands again. "You did the work, and you deserve all the credit for it. I just bolstered you a little sometimes, suggesting ideas for research or helping you find the perfect word when you needed it. You were always very good, Kate. All I did was help you to be just that tiny, little bit better."

"Gee, thanks," I snapped back. "I'll bet you 'helped' me with law school, too, didn't you?" He nodded, seemingly dazed, his hazel eyes wide. "What about the bar exam, or my legal practice? You probably even *hypnotized* the senior lawyers so I'd make partner, right?"

"Kate, it doesn't work that way," he said, soothingly, but I cut him off again.

"You're right it doesn't, and I'd be even angrier if it did," I snarled. "You flew out of my life without so much as a decent good-bye when I was just a kid, and I won't let you pretend that you're secretly responsible for everything I managed to achieve on my own after you left. And for the record, nothing you could possibly have done for me since can make up for the fact that you never bothered to come back when my mother disappeared. Gabriel, *where is my mother?*"

The archangel paused for an instant, as if listening to an inner voice, then reluctantly shook his head, his beautiful copper curls swaying gently. It reminded me of the little pauses Lucina took, and that infuriated me even more. "I'm sorry, Kate, but I can't tell you that," he answered.

"*Then what good are you?*" I raged. "You won't tell me where my mother is, and I'll bet you won't tell me anything else I want to know either, like who my real father was or why no one ever told me he existed until after Christopher Cunningham died. I'll bet you won't even tell me who left that anonymous note on my desk in New York, will you? *Will you?*"

"I did," he replied miserably.

"You *what?*" I demanded.

"I left the note on your desk, and I'm the one who wrote it," Gabriel replied. "You needed to come home to Angel Falls, and I didn't think you'd get here before Christopher died if I didn't give you a nudge. You're always so hard on yourself, Kate. I feared you would never forgive yourself if he passed away before you had a chance to reconcile with him. It didn't work—only because he wouldn't talk to you, which certainly wasn't your fault—but for both of your sakes, I thought it was important to try.

"The note was kind of a last-ditch effort," the archangel continued. "Paula had left a message for you earlier that day, but you never checked your voicemail at home. You were so completely focused on your legal work that you ignored every hint and portent I put in front of you. I happened to have dropped in on Lucina just before I wrote the note. I borrowed her handwriting and stationery. She knows nothing about this."

"You 'dropped in on Lucina,'" I echoed. "You said that like she's a friend of yours. So, she can see you and talk to you like I can?"

Gabriel nodded again. "She's the Lady of Angel Abbey, Kate. She can converse with any angel she likes."

"So, what you're saying, then," I continued, the truth beginning to dawn, "is that Lucina had nothing to do with that note on my desk. You're the one who left it there, not her. And you're probably the one who made me forget my briefcase in the cab. Am I right?"

"Not about that," Gabriel insisted. Can an archangel get defensive? "You forgot the briefcase yourself, and you're the one who chose to lie about it later. All I did was make sure the briefcase ended up back at the law firm. Choices have consequences, Kate. You needed to be reminded not to protect yourself with lies."

I had been livid before, but that last bit of sanctimonious claptrap left me so outraged I could barely speak. "So, I'm being sued for three million dollars, my legal career is in shambles, and I'm on the edge of bankruptcy because the great Archangel Gabriel took it upon himself to give naughty little Katie a lesson in *honesty?* Of all the arrogant, hypocritical trash!

"There are people in this world who extinguish cigarettes on children, Gabriel!" I cried. "There are people who torture and kill animals for fun. People who cheat, or murder, or steal millions from charity, and *they get away with it*! Why don't you punish *them?*

"Yes, I lied to Roy Blackwell," I went on, my words tumbling faster and faster. "He's a vicious bully who's as dishonest and self-dealing as anyone I've ever met in my life. You want to teach someone a lesson? Why not him? Roy Blackwell would deserve whatever you wanted to do to him. Instead, you went after *me*? How *could* you?"

"Roy Blackwell will reap what he has sown in good time," Gabriel countered, struggling for equanimity. "You can't always see Heaven's design from down here on Earth. But you can't adopt Roy Blackwell as your standard, Kate! You have to be better than that. You can't fulfill your divine purpose if you're not."

"From what you're saying, I don't want to 'fulfill my divine purpose,'" I shot back. "If 'fulfilling my divine purpose' means working with someone as self-satisfied and hypocritical as you are, Gabriel, I want no part of it. You flew out of my life once, so go fly away again. Leave me alone, Gabriel. We are *done*." I turned and stormed away, leaving the archangel behind.

Part of me, the better part, hoped that Gabriel would come after me and insist that I stop and talk with him until I had calmed down. But from what I have since come to understand about free will, stopping me or forcing me to talk was something that even the mighty Archangel Gabriel could not do. I had refused to fulfill my divine purpose, and I had explicitly told him to go away and leave me alone. The rules of Heaven required him to respect my choices, however ill-considered they might be.

I strode back up the path and through the woods, my earlier hurt and confusion transformed into a toxic cloud of fury. My pulse was pounding in my ears, and I was so angry that I could barely breathe. Even the animals of the forest could feel my rage, it seemed. Birds flew away in terror from nearby tree branches as I passed, and one poor little rabbit bolted from cover and took off through the woods when I got too close. I didn't care—my blood boiled with indignation. I stormed out of the woods, past the barn, across the courtyard to the front of Angel Abbey, and up to my car.

My earlier concerns about safety were completely forgotten. My hands were shaking so violently that I could barely open the car door, but eventually I managed. I climbed inside, slammed the door behind me, and spun out of the Abbey parking lot as fast as I could, churning gravel behind me.

Furious as I was, I managed to get home without hurting anybody. The only one there was Honoré, fast asleep on his Christmas cushion. Bella had left a note saying that she and Andrew had gone out to the movies, a rare treat for them. At least they hadn't gone to the Abbey, I thought bitterly. All I needed was for Bella and Andrew to talk to Lucina and find out what I had said to her. They would never forgive me. I tossed Bella's note aside and stomped upstairs to my room.

With all the changes we had made in the house, I still had not gotten around to redecorating my own bedroom. But now that I could remember my childhood friendship with Gabriel, the room didn't feel just juvenile and outdated. It felt downright oppressive. Everything in sight reminded me of the archangel, and I didn't like it one bit.

Looking around, I noticed the corner of my overnight bag protruding from the closet. The urge to get away suddenly overwhelmed me. I snatched up the bag and started hurling clothes into it, choosing casual things that would meet my needs for a few days. I debated taking Honoré along, but decided against it. He would be safer and more comfortable with Bella and Andrew than he would be on the road with me.

Stumbling back downstairs, I tried to decide how to explain my sudden disappearance. I rejected the idea of leaving a note claiming that something had come up around the lawsuit and that Richard had asked me to go back to Manhattan. That story would have been too easy to check. When Richard denied it, Bella and Andrew would have been left to worry and wonder where I had gone. Besides, although I would have died sooner than admit it just then, Gabriel's words about choices and consequences still echoed in my mind. Bella and Andrew had been better to me than anyone. They didn't deserve lies from me.

Finally, I scrawled a few words on the bottom of the note Bella had left for me. "Need to think some things through. I'll be back in a couple of days. Don't worry." They still would, I knew, but at least I had written the truth. I would have to leave before they got back, though. Otherwise, they would want to know what was wrong and in all probability, would try to persuade me to stay home. How could I tell them what had happened? I didn't understand it myself.

I leaned over and rubbed the top of Honoré's head. "Take care of them while I'm away, OK?" I whispered, and he purred a response. I picked up my bags, got into the Mustang, and, quite literally, drove off into the sunset, heading north and west.

Archangel Michael speaks:

It was pretty funny when Kate first turned on Gabriel. He had been so full of himself with this project, so proud of Angel Abbey and all the progress he had been making. Watching him backpedal was mighty entertaining for the first minute or two.

But it wasn't so funny when Kate kept up her rant. There are about a zillion people on Earth who would happily give their souls for the kind of special attention that Kate had gotten from Gabe. Not that they would have to. He devotes plenty of time to watching out for anybody who wants him, believe me.

But Kate? All she could see was that he hadn't given her everything she wanted the split second she wanted it. Never a "thank you for all you have done." Just a "why didn't you do even more?" A lot of people are ungrateful like that. Gabe had devoted so much love and care to Kate, though. You'd think she would have learned a little gratitude somewhere along the line.

We all knew how important Angel Abbey was to Gabe, so while he was tied up being chewed out by Kate, Raphael and Chamuel dropped by to check on Lucina. She was in pretty bad shape after the tongue-lashing Kate had given her, but they got her settled down and stable. That was important. Lucina had worked hard to stay sober. She didn't deserve to have Kate push her off the wagon.

Meanwhile, Barachiel scattered extra blessings all over the Abbey, and Raziel made sure nobody remembered seeing Kate go tearing out of the parking lot like she was on her way to a fire or something. It didn't look as if Gabe's plans for Kate were going to work out, but we wanted to do whatever we could to keep his dreams alive. What else is family for?

Even after Kate stomped off, it took Gabe a long time to come home. He must have been pretty upset. We all waited around for him, but then Metatron reminded us that the Universe wasn't going to run itself. One by one, we all went back to work.

Things were real quiet in Heaven when Gabe finally came back. Uriel, Raphael, and I were the only ones still waiting for him. He didn't fly in the way he usually does, flashing his wings and trailing the music of the spheres behind him. He just quietly appeared, looking tired and unhappy. He didn't even lift his wings when he saw us.

"That went well, don't you think?" Gabe joked, but his smile would have broken your heart.

CHAPTER THIRTY-THREE

With no clear destination in mind, I drove aimlessly for hours. The sun set, and the stars came out, one after another. The road curved north and I followed it into the Berkshires, past the New York border and into Massachusetts. I turned east for a while, stopping at a little hotel that looked reasonably clean and comfortable when I got too tired to drive anymore.

The woman behind the front desk was a motherly type in a lacy white sweater who reminded me too much of Bella. Her champagne blonde hair was perfectly coiffed, her pearl button earrings framed her kindly hazel eyes, and half-moon reading glasses hung from a woven gold chain around her neck, resting on her ample bosom. Even from three feet away, I could smell her lily-of-the-valley cologne.

The woman smiled as she reached for my room key. "It is late for you to be driving alone, dearie," she gently chastised, in a lilting Irish brogue. "Is there nobody at home you need to call before you get to bed? You would not want your folks to worry."

Worn out from driving and from anger that had burned down to ashes, I nonetheless felt an almost audible ping in my mind. There was something about the woman that was just too good to be true. "You're an angel, aren't you?" I asked her. "One of Gabriel's friends, I presume?"

The angel looked a little flustered. "Please, do not tell him you figured me out," she whispered, leaning over the desk toward me. "I have never gone undercover before, and I am not very good at it yet."

"Don't worry," I assured her, my voice crisp. "He'll never hear it from me. I'm not speaking to him. Good night." The angel's eyes widened as I snagged the key out of her grasp and marched down the hall to my room. Apparently, she had never seen anybody angry with her boss before.

The angel's advice had been sound. I really should have called Bella and Andrew to tell them where I was. It was late, though, I was bone-tired, and it was all too easy to persuade myself that it would be wrong to wake them.

My sleep that night was heavy and dreamless, as if my capacity to imagine had fled when I turned my back on Gabriel.

I woke late the following morning to a cold, drizzly day. My anger had vanished, leaving behind only a lingering, sullen regret. As I got back in my car and continued north, it felt as though the entire world around me was in mourning for something lovely that had died without my knowledge. Ridiculous, I thought.

What I could not dismiss as easily was the painful certainty that I had treated Lucina very, very badly. Furious though I might have been with Gabriel, I was sure he had told me the truth when he said Lucina had nothing to do with the note on my desk. Archangels could not lie, to my knowledge. But even if they could, Gabriel's simple admission that he was responsible for writing and planting the note, however impossible it might have seemed, made more sense than all my convoluted theories about Lucina conspiring with some unknown third party.

Trouble was, I had not just accused Lucina unfairly. I had been downright savage about it. I could not begin to imagine how to apologize to her, assuming she would even allow me into her presence again. She had been nothing but kind to me, and I had repaid her attempts at friendship with viciousness and mistrust.

What on earth was the matter with me?

It would have been easy to fall back on my usual round of excuses. My mother's disappearance, my father's insistence that I be better than everyone else every minute of every day, the losses I had suffered, the various pains I had endured. But it was now clear to me that I had also enjoyed blessings most people could not even begin to imagine. A real, live archangel had taken a personal interest in me from the time I was too small to stand. And not just any archangel, if you wanted to be really snobbish about it, but one of the most celebrated spirits in all of Creation. I had been befriended by the same archangel who was said to have announced the conception of Jesus to his mother and dictated the Koran to the Prophet Mohammed. Even though he had left me for a time, Archangel Gabriel himself had returned to me, and I had screamed at him like a fishwife before ordering him out of my presence.

What in Heaven's name had I been thinking?

Again, it would have been easy to make excuses. Blinded with rage, I had simply forgotten that Gabriel was an archangel. I treated him like an ordinary human being who had let me down, not an immortal spirit who could probably reduce me to a smoking pile of ashes. (Wasn't Gabriel supposed to have been among the angels who leveled Sodom and Gomorrah? I couldn't remember and was afraid to think about it.)

But that excuse unraveled the instant I wondered why it would be OK to treat anybody that way, archangel or mortal. Suppose Jack, for instance, had vanished from my life for years and then unexpectedly reappeared. Instead of greeting him with open arms or, at least, giving him a chance to explain his disappearance, would I have raged at him that way?

Yes—I absolutely would.

The abrupt realization that I had allowed myself to grow up into an angry, suspicious, thankless, and very demanding woman hit me hard, even harder than my early memories of Gabriel had. OK, I'd had a difficult childhood, but I had read enough books and seen enough reality TV to know that I was not alone. A lot of people had terrible childhoods. From what Lucina said, hers had been a nightmare. For all her little faults and foibles, though, Lucina was a much kinder person than I had ever been. And my early hardships had been so much milder than hers! I'd had a nice house to grow up in, plenty of food to eat, Bella and Andrew to look out for me, Honoré for company. Heck, I had even had the personal attention of a genuine archangel.

Maybe that was my problem, I thought. Maybe Gabriel came and went before I was old enough to appreciate him.

Even that excuse rang hollow. Gabriel had returned to me when I was fully grown, and I had rejected him like the spoiled, selfish brat I still was. The memory of my last words to him stung, and I could feel my cheeks growing hot. How many people had a real archangel offering to help them fulfill their destinies? How many people even had a destiny to fulfill in the first place? I had been offered the chance of a lifetime and instead of falling to my knees in gratitude, I had thrown a temper tantrum and stomped away.

The childishness and stupidity of what I had done took my breath away.

I drove and drove through the cold spring rain, my thoughts pursuing one another in dark circles of shame. Even guilt and sorrow will not stave off the body's needs forever, though. By late afternoon, I started to get hungry.

Then I heard a little chime, the Mustang's way of letting me know that its gas tank was almost empty. Where had I heard that the ringing of a bell meant an angel was near? I couldn't remember, and it didn't matter anyway. What I needed at that moment was gas for my car and something to eat.

Luckily, I found a little diner with a gas station beside it just a few more miles down the road. I pulled in and refilled my tank, then went into the diner to get some lunch.

The place was almost empty. The middle-aged waitress in the pink uniform and spotless white apron told me to sit wherever I liked. I chose a booth by the window and sat down, idly perusing the menu.

Like most diners, this one offered an amazing array of choices. The menu listed everything from all-day breakfasts to homemade Greek specialties, but the idea of eating anything that elaborate just didn't appeal. I settled on a simple cheeseburger and a diet soda, then sat back to wait for my meal, watching the raindrops slide, one after another, down the wide picture window.

The waitress dropped off my lunch, which looked and smelled remarkably appetizing. Funny, I thought, how your life can fall apart in a day but you still need to eat when the crisis is over. I took a few bites of the burger, deliciously hot under its blanket of melted cheddar and nestled in a toasted bun covered in sesame seeds, and drank about half of the soda. Then I went back to staring out the window. I needed to figure out where to go next and what to do, but I could not think of how to begin.

"You might want to try the baklava, Kate," a familiar voice said from behind me. "The owner's grandmother makes it from scratch. It is really outstanding."

I turned to see the dark-haired man from the library steps standing in the aisle beside my table. He was dressed in jeans, hiking boots, and a garnet red shirt, and he was not alone. A tall, handsome, younger-looking man with rumpled blonde curls and an open, boyish expression stood beside him. The second man wore olive cargo pants, sandals, and a sage-green Henley under his plaid shirt. "May we join you?" he asked, smiling. His voice was light and friendly, a violin to harmonize with the darker man's viola.

"Sure, why not?" I motioned them toward the empty bench across the table. I sounded calm enough, but my stomach fluttered with panic. Even if I had not met the dark-haired one before, it was easy to recognize my new companions from their many portraits at the Abbey. They were archangels for sure, and had probably come to discuss what had happened with Gabriel. That could not be good. Was I about to be turned into a pillar of salt?

I decided that if the archangels wanted to hurt me, they would have done so already. Besides, being turned into a pillar of salt would almost have been a relief. It beat having to limp home and clean up the mess I had left behind.

They slid into the booth across from me, the blond man first. I turned to the darker one. "Archangel Uriel, I presume?" I asked, remembering the name Lucina had mentioned. He nodded solemnly, and as added confirmation, the image of the garnet-clad angel from the painting in the Abbey library flew into my mind. Unlike the painting, though, the angel in my mind was radiant, shining, and vividly *alive*. "And may I ask your name?" I inquired of his companion, trying to keep a quaver out of my voice.

"I'm Raphael," the younger one replied. The image of Uriel vanished from my mind, replaced by an angel in rippling emerald robes. He had enormous, gilt-edged white wings and a halo much like Gabriel's, and he carried a lantern in one hand and a medical caduceus in the other. The image gently faded away. "I've been looking forward to meeting you, Kate. You're all the talk of Heaven, you know." He smiled, his leaf-green eyes twinkling under impossibly long golden lashes.

"It's nice to meet you, too, Raphael," I said, fearing that I might lose the battle to keep my apprehensiveness hidden. It was one thing to converse with Gabriel, whom, however improbably, I had known since childhood. He might be an archangel, but I didn't think of him that way. Sitting across the table from two other archangels whom I did not really know was something else entirely. It was marvelous and exciting—and it scared me half to death.

"Please don't be afraid, Kate. We're not here to hurt you," Raphael said earnestly. He seemed less reserved than Uriel, and friendlier, somehow, than Gabriel. Was he reading my mind? Not necessarily, I thought. Faced with two archangels, most people would probably be every bit as terrified as I was.

Raphael reached out to pat my hand, and my nervousness vanished instantly. I wondered whether he had cast a spell or something to calm me down. The mere thought sent my head spinning. Nothing in my life had prepared me for an encounter as miraculous as this.

"I'm going to have to ask you both to forgive me," I replied. "I don't really know how to properly address an archangel, much less two of them. My apologies for whatever mistakes of etiquette I make."

"You do not need to apologize to us, Kate," Uriel said courteously. "We are the ones who interrupted you. Thank you for inviting us to sit down." Just as he had on the library steps, Uriel reminded me of an Old World aristocrat, all refined gestures and lovely manners.

"We really just came to make sure you're all right," Raphael chimed in. What was it about him that was so comforting? "Most people don't have direct contact with archangels while they're on Earth, and it can be traumatizing if they aren't prepared for it. You're a special case, having played with Gabriel so much when you were little. But you had a pretty rough time at the waterfall. Are you OK? We were concerned."

"I'm fine," I told him, trying to mean it. "Just a little rattled." Raphael nodded encouragingly as Uriel calmly looked on. Sitting with the two of them, my confusion and fear slowly ebbed away. "I can't believe I'm asking this," I finally said, "because I'm still really angry with him. But is Gabriel all right?"

Uriel leaned forward. "I will not lie to you, Kate," the archangel replied gravely. "In all the millennia, I have never seen Gabriel so despondent. He has been eagerly planning his reunion with you for years. Your reaction to seeing him again came as quite a shock to him."

"But it's not your fault, Kate," Raphael interrupted earnestly. Uriel shot him a withering look. Raphael favored him with a wide, innocent grin, then turned back to me and winked. Despite myself, I laughed.

"I warned Gabriel that the patch he put over your memories of him years ago might fall apart when you saw him," Raphael said. "And that you might not be able to handle them all at once. He was so busy with his plans, though, that I don't think he really paid attention to what I said. Gabriel can be a little overconfident sometimes."

The conversation was so utterly surreal that my earlier fear was replaced by a sort of dazed amiability. "Are archangels even allowed to do that?" I asked, half-joking. "Criticize each other, or make mistakes? Aren't all of you supposed to be perfect?"

Uriel smiled broadly, revealing immaculate white teeth. "Only the

Creator is perfect, Kate, though most angels come fairly close by human standards," he said.

"Unless you count the Adversary," Raphael interrupted in a broad stage whisper. "He's about as far from perfect as it's possible to get." I laughed again—Raphael's good humor was irresistible.

Arching a dark eyebrow in Raphael's direction, Uriel pressed on. "We are *not* discussing the Adversary's shortcomings today, Raphael. He is another matter altogether. Kate, I presume you are asking about the idiosyncrasies and character traits that make each of the archangels an individual. Just like people, every angel is unique, with distinct personalities and preferences. The Creator is far too imaginative to design a Heaven filled with generic, cookie-cutter angels. Consequently, as you may be able to imagine, even the archangels occasionally disagree." His smile widened and then vanished as quickly as it came.

The briefest glimpse of tall marble columns, inlaid floors, and spectacularly colored skies filled with hosts of flying angels flashed across my mind, making me dimly remember something I had learned in a Sunday school class many years before. "Wait a minute," I asked, "aren't there four of you? Michael, Raphael, Gabriel, Uriel. Is Michael waiting outside with a flaming sword or something?"

Raphael's smile vanished, concern incongruous on his friendly face. "No, we left Michael at home. This wouldn't be the best time for you to meet him, Kate. He's not especially happy with you right now."

"What my brother *means* to say, Kate," Uriel interjected, shooting Raphael a cautionary glance, "is that there are many more than four archangels. However, you are right that the four of us are the ones humanity knows best, Michael most of all. Gabriel does his publicity, and there is no one more effective. You know that Michael is in charge of the Heavenly armies, do you not?"

I nodded, remembering Sunday school class once more.

"Michael is a warrior, Kate. He is the biggest and strongest of all of us, and he can be intimidating," Uriel explained. "He would never dream of hurting you, and he does not hold a grudge, but Raphael is correct. Michael is very protective of Gabriel, as he is of all Creation. He is not always tactful when he thinks someone has been unfair. You probably would not appreciate what he would be likely to say to you just at present." He shot Raphael another significant look, as if warning him not to say any more.

The conversation was starting to feel more and more like something out of a lost C. S. Lewis novel. Archangels with flaws, foibles, differences of opinion, and individual personalities? I could not wrap my mind around it all.

"All right," I finally said, "it sounds as though I probably ought to ask Michael's pardon at some point. Right now, though, it seems as if there are other things I need to do first. We all know that I have some fences to mend back in Angel Falls. Where do I start?"

"Where do you *want* to start?" Raphael asked.

"What do you mean?" I shot back, startled. "You're archangels. Aren't you here to give me some kind of divine directive or something?"

"We do not do that, Kate," Uriel replied seriously. "You have free will. We respect your right to make your own decisions. We can offer suggestions, but only if you want them. You were crystal clear with Gabriel about wanting him to leave you alone. He will honor your wishes. We are here to offer our help if you would like it, not to force you into anything you do not want to do. So, would you rather we kept our thoughts to ourselves?"

Coming from a human being, Uriel's comments might have felt like a cheap shot. But Uriel was an archangel, and it sounded as if he were genuinely asking what I wanted, which was amazing in and of itself. It was difficult to imagine, much less accept, that such a magnificent being could be so humble. Nonetheless, I had no doubt that Uriel was perfectly sincere.

"I came down harder than I should have on Gabriel," I admitted. "So yes, I would like your suggestions if you're willing to give them to me. There isn't a lot of precedent out there for how to patch up a friendship with an archangel, but I am sorry for the things I said. I would like to make things right with Gabriel if you think he would let me try."

Uriel shook his head, but he was smiling again. "Lawyers and precedent," he sighed. "Where did you lawyers ever get the idea that doing the same thing over and over again will lead to anything but the same result? Do not worry about precedent, Kate. Gabriel will be happy to talk with you at any time, I promise. He has undoubtedly forgiven you already. He cares about you a lot, you know."

"There's someone else you might want to talk to first, though," Raphael added earnestly, "if you're really serious about wanting suggestions from us."

"Lucina?" I asked, my heart sinking.

"I know you're embarrassed, Kate," Raphael said. "But if you don't apologize to Lucina before you talk to Gabriel, you know he'll ask you to do it. Then you'll get mad at him all over again." Raphael's beautiful green eyes widened a little, as though he was afraid he had said too much. "Sorry," he continued, "but that *is* what would happen."

He had a point. I was already feeling defensive about Lucina. Any suggestion from Gabriel to apologize would feel like a rebuke, no matter how tactfully he worded it. "Fair enough. I was way out of line, and Lucina deserves an apology," I admitted. "But honestly, what *is* it about that woman that makes everyone so crazy protective of her?" Repentant as I might be, it was hard not to be jealous of the solicitous response Lucina seemed to evoke from everyone she met.

"It's not just Lucina. Gabriel loves both of you, Kate," Raphael insisted. "And he really hates it when his favorites don't get along."

"I'm one of his favorites?" I asked. "Why in the world would that be?" Given all the wretched things I had done, I could not imagine why the Archangel Gabriel would waste another nanosecond of thought or affection on me.

"Let's just say that we archangels have an easier time seeing the best in people than you do in yourselves," Uriel replied, a smile hovering around his lips again. "You are a much better person than you realize, Kate, especially when you forget to obsess about how horrible you are."

Uriel stood, and motioned for Raphael to do the same. "Enjoy your lunch, Kate. And, if you are open to one more angelic suggestion, do not forget to leave a good tip. Doris over there"—he pointed to the waitress in the pink dress—"has been supporting her two teenage nephews since her sister died of leukemia last year. She will make good use of every penny you can spare."

Raphael leaned over and picked up my hands in both of his. I felt a wave of gentle warmth pour through my body, and I was immediately filled with happiness and hope. He winked at me, his golden lashes gleaming in the afternoon light. "It was such a pleasure to meet you in person, Kate. I'm sure I'll see you again sometime soon."

"Take care, Kate, and drive safely," Uriel said, with a courtly little bow. "We shall meet again." And then the two of them were gone, leaving not so much as a smudge on the floor or a dent in the bench cushion to show where they had been. My burger was as hot as it had been the moment they appeared, and the ice in my soda was unmelted.

I finished my lunch in a happy haze, too confounded by our conversation to think about much of anything. A few minutes later, Doris came by with my check in her hand. "Can I get you anything else, honey?" she asked.

I noticed the weary lines on her face, the graying hair that dye would no longer color, the slump of suppressed exhaustion in her posture. Doris was a lady who worked long, hard days for far too little money, all so she could take care of the people she loved. In that instant, she struck me as beautiful beyond belief.

"That's everything, Doris," I said. "Thank you for taking such good care of me today."

She brightened a little, and her smile made her look ten years younger. "My pleasure, honey. Come back and see us anytime. You can just leave the money here whenever you're ready to leave."

My lunch had cost less than ten dollars. I left that, along with a hundred-dollar tip, and went out to my car for the long drive back to Angel Falls.

Opening the car door, I discovered that the archangels hadn't vanished without a trace after all. On the driver's seat inside my locked car sat a large white feather, immaculate and beautiful. Smiling, I unlocked the car door and slipped inside, tucking the feather into my hair. The Mustang started immediately, and together we headed for home.

Archangel Gabriel speaks:

Kate was right that archangels can't lie. We aren't supposed to despair, either. In a universe with infinite opportunities for redemption, there's always reason for hope. Besides, archangels stand closer to the Creator than you do, and we see miracles every minute. There's no excuse for an archangel to lose faith, not ever.

So, by the time I got back to Heaven I was already starting to develop contingency plans for Angel Abbey. My heart really wasn't in it, though. I had been so sure Kate was the one—but she had been very, very clear that she wanted nothing more to do with her divine purpose or, for that matter, with me. I didn't like her decision, but I had to honor it. Only the Adversary and his minions try to coerce people after they say no.

So I was sitting by myself, staring out at the Infinite Void and trying to come up with a workable alternative, when I felt a hard thump between my wings. It had to be Michael—nobody else in all of Creation would dare get my attention that way. "Look, Mike, I'm really not in the mood," I began, but he cut me right off.

"Gabe, come with me. Right now. You've got to see this." He yanked me to my feet—Michael's very strong when he wants to be—and pointed toward New England. "Look down. Now."

I followed the angle of his finger down to a diner in Massachusetts. Kate's car was parked in the lot, and I groaned. "Let it go, Mike! You heard her. She doesn't want anything to do with me, and you know I can't interfere with her free will."

"Just shut up and look in the diner," he insisted. Sometimes I forget that Michael is the commander of the Divine Armies, but he always finds ways to remind me. So, sighing, I took a look inside.

Uriel and Raphael were in the diner, sitting in a booth across the table from Kate and having a perfectly rational conversation. That was amazing all by itself. If you had asked me, I would have told you that Kate would never willingly talk to an archangel ever again. I leaned in to get a better look.

"Listen," Michael barked.

So, I listened, and heard every word Kate had to say. She agreed to apologize to Lucina and, hallelujah, she even wanted to patch things up with me! By the time she took off in her little Mustang, I could have flown from Earth to Sirius and back without even breaking a sweat, I was so happy.

And oh, by the way, Uriel and Raphael didn't leave Kate that feather. I did. If she could apologize, well, so could I.

Do I have the best brothers in all of Creation or what?

CHAPTER THIRTY-FOUR

It was well after midnight when I parked the Mustang in our garage. The rest of the household was quiet as I crept quietly into the house. I tiptoed upstairs, slipped into bed, and was fast asleep in minutes.

I woke the next morning to the sound of Bella talking on the phone. "I'm sorry, Richard," she was saying, "but I really don't know where she is. She took off two days ago." There was a pause, when Richard must have been talking on the other end. "Yes, she left a note, but she didn't say when she would be back," Bella said. Another pause, a little longer this time. "No, Richard, I haven't called the police. Kate is an adult. If she wants to go somewhere on her own, Andrew and I can't stop her. And for what it's worth, we're every bit as worried as you are."

The tension in Bella's voice could have cracked walnuts.

"Bella, wait," I called. "It's OK. I got in late last night after you went to bed. Tell Richard I'll be right there."

I threw a bathrobe over my pajamas and ran downstairs to take the phone. From the expression on Bella's face when she saw me, it was pretty obvious that the note I had left telling her not to worry had just the opposite effect. She handed me the phone and turned away, looking as though she was struggling not to cry.

"Richard, what's up?" I asked, trying not to sound too breathless.

"Kate, how fast can you get over here?" He sounded excited.

"Maybe twenty minutes," I answered, trying to figure out how quickly I could get in and out of the shower. "What's so urgent?"

"Remember Jeanine Powell?" he asked.

"Of course. Why?"

"Because she's sitting in my office, that's why. Just get here, OK?" He hung up before I could even say good-bye.

When I hung up the phone, Bella was watching me with reddened eyes. "Look, Bella, I'm really sorry—" I started, but she cut me off.

"No, Katie, don't even say it," she answered, her voice clipped and hard. "It's just like I told Richard. You're an adult. You can make your own choices, which apparently include vanishing for days at a time without telling us where you are going, how to reach you, or when you will be back. Oh, and then there's whatever happened at the Abbey. No one has seen the Lady since you left. Did you have another falling out with her?"

It was tempting to deny it, but I could not lie to Bella. "Yes, and it was entirely my fault," I confessed. "I jumped to conclusions and accused Lucina of something she hadn't done. As soon as I'm done in Richard's office, I will go over to the Abbey to apologize, if Lucina will talk to me.

"And Bella," I added, shamefaced, "I'm sorry I worried you and Andrew by taking off like that. I've got an awful lot going on right now. I just needed to get away and try to get some perspective on everything."

Bella's eyes narrowed. She nodded, not entirely convinced. "You know, you're right," she finally said. "You needed to get some perspective, and I sincerely hope that you did.

"You've had a rough time in a lot of ways, Kate," Bella continued. "I wouldn't wish on my worst enemy some of the things that have happened to you. But you're not a little girl anymore. It's time you got over the idea that having a less than perfect childhood entitles you to behave badly toward the people who love you. You're not the only person who has suffered, Kate. You need to grow up, get over the past, and start taking responsibility for your actions.

"Now, go find out whatever it is that Richard thinks is so important," Bella said firmly. "And when you're done, see if you can patch things up with Lucina. You've been suspicious of her from the minute you met her. But she's very important to a lot of people, including Andrew and me, and she does a world of good for our community. If you can't get over this idea that you're entitled to pass judgment on Lucina and that you know better than all the people who think well of her, let's just say that I'm going to be very, very disappointed." She turned and walked into the kitchen, leaving me alone with my shame.

I stood there, silent, for a moment, letting her words sink in. Then I took a deep breath and headed up the stairs. There would be time for contrition later. Right now, I had fences to mend.

After grabbing a shower, I took a quick look through my closet for something to wear. The beautiful, arty dresses Bella had bought for me all felt inappropriate. Those clothes were for a happy woman with loving friends and fun things to do. Before I could enjoy them again, I would have to earn them back.

Instead, I threw on jeans, loafers, and a simple beige sweater, and then dragged my hair back into a plain, practical ponytail. Dressed, I hurried downstairs, got into my car, and drove to Richard's office.

When I got there the door was slightly ajar, so I knocked and let myself in. Richard and Jeanine were sitting across his desk from one another, laughing over big mugs of coffee. Richard has an amazing way of ingratiating himself with people, I thought, and resolved to put my lingering upset aside. "Sounds like I'm late for the party," I said, forcing a smile and sliding into the empty chair next to Jeanine's. "Good to see you, Jeanine. Thanks so much for coming."

Jeanine turned to look at me, and her lovely eyes widened. "Kate? Wow, you look different! What happened to you? You could almost pass for a human being now."

Tempting as it was to snap back at her, I bit my tongue. What could I honestly say, anyway? She was right, and the look Richard shot my way warned me not to indulge my temper for once. "It's good to see you," I said, forcing another smile. "You look great, Jeanine. Amazingly enough, life has actually been better for me since I got fired. How about you?"

Jeanine rolled her eyes. "Kate, neither one of us belonged in that hellhole in the first place," she retorted. "I would have said that to you back then, if you hadn't stopped talking to me when you made partner. Once that happened, I figured you deserved whatever you got."

My smile faded. "You were right about that, and I'm really sorry," I said. "I let the firm culture get to me, and I was dead wrong to do it. But if you're that angry with me, Jeanine, why are you here?"

"Who said I was angry?" she fired back. "I'm just telling you the truth. I figured out pretty quickly what was going on with you, Kate. A lot of us did. Anybody who had to work that closely to Blackwell had no choice but to cover her backside any way she could. If you were seen talking to the peons, Blackwell would've made your life even worse than it already was.

"It's just that I looked up to you, you know?" she went on, her voice softening. "You were always so strong, so sure of yourself. I wanted to have that kind of confidence more than anything. It hurt when you cut me off, but I understood why you did it. I couldn't even blame you, really.

"So when I heard that your lawyer had called my house, I decided I'd better find out what was going on," Jeanine continued. She turned to Richard with a wicked little smile. "Sounds like my mother really tore into you, counselor. Sorry about that! She gets awfully protective where her kids are concerned."

"Apology accepted," Richard said, smiling. "I understand about mothers. But Jeanine, tell Kate what you told me about why you left the firm."

Jeanine sat back in her chair, took a big swallow of coffee, and told us her story. It soon became clear that I was not the only young woman lawyer Blackwell had bullied.

Jeanine had been assigned to work on a lawsuit against one of the firm's major clients, a big, multinational IT company. The plaintiff, a small software-design company, claimed that our client had stolen one of its best products, a virtual world that allowed hundreds of users to work online together to create a sustainable utopia. The program had been designed for universities to use in training students, and the plaintiff had been selling it for almost nothing, so schools around the world could afford to buy it. According to the plaintiff, our client had illegally hacked into the plaintiff's computer system, stolen the program, and transformed it into a video game. Our client then posted the redesigned game online, where it was bringing in millions of dollars every month from addicted gamers.

It was Jeanine's job to read through the documents that our firm would have to hand over to the plaintiff's lawyers. While going through box after box of innocuous junk, she came across what lawyers call a "smoking gun." In this case, the damning evidence was a chain of e-mails between our client's CEO and various other executives in the company proving that our client had, in fact, deliberately stolen the program exactly as the plaintiff claimed. Those e-mails would have proven the plaintiff's case beyond any doubt.

When Jeanine brought the e-mails to the attention of Adrian Martin, the partner in charge of the defense, Martin ordered her to shred them and destroy any record of them in our files. Jeanine flatly refused. Within minutes, Roy Blackwell was in her office, threatening to fire her for leaking confidential information to the other side if she did not do what Martin had directed.

"Kind of a one-trick pony, isn't he?" Richard observed, smirking. "It's always about leaks with him."

Rather than be forced out, Jeanine chose to resign on the spot. Ruth Martingale tried to talk her out of it, but Jeanine said there were personal reasons for her decision to leave and walked out the door. The lawsuit was settled soon after, she had heard, but she didn't know much more about it.

"I never liked being there anyway," Jeanine declared. "That law firm is a snake pit. What kind of lawyers try to make you lie just so they can win some lawsuit for a dishonest client? Good riddance, is what I say."

It occurred to me to ask Jeanine why she hadn't come and talked to me when Blackwell tried to pressure her, but I already knew the answer. Would I have done anything to help her if she had? Probably not. "You had more guts than I did, Jeanine," I admitted. "I'm so sorry not to have been a better friend to you."

"Hey, that's business, right?" she replied. "But you helped me out a lot when I got started, Kate. That's why I'm here. I wanted to return the favor.

"Unfortunately, though," Jeanine continued, "I'm sure those e-mails are long gone by now. Nobody else knows what happened, so it's a 'he-said, she-said' thing between Blackwell and me. Ruth probably figured it out. She won't be much help to you, though."

"Why not?" Richard asked. "I tried calling her a couple of times, but she never got back to me."

"That's because she can't, at least not right now," Jeanine explained. "You probably don't know this, Kate, but Ruth had a stroke a couple of weeks after Blackwell fired you. She's still alive, but she can't write, and when she tries to talk it comes out all jumbled. The doctors say she may recover eventually, but it's going to take a while."

"You left before I did, Jeanine. How do you know that?" I asked, puzzled.

"Mark Davenport called and told me," Jeanine replied. "He's a nicer guy than you ever gave him credit for, Kate. He just got stuck working with Blackwell, same as you did, and he knew he would never make it in the firm if he tried to get reassigned. You two might really like each other if you ever got together over a drink, you know."

Jeanine stood up, gathering her purse and setting her empty mug on Richard's desk. "Listen, Richard, if you want me to testify I'll do it, though I don't know how much it will help. Ruth is the one you really want, if she ever gets well enough. For now, though, I have to go catch my train."

"You mean, you came all the way up here from North Carolina just to talk to Richard and me?" I asked.

"You sound so shocked, Kate." Jeanine was clearly amused. "I didn't come up *just* to talk to Richard and you, but yes, that's why I'm north of the city. All of a sudden, I got this strong feeling that you needed my help, and I don't like to let those feelings go unanswered. I'm going to stop in the city on the way back, catch up with friends, and maybe take in a show. My mother likes the red velvet petit fours they sell at Zabar's. As long as I'm in Manhattan, I might as well stop by and get her a box." She dipped into her purse and then handed Richard a piece of paper. "Here," she said to him, "that's all my contact information. You let me know if you need me to come up again."

Jeanine started for the door and then turned back. "Kate," she said firmly, "you win this thing, OK? And for whatever it's worth, you look a whole lot better now than you ever did in New York." And then she was gone.

Richard and I looked at each other, nonplussed. "Well, that was interesting," I finally said.

Richard shook his head. "She's a pistol, that's for sure. But she's probably right that her testimony won't mean much if it's just her word against Blackwell's. At least we know why Ruth Martingale never got back to us. Any chance you could find out where she is and how she's doing?"

I thought for a moment, and then the light dawned. "Probably not, but I might know somebody who could. Let me see what I can do."

Richard glanced down at his watch. "Yikes, it's almost two o'clock. Are you hungry, Kate? Maybe we could go grab some lunch somewhere."

It was the first time in months that Richard had invited me anywhere, and I would have loved to accept. But I owed Lucina an apology, and I wasn't going to be any less steadfast than Jeanine had been in coming all the way from North Carolina to Angel Falls based on a mere "feeling" that I needed her help (something I strongly suspected Gabriel might have had a hand in). "Thanks, Richard," I replied, "but I need to take a rain check today. Let me call you later when I know more about finding Ruth. Right now, I'm overdue at Angel Abbey." Shouldering my purse, I headed for the door.

Archangel Gabriel speaks:

It was so refreshing to deal with Jeanine! My angels dropped a couple of tiny hints into her dreams, and she traveled all the way up to Angel Falls to answer our call. Now, that's a lady who can really hear the angels sing!

We talk to you all the time, you know. It's not that we want to dictate every step you take. We just want to help you when we can. If you would only stop long enough to listen or, better yet, even ask our advice, we would be able to spare you so much grief! Mortal life is hard enough—there's no need to make it worse.

Nobody was better than Kate at making things harder than they had to be. She had a positive genius for it! Still, she was always willing to admit to her mistakes—eventually—and try again. That's something a lot of you won't do. We angels don't really understand why people are so stubborn, but we've seen enough to know that we can't persuade you to admit to error and ask for help unless you're good and ready. All we can do is wait, hope, and pray.

Here's a thought for you, though. It's a lot easier to admit to a mistake everyone already knows you've made than to go to all the trouble of pretending it never happened. The truth will come out, sooner or later, because it always does. Might as well accept the inevitable and just 'fess up, don't you think?

CHAPTER THIRTY-FIVE

On my way to the Abbey, it occurred to me that it might not be a bad idea to bring Lucina a peace offering. There was a florist en route, so I stopped and picked up half a dozen roses, cream-colored, with a hint of pink at the tips of their petals, and tied in a sheer ribbon of deeper pink. They looked almost exactly like the roses I had brought on my maiden visit to the Abbey, and I debated for a moment whether to choose something else. But I was really hoping that Lucina and I could start over. Bringing her the same gift I had brought the first time we met seemed fitting, somehow.

I parked in front of the Abbey and walked up the broad front steps, noticing that the gardens were coming into their first spring bloom. The weather vane at the top of the barn swung lazily in the breeze. It was disconcerting to know exactly whom it represented, but there was no doubt that the artist had captured Gabriel's image to perfection.

Just as she had on my very first visit, Amy opened the front door before I could quite touch the knocker. She wasn't smiling this time, though. "Are you here to see the Lady?" she asked, more formal than she had been with me in a long time.

"If she's available," I replied. Was Amy going to stop me at the door? She seemed to consider it for an uncomfortable moment, but then she stepped aside.

"Wait in the sitting room," Amy said. "I'll go find out if the Lady can see you."

She turned and left abruptly, but there was no need for Amy to escort me. I would have known the way blindfolded. I went down the hall and into the sitting room, strolling around and looking at the furnishings while I waited for Amy's return.

Everything looked very different now that I had met a few of the angels who appeared in the Abbey's art collection. In the sitting room alone I found two portraits of Uriel, looking solemn and thoughtful, three portraits of Raphael's friendly, smiling face, and at least five portraits of Gabriel. How had I failed to recognize them before? Maybe it hadn't been a failure to recognize them so much as a simple refusal to look.

Amy came back in about fifteen minutes. "The Lady asked you to wait," she said, even cooler than before. "And you might as well give me those roses. I don't think she wants them."

So much for my peace offering, I thought, silently handing them over. Amy took the roses and left the room without saying another word. I sat down in the chair I had first occupied when Lucina invited me for tea and waited, empty-handed.

Hours went by. The Abbey was unusually quiet that day. Any voices I heard were muted, as if they came from the other side of the building, and I didn't recognize them. No one I knew came in or walked by. No one stopped in to ask whether I needed anything, a remarkable omission in the normally hospitable Abbey. I started to regret refusing Richard's invitation to lunch, as hunger set in, but I didn't move from the sitting room. If this was a test, I was determined to pass it.

The sun had long since set when Lucina finally came in. "You wanted to see me, Kate?" she asked. She looked and sounded exhausted. I felt a stab of guilt, both for the ugly things I had said to her and for making her come talk to me when she so clearly needed to rest.

"Thank you for seeing me, Lucina. I wasn't sure you would," I began, trying to be as humble as possible. "I want to apologize for the terrible things I said to you. I was vicious and hurtful, and I didn't even have my facts straight. I lit right into you and didn't have the decency to let you respond. The things I said were unforgivable, but I want you to know that I'm very, very sorry."

I stood up and faced her again. "I'll leave now, and you won't ever have to see me or talk with me again. Thank you for trying so hard to welcome me to the Abbey. You paid me a great honor, and I'm very sorry not to have deserved it." I turned and started to leave.

"Oh, for pity's sake, sit down," Lucina snapped, pointing at the chair I had just occupied. She had never spoken to me so harshly before. Shocked,

I sat, and she settled into the other chair facing mine, the one where she had sat for tea so many months before.

"You're right about one thing, Kate," Lucina began, her voice hard. "You never gave me a decent chance to tell you my side of the story. If you meant one word of what you just said, however, you're going to do it now.

"That's why I asked you to wait," she continued. "We have things to discuss that other people at the Abbey can't hear. I thought it best to put off talking to you until everyone else went home. I realize that this isn't a private room. After what happened last time, however, it didn't seem like an especially good idea to invite you to my office."

She had a point there. It stung, but I wasn't about to say so. Lucina looked up at the ceiling for a moment, blew out an exasperated puff of air, and continued. "You don't need to explain the things you said to me. Raphael and Chamuel told me the whole story. It makes sense, I suppose. If you really believed that I was somehow involved in a secret plot to destroy your career, no wonder you were so upset."

Lucina leaned forward, pinning me with her gaze. "Let me be perfectly clear, Kate," she said, emphasizing every word. "I had nothing whatsoever to do with that note or anything that happened to you after you found it. *Do you understand that now?*"

I nodded, wide-eyed.

Lucina leaned back, apparently satisfied with my response. "Good. Let's put that behind us, then.

"There's one thing I don't understand, though," she continued. "And I frankly doubt you can explain to me. Why would you ever imagine that anything so bizarre had happened in the first place? Why would I have any interest in ending your legal career? And why in Heaven's name would anyone go to such lengths to get you fired? Surely there would have been simpler ways to make that happen."

"The note was just so mysterious, Lucina," I replied. "It wasn't signed, so I couldn't tell *who* had written it. And it kept turning up out of nowhere, even after I was sure I'd thrown it away. Somebody had to be up to something, playing games somehow. I couldn't tell who it was or what they wanted, and all the uncertainty just made things worse."

Lucina cocked her head to the side for a moment, as if considering what I had said, and then nodded. "All right," she replied, a little less grim. "That must have been pretty disturbing. But why accuse *me*? Surely there were better candidates to be the anonymous author."

"It never occurred to me that you might have written it until I saw your stationery in your office. It's the same paper as the note, and the handwriting is identical too." I raised a hand to stop her before she could interrupt. "I know you didn't write it, Lucina. Gabriel did. He admitted that he borrowed your paper and handwriting. It was convenient, I guess."

Lucina blew out another puff of air. "Ah, Gabriel," she said, a touch of exasperation in her voice. "He can be such a show-off, always sending signs and portents when a simple visitation would do.

"Then again," she went on, "maybe a visitation wouldn't have been a good idea. Raphael said that the two of you hadn't talked in years. Heaven only knows how you would have reacted if Gabriel had appeared on your doorstep out of the blue."

It occurred to me that anyone watching the two of us, talking about archangels as casually as if they were our next-door neighbors, would have thought we were completely insane. "Not well," I admitted. "You may not know this, but after I left here I went down to Angel Falls to calm down. Gabriel appeared out of the waterfall, and all of a sudden I *remembered* him. It was pretty unsettling. What I said to you was nothing compared to the chewing out I gave Gabriel when he showed up out of nowhere."

Lucina's mouth quirked. "Really? I'd have given a great deal to listen in on *that* conversation." Her smile faded. "Seriously though, Kate, it's long past time that you and I were more straightforward with each other. I had been asked not to talk with you about the angels, but you see where that's gotten us. Time for me to straighten my spine and exert my own free will, don't you agree? So, I'll tell you about my angel encounters if you'll tell me about yours. When did you first meet Gabriel?"

"Not sure," I replied. "I remember him leaning over my crib when I was a baby, but he might have been around even before I was born. You?"

Lucina smiled and looked away. "It wasn't until I joined Alcoholics Anonymous. You never did ask me who my sponsor was."

"Whoa! Your sponsor was Archangel Gabriel?" I asked. "That must have been incredibly weird."

"You have no idea," Lucina replied dryly. "He didn't tell me who he was at first. He was just this handsome, amazingly nice guy in the AA group, who treated me well and never tried to get me into bed. He helped me get back on my feet, found me a decent job and an apartment, and was always at the other end of the phone when the urge to start drinking again hit me." She leaned in confidentially and whispered, "To be honest, Kate, I thought he was probably gay."

That sense of the madness of it all swept over me again, and I started to giggle. To my enormous relief, Lucina joined in, and soon the two of us were laughing uncontrollably. "Ah, that's better," she finally gasped. Then she turned to me with a wistful smile. "I've missed you, Kate, prickly pain in the neck that you are." I smiled back sheepishly, glad that Lucina seemed willing to forgive me.

"Anyway," Lucina resumed, "it took me a few years to get stabilized. Then Gabriel invited me out for dinner one night. Over dessert and coffee, he started to tell me who he really was. I thought he was joking, but then everything in the room stopped, like we were in a freeze-frame in a movie or something. Gabriel started to glow all over, almost as if there was a spotlight on him but *inside* of him at the same time. You've seen him—you know what I mean. The glow got stronger, especially around his head and shoulders, until he suddenly had a real, live halo. Then his wings started to appear."

"What did you do?" I asked, mesmerized.

"I jumped up, screaming, and ran out of the restaurant as fast as I could," Lucina replied, laughing. "I have no idea whether anybody ever paid the check. Gabriel was smart enough not to come after me right away. He let me walk for a while by myself. To my own credit, though, I didn't go looking for a bar or a liquor store to drown out the shock. I actually managed to handle it all on my own. It may have been a test of some kind. I really don't know.

"When I finally calmed down and went back to my apartment, Gabriel was waiting for me, with a bunch of roses like the ones you brought," Lucina went on. "They're my favorite flowers—trust an archangel to know something like that. I still didn't believe he was an angel, but he had managed to get into my locked apartment somehow. I couldn't just explain that away.

"The whole situation was so unbelievable that I finally decided he had to be telling me the truth," Lucina continued. "Especially when he started doing little miracles for me, like reviving the dead fern sitting on my windowsill. You wouldn't know it from the gardens at the Abbey, but I've got a horrible black thumb. Nothing short of a miracle was going to bring that poor plant back to life."

Lucina paused for a moment, her eyes unfocused, as if she were looking back to the resurrection of her wilted fern. "When I finally calmed down enough to be able to listen to what he had to say, Gabriel said that he wanted me to be part of a very special project he had engendered centuries ago. He wanted there to be a place that would be a beacon of hope, somewhere anyone could come to find what they needed most. He started the place in the 1700s when he appeared to Jacob Wittesteen and told him to build a town here."

"Wait a minute," I interrupted her. "You mean Gabriel created Angel Abbey more than three hundred years ago?"

"He's immortal, Kate," Lucina replied, a touch tartly. "The archangels' sense of time tends to be different from yours and mine. Three hundred years for us is about three months for them.

"At any rate," she continued, "Gabriel told me that he needed someone to come to the Abbey and be its mistress, if you like, someone people could identify as its visible face. After working with Jacob Wittesteen, who apparently was a real pill, Gabriel decided it would be better for the head of the Abbey to be a 'Lady.' He asked if I would do it. After a whole lot of hemming and hawing and 'why me?' and 'I'm not good enough,' I finally agreed. He installed me as the Lady of Angel Abbey, and I have been here ever since."

"How long has that been?" I asked.

"Twenty-five years on Midsummer Night," she said proudly.

It was a lot to take in. "Lucina," I finally asked, "how is it that I never heard of the Abbey when I was growing up in Angel Falls?"

"Why would you have, Kate?" she asked me back. "Your father was a wealthy, powerful man, so your family never needed charity from us. You were already busy at school, so our classes and get-togethers wouldn't have been of interest. When your mother disappeared, no matter how badly you needed her, you wouldn't have found her here. You did get one thing from us, though. Any idea what that might be?"

A sudden flash of insight hit me. "My cat?" I asked.

"Yes," Lucina confirmed. "Archangel Ariel dropped by one night with a little male Siamese kitten. She had found him on the side of the road, starving and soaking wet. Bella and Andrew were already volunteering at the Abbey once in a while, and Bella offered to take him, because she thought having a kitten might be good for you. She brought the little fellow home and talked your father into giving him to you. You had been pretty angry with your father by all accounts, blaming him for your mother's disappearance. Everyone hoped you might be a little more forgiving if he gave you a pet. Did it work?"

I thought back to Christopher Cunningham clumsily shoving a tiny, fawn-colored ball of fur into my hands. It abruptly occurred to me that it had been Bella, not my father, who had been at the ready with a litter box and food. "Maybe," I admitted. "Things were never great between my father and me. But our relationship might have been even worse if he hadn't given me Honoré."

Lucina smiled. "Let's decide that it worked, then," she said. "Sometimes, Kate, interpreting your memories of the past in the best way rather than the worst is a very good strategy. It can save you a lot of resentment and regret."

She leaned forward again. "The other reason you didn't know about the Abbey before, to be honest, is that you weren't much interested in helping out here. Bella mentioned it to you a few times when you were growing up, but you never took the hint. You were too busy with your schoolwork and extracurriculars.

"I'm not criticizing you," Lucina said, raising a hand to stop me from interrupting to defend myself. "Most teenage kids are the same way, all wrapped up in their own lives. Then you went off to college and law school and on to Manhattan. You didn't come back here for years. Other than your cat, Angel Abbey didn't have much to offer you until now."

It made sense when she put it that way, though I was a little ashamed to have been so self-involved. That was emerging as a bad habit I would definitely have to break. "Fair enough," I admitted. "But speaking of 'why me?' and 'I'm not good enough,' do you have any idea why Gabriel would have taken such an interest in *me*, of all people?

"It makes perfect sense with you, Lucina," I hurried to add. "Even though I haven't done a terrific job of showing it, I think you do amazing things here at the Abbey. Everybody *loves* you. Honestly, if they loved you a little less, I probably would have liked you more at first. I can get pretty competitive." Lucina chuckled. "But, as we've pretty much established, I'm a self-centered, suspicious, impatient, intimidating, and often unreasonable pain in the neck. Why would the great Archangel Gabriel waste even an instant on me?"

Lucina sat back and looked at the ceiling for a moment or two, clearly gathering her thoughts. "You know," she finally admitted, "that's a really good question."

Ouch.

"I'm not going to contradict anything you said about yourself, Kate, so if you're hoping for that, get over it," Lucina said flatly. "What I *can* tell you, though, is that the archangels are able to see virtues in us that we don't necessarily see in ourselves or one another. They somehow manage to coax the best out of us, if only we'll let them.

"Honestly, you wouldn't have been my choice, and you're really going to have to get your temper under control if you're going to succeed here," Lucina went on. "Gabriel wants you, though, and I've learned not to argue with him. The other archangels swear that no matter how far-fetched his ideas might seem to be, Gabriel's always right in the end."

Lucina certainly hadn't pulled any punches. I hadn't asked her to, though, and I deserved every criticism she could fire my way. "OK. But I still don't understand, Lucina. What is Gabriel right about?" I asked weakly.

She leaned back and looked at me, surprise blossoming on her face. "You don't know, do you?" I shook my head.

"Whew," Lucina said, shaking her head in turn. "I'm really going to be in for it when Gabriel comes by next. I honestly thought he would have told you at the waterfall, but maybe you didn't give him the chance. Whatever. I'm not going to keep you in suspense at this point."

"Keep me in suspense about what?" I asked, trying not to show my growing impatience. "Lucina, what are you talking about?"

Lucina took a deep breath. "I'm leaving, Kate. It's time for me to move on, and I'm stepping down," she said. "Gabriel wants you to succeed me as the Lady of Angel Abbey."

Archangel Raphael speaks:

Oh, the expressions that played over Gabriel's face as he watched his two protégées talking together–what a hoot! Gotta say, it was just priceless. One of the things we angels have in common with you folks is that we don't know exactly what people think of us. We can guess, but we don't read minds any more than you do. That's the Master's province, not ours.

Anyway, Gabriel had been looking forward to telling Kate about her glorious future at the Abbey from the time she was a tiny baby. He never expected that she would hear the message from someone else. And when Lucina so blithely dismissed all his signs and portents! Let's just say that if Gabriel had been human, it might have dealt him a mortal blow. He's so proud of his showmanship! He was downright crestfallen, though it didn't last long. Good thing he bounces back fast.

Kate and Lucina both loved Gabriel a lot, though they might not have known it themselves just then. They knew how to handle him, too–Lucina especially. I've always liked Lucina. Sure, she's fragile, but there's enough strength in her soul that she was able to fight her way back from alcoholism. That isn't easy. And she's especially sensitive to other people's feelings, probably because she's had such a tough time herself. Lucina would have made a fantastic healer if Gabriel hadn't grabbed her first.

But then, Lucina might still end up on my team. Only the Master knows for sure what's yet to come. Part of the fun of being an archangel is getting to watch as the Divine Plan unfolds. If Lucina decides she wants to get into healing before she comes home to Heaven, my angels and I will be happy to work with her.

Wonder what Gabriel would have to say about that?

CHAPTER THIRTY-SIX

"*What?*" I gasped.

"You're not deaf, Kate," Lucina replied calmly. "You heard perfectly well what I said."

"Yes, but—well, he—I mean, well—it's just that… Lucina, why are you leaving the Abbey? And where are you going?" I finally asked. I could not get my mind around her second statement. *Me*, the Lady of Angel Abbey? The idea was utterly absurd.

Lucina seemed to understand my incredulity, perhaps because she had been in the same position twenty-five years before. "Apparently, I'm being promoted." She smiled almost girlishly. "Gabriel is so happy with the way the Abbey has been running that he wants me to help him open another place somewhere west of here."

"That's great," I replied, still dazed. "But Lucina, what could he possibly be thinking? I'm about the last person I'd pick to be your successor. He'd be better off with Amy, or Bella, or Miss Flo, or even Violet. Why *me*?"

"Why *not* you?" Lucina countered, as unruffled as I was agitated.

"For all the reasons you pointed out to me not ten minutes ago!" I fired back. "You said it yourself, Lucina—I'm self-involved, suspicious, impatient, intimidating, angry, and unreasonable. I can't think of anybody who would be a worse choice than me!"

"Actually, Kate, I didn't say any of those things," Lucina replied evenly. "You did. I just called you prickly and said you would need to get your temper under control if you were going to succeed here. Both of those things are true, in my opinion, but they're not all that important. A great many people, myself among them, enjoy your company and care about you a lot. The only person who thinks you're irredeemably obnoxious is you.

"You're just *human*, Kate," Lucina went on. "You're an imperfect human being with flaws and baggage like the rest of us, but you're nowhere near the monster you believe yourself to be. Gabriel wouldn't have picked you if you were. Honestly, when you put away your 'lawyer hat' and forget to be defensive, you're a delight. Maybe if you stopped defining yourself as a lawyer first and a human being second, a lot of those qualities you dislike so much in yourself would disappear."

It was food for thought, but I could not get past the shock of Gabriel choosing me to succeed Lucina. "All kidding aside, why would Gabriel choose me?" I asked. "Even when I'm on my best behavior, I'm nowhere near as gracious as you are. Everybody adores you."

Lucina laughed. "Oh, come now! People who come to the Abbey love the 'Lady,' but it's the angels' magic that really draws them here. You figured out months ago that the 'Lady of Angel Abbey' is a role I play. Do you think you're the only person who ever saw through the performance? Or, for that matter, that I'm the only one who can do it?

"You would be a different Lady than I am, but who knows? You might be even better," Lucina continued. "Ask your friend Jack. Every role, whether it's on the stage or in life, can be played by more than one person, and each one brings her own personality to the part. Maybe the Abbey is going to need a Lady who's more like you than me. I don't know. But Gabriel does, and I trust him to make a good choice.

"Besides, Kate, I get a lot of support from the archangels, and so will you," Lucina assured me. "One of the perks of the job is that I can pretty much call on any of them anytime for whatever help I'd like. They give me advice whenever I need it, and sometimes even when I don't." She smiled wryly. "If Gabriel hadn't been an archangel, he would have made a great film director."

That explained those little pauses she frequently took—she must have been listening to angelic prompts. "The whole 'ask the archangels' thing sounds a little weird to me, I have to admit, but let's put that aside for now," I said slowly, shaking my head. "Lucina, nothing in my life has prepared me for this. I wouldn't know where to begin."

"Really?" Lucina retorted. "Being blessed from infancy with the personal protection and companionship of the great Archangel Gabriel, founder of

Angel Abbey, hasn't prepared you? You've got to be kidding me, Kate. What better preparation could there be?"

"But Lucina," I said weakly, "I've made so many mistakes, hurt so many people, and suffered so many losses. I'm damaged goods. How could I possibly be strong enough or *good* enough to do this?"

Her answering smile was fond and a little sad. "We've all had losses Kate, and everyone on this Earth makes mistakes. I'm living proof of that. You don't have to be perfect to contribute to the welfare of the world. You just have to show up with a willing heart and do the best that you can.

"But it's not my responsibility to convince you to take this on, and I'm not going to try," she continued, suddenly brisk. "Being the Lady of Angel Abbey is the last job in the world that anyone should take with an uncertain heart. There is someone else you need to talk to."

"Gabriel?" I asked, trying to keep my voice neutral. I really did want to patch things up with him, but I wasn't quite ready to talk with him yet.

"No, not Gabriel," she replied. "We already know what he would like you to do, but it really isn't up to him. We need to kick this upstairs. Follow me." When she stood up and walked away, there was nothing for me to do but follow.

Lucina hurried me along, down the long corridor and into her office. Reaching into her desk, she pulled out a big, heavy metal key. Its shaft appeared to be engraved with some kind of writing I did not recognize, and the head was set with gemstones, rubies, emeralds, and sapphires surrounding a larger clear stone. It reminded me of the necklace Lucina had received on New Year's Eve, but older and stranger somehow.

Turning, Lucina fitted the key into the brass lock of the old wooden door on the far wall. It swung open silently—I was half-expecting an ominous creak—to reveal a steep, curving flight of stone steps. "This leads up into the turret," she explained. "You'll need to go upstairs by yourself. Are you hungry or thirsty, Kate? You could be there for quite some time."

I was hungry and thirsty both, but my curiosity about what might be up those stairs won out, and I shook my head. Almost to the door, though, I stopped. "Before going up there, I need to call home," I told her. "I scared Bella and Andrew half to death by taking off on my own a couple of days ago. It would be horrible to do that to them again."

Lucina smiled. "We'll make a grown-up of you yet," she replied. "Go ahead up. I'll call them for you and let them know you're here." She pointed toward the door, and I started up the stairs. "Knock when you're ready to come down," Lucina said, swiftly closing the door behind me. I could hear the key clicking in the lock.

It looked as if I was really going to have to go up there alone.

The stairs seemed to continue forever, spiraling up and up as I climbed. When Lucina closed the door I expected to be engulfed in darkness, but a warm, golden glow hovered above me, casting enough light onto the steps to let me find my way. I climbed toward the glow—it grew brighter with every step—until I reached the top.

The stairs ended at an open, arched doorway like something out of a Gothic cathedral. Golden light gleamed cheerily within. I took a deep breath and then stepped across the threshold.

The room I entered was a round chapel, about forty feet across and fifteen feet high. The floor and walls were made of chiseled blue-gray stone that looked centuries old. Heavy candles glowed from wrought-iron sconces on the walls, although when I looked at them closely, they didn't actually seem to be burning. The room was redolent with the scents of melting beeswax, roses, and lilies, even though there was nary a flame or flower to be seen.

Five stained-glass windows were set deeply into the walls at evenly spaced intervals. Even though it was dark outside, they glowed brilliantly, as if lit from behind by the afternoon sun. Four of the windows represented archangels. On the far left was Raphael, his robes shining emerald green, his friendly face alive with humor and compassion. Next to him stood Gabriel, brilliant in gilt-embroidered white and brandishing an enormous golden trumpet, his face so familiar that I almost expected his portrait to turn to me and speak. To the far right was Uriel, his expression noble and wise, dressed in the garnet robes he wore in the library painting. Rendered in stained glass, they glowed like rubies. Next to Uriel stood a tall, broad-shouldered angel in silver armor and a vivid blue cloak. His handsome face was strong and proud, and he brandished an unsheathed sword, clenched tightly in one hand. Without ever having met him, I had no doubt the window was an exquisitely accurate portrait of the Archangel Michael. Swallowing hard, I wondered if I would ever dare speak to such an imposing angel.

But it was the fifth window, directly across the room and centered between Gabriel and Michael, that caught my attention. Taller than the others, it was deceptively plain, an elongated triangle of amber glass set in the center of what looked like a clear, midnight-blue sky and topped with a sparkling glass star. Rippling rows of aqua, blue, and green glass were set at uneven angles in the lower portion. The window seemed to represent a beam of light playing on moving waters.

It was a simple picture, pretty enough but far less detailed than the portraits of the archangels that stood to either side. As it held my gaze, though, I started to feel the starlight and the waves beneath it *moving*, pulsing as if with an inner vitality. It was as though the glass could barely contain the joyous, living glory hidden behind it.

All at once, I found myself standing in an open, semicircular glade, surrounded by fragrant pines. Damp sand crunched beneath my unexpectedly bare feet. A wide lake lapped a few feet away, silvery in the darkness, and a cool breeze whispered through the treetops. A single star, almost unbearably brilliant, sparkled in the sky above, casting down beams of light to dance on the ripping water. Everything smelled fresh and clean, like a clearing in the deep woods. In the distance, I heard the soft cry of what might have been a dove.

Then, somewhere from behind that sparkling star, a voice spoke to me, an enormously powerful yet intimate voice that was infinitely knowledgeable, loving beyond measure, completely forgiving, and utterly unlike anything I had ever experienced before.

I won't tell you everything the voice said to me that night, in part because I can't. Human language is nowhere near expansive enough to encompass what that incomparable voice had to say. But mostly, I won't tell you because your path is your own, different from mine, and anything I say could confuse or frighten you. Even worse, you could decide to settle for my truth, closing your mind and heart to that same voice when it whispers to you. If you did, you might just miss your own divine purpose, and that would be a tragedy. If you listen for that voice and let it speak to you, your conversation will be different from mine. That much I guarantee.

But there is one thing I can tell you, which I *must* tell you, in fact, to honor the conversation I had on that extraordinary night. That one thing is this:

All of our faults and foibles, the mistakes we make, the balls we drop, the physical flaws and personal shortcomings that make us writhe in shame, the nasty little grudges we carry, and the petty resentments we so jealously guard amount to less than nothing in a loving, infinite Universe. We were never meant to be perfect in the sense that we think of perfection. Indeed, our most cherished notions of perfection are so small and shabby that they are downright laughable to the Divine.

If you could see yourself through the eyes of the Creator—of course none of us can—you would find yourself watching a stubby little creature made of mud and water, endearingly ridiculous as it struts and crows and insists on getting its own way. You would also see a glimmering, eternal spirit, brighter than winter starlight, more graceful than a falling leaf in the autumn wind, more beautiful than the breaking dawn. That is the paradox in which we are suspended, and we are blessed indeed not to be only one or the other. We are both. And to our Creator, there is nothing more beautiful.

We are loved beyond deserving, beyond reason, beyond hope. And our only task in life is to pass that love along to one another, in whatever way our hearts and spirits lead us. Love alone is eternal. Nothing else endures and nothing else is asked of us, because nothing else is needed.

In regard to Angel Abbey, some things were made exquisitely clear to me. The owner of the voice from beyond the stars knew me to the depths of my being, loved me without reservation, and would be overjoyed if I chose to serve as the Lady of Angel Abbey. However, I was under no obligation to consent. The decision was entirely mine, and should be made without fear or any misplaced sense of duty. Should I refuse, there would be no blame. I would never be punished or loved any less for my refusal. If I agreed and later came to regret my decision, I would be free to walk away without recrimination. Whatever decision I made, the Creator would delight in my exercise of free will. I would be blessed no matter how I chose, and all would be very well indeed.

It was also made clear that no matter how I begged, I would not be given supernatural insight into where my mother might be or why she had left. If and when she wanted me to know where she was, she would tell me. Accepting Gabriel's invitation would not change that, so my decision should not be made in the expectation that I would be rewarded with knowledge of my mother's whereabouts. I was not being threatened, just informed so I could choose that much more wisely.

If Gabriel had said as much, I might not have believed or accepted it. With it coming from the Divine voice, I could do both.

It is impossible for me to say how long I stood in that clearing, deep in conversation with that tender, impossible voice. Lucina had already taught me that the archangels' sense of time is vastly different from ours. I suspect that the owner of that matchless voice has an even more expansive understanding of time and space than the archangels do.

Eventually, though, dawn seemed to break softly over the lake. The star faded into the brightening sky, the breeze gently tousled my hair for the last time. Then I was back in the chapel, sitting on the floor and watching the rising sun shoot vivid darts of ruby, emerald, sapphire, and amber light through the windows and onto the walls.

My loafers lay abandoned next to my feet. A few grains of sand still clung to my bare toes. Wherever I had been, my conversation with the Divine voice had been real. I sat there for a long time, mulling over everything the voice had said and thinking carefully about what to do.

Eventually I stood and shoved my loafers on. Then, on impulse, I bowed to each of the windows in turn, first to the center, then left and right, and then back to the center again. "Thank you," I whispered, and started down the stairs.

It seemed to take considerably less time to reach the bottom of the stairs than it had to climb to the top. When I got to the closed door I knocked once, and Lucina opened it in an instant. She had been waiting for me the entire time. "Well?" she asked, watching me closely.

"I still think Gabriel is crazy to have chosen me," I replied, my voice hoarse from lack of sleep. "But I'll do it.

"Now, what's for breakfast?" I asked. "I haven't eaten since lunch two days ago and I'm starved."

Archangel Metatron speaks:

It always pleases me to see human beings express their thanks to the Creator. No amount of deference entirely suffices when directed toward the organizing Intelligence of the Universe. Nor do we expect human beings to understand the full magnificence of the Infinite. The mortal mind simply was never intended to stretch that far. Still, basic gratitude and awe are definitely in order when addressing the Master, something too many modern souls seem to have forgotten.

Consequently, I was gratified to see Gabriel's little protégée begin to demonstrate some sense of decorum. Until then, it had seemed to me as though all the child could manage was to swing between temper tantrums and tears. The drama surrounding her had distracted too many of the archangels from their other responsibilities, even allowing for their ability to focus on a million or more things at once. It was an ability they were not exercising well enough, in my opinion. I was not about to allow all of Creation to fly apart while the archangels fixated on the antics of one unstable, self-centered little girl.

Kate acquitted herself well in her conversation with Raphael and Uriel, however. She apologized appropriately to Lucina. She showed courage in mounting the stairs alone. Most important, our Master seems well pleased with her. Next to that, nothing matters.

Perhaps Gabriel was right to be so optimistic about Kate. It will be a cold day in Heaven before he hears that from me, though. Some concessions are simply too much to be made.

CHAPTER THIRTY-SEVEN

Lucina had breakfast waiting in her office; fruit salad and a basket of freshly baked croissants were accompanied by a crock of Violet's superb raspberry jam and an enormous pot of steaming coffee. We ate together in companionable silence. At the time, it struck me as odd that she didn't ask what had happened to me. Now I know that such a conversion is to be treated with the utmost respect, revealed only when the one who went through it is ready to share. It would be a long time before I could bring myself to relate even the briefest description of my experience in the turret chapel. The sacred is not to be divulged lightly.

One thing I did learn that day, however, is that encounters with the Infinite can be utterly exhausting. After breakfast, I thanked Lucina, hugged her good-bye, and stumbled wearily out of her office and down the hall. Unlike the previous day, the Abbey was jammed with busy people. All of them stopped to greet me cheerily as they went about their various activities, seemingly oblivious to my fatigue. Amy, in particular, was every bit as friendly when she saw me as she had been aloof the day before. I started to wonder why, but then shrugged and let the question go. Angel Abbey was full of mysteries—Amy's moods were hardly the most significant. Seeing her reminded me of my meeting with Richard, though. Had it been only the previous day? It felt as though a month had passed.

After wishing her a good morning, I asked Amy for a favor. "Amy, you were nice enough to set up my e-mail account and make Honoré an overnight sensation, so I know you're a whole lot better with computers than I am. How are your online sleuthing skills?"

"Pretty good," Amy answered, too modest to boast. "What are you looking for?"

"Not what, whom," I answered. "There's a lady from New York City named Ruth Martingale who is a former colleague of mine. I've just found out that she had a stroke a few months ago, and I'd like to get in touch with her. She's not at home, which means she's in a hospital or rehab facility somewhere. Could you possibly find her for me?"

Amy thought for a moment and then shrugged. "Maybe. Let me see what I can do, and I'll let you know. E-mail you later—I'm late for a meeting." She smiled and bounced away, leaving me to marvel at her energy as I dragged myself out to my car.

Someone must have sent angels to watch over me as I drove, because I managed to make it home safely despite my exhaustion. Whatever Lucina had said when she called the night before must have satisfied Bella. She was all smiles as she bundled me off to bed the instant I walked in the front door. Too tired to object, I let her happily fuss over me. My last waking thought was that at last I understood why Lucina sometimes seemed so frail. Serving as the Lady of Angel Abbey might be tougher than it seemed. I fell asleep before Honoré could even curl up on my shoulder.

When I awoke several hours later, the sun was beginning to set and Honoré had gone to look for his dinner. I went downstairs to find Bella and Andrew in the parlor, talking worriedly. "What's the matter?" I asked.

Bella looked up, her face concerned. "We went over to the Abbey this afternoon, Katie. You were sound asleep, so we thought it would be a good idea to get out of here so you could have some peace and quiet. Anyway, there's a rumor going around that the Lady is leaving us, and everyone is terribly upset. Did she say anything to you about it?"

"As a matter of fact, she did," I answered, choosing my words with care. Things seemed to be moving awfully quickly all of a sudden. Maybe Gabriel was afraid I would change my mind if he gave me a chance. "The rumor is true, Bella. Lucina is leaving Angel Abbey, though I don't know exactly when."

Bella's lower lip trembled. "Everything will be fine, sweetheart," Andrew said to her in a reassuring tone, wrapping a comforting arm around her shoulders. "I'm sure Lucina will pass the place along to someone who will continue all the good work she has done there. She wouldn't just up and leave everything behind. She'll find a worthy successor, you'll see."

I grimaced a little at that, but could not keep silent. They were going to find out sooner or later—might as well hear it first from me. "I'm not sure how 'worthy' her successor is," I told them, "but she has already found somebody."

"Really?" Bella asked. "Do you know who it is?"

Taking a deep breath, I answered. "Yes, as a matter of fact, I do. It's me. Lucina has asked me to be her successor, and I've accepted. I'm going to be the next Lady of Angel Abbey."

The silence that followed was positively deafening.

Andrew and Bella took a long, slow look at each other while I stood there, staring at my feet and dying of shame. It was every bit as bad as I had anticipated. Gabriel meant well, no doubt, but he had picked the wrong woman. The two people in the world who knew me best both knew that I could never, *ever* be good enough for Angel Abbey. I might as well just jump off a bridge—it would save everyone, myself included, a whole lot of time and discomfort.

Bella spoke first. She seemed a little breathless. "Really, Katie? She chose *you*?" I nodded, shamefaced.

"And you're sure you really want to do this, Miss Kate?" Andrew asked. I looked up and gave him another uncomfortable nod, wishing I could disappear into the floor.

Bella's face lit up like Christmas morning, and Andrew's was almost as bright. "I knew it!" she crowed. "The minute I heard about her leaving I thought of you! The two of you have had such a rocky time of it, though, that I was afraid she wouldn't ask or you wouldn't agree to do it." She jumped up and threw both arms around my neck. "Katie, congratulations! You're going to do such an amazing job, and I am so, *so* proud of you!" Then Andrew was hugging both of us, and Honoré was twining around our ankles, purring, and I was happier than I had been in a long, long time.

That was just the first of many conversations to come. In the days that followed, I learned that gossip passes faster than lightning among the good people of Angel Abbey. News of Lucina's impeding departure spread like wildfire, and speculation about whether she would be succeeded—and, if so, by whom—was on everyone's lips. It didn't take long for word to get out that she had selected me.

Despite Bella and Andrew's enthusiastic reaction, I was convinced that a significant segment of the Abbey community would be unhappy with

Lucina's choice. There were a few raised eyebrows and forced smiles, but not many. That came as a pleasant surprise. I learned later that the mother of one of the children who had found me too intimidating as a tutor asked to have her name removed from the Abbey's mailing list when she heard I would be stepping in. Her reaction was less amazing than the revelation that the Abbey even *had* a mailing list (compiled by Amy, of course). Both were less astonishing than the fact that hers was the only overt departure. Most of the Abbey regulars accepted Lucina's choice, and a lot of them went out of their way to assure me that they would be delighted to help in any way that they could after I was installed.

At one point, a picture flashed into my mind of Gabriel and a score of angels striding through the Abbey tossing fistfuls of glittering white feathers into the air. The feathers, it seemed, were intended to disseminate good humor and harmony. It was all I could do not to laugh out loud.

Apart from that one brief vision, however, I didn't see or hear from Gabriel at all. He had to know what was going on at the Abbey. I kept expecting him to show up at any minute, but he never did. Perhaps, I thought, he was waiting for me to call upon him. If so, he would have a while to wait.

The little Lucina had said about Gabriel gave me the distinct impression that he was going to be a handful. I was sorry that our last conversation had been so unpleasant and had every intention of setting things right. My decision to take over the Abbey had changed things, though. I had been bullied by bosses before and was not going to stand for it again, not even if my new boss was an archangel. If I was going to succeed at the Abbey, some firm boundaries needed to be drawn. Better to let Gabriel stew in his own juice for a while.

The only person who failed to warmly congratulate me was Richard. He called a few days after word got out that I was taking over the Abbey. "Are you sure you want to do this, Kate?" he asked in a skeptical tone. "It's a pretty big change from life in a Manhattan law firm."

"Yes, Richard, I am," I replied. "It's time for me to make a change, and this isn't the kind of opportunity that comes around every day. It will be a fresh start for me. You don't think it will ruin my defense, do you?"

Richard sighed. "No, probably not," he admitted. "We'll just have to emphasize the community-service aspects of the Abbey, and not the 'woo-woo' angel stuff. It might even make you more sympathetic to the jury. Let me think about how to present this, OK? Best of luck with it, Kate." He hung up the phone without saying good-bye.

It was only then that I remembered what Richard had said on New Year's Eve about his mother's fascination with angels. Maybe he thought I had gone as loopy as she had. Then again, maybe he had just been too gentlemanly to say that I was jeopardizing the lawsuit by taking on a "flaky" job. One way or the other, he would tell me eventually—Richard was at the Abbey too often to avoid me forever. I decided to wait until he brought it up again, telling myself that it would be wrong to push him. Truthfully, though, I was not at all eager to hear what he might have to say.

Meanwhile, someone at the Abbey suggested having a party to wish Lucina *bon voyage* and welcome me in. The idea caught fire, and within days a date had been selected, Midsummer Night, to bring Lucina's time at the Abbey full circle. Committees were appointed, tasks were duly assigned, and I was told nicely but in no uncertain terms to butt out and stay home. Preparations would be handled by others. My sole responsibility, as Miss Flo kindly put it while she patted my hand, was to "show up and look pretty for the party." There was no polite way to argue with her, especially when she had so generously volunteered to take charge of all the arrangements.

Miss Flo's edict left me with time on my hands, as the days leading up to the party ticked past. I spent more time than I should have looking for something to wear, partly because I didn't have much else to do and partly because neither Bella nor I could decide what would be appropriate. I was about to take on a very unusual job for which there was no dress code, to my knowledge. In the law firm, I had known exactly what young attorneys were expected to look like and had dressed accordingly. But what is the "visible face" of a place like the Abbey supposed to wear?

Lucina had adopted a "mystical high-priestess" style that looked great on her. It wasn't really my taste, though, and I was still uncomfortable with the whole "Lady of Angel Abbey" thing. Dressing up like a medieval seer just didn't work for me. There was nothing in the local stores that I liked, though. Nothing online especially appealed to me, either. At one point I even asked Lucina what I should wear to the party, but she just smiled cryptically and told me that I would know it when I saw it. Not exactly illuminating.

Eventually, I settled on a plain blue dress that I found in a catalog. It wasn't anything special, but it was reasonably priced and would do well enough. I already had shoes and jewelry that would look fine with it. With no better options available, I gave up and ordered the dress, ignoring the little voice inside that insisted it was not good enough.

My other problem was deciding what to give Lucina as a parting gift. It was not strictly necessary for me to give her a present, but a major chapter in both of our lives was drawing to a close. It was entirely possible that we would never see each other again. We'd had our differences, Heaven knew, but the thought of having her disappear from my life was unexpectedly upsetting. I wanted to give her something tangible to remember me by.

After many hours and a lot of thought, I finally dragged out the box of Christmas ornaments and carefully wrapped up the tree topper that I now recognized as Archangel Gabriel. The Abbey was full of angels. Family heirloom or not, I would have so many that I wouldn't miss this one. And what better gift to give Lucina than a memento of our Christmas dinner together in the shape of the archangel who had united us as unlikely friends?

Meanwhile, Amy continued her online hunt for Ruth Martingale, but without success. Richard called to say that he had filed more paperwork in the lawsuit, but it would be months, perhaps as much as a year, before anything substantive would happen. He also promised to be at my upcoming installation party. That was a good sign, I thought. Maybe the idea that I was taking over the Abbey had grown on him.

As the days slipped past, I continued to look halfheartedly for a job, but mostly postponed my efforts until after the party. It was not clear to me how much time I would be expected to devote to the Abbey, or whether I would need some sort of "day job" to support myself. Did the Lady of Angel Abbey get a stipend? I wondered, but I never found a ready opportunity to ask Lucina. There would be time for that later, I told myself. It almost didn't matter what the job actually entailed, for despite what the Divine voice at the lake had said, there was no way for me to gracefully back out even if I wanted to, now that my appointment had been announced and party preparations were fully under way.

And I didn't want to back out, despite knowing so little about what was in store. My experience in the chapel had changed me in ways that I would not come to understand until much later. All I knew then was that for the first time in my life, I was taking on a responsibility entirely of my own choice. The Divine voice had been very clear that my acceptance would be joyously welcomed, but only if it was freely given. Funny, I thought, how the complete absence of pressure to accept had made accepting so much more palatable. Perhaps if my father had been less insistent that I follow in his footsteps, I would have been happier to do so.

The afternoon before the party, I was sitting on the couch in the parlor, carelessly sketching some possible poses for a new statue of Honoré, when the doorbell rang. Bella answered it before I could even get up, and came in carrying a big rectangular box. "It must be that dress I ordered," I told her, trying to ignore the sinking feeling in the pit of my stomach. There was nothing *wrong* with the dress, I sternly told myself. It was pretty enough, and certainly better than the power suits I had crammed myself into to satisfy the expectations of my former law partners.

Bella placed the box gently on my lap, as I set my sketchbook and pencil aside. It was made of thick, parchment-colored cardboard, and the address label was deeper beige with an antique-gold band across the top. My name was written on the label in a sophisticated script, but there was no address. There was no return address for the sender, either. Only the words "Chez J" swirled across the gold band, accompanied by a delicate drawing of a feather.

What was the name of the company where I had ordered the dress? I could not remember, but I was pretty sure it wasn't "Chez J." There had to have been some mistake. Still, the package was addressed to me, and curiosity about what might be inside overcame my reservations. I could always seal it back up, after all. Carefully, I opened the lid.

The contents of the box were packed in layers of antique-gold tissue paper, held together with a gleaming gold paper seal, embossed with another capital letter "J." A delicate floral fragrance wafted from the tissue, growing stronger as I carefully broke the seal. I pushed the tissue aside, and Bella and I gasped simultaneously.

Inside the box was a dream of a gown, of sheer, cream-colored organza layered over heavy, deeper cream silk. The organza was embroidered here and there with raised ivory flowers, each with a copper-bead center and touches of antique rose at the tips of its five petals. More five-pointed flowers were embroidered on swirling, pale green vines that ran across the hem and up the back, so beautifully crafted and artfully arranged that they looked almost alive.

The gown was accompanied by a pair of slippers that would have driven Cinderella mad with envy. They were the same deep cream as the gown but made of the softest possible leather and heavily embroidered with the same five-pointed, copper-centered flowers. The heels, inlaid with polished copper, were the perfect height for dancing. There was jewelry, too, delicate earrings and a filigree necklace set with pearls that, impossibly, had been coaxed into the same teardrop shape as the petals of the flowers that adorned the shoes and gown. There was even a tiny crystal bottle of the perfume that had wafted from the tissue when I first opened the box, its cap topped with a dancing golden angel.

Without even trying them on, I knew the gown and shoes would fit me perfectly, because they had so clearly been designed and made just for me. No human hands could possibly have created anything so flawless—they had to be the work of angels. The idea simultaneously thrilled and frightened me. On the one hand, there would be no drab little blue dress. I would go to the party dressed in a one-of-a-kind confection that even the wealthiest princess could not buy.

On the other hand, I'd had no say at all in selecting what I would wear to the party. The idea of having invisible angels playing dress-up with me as if I were some kind of Barbie doll was more than a little unnerving. I could feel my old obstinacy starting to rise, and was tempted to refuse to wear anything I had not chosen myself. It wasn't stubbornness, the pigheaded part of me insisted. It was a matter of principle.

Ultimately, though, the sheer beauty of the gown and accessories overcame my annoyance at effectively being told what to wear. I carefully pulled the dress out of the box and held it up, almost afraid to touch such a gorgeous thing.

"Katie, who sent you this?" Bella whispered in awe.

"I'm not sure, but I can make a pretty good guess," I replied. The clothes had to be from Gabriel. Were they a peace offering, or just an effort on the archangel's part to make sure I would be presentable at the party? That idea irritated me, but in fairness, Gabriel had never done anything of the kind before. Maybe he was just trying to be nice.

"There's a note in the box," Bella said. She reached in and pulled out a parchment envelope, longer and a shade or two darker than the notepaper Lucina used. My name was scrawled across the front in the same sophisticated script on the address label, and the envelope was secured with another golden, J-embossed seal.

I lay the gown on the couch, then took the envelope from Bella and opened it. The letter inside read:

> *My darling Kate,*
> *Forgive me for presuming, but it broke my heart to see you settling for that sad little rag you had selected. This is a celebration, sweetheart, and you deserve to be your most beautiful self on your very special night. My angels and I designed these just for you. It would honor us if you would wear them. Our dear G. had nothing to do with this—the idea was entirely mine.*
>
> *Enjoy the presents, and when you have a minute tomorrow night, do remember to save a dance for me. We have much to discuss and more friends in common than you know. Looking forward to seeing you, gorgeous!*
>
> *À bientôt,*
>
> *Jophiel*
>
> *P.S.: If you are willing, do wear your hair down, darling! Nothing suits you better. J.*

Bella had been reading over my shoulder. We looked at each other in utter astonishment. "Katie," she asked carefully, "who is this 'Jophiel'?"

"Lucina's personal stylist, I think," I managed. "No wonder she always looks so good."

Bella shook her head. "Well, it is certainly a beautiful dress. But Katie, this is all very, very strange."

"Bella, you have no idea," I muttered. "And I think it's going to get a whole lot stranger before it's over." I placed the gown and the note gently back in the box, and carried my new presents upstairs to my room.

Archangel Jophiel speaks:

Well, really, you did not think I was going to let our girl settle for that dreadful little number she had so reluctantly chosen, did you? We were about to install a new Lady at Angel Abbey, for Heaven sake! She deserved to show up in something finer than she could find in some tacky paper catalog.

Designing and whipping up that ensemble for Kate was such fun for my angels and me. There is nothing we enjoy more than enhancing the loveliness of a lady. And never for one instant imagine that appearances do not matter! People judge one another by their looks all the time. Trust me, darlings, clothes have been symbols of power and social standing ever since those first limp little fig leaves all those millennia ago. If Kate had failed to arrive at the party looking like a queen, the people who adored Lucina would have been that much less willing to support her. Beautiful garments may not make the woman, but until the Creator comes up with a remedy for sexism, they certainly do not hurt.

Gabriel loved Kate, and we all love Gabriel. The least I could do was help dress up his darling for her debut. And what fun to anticipate how beautiful she would be!

CHAPTER THIRTY-EIGHT

The morning of the party dawned clear, warm, and sunny, perfect for an outdoor gathering in June. I tried to sleep late, but a mix of eager anticipation and near-paralyzing stage fright had me wide-awake at six a.m. I lay in bed for a while with my eyes closed, trying to doze off, but it was no use. Sighing, I got up and dragged myself down to the kitchen for coffee.

Bella was up too, clearly as nervous as I was, and Andrew had already left to get the Lincoln washed and waxed. Only Honoré was his usual dignified self, calmly watching Bella and me as we sat across the table from each other, sipping coffee and pretending to pick at toast and scrambled eggs. We both knew it would be hours before we could decently start getting dressed for the party. It promised to be a long, uncomfortable day.

I decided to spend the morning in what was left of my father's library, to see whether I could find something, *anything*, to distract me and settle my nerves. Even though we had donated cartons of books to the Abbey, there were still plenty left. Browsing through the shelves, I came across an old, leather-bound copy of John Milton's *Paradise Lost*, with beautiful woodcut illustrations. It didn't strike me as the sort of thing Christopher Cunningham would have preferred, but it might have been a gift or even something my mother had chosen. On a whim, I pulled the book off the shelf and settled down to read.

Paradise Lost was written in the late 1600s, and the dense, Elizabethan language was challenging. I persevered, though, and was soon deep into the story of Adam and Eve, through which Milton interwove a darker tale. Not having touched the book since college, I had forgotten that Milton had portrayed Satan as complex and charismatic, brooding over his exile from Heaven even as he plotted revenge through humanity's downfall. But there he was, a disturbing reminder that the angels I had met up to that point were not the only ones out there. Raphael and Uriel had said something about "the Adversary" during our meeting at the diner, hadn't they? They must have been referring to their fallen brother. He had to be as real as they were. Just the thought of it made me shiver.

Fallen or not, Satan was not the only archangel in *Paradise Lost*. The poem mentioned Uriel and Michael, while Raphael had a major role, describing the war in Heaven to an enraptured Adam and Eve. Milton's description of Raphael as the "affable archangel" was so apt that I wondered whether Raphael had appeared to him, too. I would have to ask Raphael sometime, I thought, and then realized what an astonishing notion that was. Casual conversation with an archangel? Incredible.

Paradise Lost also featured Gabriel, whom Milton described as the leader of the angelic hosts of Heaven. That surprised me—I thought Michael commanded Heaven's armies. Maybe Gabriel moonlighted or something.

The book was illustrated with a detailed woodcut of Gabriel and Uriel talking together in the Garden of Eden. Their faces were instantly recognizable to anyone who knew them. I leaned down to take a closer look.

There he was—Gabriel the mighty, Gabriel the magnificent, Gabriel the Archangel of the Annunciation, an infinitely formidable spirit of such power and glory that a single blast of his trumpet could bring about the end of all things. He was among the greatest of the archangels. But instead of falling to my knees in awe when he appeared, I had scolded him as if he were a naughty child.

Unbelievable.

I was still marveling at my own staggering arrogance when Bella stuck her head in the library door. "Katie, could you come into the parlor for a minute? Lucina's here, and she wants to talk with you."

"Coming," I answered, putting down my book with considerable relief and following Bella down the hall. There would be plenty of time to contemplate my own stupidity later.

Lucina was seated on the couch in the parlor stroking Honoré, to his obvious delight. "So, this is that same little kitty we gave you all those years ago," she said, looking up at me and smiling. "I didn't recognize him at Christmas dinner. He certainly doesn't look his age."

"Honoré never changes," I replied. "But yes, he is the same cat, and thank you for him. He has been my closest companion for a long time. I don't know how I would have managed without him all these years."

"That's wonderful," Lucina said warmly. "I'm glad he has been such a good friend for you." She glanced over her shoulder to see if Bella was listening, but she had left us to talk undisturbed. "Did you like the gown?" Lucina asked, in a low, conspiratorial whisper.

"It's gorgeous," I whispered back. "Was that your idea?"

"No, but I'm relieved that you like it. Jophiel was so excited about helping with your installation, I didn't have the heart to tell him you might prefer to choose something yourself."

"Believe me, the dress I had picked out looked like a thrift-shop castoff compared to what he sent. Did Jophiel and the angels, uh..." I trailed off, not sure of how to ask what felt like a bizarre question.

"Are you asking whether the angels made the dress?" she whispered, her eyes dancing.

"Well, yes," I replied.

"Of course they did!" she assured me. "Jophiel would never have left something that important to mortal hands. He takes incredible pride in his work, and he really wanted to make you happy."

"Lucina, doesn't it seem a little strange to you to know you're wearing something that wasn't made by, well, *people*?" I asked.

Lucina laughed. "Trust me, you'll get used to it," she replied. "I thought it was a little strange at first too, but everything they create is so incredibly gorgeous that your vanity will soon insist on nothing less.

"But I didn't come over here just to gossip about clothes, Kate." Lucina's face grew more serious. "There's one last thing that we have to address before tonight. It's about your name."

"My name?" I asked, perplexed.

"Yes. Kate, what is your name?"

"Katherine Patricia Cunningham," I replied.

"Really, Kate? Are you sure?" she persisted.

"Of course I'm sure, Lucina," I said, a little exasperated. Where was she going with this?

"Kate, we both know that Christopher Cunningham wasn't your natural father. So, why do you continue to use his last name?" she asked.

The question stunned me. Despite having come to terms with the revelation that the man I had always thought was my father really was not, it had never occurred to me to relinquish his surname. "That's an amazing question, Lucina. Why are you bringing it up now?" I asked, reverting to the lawyerly trick of answering a question with a question to avoid committing myself to a response.

Lucina leaned forward. "After this evening, Kate, Angel Abbey will be yours by law. Your name will be on the title, the deed, all of the documents. This is your opportunity, as the Lady of the Abbey, to get a fresh start and become whomever you choose. Gabriel gave me that chance twenty-five years ago. Now it's your turn.

"Before I met Gabriel, my name really was Lucy Stevens," Lucina went on. "Gabriel gave me the chance to redefine myself, to be reborn, if you like, as a better person than I had been before. It's part of the magic of Angel Abbey. When you become the Lady, it's customary to take a new name to symbolize your commitment to what the Abbey stands for. 'Lucina' means 'light,' and I'm sure you can guess what 'des Anges' means."

"It's French, isn't it?" I asked. "It means 'of the angels.'" She nodded.

"That's right. The 'des Anges' name has been handed down from one Lady of the Abbey to the next for generations. It binds us together into family of sorts. You can join our family tonight, Kate, if you'd like. But the choice is entirely yours. Whatever name you give me will go on the documents. The Abbey will be yours, no questions asked."

It was a lot to take in all at once. My initial reaction was to refuse, but I realized almost immediately that the impulse was coming from that mistrustful part of me that rejected anything I had not thought of myself. The idea of changing my name was unexpected, but that didn't mean it was bad. Lucina watched me quietly, careful to keep her expression neutral, as I debated what to do.

Once I put my suspicions aside, it didn't take me long to reach a conclusion. Lucina was right. Christopher Cunningham was not my father, and he had not been at all happy about being saddled with me after my mother left. His final letter to me made it perfectly clear that he did not consider me to be his daughter, so why should I continue to pretend that I was? There was no reason for me to keep his last name, nor was I interested in taking the last name of my natural father, whoever he might be. My mother's maiden name was a possibility, but I had strong, conflicted feelings about her disappearance. I didn't even know who she was anymore. Taking her maiden name would be almost as false as continuing to use Cunningham.

Unbidden, an image of *Paradise Lost* flashed into my mind, and I realized I was being presented with a very significant decision. Changing my name would demonstrate my commitment to everything that the Abbey stood for and, although Lucina had not said so, to the archangel who had conceived of and created the Abbey in the first place. Taking the 'des Anges' name would bind me forever to the Abbey family. Put that way, there was only one choice I could make.

"When I was born, my mother wanted to name me Caitlin for her maternal grandmother," I told Lucina. "But her husband thought it was too 'old country.' So, they settled on Katherine instead. I'd like to honor my mother's original intention by taking the name Caitlin."

"A lovely choice," Lucina said.

"And for my last name, I accept. I'd like to use 'des Anges,'" I continued.

Lucina positively beamed. "You honor me, Kate, and every Lady before me. This will truly make us family. Thank you so much. All the papers will be delivered to you in the morning."

"Wait a minute," I said, "don't I have to sign them first?"

Lucina leaned in again, her eyes sparkling. "It will all be taken care of, believe me," she whispered, careful not to be overheard. "If you're impressed with Jophiel's skills as a fashion designer, just wait until you see what Raziel can do with a deed."

Dresses, deeds, and miracles... It was all a little overwhelming.

Lucina stood up, treating Honoré to a final tickle under his chin. "That's settled, then. Wonderful! Now, it's time for me to go so you can get ready for the party. See you at the Abbey, Kate, and thank you for joining our family." She gave me a quick hug and left, leaving behind the faintest whiff of her spicy perfume. Archangel Jophiel, I suspected, had cooked it up just for her. The thought still unsettled me.

Honoré sat on the couch next to me, purring softly, his eyes blissfully closed. "You know," I told him, scratching behind his ear, "I've never really thanked you for being my friend. You probably don't understand what I'm saying, but I love you and I'm so grateful to you. You've been one of the very best things in my life for as long as I can remember. So thank you, Honoré. Thank you for being my friend." His purr deepened, and I went upstairs to dress.

I expected to be all thumbs getting ready, nervous as I was. But there must have been angels hovering close to help me, because my hair tumbled into perfect place—styled down, as Jophiel had suggested—and my makeup practically applied itself. I applied a little of the scent that Jophiel had provided, and was instantly surrounded in a cloud of light, floral fragrance. It was very different from Lucina's perfume, and I absolutely loved it. Amazing what an archangel can do, I thought, bemused.

As expected, the shoes fit perfectly, so comfortable that walking in them felt like strolling barefoot on the beach. I slipped into the gown, which molded itself to me as if it had been made for me—which, of course, it had. The strapless bodice left my neck and shoulders bare, hugged my torso, and came to a deep V below the hips. The skirt was fitted at the top but flared dramatically at the bottom, stopping just a hair's breadth above the floor and ready to swish around my ankles with every step I took. After adding the earrings and clasping the necklace at my throat, I went to the mirror to see how I looked.

The woman who peered back at me looked like someone out of a Celtic legend, ethereal and lovely as the Faerie Queen herself. And yet, there was nothing costumey about my ensemble. The dress, the shoes, and the jewelry just came together to make me something more than I would be without them. I was still myself, but presented in a way that people at the party would recognize and remember as a living symbol of what the Abbey itself was all about.

"Jophiel," I whispered, transfixed by the image the archangel had created, "you and your angels certainly know how to dress a lady. *Thank you.*" I turned to go downstairs but then stopped. There was one more thing that needed to be done.

I walked to my bedroom window, the one I had closed in despair so many years before on the night when I finally admitted that my mother was never coming home. I pulled it open, leaned on the sill, and stuck my head out into the fresh evening air.

"Gabriel," I called into the twilight, "can you hear me? If you can, please forgive me for taking so long to understand what you wanted me to do. I'm honored that you've chosen me, and humbled that you've put the well-being of the Abbey into my hands. Please help me to fulfill my new responsibilities well.

"And tonight," I continued, "if you can forgive me for all the horrible things I said to you, please come to the party and bring your friends. I'd like to tell Jophiel how grateful I am for these beautiful clothes. I'd like to thank Uriel and Raphael for coming to help when I needed their insights. And mostly, I want to thank you for this opportunity, Gabriel. I'll do my very best to be worthy of it."

I listened for a moment, but there was no sound except the chirping of crickets in the yard below. If Gabriel had heard me, he had not chosen to respond. I deserved his silence, but it still hurt a little.

Sighing, I pulled my head back into my bedroom and started to close the window. On a whim, though, I decided to leave it open just an inch or two. After all, you never know when an archangel might want to come inside.

Bella cried when she saw me coming down the stairs, and Andrew quietly said, "*Wow.*" I picked up my present for Lucina, and we all stepped outside and got into the Lincoln. We drove off to the Abbey together, and I felt like Cinderella headed for the ball.

We arrived at the Abbey just at sunset. Lucina was already there, of course, resplendent in a moss-green gown that set off her beauty to perfection. The angel necklace she had received at the New Year's Eve party gleamed at her throat. As she embraced me to the applause and cheers of the assembled guests, the thought occurred to me that our dresses had been created to look gorgeous together, without being even slightly similar in design. Archangel Jophiel could teach our best couturiers a thing or two.

The courtyard had been decorated with thousands of white lights that shimmered like fireflies in the darkness. A few musicians had been set up against the barn wall, where they were playing sedately. Everyone I knew at the Abbey was there, along with a lot of people I did not, all laughing, talking, and enjoying the fine summer night.

Richard was off in one corner, deep in conversation with Pastor St. James. He waved to me and started to come over, but the rector caught him by the sleeve and pulled him back into their conversation. Oh, well, I thought, Richard and I could always catch up later. There were many other people waiting to offer their good wishes. It would have been rude of me to cut across the crowd just to say hello.

It soon became apparent that serving as the new Lady of Angel Abbey was going to be a strenuous job. For what seemed like hours, I went from guest to guest, shaking hands or exchanging hugs and making friendly conversation. It was a beautiful party and all the attendees seemed to be enjoying themselves, but I could not shake the sense that underneath the polite chitchat, people were *waiting*, somehow, for something special to happen. Were there going to be speeches or something? I hoped not. It had never occurred to me that I might be called upon to make a speech, and I had not written anything down.

Then, a hush settled over the crowd. The band stopped playing, the stars seemed to glow more brightly, and the voice of the midsummer breeze, dancing gaily through the treetops, grew louder. Everyone looked up into the sky, though I am certain no one could have told you exactly what they were looking for—or rather, no one except Lucina and me.

Out of the sky they came, flying in a magnificent spiral of radiant, gilt-edged wings. They circled overhead once, twice, three times. The heavens glowed and the Earth trembled as flights of angels and archangels soared over Angel Abbey, then lightly touched down and stepped forward, smiling, to walk among our mortal guests.

I recognized Uriel and Raphael instantly, their faces joyful, robes shimmering with unearthly color. They were accompanied by a broad-shouldered, armor-clad archangel in blue who could only be Michael. I remembered what Uriel and Raphael had said at the diner, and wondered how to ask him to forgive me for treating Gabriel so harshly. Before I could say a word, though, Michael shot me a broad smile and a wink. Whatever lingering fear I'd had of him vanished in a flash. Invincible warrior he might be, but I knew in that instant that for the rest of my life, Michael would be the protective big brother I had always longed for and never had.

They were followed by a small army of archangels, each of whose names flashed into my head as they came to greet me. The archangel in embroidered golden robes with the patrician face was Jophiel, who beamed when he saw me. *You look gorgeous, darling,* his voice laughed in my mind. *Cannot wait to see you dancing!* Behind him came an almond-skinned, tawny-haired archangel in leaf-green robes, who introduced herself as Ariel. She greeted me with a friendly nod, and something about her made me think of Honoré. Her companion, a blonde archangel dressed in diaphanous blue, introduced herself as Haniel, the Archangel of Grace. *I am glad you are here,* I told her silently. *Everyone is expecting me to dance, and I'm scared to death. Do not be,* she replied kindly. *When the time comes, you will be fine.* She gave me a dazzling smile and passed on.

Next came a dark-haired angel in forest-green robes. He smelled of roses, and his face seemed to sparkle with laughter. *I am Barachiel,* he informed me, *bestower of Divine blessings. It will be my joy to help you, Lady! Call upon me anytime.* The dark-skinned archangel beside him in pink robes with the irresistible grin was Chamuel. He led me to understand that he was the archangel of romantic love.

Next came a slender archangel in rainbow-hued robes, with white hair and a long beard that glowed like starlight on snow. *I am Raziel,* he told me silently. *Your secrets are safe with me.* He bowed slightly, gave me an enigmatic smile, and passed.

Accompanying Raziel was an archangel in cream-colored robes with a patient, humble expression. *I am Azrael, the Angel of Death,* his quiet voice informed me. *Fear not. None of your guests will be leaving with me this evening. I have been watching and wishing you well for a long time, though, and I would be honored to join in your celebration. Will you welcome me here?*

Absolutely, I thought back. *Thank you so much for coming.* Azrael smiled and squeezed my hands in his. He was so gentle that I wondered how anyone could possibly fear his embrace. *Azrael,* I asked, fearing the answer but wanting to know, *is my mother with you?*

Azrael shook his head. *No, Caitlin, she is still among the living. However, the man you knew as your father is with us. He has been watching you since his death and, I think, is beginning to appreciate you as you are, not as he would have had you be. Do not grieve for either of them, especially tonight. You have made a joyful choice. Celebrate it.* The archangel bowed to me, and went on his way.

A broad-built archangel in orange robes approached next. He looked me up and down with such an air of command that I blushed. Then he abruptly picked up my hand and kissed it. *Gabriel chose wisely,* a regal voice in my mind informed me. *I am Metatron, the Creator's chief administrator. Call upon me whenever I can be of assistance to you.* It was a generous offer and I thanked him for it, but I will admit to breathing a little easier after Metatron passed by.

Next came an especially tall, almost lanky archangel in robes that seemed to change color with every step he took. He had sparkling, hazel eyes and a warm, infectious grin. *Sandalphon at your service,* he informed me. *I am Metatron's brother and, among other things, the Archangel of Music.*

Sandalphon looked at the band, and they all looked back at him, silent and visibly confused. *Let us see if we can't liven things up a little,* he said in my mind, and strolled over to talk to the musicians. In less than a minute, the archangel had tactfully supplanted the bandleader and was swinging a baton as the band broke into a lovely reel.

As the archangels greeted me, the angels who had accompanied them dispersed through the crowd. The archangels towered over our human guests by a foot or more. The angels were a little smaller but no less beautiful, alive with light and dressed in shimmering, vividly colored robes. Their wings glowed as if with fire, and their faces were lit with joy. But only Lucina and I could see them as they were. Our party guests saw ordinary people like themselves, who had come to wish Lucina well and welcome me in.

I wondered about what Azrael had said. Was Christopher Cunningham watching me? And if he was, what did he think of my decision to leave the law for Angel Abbey? The man I had known would never have forgiven me for abandoning his chosen profession. Was he still the relentless taskmaster I remembered, or had death given him a kinder perspective than he'd had in life?

Suddenly, I missed Jack. Unlike Christopher Cunningham, Jack would have applauded my decision to take on Angel Abbey. My fanciful friend was the only other person I knew—except Lucina, of course—who might have been able to see the angels and archangels as they really were.

I had convinced myself that Jack would not want to come all the way up to Angel Falls for my modest little reception. Truthfully, though, I had not wanted to introduce Jack to Richard, or even to consider why that might be. But as I watched the angels and archangels milling around in the courtyard, I regretted my decision. Richard or no Richard, I wished with all my heart that I had invited Jack to come to the party. He would have loved it.

Even without Jack, it should have been a perfect moment for me. Most people never meet a single archangel in a lifetime, and I had just made the acquaintance of half a dozen. It was an extraordinary blessing.

One special guest still had not made an appearance, though, and I was starting to fear he never would. Yes, I'd had reason to be angry, but I had been so ungrateful when he had offered me so much. Even an archangel might be hard-pressed to forgive the things I had said. Anxiously, I searched the sky, but it was empty apart from a handful of stars and the shining crescent moon. Apparently, all of the angels who were coming to the party had already arrived. Gabriel was not coming.

But then, without warning, the sky exploded in a flash of brilliant gold. From everywhere and nowhere came a blast of triumphant trumpet music. The melody soared, spun, and spiraled around itself, as the golden light coalesced into swirls of stardust, before coming together into a single, radiant beam that stretched all the way from Heaven to Earth below.

Down that beam he slid, white robes incandescent, auburn hair shining as brilliantly as the halo behind it, wings stretched wide to catch and reflect back every flicker of light. His golden trumpet pointed into the sky as he played one final, joyous crescendo before alighting on the grass before me, resplendent in infinite joy. Archangel Gabriel, my protector, my mentor, my sometime antagonist, and ultimately, my friend.

"You certainly know how to make an entrance," I greeted him, smiling. The depth of my relief astonished me.

"Nothing but the best for the new Lady of Angel Abbey," Gabriel replied, grinning back. "You look fantastic! Jophiel make that for you?"

"Who else? He's incredible." I swallowed hard. "But listen, Gabriel, there's something I need to tell you. I'm so sorry for all the terrible things I said to you that day at the waterfall—"

"Gone and forgotten, Cate," he interrupted, and I could see that he meant it. "I heard you the first time, when you called out your window. And I'm sorry too. I got so carried away with my plans for Angel Abbey that I took your participation for granted. I should have treated you more respectfully. But we're here, the Abbey will continue, and everything is just as it should be. I think that's cause for celebration, don't you?"

I nodded, too relieved to speak. Angry as I had been with Gabriel, I treasured him, too. The idea of losing him again was more than I could bear.

Glancing around, I expected to see the crowd in shock, but everyone else at the party seemed engrossed in their separate conversations. How had they missed Gabriel's showstopping arrival? Then Lucina caught my eye and winked. She had seen it all, and so had the archangels, but none of our party guests had. That incredible spectacle had been just for me.

Gabriel looked around too, and his grin widened. "Pretty dull gathering, it seems," he said. "Let's get this party started. Hey, Sandy," he called to the tall archangel conducting the band. "Give us something lively, will you? It's time to *dance*!"

Archangel Azrael speaks:

No one alive, in Heaven or on Earth, can produce a better celebration than our Gabriel! It had been far too long since the angels and archangels had gathered simply to celebrate, and Gabriel had outdone himself, with a little help here and there from our very willing brothers. The party at Angel Abbey would be the talk of Heaven for a long time to come.

As much as I enjoyed the spectacle, though, the best part of the celebration for me was Caitlin's immediate, unqualified welcome. As you can imagine, the Archangel of Death does not get a lot of invitations. She would be a more gracious Lady of the Abbey than some of us had anticipated. I looked forward to becoming her friend.

My angels told me later that Christopher Cunningham watched every instant of the party without moving so much as an eyelash. He never said a word about Caitlin or the choices she had made, though he certainly must have had some opinion about them. Some of my angels asked him what he thought of her becoming the new Lady of Angel Abbey, but he just shook his head and refused to answer.

His silence might have meant many things, but only Christopher and the Creator know what they were. He can keep his secrets as far as I am concerned. Now that I know firsthand how lovely Caitlin is, I do not much care what he thinks.

CHAPTER THIRTY-NINE

Sandalphon waved a cheery assent to Gabriel. He raised his baton, and on the downbeat, every angel at the party drew out a soft ball of sparkling feathers and tossed it into the air.

In an instant, our sedate little gathering was transformed into an all-out bash. The band struck up a dance tune like nothing I had ever heard before, a cross between a waltz and a fox-trot with a jazzy overtone. Whatever it was, it was irresistible—just a few notes were enough to start everyone at the party dancing joyfully.

"What do you say, Cate? Bet you've never danced with an archangel before," Gabriel said jauntily. He was right, but the idea of taking the floor with everyone watching paralyzed me with fear. I had never danced. I *couldn't* dance. Gabriel knew that, didn't he?

"Let me handle this, brother," said a melodious voice behind me. I turned, and there was Uriel. "There are *two* Ladies of Angel Abbey at the moment, and it would not do for you to neglect either one," he told Gabriel. "Go dance with Lucina. She has been looking just the slightest bit dejected. You would not want her to think you do not love her anymore."

"She knows better than that," Gabriel exclaimed, but he gave me a quick nod and went off to look for Lucina. Relieved, I turned to thank Uriel, who seemed to be studying me closely.

"You have never been able to dance, have you, Caitlin?" the archangel asked. His voice was kind.

I shook my head. "My ballet teacher kicked me out of class when I was seven," I admitted. "And I've always been too clumsy anyway. Anybody who tried to dance with me would end up limping for a week."

Uriel's face remained still, but I thought I saw the hint of a smile in his gray eyes. "Dancing is less difficult than many things you have learned to do well, Caitlin. But I can understand why you might not want to begin with Gabriel as your partner. He can be a trifle overexuberant, do you not agree? My brothers say I am an excellent teacher. If you are willing to take a chance on dancing with me, I promise to take it slow. Do you trust me?"

A flash of soft blue caught my eye from over Uriel's shoulder. It was Haniel, who gave me an encouraging smile. *You will be fine, Caitlin,* her voice whispered in my mind, and a little tingle shot through my toes.

"What the heck," I said. "If you're willing to put your feet at risk, I can do the same with my vanity. Lead on, Uriel."

"Then take my hand," he said, bowing slightly and extending long, luminous fingers. I placed my hand on Uriel's palm, and those fingers closed around mine. The archangel placed his other hand gently at my waist and slowly, gently, urged me to take a step.

We began with a simple waltz, one-two-three, one-two-three. In what felt like mere seconds, though, Uriel had me whirling around the floor like I had been dancing all my life. We swirled, dipped, and he even lifted me up in the air once or twice. It was impossible to concentrate on every step—we were moving too fast and covering too much space. It was scary but exhilarating, and I loved it. Thanks to Haniel, I felt perfectly free to relax and trust Uriel to lead me wherever we needed to go.

Once or twice, I saw Lucina dancing with Gabriel, her head thrown back in breathless laughter, and I was glad to see her so happy. I couldn't watch for long, though—every time I got a glimpse of them, Uriel would swing me in another circle and we would go flying off again.

Soon, everyone at the party had stopped to watch the two Ladies of Angel Abbey dance, smiling and cheering us on. As we whirled around and around, I caught glimpses of the people I had come to love at the Abbey—Amy, Miss Flo, Mr. Han, Richard, Pastor St. James, Violet. And, of course, Bella and Andrew, who watched me with beaming smiles.

I also caught flashes of the angels who had come to the party, and sometimes their faces would shift into mortal guise. I saw one pretty angel in a green robe become Nurse Paula, who had cared so tenderly for my father in his final months. Another angel, also in green, became the elderly lady who had spoken to me on the train when I first came home from Manhattan. A tall angel in white robes turned out to be the busker from the subway. I saw the chestnut vendor who had told me to be brave, the motel clerk who had urged me to call home. She shot me a grateful smile—apparently, Gabriel did not know or did not care that I had figured her out.

One angel in bright blue robes turned into the Russian cabbie who had kept my briefcase, setting off the chain of events that brought me to Angel Abbey. It occurred to me for an instant to be angry with him, but the thought instantly dissolved. At that moment, there was nowhere on earth that I would rather have been. I could not blame anyone who had helped me to get there.

The song ended to thunderous applause and cheers from our guests, and Lucina and I fell into each other's arms, breathless and laughing. She returned to Gabriel, and I stepped back to Uriel, who was waiting for me as calmly as ever.

"I thought you said you were going to take it slow," I laughed, trying to catch my breath.

"And I thought *you* said you could not dance," Uriel retorted, smiling a little. "It is remarkable, really, how easy things are if you remember not to think so much." He offered me his arm and led me away from the party into the cool, soft night.

"Uriel," I asked him, "what do other people see when they look at you? Do they know that Lucina and I were dancing with angels, or do they think we were out there alone making fools of ourselves?"

"Ah, always so concerned about what other people might think. You really need to get over that, Caitlin," he told me gently. "People saw you and Lucina dancing with two gentlemen who had come to the party. They will not remember what we looked like, and they will not try. They will just look back on a marvelous evening and be happy for the memory.

"But if you want to make sure they do not try to figure it out," Uriel continued, "the best thing would be for you to dance with as many of your guests as you can tonight. Your friend Richard is dying to ask you, and none of us will hear the end of it if Jophiel does not get his turn before the evening ends." He extended his arm to me again. "Shall we?"

"We shall," I replied, and back to the party we went.

And so I danced. I danced with Richard first. "You look incredible," he said to me. "And you seem really happy. But this is such a change for you. Are you sure it's what you want?"

"Absolutely," I assured him. "It'll probably be a stretch at first, and people are going to have to get used to a new Lady. Lucina and I have very different styles. But it's going to be important for me to do the job my way."

"OK," Richard said, still sounding a little skeptical. "Maybe you're just what the Abbey needs. You'll know how to run the place more like a community outreach organization than an extended house party. Just don't start talking to angels, OK? It's bad enough that my mother has gone completely around the bend. Two 'angel ladies' in my life might be the death of me."

I swallowed hard and wondered what to say to that. Then I noticed Jophiel watching from nearby. The archangel's lips quirked into a conspiratorial smile. *Do not worry, darling girl,* his voice chuckled in my mind. *His mother and I will take care of everything. For now, just keep dancing. You are the very picture of grace.*

The song ended, and I excused myself from Richard, explaining that I had a lot of guests to attend to. I danced with Andrew and Mr. Han and Pastor St. James. I danced with men from the book club and AA and volunteers from the food bank and the homeless shelter.

I danced with Jophiel, discovering him to be a deliciously witty conversationalist. "Thank you so much for these incredible clothes," I said to him. "And especially for your note. It meant a lot to me that you gave me a choice about whether or not to wear them."

"Well, of *course* I did, dear heart," the archangel laughingly replied. "If you did not want to wear them you would have been miserable all night. We could not have that, now, could we?

"Still, I am just delighted with how well everything fits you," Jophiel went on. "It is all perfect on you, but then, you could wear absolutely anything. You are just gorgeous, you know. Designing for you is going to be *such* fun!"

After Jophiel, I danced with dear Chamuel, laughing Barachiel, sweet Raphael, and gentle Azrael, who was so shy that I had to take the lead. Dancing with Michael was an adventure. Unlike Azrael, Michael *loved* to lead, and had no qualms whatsoever about picking me up and tossing me around. "My brothers tell me that you've been a little bit scared of me, Caitlin," he boomed cheerfully. "Don't be—I never drop my partners." That was reassuring, I thought, but I still would never want to get on Michael's bad side.

I danced a stately waltz with Metatron, who proclaimed himself well pleased with my appointment. I did not need Raziel to tell me that I had just received the highest compliment that Metatron had to offer. Still, Raziel told me anyway, even as he warned me that he was not likely to disclose any other secrets anytime soon.

I even danced with Ariel and Haniel in a sort of line dance that I had never done before and could not remember the following day. "You have taken good care of our kitten friend," Ariel said approvingly. "I love people who appreciate cats. Feel free to call upon me anytime." She kissed me on the cheek and walked away, leaving me to wonder if she had ever been worshipped as Bastet, the cat-goddess of the ancient Egyptians.

The hours slipped away as we danced, and drank, and ate, and celebrated. Everyone wanted to meet the new Lady of the Abbey, so I barely had a moment to myself all evening. Richard and I managed to catch one more dance together, but even that lasted for only a few minutes. Then, Lucina walked into the center of the crowd. She raised her hands for silence, and the musicians stopped playing and the crowd fell still.

"Beloved friends," she said, raising her voice to be heard, "thank you for this lovely party, and for all of the special moments that we have enjoyed over our years together. My time here is ending, but I am certain that the good work of Angel Abbey will continue in the talented hands of my sister in spirit, Caitlin des Anges." I glanced at Bella and Andrew, but they showed no confusion at the name Lucina called me. Had the angels been whispering to them, too?

Lucina went on. "Each of you has brought many gifts to the Abbey, not the least the gifts of your time, talents, and commitment to our community. I have heard it said many times that anyone who comes to Angel Abbey finds what he or she needs most. That may be something different for each of us, but I believe that the best thing the Abbey offers is the opportunity to give of ourselves, and to find meaning and purpose in a challenging world."

The guests cheered, but Lucina raised her hands once more, and they quieted. "I have loved every minute here, and I am going to miss every last one of you. But this is a celebration, not a farewell, so let me close by thanking you for your kindness, your generosity, and your love, and with the promise that, no matter where our separate paths may take us, we are certain to meet again. Thank you for gracing Angel Abbey."

As the crowd clapped and whistled, Lucina lifted her arm. Fireworks burst out of the sky, shimmering and sparkling against the darkness. Silver, gold, amber, ruby, sapphire, and green, they tumbled in blazing cascades of stars, bursting and falling again and again. It was a breathtaking display, and a magnificent finale to the most memorable evening of my life.

It was long past midnight when the fireworks ended, and the sun would soon be coming up. Lucina and I said goodnight to our guests, who stumbled out in twos and threes, happily exhausted. When Bella and Andrew approached, I started to go with them, but Lucina caught my hand.

"This is your home now, Cate," she said, "and you should spend your first night as the Lady here at the Abbey. Everything you'll need is upstairs in the Lady's chamber." Turning to Bella and Andrew, she hugged them both. "Thank you for giving us Caitlin," she said quietly.

Bella hugged her back hard, fighting tears. "You're welcome. We're going to miss you, Lady."

"Not forever, Bella," Lucina replied fondly. "With friends, good-bye is never forever."

Bella and Andrew each kissed me on the cheek. "We are so *proud* of you, Catie," Bella said fondly.

"Just behave yourself, Miss Cate, you hear?" Andrew said, his eyes twinkling. "We'll be over to see you in a day or two." He took Bella's arm, and they walked off together. Of all the things that happened that night, their departure drove home to me most how much my life was about to change.

I almost went after them, but Amy caught my arm. "I'll be over around ten, Miss Caitlin," she said, all business. "There are some important things that we'll need to discuss in the morning." Suddenly she giggled. "This is going to be such fun!" She dashed away, leaving me to shake my head and smile.

I turned to Lucina, who was also smiling as she watched Amy go. "Lucina, I have something for you," I said. "Just give me a moment to go get it."

It took me several minutes to find the package I had brought for her, sitting on one of the tables in the courtyard. Luckily, it had not suffered any damage in the revelry. I brought it back and placed it into her hands.

"Oh, Caitlin," she said, after opening it and seeing the angel tree topper inside. "I remember this from your Christmas tree. It's beautiful and I am touched, but are you sure you want to part with it?"

"Absolutely," I assured her. "Please keep it, Lucina, and think of me sometimes. We've had our differences, but I'm very glad you're my friend, even if I haven't always shown it."

"And I'm glad you're mine, Caitlin," Lucina responded. "I'm honored by your gift. And you'll do an incredible job here. I would warn you not to let Gabriel push you around, but somehow I don't think that's going to be a problem." We laughed like sisters.

Then one of the last stragglers called my name. I turned to say good night, and when I looked back, Lucina was gone.

The courtyard was far from empty, though. The angels and archangels still lingered, casting a gentle, golden glow that mingled with the sparkling white lights in the trees. The human musicians had long since departed. But several of the angels, instruments in hand, had clustered around Sandalphon. He lifted his baton once more, and they began playing a slow, sweet tune. Gabriel appeared at my elbow, smiling.

"We never did have that dance, Cate. Can you manage one more?" he asked.

"Do I have a choice?" I asked him, careful to keep a straight face.

"Of course," Gabriel replied, grinning. "Always."

"In that case, I'd be delighted," I said, laughing. "By all means, Gabriel, let's dance."

And so, as dawn began to break over Angel Abbey, I enjoyed one last, leisurely waltz with the Archangel Gabriel, turning around and around together like figurines dancing inside a music box, as the hosts of Heaven looked on in joy.

Archangel Michael speaks:

Wow, what a shindig! Gabe really pulled a rabbit out of his hat this time. That new Lady of his is going to be a handful, though. It'll be good for Gabe—he's always at his best when something or somebody is keeping him on his toes.

It was a great time, and we were all glad that Caitlin was finally starting to figure out who her friends were. She had a lot more than she realized, especially considering all of us angels. None of you folks know how many of us there are rooting for you. If you did, maybe you wouldn't let the small stuff bother you so much. And take it from me, compared to what is waiting for you in Heaven, it's all small stuff. When you get here, you'll see what I mean.

I overheard an interesting conversation after the party ended. Raphael and Uriel were talking with Gabe, congratulating him on how well everything had turned out. Then Raphael said, "Gabriel, there's just one thing I don't understand. Didn't Lucina send Caitlin a written invitation to the Abbey right after she got to town?"

"Yeah," Gabriel answered, shrugging a little. "What about it?"

"Well, Lucina always uses that same paper, right? And her handwriting wouldn't have changed."

"Both true," Gabriel replied. "So what's your question, Raphael?"

"Well, if Lucina wrote the invitation on the same paper you used for the note you put on Caitlin's desk, and her handwriting was the same as you used, why didn't Caitlin make the connection then? Why did it take her so long to figure out that something was going on?"

"Ah, you noticed that, did you? Very perceptive." Gabriel winked at Raphael and then flew off without answering his question.

So, did Gabe actually plan everything that happened, or did he just have to wing it? The only one who knows for sure is Gabe, and maybe Raziel. But you can bet those two won't be telling anytime soon.

CHAPTER FORTY

Several hours later, I woke in a strange but supremely comfortable bed, dressed in a beautiful nightgown I had never seen before. Another present from Jophiel? Wherever it came from, it was certainly pretty—delicate white muslin festooned with ribbons and lace.

The warm, familiar weight on my shoulder proved to be Honoré, who glanced up at me contentedly before falling back to sleep. How had he gotten there? Someone must have brought him to the Abbey during the party, I thought. Archangel Ariel, perhaps. Whoever it was, I was grateful to have him there.

After easing Honoré onto my pillow, I sat up and looked around.

We were in a large round room, with a high ceiling and tall windows. The walls were painted a pale, creamy peach that glowed softly in the morning sun. A round oriental rug in soft shades of melon, gold, and sage covered the floor. There was a chaise longue upholstered in copper-colored silk and loaded with pillows, a low bookshelf, a dressing table and chair, a large armoire, and a matching dresser with what looked like a jewelry box on top. The ceiling was a masterpiece, a gorgeous mural of the heavens, stars twinkling in the night sky at one side as the first rays of dawn tinted the other. Across the room, an open door revealed a sumptuous bath, all done up in shades of ivory and blush. Everything was rich, luxurious, and almost indecently comfortable.

So this is the Lady's chamber, I thought. Judging from the shape of the room, it had to be somewhere in the tower. Was it over the chapel, perhaps? I wondered how I had gotten there and who had dressed me for bed. An image of invisible, angelic hands wafting me upstairs and into my nightgown popped into my head. The idea was unnerving enough that I quickly decided not to think much more about it. Had the angels always watched me as I went about my daily life? How much had they seen? This business of being surrounded by invisible companions everywhere I went was going to take some getting used to.

A small nightstand sat beside my bed, with a pretty brass reading lamp on top. I noticed a little white silk bag resting against the lamp, propping up a notecard. The envelope bore my name in a script that was unmistakably Lucina's—unless Gabriel was playing games again, I thought wryly. I picked up the note, opened it, and read.

> *Dear Caitlin,*
>
> *This morning begins your tenure as the Lady of Angel Abbey. What an adventure you are about to have! I wanted to leave you a little gift, as both a remembrance and a reminder to enjoy your new role. I have no doubt you will fulfill your responsibilities admirably—you always do. Just don't forget to have some fun along the way.*
>
> *The ability to see and speak with angels is a consummate blessing. The power to invoke them is an incredible responsibility. Use that power well and wisely.*
>
> *We will meet again, I have no doubt. You don't care much for "the Lady's blessing," I know, so I won't presume to confer it on you. Instead, just remember until then that my friendship and good wishes are yours always.*
>
> *Fondly,*
> *Lucina*

I set the note aside and picked up the little silk bag. Had Lucina left her angel necklace for me? It was a beautiful piece that I would be proud to wear, but the better part of me hoped that she had kept it for herself.

The bag opened, and its contents slid into my hand. Lucina had indeed left me a necklace, but not her own. An abstract golden angel, its wings outstretched, danced on a small, round diamond. A pink tourmaline glowed at its heart, and it held another round diamond high above its head. There could not be a better reminder to dance now and then, I thought, carefully fastening the chain around my neck. The little angel settled against my throat, and I smiled.

"I hope you like your quarters, Cate," a familiar voice said from a few feet away. "If not, we can always redecorate."

Turning, I saw Gabriel seated casually at the dressing table, his wings elegantly draped across the carpet. I smiled again. "Maybe later," I told him. "Let me get used to all the opulence first. It's a lot to take in."

"You'll adjust," he smiled back. "You were always a quick study."

"Gabriel," I said, "thank you for all this. It still feels as though I haven't told you enough how grateful I am. It's strange, though. Nothing in my life ever prepared me for something like this."

"That's where you're wrong, Cate," he answered. "*Everything* in your life prepared you for this, and you're going to do an amazing job. I won't keep popping in on you unannounced, though. You're going to need some time to get used to being the Lady, and people at the Abbey are going to need some time to get used to you. It'll be important for you to make the Abbey your own. Some people may have trouble accepting the change at first, but you'll manage. It's time for me to step back and let you find your own way for a while."

Just the thought of having Gabriel disappear again sent a pang of anxiety through me. He had only just come back, and I wasn't prepared to let him go twice. "But what if there's a problem?" I asked. "What if something comes up that I can't handle? Or what if... well, what if I just want to talk with you sometimes?"

Gabriel laughed. "I said I was going to step back, not vanish altogether!" he answered. "When you want to talk, just call me. I'll be here in an instant. Besides, it'll be a cold day in Paradise when something comes up that Caitlin des Anges can't handle."

The archangel stopped, seeming to listen for a moment. "Cate, you had better get up and get dressed," he told me. "You've got a meeting in about an hour."

"A meeting? With whom?" I asked, puzzled and a little nervous.

"The Abbey's biggest benefactor," Gabriel replied. "But don't worry—everything will be just fine." He started to fade into a cloud of golden light.

"Gabriel, wait!" I said, starting to panic. "I haven't properly thanked you yet. The party, the Abbey, the people here—it's all incredible."

"You're welcome, Cate," he said. I could not see him any longer, but I could hear the smile in his voice. "If you like Angel Abbey, just wait until you see what my boss can do."

And then Gabriel was gone, leaving a sunbeam behind to dance across the carpet. Sighing, I got up, moving slowly so as not to disturb Honoré, and went off to bathe and dress.

The bathroom was a decadent delight, all soft towels, thick rugs, and luxurious toiletries. There was a deep marble tub spacious enough for three people, a separate shower, and a wide skylight to let in the morning sun. The shampoo, soap, and lotion had all been scented with the same light floral fragrance Jophiel had sent for the party. Apparently, it was intended to be my signature scent, the way Lucina's spicy perfume had been hers. I started to get indignant—I would pick my own perfume, thank you—then realized how ridiculous I was being. Jophiel's scent was beautiful and exactly what I would have chosen for myself. So why not just accept the gift with thanks?

On the side of the tub sat a small tray with breakfast. A warm croissant, apricot jam, a big cup of steaming coffee, and a pink rosebud in a silver vase were all prettily arranged on the Abbey's china. The angels, it seemed, had thought of everything. I ate the croissant while the tub filled and then sipped my coffee while up to my neck in fragrant bubbles.

It was all so indulgent that it was tempting to linger, but I forced myself to bathe quickly. It wouldn't do to keep the Abbey's biggest benefactor waiting, whoever he or she might be. I pushed aside a frisson of nerves. I had been in meetings with important clients before. How much more difficult could this mysterious benefactor be?

A quick inspection of the armoire and dresser confirmed what I had already suspected. The angels had thoughtfully provided me with a full wardrobe, all beautifully designed and crafted. My gown from the party hung at one end of the armoire. I looked at it closely. Even after hours of vigorous dancing it was immaculate, without a single spill, stain, or smudge. My dancing shoes were pristine, too. I was starting to feel like a character in a fairy tale, waited upon night and day by invisible servants. Amazed, I started to dress.

Jophiel understood my taste. All of the clothes he had provided were simpler than Lucina's, less blatantly mystical. Lucina was an actress, after all—it made sense for her to dress more flamboyantly than I comfortably could. I settled on a plain, sandy-beige dress with a ballet neckline and matching shoes. The angel pendant from Lucina rested perfectly in the neckline. The skirt swished gracefully around my ankles when I walked, sending up a subtle hint of Jophiel's perfume. If clothes made the woman, I was fast becoming the Lady of Angel Abbey.

Everything in the closet was beautiful, and I was grateful for the angels' generosity. Still, I missed my clothes at home, all of which Bella had selected with so much love and care. *Don't worry, darling girl,* I heard Jophiel drawl in my mind. *You can bring those things here or wear them at the other house, whichever you prefer. We would never ask you to give up anything you loved. Just let us know what you would like.*

Yes, having archangels talk to me from out of nowhere was definitely going to require some adjustment on my part. "Thank you, Jophiel," I replied aloud. "These things are lovely, and I appreciate all the trouble you took to make them for me. But if you'll excuse me, I have a meeting to go to."

Of course, dearest, I heard again. *Just call when you need us.* And then he was gone.

Jophiel had barely departed when there was a soft knock at my bedroom door. When I opened it, Amy was standing there. "Good morning, Lady. I hope you slept well," she began.

"Good morning, Amy, and don't call me 'Lady,'" I replied, cutting her off. "Maybe Lucina liked it, but you and I are better friends than that. Please just call me Cate, OK?"

She paused, my request clearly violating her sense of propriety. "Well, all right," she finally said, a little grumpily. "But only when there's no one else listening. You have a position to consider, you know." She was so earnest that it was tempting to laugh, but I managed to keep a straight face. "At any rate, there's someone here to see you—"

"—the Abbey's biggest benefactor," I interrupted, completing her sentence. "Yes, I know. What I don't yet know, however, is how to get out of this beautiful new room and into the Abbey proper. I'll have to follow you for now. Let's go downstairs, shall we? We shouldn't keep our guest waiting."

Amy led me down a spiraling flight of stone stairs. At one point we crossed a landing with an arched door. Was it another way into the chapel? I made a mental note to check later, while continuing the climb down. At the bottom, the stairs connected to a short hall that ended in another door. Amy opened it, and we stepped out into the main corridor.

Amy led me down the hall at a brisk pace. "Tell me about this benefactor,"

I said, puffing a bit behind her. "What should I know about him? Or should I say 'her'?"

"Oh, no, definitely 'him,'" Amy replied over her shoulder as she trotted ahead of me. "He's a lovely old gentleman, always very courteous and kind. He has old money, I think, lots of it. They say his family has donated to the Abbey for generations. He doesn't live around here anymore, though. I think he and his family moved downstate when he was a boy."

"Amy," I asked, trying not to let impatience creep into my voice, "what's his *name*?"

"Oh, I'm sorry," Amy exclaimed. "Didn't I tell you? Well, let me introduce you, then. He's right here."

I had been so intent on learning whatever Amy could tell me that it was almost a surprise to arrive in the Abbey's sitting room. Our mysterious benefactor was waiting, seated with his legs crossed, facing away from me in one of the high-backed chairs. A tray laden with coffee and cookies sat on the table beside him. I saw a leg clad in blue striped seersucker, a foot shod in white buck, and the top of a fine head of thick silver hair. Amy walked around to the front of his chair, and said, "Excuse me, sir. May I introduce you to our new Lady?"

The Abbey's biggest benefactor stood, turned, and took one look at me before his face lit up with a delighted grin.

"Why, if it isn't my dear friend Cate!" Dr. Grandy exclaimed, taking my right hand and shaking it enthusiastically with both of his. "This is an unexpected pleasure. Blackwell told me you had left the firm, but no one could tell me where you had gone. It's so very good to see you. How *are* you, my dear?"

Archangel Verchiel speaks:

You will not have heard of me. I am nowhere near as famous as many of my brothers, and that suits me just fine. My particular specialty is creating and delivering wonderful surprises of every kind, so my angels and I prefer to fly under the radar. We are not trying to hide, you understand.

It is just that if you knew all about us, you might start watching for us. It would be a harder to amaze and delight you that way.

When Gabriel asked me to help with a little surprise for Caitlin, I was thrilled to do it. Every archangel in Heaven knew about the goings-on at Angel Abbey. And oh, the look on Caitlin's face when she saw the doctor! It was the best surprise we had delivered in ages. My angels and I reveled in it for months.

So, the next time you receive a happy surprise—a gift, a party, a call or e-mail from a friend you have not seen in far too long—take a quick look around. You will never see us coming, but you just might catch the merest glimpse of a feather as we leave you. If you listen hard, you might hear the soft swish of wings or even a happy cry of "Surprise!" before we fly away.

As my brother Barachiel likes to say, miracles are never far away. And we angels just love it when we catch you by surprise.

CHAPTER FORTY-ONE

It was shock enough just to see Dr. Grandy sitting there, but his obvious delight at seeing *me* was positively staggering. For a moment, I was stunned into speechlessness.

"Hello, Dr. Grandy," I finally stammered. "It's nice to see you, too, I suppose. However, I'm not sure I should even be talking with you without my lawyer present."

Dr. Grandy looked puzzled. He had always been one of my favorite clients, someone I was invariably glad to see. I had never greeted him so coolly before.

"Your lawyer, you say? And why would that be, Cate?"

"Well, Dr. Grandy," I pointed out, "you *are* suing me for three million dollars. If I were my own lawyer, I'd instruct me not to talk to you." That didn't make sense, exactly, but it was pretty clear what I meant.

It was Dr. Grandy's turn to be astonished. "Three million dollars? What are you talking about, Cate? I am not suing anyone to my knowledge, but even if I were, it certainly would never be you."

When Dr. Grandy said "to my knowledge," a tiny chime, pure as crystal, rang sweetly in my mind. It was the first of many times the angels would ring that chime as a sign to pay special attention. One of the perks of being the Lady of Angel Abbey, I came to learn.

"Dr. Grandy," I replied slowly, "a few months ago, Roy Blackwell filed a lawsuit against me on your behalf. He's asking the court to make me pay you three million dollars. Are you saying that you don't know anything about this?"

Dr. Grandy shook his head. "Cate, upon my beloved mother's grave, I assure you that I know nothing about any lawsuit. Are you quite certain about this?"

"Quite," I replied, and then turned to Amy, who was still hovering at my elbow. "Amy," I asked, working hard to keep my voice steady, "would you please get Richard Helmsworth on the phone and ask him to come by the Abbey *right now?*"

"Yes ma'am," Amy replied, her eyes wide. She hurried away.

Turning back to Dr. Grandy, I smiled sweetly and sat down in the chair beside him. "While we're waiting, Dr. Grandy, may I offer you another cup of coffee?" He nodded, and I felt as graceful as Lucina as I poured.

Richard must have broken every speed limit in town, because he arrived at the Abbey less than fifteen minutes later. By then Dr. Grandy and I were chatting away merrily about his family's connection to the Abbey. "My father moved us to Yonkers when I was at Yale," Dr. Grandy told me, "but I grew up in Angel Falls and my family has supported the good work of Angel Abbey since my great-great-grandfather's time. Why, my dear mother was a Wittesteen before she married into the Grandy family."

The image of a grinning Gabriel, accompanied by a smiling archangel in salmon-colored robes, flashed before my eyes. *This is my brother Verchiel,* Gabriel's voice whispered in my mind. *Surprise!* Verchiel cried, waving gleefully. He vanished in a puff of sparkling pink smoke, taking Gabriel with him.

The Heavenly hosts were larger than I had realized.

Looking toward the door, I saw Richard barreling into the sitting room, clutching his briefcase. "Richard," I called cheerfully, "come and meet my old friend Dr. Grandy. It seems we've had something of a misunderstanding. Would you care for some coffee while we chat?"

Richard's eyes nearly popped out of his head, but he nodded dumbly and took a chair. I poured him a cup of coffee as Dr. Grandy reiterated that he had never authorized Roy Blackwell to sue me and, until just moments before, had had no idea that a lawsuit against me had been filed in his name. "I always suspected that Blackwell might be a bit of a scoundrel," Dr. Grandy said, "but my father swore by that law firm. Besides, my legal work always seemed to be done well, which was probably due more to you than to him, Cate. I am terribly sorry you have been so badly treated. Please let me know what I can do to set things right."

"Just tell Richard what he needs to know, Dr. Grandy, and he'll do the rest." I sat back to watch what promised to be a *very* gratifying conversation.

Within thirty minutes, Richard had gleaned all the information from Dr. Grandy that he could possibly need. He was, as my erstwhile father had recognized, a really outstanding lawyer. "Can I borrow you for a minute?" he asked me. "Pleasure to meet you, Dr. Grandy." The men shook hands, and I walked Richard to the Abbey door.

"This is incredible, Cate," Richard whispered to me. "You know this will blow Blackwell's case wide open, don't you?"

"I do, and I couldn't be happier," I replied, feeling like a cat that had unexpectedly been presented with a gift-wrapped bushel of canaries. "Go forth, counsel, and beat the son-of-a-gun for me, OK?" Richard nodded, grinning, and sailed out the door. Breathing a deep sigh of relief, I returned to my visit with the Abbey's biggest benefactor.

Dr. Grandy and I spent another two hours chatting about the Abbey and reminiscing about growing up in Angel Falls before he finally got up to leave. "This has been a real pleasure, Cate," he said, taking my hand and patting it kindly. "I must say, you look much happier here than you ever did in the city. It cannot have been easy, working so closely with a villain like Blackwell. Life at the Abbey seems to suit you far better."

"It does indeed, Dr. Grandy," I answered. "I've enjoyed having this opportunity to get to know you in a more congenial setting. Please come back and see us anytime—you will always be welcome at Angel Abbey." I smiled serenely and escorted him to the door, then waited for him to get out of earshot before letting out a whoop of sheer joy.

The next day, Richard called to update me on my court case. He had filed a motion to dismiss the lawsuit and, for good measure, asked the judge to order Roy Blackwell to show cause why he should not be held in contempt of court for fraud and abuse of process. He had also filed a lengthy ethics complaint against Blackwell with the New York bar. "I thought about giving him an opportunity to withdraw the suit on his own," Richard happily said. "But it didn't seem right to let him wriggle out of the mess he had made. Blackwell deserves a healthy dose of his own medicine." After we hung up, I reflected that my friend Richard could get downright antagonistic under the right circumstances. It might be a good idea to keep that in mind.

I spent the rest of that day doing what I was already beginning to think of as "Lady things." There were a lot of them. Between greeting visitors, dropping in on meetings, stopping by to thank Violet for the delicious food at the party, and spending a few minutes with Mr. Han's sculpture class, my entire afternoon was occupied. It was all a lot of fun, though I wondered whether I would get bored once the novelty wore off.

Honoré padded around the Abbey as if he had always lived there, sometimes shadowing me, sometimes sprawling majestically across one piece of furniture or another, while our visitors admired him. Amy was thrilled to have him there, and he graciously accepted her praises and petting.

The afternoon was drawing to a close when I turned and saw Bella and Andrew, who had appeared seemingly out of nowhere. "We thought we would drop by and see how you're doing, Miss Cate," Andrew said. His voice was jovial, but there was a trace of concern in his eyes.

"We've missed you, Catie," Bella echoed. It was clear that she was working hard not to reproach me, but I could have kicked myself. Between the excitement of Dr. Grandy's visit and the distraction of all my new duties, I had neglected to call them. That was one fence I would need to mend right away.

"I'm so glad to see you!" I said, hugging Bella and then Andrew. "It's been a crazy couple of days, but I have lots of good news. Can you stay for dinner?" I asked, fervently hoping that the Lady of Angel Abbey could arrange a last-minute meal for her closest friends.

Fortunately, dinner proved to be no problem. Bella, Andrew, and I were soon seated comfortably in the dining room, enjoying soup, salad, and warm bread that appeared out of the kitchen as if by magic—perhaps, I reflected briefly, it had. As we ate, I told them about Dr. Grandy's revelation and how eager Richard was to give Roy Blackwell a taste of his own medicine. Bella and Andrew were both clearly pleased with the news, but my sense that something was not quite right still lingered.

Finally, when dinner was over, I asked, "So, is everything OK at the house? You two seem a little worried."

Bella and Andrew looked at each other for a moment, and then Andrew cleared his throat. "Well, Miss Cate, we've been talking," he said. "Now that your father is gone and you're settled in here, there doesn't seem to be much reason for Bella and me to keep taking care of that drafty old house. You've never liked the place, and we wondered what you wanted to do with it."

"We don't want to create a problem for you, Catie," Bella interjected. "But the house really isn't ours, and we have looked after it for such a long time. You've had a change, and we think maybe we should too. We'll stay there as long as you need us, of course, but it's time we figured out where we should go next."

The minute Bella spoke, I realized that I had overlooked the obvious yet again. Of course they didn't want to keep maintaining a cold, empty house. The idea of losing them altogether, though, was heartbreaking. I had finally realized that they had been far better parents to me than Christopher Cunningham or my missing mother. It would be horrible to lose them just when I had started to appreciate how much they really meant to me.

"Well, of course you should do whatever would make you happy," I started, remembering that, however much I might love them, Bella and Andrew were not my biological family. If they didn't want to stay, it would be wrong of me to pressure them. "The thing is, though…"

An image of the empty carriage house across the courtyard from the Abbey popped into my head, unbidden. *Go ahead, Cate,* Gabriel's voice whispered in my mind. *They're just waiting for you to ask them.*

Bella and Andrew were exchanging a worried glance, and I realized that I must just have taken one of those little pauses of Lucina's that had so annoyed me. *We are going to need to come up with a less obvious way to do this,* I thought, and heard Gabriel chuckle. "Sorry, I lost my train of thought for a moment," I told them, and they nodded, apparently relieved.

"As far as the house goes," I continued, "I could not care less about it. It's high time I got rid of that awful old place. We can put it on the market tomorrow, if you like.

"The thing is, though," I continued, trying not to let my nervousness show, "the two of you are like parents to me. You've taken care of me for almost my entire life. I love you both, and I don't want to lose you unless you really want to go somewhere else. This isn't to pressure you or anything, and it has to be your decision. But I was wondering… How would you feel about moving to the Abbey?"

Andrew grinned, and Bella's face lit up with joy. "Catie," she said, "we were so hoping you would ask." She leaned over and threw her arms around my neck.

Well done, Caitlin, Gabriel whispered to me. *Very well done indeed.*

Archangel Gabriel speaks:

Miracles happen every day. Every blade of grass, drop of water, handful of earth, glimmer of sunlight, or living being you encounter is a miracle. Every act of courage or kindness is a miracle too. Every last one of you is surrounded by miracles, but you're so accustomed to them that you forget to see the magic sometimes.

It's easy to lose your way when you forget who you are and why you're here. Caitlin lost herself for a while, and it took a lot of effort from a whole lot of angels to bring her back. Don't get me wrong, though–I'm not complaining. It was our joy and our privilege to help Caitlin find her way back to her Divine purpose. Her adventure was just beginning, and I couldn't wait to watch her dance down the path the Creator had set for her.

Your path isn't Caitlin's, of course. Your path is your own, and thanks to the Creator's grace, you're free to walk it, abandon it, circle around it, run away from it, or pretend that it isn't there. But whenever you're ready to dance down the road to your best and finest self, remember that we angels are right here, just waiting to dance with you.

All you have to do is ask.

CHAPTER FORTY-TWO

It took only a few short weeks for Roy Blackwell to get his comeuppance. Once Richard filed his motion and our side of the story got out, the other partners in the firm—many of whom detested Blackwell—launched an internal investigation. They soon discovered that I was not the only person Blackwell had victimized. He had been lining his own pockets for years by padding the legal bills he sent Dr. Grandy and several other clients, while taking bribes from opposing counsel whenever he could. The real estate deal I had fought so hard to prevent turned out to be just one of Blackwell's many scams. He would talk clients into buying properties for an inflated price, knowing full well that they were terrible investments, in exchange for hefty kickbacks from the sellers. He had carefully covered his tracks along the way, bullying and threatening younger attorneys whenever he feared they were coming too close to catching him.

The truth came out, though, as Archangel Michael assures me it always does. Mark Davenport turned out to be the most damning witness against Blackwell, finally free to tell the partners about all the horrible things he had been forced to do. Mark left the firm shortly thereafter, and has since joined a legal-aid clinic, where he uses his litigation skills to help the homeless.

The partners did not wait for the court to rule, summarily firing Blackwell from the firm. Ultimately, he was barred from the practice of law. Raziel usually doesn't say much, but he quietly let me know that Blackwell was starting to regret some of the terrible wrongs he had done. In return, I promised not to tell the other archangels that Raziel had shared such an important secret with me. After all, he has a reputation to protect.

Revenge is not supposed to be sweet to those who commune with the archangels. I will admit to sleeping better, though, knowing that Roy

Blackwell would never again abuse another young attorney the way he had me. What can I say? Even the angels' good influence can't keep me from being human.

Blackwell's lawsuit and the bar complaint against me were both dismissed. I was even offered my old job back, as were Jeanine Powell and several other young lawyers Blackwell had forced out. Many of them went back, but Jeanine and I both politely declined. Last I heard, Jeanine had enrolled in seminary. She'll make a fabulous minister, that's for sure.

Although Amy never found Ruth Martingale, Raphael did, with ease. At my request, he and his angels gave her doctors some extra angelic assistance. Ruth recovered completely from her stroke, but chose to retire rather than return to the firm. She lives on the Maryland shore now, close to a niece who looks after her from day to day. Ruth was delighted to learn that Roy Blackwell had finally been taken down, crowing about it far more triumphantly than I felt I decently could. We e-mail regularly, and I am happy to call her a friend.

Jack's play opened to rave reviews and sellout audiences. My good friend from college is now a leading man on Broadway, and he has already set his heart on taking Hollywood by storm. Gabriel positively dotes on Jack. He is likely to go far in the performing arts, with an archangel supporting him.

Bella and Andrew moved into the pretty little carriage house just as Gabriel suggested, and came to work at the Abbey full-time. Andrew oversees the volunteers' work on the gardens and grounds. Bella has taken over the kitchen. I worried that Violet might be offended, but she was grateful to have more time for her pastry shop. Violet still comes by to help with food-bank donations, and I regularly join her and Bella for coffee and gossip.

After Bella and Andrew moved out, I sold Christopher Cunningham's monstrous old house to a dot.com millionaire from India, Arjun Dahari. It turns out that Archangel Chamuel isn't just good at love—he's a whiz at finding things. It took Chamuel less than three days to produce Arjun after I asked for help locating a buyer for the place. The sale went through with amazing ease.

Arjun cheerfully explained to me at the closing that he wanted a place that was close—but not too close—to his parents in Yonkers and his girlfriend, a medical student in Albany. Christopher Cunningham's house was the perfect solution. Arjun has painted the exterior trim a brilliant purple, which looks remarkably attractive next to the stone walls and verdigris roof. Better still, he has finally defeated the house's gloomy spirit, filling it with sheer chiffon draperies, bright colors, and raga music. Just the thought of it is enough to make me smile.

My beloved Honoré passed away some months after we moved to the Abbey, his little cat body too old and frail to sustain his enormous, loving heart. I was working at my desk one afternoon when he jumped up and pushed between me and the papers I was reading, something he had not done in many years. He reached out and rubbed one cheek gently against mine. Then, he hopped back down and went to settle on his blue Christmas cushion, just a few feet away. When I went to pet him an hour or so later, he was gone.

We buried Honoré in the Abbey garden, and Archangel Ariel herself blessed his final resting place. He continues to visit me in dreams sometimes, healthy, happy, and the size of a lion. I have no doubt that he is well.

Still, Honoré was my closest friend for many years, and the loss of him hit me hard. But this is Angel Abbey, and no one can be here for long without receiving what he or she needs most. Dr. Grandy got word of Honoré's death through the Abbey grapevine. On his next visit, he presented me with a beautiful pair of Siamese kittens. I named them Gaston for Honoré's nephew and Gigi for the gamine he loved, the leading characters in the movie that was once my mother's favorite. They thunder through the Abbey, merrily spilling drinks, scattering papers, and creating happy chaos wherever they go.

Richard showed up at the Abbey one afternoon with a big bouquet of flowers and a card. Inside were two movie tickets and the dollar I had given him when he first agreed to represent me, little red smudge and all. (Had that smudge always been shaped like a lopsided heart, or had my lawyer been guilty of defacing currency? Either way, the sight of it made me smile.) Sure enough, Richard had thought he should not date a client, but now the litigation was over. We went to the movies that evening, and have been seeing each other ever since.

I do not yet know whether our relationship will evolve into something closer, or if it even should. I have been blessed with the ability to speak with the archangels, a precious responsibility that I freely chose and would never willingly set down. Richard doesn't believe in angels and isn't comfortable with those who do. Unless that changes, our friendship isn't likely to deepen. But Chamuel keeps telling me to wait and see what happens. According to my archangel friend, love prospers best when you let it blossom in its own time.

Lucina has settled west of here, though I'm not quite sure where. According to Gabriel, she is working with the archangels to establish a new place, different from Angel Abbey. I think of her often and wish her well. Only time will tell whether, and when, we will ever see each other again, but I'm grateful for the goodwill she left behind.

The regulars at Angel Abbey are still adjusting to their new Lady. Despite my best efforts I am neither as patient nor as gracious as Lucina, and I have accidentally bruised a few feelings here and there. Gabriel tells me not to worry and promises that things will work out for the best. After all, he reminds me, I have all the archangels in Heaven to help me. His optimism is appreciated, but sometimes I wonder if it's entirely justified.

The table that sits beside my bed has a little drawer. In it I keep the white silk bag and note from Lucina, along with a small leather box that holds an antique pocket watch, two sets of cuff links, and three rings. No matter how much I study the contents of that box, they remain a mystery. Despite what the Divine voice at the lake told me that magical night, I keep hoping that my mother's whereabouts will eventually be revealed to me. When I ask the angels about her, though, they lovingly refuse to tell me more.

I still don't know who my natural father was. I don't know where my mother went, or why she left, or whether I will ever see her again. But what I do know is that people are complex, puzzling, sometimes annoying and always cherished, even when they don't know or can't accept it themselves. My parents have their own paths to walk, and only Heaven knows if those paths will ever cross with mine. But I have friends who love me, good work to do, and the gentle advice of the archangels to guide me along the way. What more could anyone ask?

My name is Caitlin des Anges, and I am the Lady of Angel Abbey.

I am content.

Appreciations

If I have learned one lesson from writing *Dancing at Angel Abbey*, it is that the angels delight in gratitude. My name may be on the cover of this book, but a great many angels, human and otherwise, contributed to its creation. As Archangel Metatron might say, appreciations are definitely in order.

First, special thanks to my beloved Tatyana and Lance, who cheerfully put up with many hours of keyboard clatter, take-out meals, and distracted responses from Mama while this story took shape. The two of you are my most cherished angels, and I am so grateful for you both!

Thanks to Mom and Dad for being nothing like Cate's parents, and for making a loving home for a daughter who still hears angel voices long after sensible people have been deafened by adulthood. Thanks to Steve for staying a kid right with me, and for being the best brother anybody ever had. Thanks to Tanya for bringing your warm, generous spirit to our family and for making my brother so happy.

Deepest gratitude goes to daughter-in-spirit Valerie Holt, who read through early drafts of the manuscript and offered comments that were both candid and tactful. Val, thank you as well for inspiring one of my favorite characters in the book. Without you there would have been no Amy, and Cate would have been *very* cross with me.

Special thanks to my dear friends Steve Benkin, Ilana Feinberg Cardin, Tina Firewolf, Nancy and Bob Rietz, Charla Rowe, Corry Weierbach, and John Yoegel for reading the first draft of the novel and giving me your thoughtful suggestions. Thanks to publicist Sara Sgarlat for assuring me that the book was something readers would enjoy. Thanks as well to my angel editor, Amy K. Hughes, and to my friends at Balboa Press for your hard work to bring *Dancing at Angel Abbey* into the world.

Thank you to Diana Cooper and Doreen Virtue, whose inspiring books and uplifting workshops taught me much of what I know about the angels. Thanks to the cast and crew of *Touched by an Angel,* especially the lovely Roma Downey and the sublime Della Reese, for being a bottomless source of spiritual encouragement. Thanks to the cast and crew of *Michael,* especially John Travolta, for showing me that archangels can be funny as well as divine. And particular thanks to the incomparable Donna Murphy, whose graceful onscreen presence inspired Lucina des Anges.

Not all angels take human form. My love and gratitude must also go to Sabrina, Sherman, Gareth, Nimuë, Tess, Robyn, Lancelot, Soleil, Remy, Mufasa, Atticus, and Katniss. Together, you embodied Kate's beloved Honoré, and brought me a lifetime of love, laughter, and wonderful memories. It has been said that every life should have nine cats—in being owned by all of you, I have been especially blessed.

Finally, I will leave it to the reader to decide whether the angels and archangels who offer their thoughts throughout this book are real or imaginary. But these appreciations would be incomplete if I failed to express my heartfelt gratitude to them. So, thank you Archangels Ariel, Azrael, Barachiel, Chamuel, Jophiel, Haniel, Metatron, Michael, Raphael, Sandalphon, Uriel, Verchiel, and most especially Gabriel! Thank you to the angels who serve under you, and above all to the Master you so devotedly serve, for allowing me to walk a little way in your company. You have given me a glimpse of Heaven, and I am forever grateful.